In Dreams, We Love Again

By Casey L. Bennett

CB
CK
Creative

CBCK Creative
www.cbckcreative.com

This is a work of fiction. Names, characters, places, and events are the product of the
author's imagination or used fictitiously. Any resemblance to actual persons (living or
deceased), locations, or events is entirely coincidental.

ISBN: 979-8-9998791-1-0
First Edition, 2025
Printed in the United States of America

For Courtney A. Kratzer

You were the first spark, the reason I didn't give up,
the reason this story found its voice.

Some truths do not fade.
Some names never leave us.
Some moments change everything.

This one was yours.

For James M. Braun

The road ended too soon,
but your memory is in every step that followed.

This story is for the ones who never got to finish theirs.

To die, to sleep;
To sleep, perchance to dream. Ay, there's the rub...
— William Shakespeare, Hamlet

Chapter 1

Sunlight striped the kitchen tile as he flipped the eggs. His phone buzzed beside the burner. He didn't look up.

Emily crossed behind him, barefoot and silent. A crooked photo on the fridge made her wince.

"Something smells good." She pulls him close, resting her chin between his shoulder blades, her arms tightening around his waist.

"Trying this new thing where I actually cook breakfast instead of grabbing coffee on the run." Zane slides the eggs onto two plates, already loaded with toast and fresh fruit.

The kitchen shows signs of their merged lives. Emily's collection of mismatched mugs sits next to Zane's precisely arranged coffee gear, her colorful dish towels brightening up his once-minimalist space. A magnet board on the fridge displays their shared calendar, covered in Emily's neat handwriting marking dinner dates and appointments.

Zane pours two cups of coffee, setting one by Emily's plate. She flashes a grateful smile before tucking a leg beneath her and sitting down.

"True. Though I think your definition of excitement is just being able to order takeout at 3 AM," she said, smiling over her cartoon cat mug.

Zane laughs, the sound mixing with the quiet hum of the fridge. He takes a bite of toast and gestures toward her plate. "Eat. It's a peace offering."

The kitchen feels warmer now, lived in. Photos on the fridge tell their story. Emily laughing at a rooftop party, bundled together in

Central Park, a vacation selfie. It was no longer just Zane's space, it was theirs.

Emily stirs her coffee. The spoon clinks against the ceramic, punctuating the silence between them.

Zane thumbs through his inbox. The phone's blue glow bouncing off his coffee mug. A brief needed approval, and the design team had flagged something urgent. His collar feels stiff, probably over-starched again.

Emily doesn't comment on his phone use. She's gotten used to it, like the distant rumble of traffic outside their window or the way their upstairs neighbor always vacuums at 6 AM.

Still, she watches him.

Zane sets his phone face-down, but his fingers twitched when it buzzed again. "Point taken."

Emily returns to her seat, wrapping both hands around her coffee mug. "Speaking of breaks... I was thinking about that bed-and-breakfast you mentioned last month?"

Zane's phone buzzes again. Another email from design. He skimmed it, fingers tapping the table. The Johnson pitch needed a full overhaul.

"Yeah, maybe after this project wraps up." He doesn't meet Emily's eyes, already calculating how many hours he'll need to re-work the presentation. "The client's particular about their branding, and Park and I need to nail this one."

Emily's hand slips from his wrist. The light shifted, shadowing her features. She pushes back from the table, chair legs scraping against the floor.

"That's what you said about the last project." She carries her mug to the sink, her back turned. "And the one before that."

Zane stays focused on his phone, scrolling through mock-ups. The fridge photos blur, weekends buried beneath deadlines.

Emily shoulders tense beneath the green blouse she wore on their first date, though Zane doesn't notice anymore.

Zane scrolls through his inbox again. Subject lines blur: Reminder. Urgent. Please Review.

Emily traces her mug, watching Zane's eyes flick across his screen.

Zane mumbles something about changes the client wants, but Emily doesn't respond. Her eyes follow a pigeon on the sill until it flies into the city.

"One of my students did the sweetest thing yesterday," she says, tone light, like she's testing the air between them.

Zane doesn't look up. "Yeah?"

"Remember Tommy? The shy one with the dinosaur backpack?"

He nods, eyes still on his screen. "Sure."

"He brought in this little origami crane his grandmother taught him to make. Spent recess showing the other kids how. By the end of the day, my desk was full of them. Twenty-seven little paper cranes, all different colors."

"That's nice," Zane says, barely glancing up, his smile fading behind the glow of his screen.

"I kept one." Emily pulls a small blue crane from her purse, wings slightly bent. "Tommy said blue ones bring good luck." She sets it on the table and gently fixes the wings.

Zane looks up, smiling warmer this time. "Sounds like you're making progress." His phone buzzes and his eyes return to the screen.

Emily's fingers linger on the paper crane.

She'd spent nearly an hour yesterday arranging all twenty-seven cranes on her classroom windowsill, carefully spacing each one, proud of the breakthrough. But that part of the story stays with her now.

She folds the crane's wing back into place, then places it on top of her purse. The moment passes, quiet and unnoticed, like so many others between them.

Emily stirs her coffee in slow, steady circles. Clink. Clink. Clink.

Zane zips through his phone, replying to another urgent email.

A siren wails below, muffled by the windows. Emily watches steam curl from her cup and vanish. Her hair falls forward, hiding her face.

Clink. Clink.

Emily glances at the fridge calendar—her neat handwriting marking dinners and movie nights now crossed out. Red Xs have piled up like fallen leaves.

Zane mutters something about client revisions. His coffee sits untouched, a brown ring clinging to the mug.

The spoon slows. Clink... Clink... Each circle is more drawn out than the last.

Emily opens her mouth, then shuts it. Her hand traces the table's grain.

Zane catches Emily's reflection in the glass—face down, fingers tight on her mug. Daylight reveals exhaustion he hadn't noticed. His phone buzzes again. He flips it over and ignores it.

"You know what this reminds me of?" He gestures to his half-eaten breakfast. "That disaster brunch I tried to make when you first moved in."

Emily glances up, a hint of amusement breaking through her clouded expression. "You mean when you set off every smoke detector in the building?"

"Hey, those pancakes were just... extra crispy." He leans back, loosening his tie. "The fire department said they'd never seen such perfectly carbonized breakfast food."

"Mrs. Peterson from 12B still gives you suspicious looks in the elevator." The corner of Emily's mouth twitches upward.

"She should thank me. I gave her bridge club material for weeks." Zane lifts the crane carefully. "Though my cooking hasn't improved much."

Her smile is playful, but her expression stays guarded. She cradles her mug. "At least you didn't burn the eggs this time."

"Progress, right?" Zane sets the crane down. "Maybe by next year I'll figure out how to make toast without turning it into charcoal."

Her laugh is genuine this time, even if it doesn't completely erase her shoulder tension. "Baby steps."

Emily sets her mug in the sink with care. A soft click against the basin. "I should get going soon. Staff meeting this morning.

We're planning the science fair." She moves through their routine, grabbing her bag and checking for her metro card.

"The kids are building volcanoes this year. Less messy than last year's ecosystem projects," she says. Her voice is light, but the tension stays. "Remember Tommy's origami? He wants to do a project on the physics of paper airplanes."

Zane's phone lights up again, but Emily continues as if she doesn't notice. "I told him about that documentary we watched. The one about Japanese paper art? He's already started researching different designs."

She slips on her flats, steady and slow. Sunlight hits the silver bracelet he gave her last Christmas as she checks her watch.

"Maybe he'll revolutionize aerospace engineering with his paper airplanes." Emily's smile is honest now, focused on her student's enthusiasm. "But right now he's mostly interested in seeing how far they'll fly across the playground."

Zane watches her gather her things. Her posture feels heavier. That distance in her expression twists something in his chest. When did that shift happen? He's not sure.

His phone flashes again. The Johnson account could mean a promotion. A corner office. Better pay. Benefits. A future where Emily doesn't have to stretch her teacher's salary.

But Emily's words rattle in his mind: "Things never calm down."

He looks at the fridge—red Xs mark dinner plans. Each canceled for meetings, deadlines, calls. All for their future, he tells himself. Every missed moment, an investment.

The paper crane catches his eye, wings slightly crushed. Emily's student shared something of himself. When did Zane last do the same?

His fingers rest on his phone case. The pitch needs revisions. The client won't wait. Emily won't either, he thinks.

"It's temporary," he mutters, straightening his already-straight tie. He hears the hollowness in his voice. How many times has he made that promise?

But the thought of stepping back, of letting even one ball drop in his carefully juggled career, sends anxiety crawling up his spine. Success requires sacrifice. Emily will understand once he lands this account, once he secures their future.

Won't she?

Zane downs his coffee, cold and bitter. The mug clinks as he sets it down. His phone lights up again. Another message from Park, but he ignores it.

Emily zips up her bag, tucking a folder of student assignments inside. Her auburn hair hits the morning light, and for a moment, Zane remembers their first breakfast in this apartment. How she'd laughed when he couldn't figure out the fancy coffee maker she'd brought from her old place.

He rises, slinging his laptop bag over his shoulder. The silence sits heavily between them. No time to fix it. The N train won't wait. Neither will his clients.

"Thanks for everything," he says, softer than planned. He steps closer, breathing in her lavender-sweet shampoo. His lips brush her forehead, lingering.

Emily's eyes close at the contact. Her hand finds his arm, squeezing gently. "Have a good day." The words carry both warmth and worry, a contradiction he's grown used to hearing.

She walks him to the door. Emily stands against the doorframe, watching as he checks his pockets—phone, wallet, keys. He's always misplacing something.

Zane catches her expression, that blend of love and concern he knows too well. She studies his face, searching for something long gone.

He steps into the hallway, adjusting his tie. The elevator dings. Still, he glances back—Emily framed in the doorway like a memory.

Emily lingers in the doorway until Zane disappears. The elevator doors close, leaving her alone with the sunlight and cooling coffee cups.

Back at the table, she circles the top of Zane's abandoned mug. His chair sits empty, A jacket draped over its back, the brown one with the worn elbows he keeps forgetting to take to the cleaners.

Her fingers find her phone, muscle memory pulling up their photo album.

The screen fills with a photo from last summer—Zane's arms around her waist, both laughing in Central Park. His tie loose, top button undone. They'd skipped a networking event to feed ducks and eat hot dogs. His phone stayed in his pocket for hours.

Emily watches a pigeon on their windowsill. It pecks at nothing, then takes flight, vanishing into the canyon of buildings.

Her thumb hovers over the photo. That version of Zane feels distant now, like someone else's story. She sets the phone face-down and pushes back from the table.

Down in the lobby, the elevator deposits Zane into the morning rush. He joins the stream of suits and briefcases flowing toward the subway, his phone already in hand. The Johnson pitch dominates his notifications, with urgent messages from Park about color schemes and font choices.

The memory of Emily's smile fades beneath the weight of client expectations. His tie feels too tight, but he doesn't loosen it. Sacrifice, he reminds himself. The promotion will make it worth it.

The N train rumbles beneath his feet as he descends into the station, leaving the morning's quiet moments behind.

Chapter 2

THE BELL ABOVE THE Beanie Café door chimes as Zane enters, a gust of air trailing him. Warm coffee air meets the chill outside. His laptop bag bumps against his hip as he fumbles for his worn loyalty card.

Dark wood panels reflect the glow of pendant lights. The morning crowd hunches over laptops with headphones on. The barista's practiced movements behind the counter provide a steady rhythm: the hiss of steam, the tap of grounds, the clink of ceramic.

His eyes find Park at their corner table, already settled in with what looks like his second cappuccino. The familiar view through the window frames his friend—the brick building across the street, the small florist shop with its colorful display. Their table sits apart from others, perfect for their regular catch-ups.

Zane weaves between chairs, dodging a toddler who's escaped parental supervision. His shoulders ache from tension. Emily lingers at the edge of his thoughts, but Park's calm smile helps push it aside.

Floorboards creak as Zane approaches. Park's laptop screen displays the Johnson pitch—splashes of color and text that will need hours of refinement. Their corner feels like a sanctuary, removed from both home and office, where problems seem more manageable over steaming cups of coffee.

Park glances up from his laptop, blue eyes shine with mischief. "Well, if it isn't GQ's newest cover model. Did you iron those jeans too?"

Zane sits in a chair across from him, the wood creaking beneath his weight. The familiar scent of Park's cologne mingles with coffee grounds and freshly baked scones.

"Some of us actually care about first impressions." Zane tugs at his crisp button-down. "Unlike certain people who think hoodies count as business casual."

"Hey, this is designer." Park spreads his arms, showcasing the well-worn gray fabric. "And I closed three accounts last month looking exactly like this. Meanwhile, you're dressed like you're meeting the Queen."

"The Johnson pitch—"

"Yeah, yeah." Park leans back, crossing his arms. "You've got that 'I skipped breakfast to color-coordinate my socks' look again."

"I made breakfast, actually." The words slip out before Zane can catch them.

"Ah." Park's expression shifts, the teasing edge softening. "And you were too busy checking emails to eat, right?"

A flush rises up Zane's neck. He pulls out his laptop, the metal cool in his hands.

"That's what I thought." Park drums his fingers. "You know, for someone who spends hours perfecting presentation slides, you're pretty terrible at reading the room at home."

Zane pushes away from the table. His chair scrapes the wood. "The usual?"

"You know me too well." Park's fingers tap across his keyboard, eyes fixed on the screen. "Extra shot this time. These metrics aren't making sense."

Zane faces Maya, purple-streaked hair tucked under a black cap. Her hands don't stop moving, guided by muscle memory.

"Let me guess." Maya's silver nose ring glints in the light as she grins. "Black coffee, no room for cream, and that ridiculous latte with three shots, and—"

Zane pulls out his wallet. "Make it four shots today. Park's wrestling with spreadsheets."

"Ah, a numbers emergency." She punches in their order without looking at the register. "You two are so predictable, I could probably make your drinks in my sleep. Same corner table, same drinks, same times every day."

"Creatures of habit." The familiar aroma of fresh grounds fills his lungs as Maya moves to the espresso machine. "Though Park claims his hoodie is different today. Apparently it's designer."

Maya snorts, her hands dancing over levers and buttons. "That thing? He's worn it at least twice this week already. But don't tell him I said that."

Steam hisses as she froths milk. The whir of the machine drowns the café's chatter, giving Zane a brief barrier from his thoughts. He watches her pour with precision, forming a perfect leaf.

"There." She slides both drinks across the counter. "One boring black coffee and one 'I'm too important for sleep' latte. Try not to make any life-changing decisions before the caffeine kicks in."

Zane balances the drinks on the way back to their corner, careful not to spill Park's latte. The foam leaf starts to dissolve, bleeding into abstract shapes.

"Speaking of designer..." Park closes his laptop with a snap. "That's what, the third new shirt this week? The marketing budget isn't covering your shopping sprees, is it?"

"It's called professionalism." Zane slides Park's drink across the table. "You should try it sometime."

"Oh, please." Park wraps his hands around the mug. "The only relationship you're in right now is with your career. When's the last time you took Emily somewhere that wasn't connected to a client meeting?"

Zane opens his laptop, the screen glowing with unread emails.

"That's what I thought." Park leans forward, elbows on the table. "You know what your problem is? You've got your priorities so backwards, you probably scheduled 'spontaneous romance' for next quarter's planning meeting."

"I'm focused." Zane's fingers hover over the keyboard. "There's nothing wrong with taking work seriously."

"Focused?" Park snorts into his latte. "You're practically married to your inbox. I bet you sleep with your phone under your pillow, whispering sweet nothings to the calendar app."

"At least I'm moving up the ladder."

"Yeah, while your actual relationship gathers dust in the corner." Park's eyes sparkle with mischief. "Do you and Emily even remember what date night looks like? Or do you just sync your Google calendars and call it quality time?"

Zane sips his coffee, letting the bitterness ground him.

"That's it." Park snaps his fingers. "We should start a betting pool at the office. How many times can Zane mention the Johnson pitch during dinner? My money's on at least five times before dessert."

Park sets his mug down, foam clinging to his upper lip. "You know what would really impress the higher-ups? A power move like getting engaged. Nothing says 'corner office material' like putting a ring on it."

Zane's stomach tightens. He takes another sip, buying time.

"Emily has very particular ideas about proposals."

"Oh?" Park wipes his mouth with a napkin. "Let me guess - something Pinterest-worthy? Hot air balloon at sunset? Flash mob in Times Square?"

"She mentioned once that her parents got engaged at the Met," Zane says, tracing the rim of his cup. "During some fancy exhibit opening. Her mom still talks about it.""And you're using that as an excuse because...?"

"It's not an excuse. She deserves something special." The words fall flat even to him. "Something memorable.""Right, because waiting for the perfect moment is working out so well." Park leans back. "You've been together what, three years now? That's longer than most Netflix shows survive."

"Two and a half." Zane's correction comes automatically.

"My point exactly. You've got the timeline memorized, but can't pull the trigger." Park's voice softens. "Come on, man. What's really holding you back?"

Zane stares into his coffee. The morning replaying—Emily's patient smile, stirring even after the sugar had dissolved.

"The timing just isn't right." He straightens his sleeve, smoothing an invisible wrinkle. "With the Johnson pitch coming up—"

"There's always going to be another pitch." Park drums his fingers against the table. "Another deadline, another project. Meanwhile, Emily's still waiting for you to figure out that life isn't a quarterly review."

Zane shifts, the wood creaking. His eyes dart to Maya behind the counter, a convenient escape.

"What about you and the artistic barista? I saw how she drew that leaf in your latte. Very... personal."

"Nice try." Park's eyes crinkle at the corners. "Maya's got a girlfriend who teaches yoga in Brooklyn. They're adopting a rescue pit bull next week."

"Since when do you know so much about her life?"

"Since I actually talk to people instead of hiding behind spreadsheets." Park takes another sip of his latte. "But we're not done discussing your relationship amnesia."

Zane's fingers drum against his coffee cup. "There was that girl from accounting—"

"Who transferred to Boston last month." Park waves his hand. "And before you bring up Sarah from legal, she's engaged now. To a woman, by the way. Shows how much attention you pay to office gossip."

"The point is—"

"The point is you're deflecting." Park leans forward, his designer hoodie catching on the edge of the table. "And doing a terrible job at it. I mean, seriously? Trying to set me up with Maya? That's amateur hour, even for you."

Heat creeps up Zane's neck. He tugs at his collar, suddenly too tight.

"At least my dating disasters make for good stories." Park grins. "Remember that chef who tried to 'elevate' my palate with fermented fish paste? Or the cyclist who measured everything in kilometers? Those are solid gold entertainment. Your love life? More like watching paint dry in slow motion."

"My relationship is fine."

"Sure, if by 'fine' you mean 'slowly suffocating under a pile of unread text messages and missed dinner dates.'" Park's voice carries a hint of genuine concern beneath the teasing. "But hey, at least your PowerPoint transitions are on point."

Park watches Zane turn his cup in slow increments. Light from the window highlights the exhaustion under his eyes and makes his skin look washed out.

"Look, I give you grief because I care." Park pushes his half-empty latte aside. "Remember when we first started at the firm? You used to talk about Emily for hours. The way her eyes squint when she laughs, how she can quiet down an entire classroom of kids with just a look."

Zane keeps his hands around his cup.

"But when's the last time you told her?" Park leans forward, his voice dropping. "You've got this amazing woman who somehow puts up with your obsession with client demographics and marketing metrics. She makes you breakfast, for crying out loud. Real breakfast, not just protein bars and coffee."

Park's words land hard. Zane remembers this morning: Emily's gentle touch on his shoulder and how she tried to meet his eyes across the kitchen table.

"You're not wrong." The admission comes out.

"Of course I'm not wrong. I'm never wrong." Park's grin returns, but his eyes stay serious. "Emily's not some quarterly report you can put off until next week. She's not going to wait around forever while you chase promotions and perfect pitch decks."

A lump rises in Zane's throat. The café's warmth presses against his collar.

"The thing about relationships," Park continues, "is they're like those plants Emily keeps trying to grow on your balcony. Ignore them too long, they wither. No amount of last-minute watering can fix dead leaves."

Park glances at his phone. His smile fades and shoulders sag. "Speaking of dates..." He traces the coffee ring on the table, his finger following the perfect circle. "Next week. It'll be two years."

Zane tenses. The café feels stifling as memories flood in: screeching tires, shattered glass, the metallic taste of blood. His coffee sits untouched and cold.

"Mike would've loved this place." Park's voice comes out rough. "Remember how he used to rate coffee shops based on their Wi-Fi speeds? Said it was the only metric that mattered."

The corner of Zane's mouth twitches. "He'd hack their networks just to run speed tests."

"Got us kicked out of that place in Brooklyn." Park's finger stills on the table. "The one with the pretentious barista, who insisted on calling everything 'artisanal.'"

Light spills through the window, casting shifting patterns across Park's face. His usual composure slips under the weight. The café's hum fades as memories take hold: Mike's grin, relentless puns, and uncanny timing with food.

"I drive past that intersection sometimes." Park speaks softly, eyes fixed on the fading foam in his cup. "Can't help it. Office route goes right by it."

Zane clenches his cup, knuckles white. The scar on his cheek tingles with phantom memory. His throat tightens, words failing as Park sits quietly.

Grief settles between them, heavier than the morning's earlier banter. Park's designer hoodie looks like armor against the memories.

Zane's fingers circle the edge of his cup, the ceramic's warmth long faded. "I haven't been to see him." The words scrape against his throat. "Not since..."

"The funeral?" Park's voice stays gentle, unlike his usual teasing tone.

"March." Zane's scar burns with phantom pain. "I drove there, sat in the parking lot for an hour. Couldn't get out of the car."

Zane gazes into his coffee as his shoulders sink.

"I keep meaning to go. Buy flowers or... something. But every time I try..." The words knot in his chest.

Park reaches across, grounding Zane with a hand on his arm.

"I should have been there more." Zane's voice cracks. "He deserves better than—" Zane gestures at himself. "Than this. Me forgetting, buried in work and pitches and..."

His throat tightens. The polished exterior cracks, guilt showing through.

Park's grip on Zane's forearm tightens, his thumb pressing against the crisp fabric of his shirt. "You know what Mike would say right now?" His voice carries a familiar warmth. "He'd tell us we're being dramatic idiots who need to get back to work."

A ghost of a smile appears on Zane's face. "Probably throw in some comment about our coffee choices too."

"'Four shots of espresso? What are you, a machine?'" Park's impression of Mike's voice breaks through the heaviness. "'Real hackers drink energy drinks, you corporate sellouts.'"

Zane's shoulders ease. Morning sun lights the rising steam, curling like tangible memories.

"He lived more in twenty-six years than most people do in eighty." Park lets go of Zane's arm and leans back. "Remember that time he convinced the entire IT department to wear Hawaiian shirts for the quarterly review?"

"The CEO's face when they all walked in..."

"That's who Mike was. He didn't waste time worrying about what could have been." Park meets Zane's gaze, steady and sure. "He'd want us moving forward, not sitting in parking lots or avoiding intersections."

Park's words settle between them, lighter than grief but just as lasting. The café sounds return—espresso hissing, Maya's laugh, cups clinking.

"Besides," Park adds, his voice softening, "he'd be the first one telling you to get your head out of spreadsheets and pay attention to what matters. Like that amazing woman who makes you breakfast and puts up with your workaholic tendencies."

Park finishes his drink, foam clinging to his lip. "If Mike were here, he'd have plenty to say about your expensive taste in shirts.""Don't." Zane's lips twitch.

"'Did your closet throw up a J.Crew catalog?'" Park's impression of Mike's voice cracks through the heaviness. "'Or are you auditioning for Wall Street: The Musical?'"

A real laugh breaks from Zane. "He used to call my ties 'corporate nooses.'""Remember when he reprogrammed your work calendar to remind you every hour to 'loosen up, you stuffed penguin'?" Park rubs his nose. "IT couldn't undo it for weeks."

"The notifications kept getting more creative." Zane shakes his head, smile growing. "'Warning: Stack overflow detected in stick-up-ass parameter.'"

"'Emergency alert: Fun levels critically low. Prescribed treatment: Remove head from spreadsheet.'" Park's eyes crinkle. "He had your phone playing the Imperial March every time the CEO walked by."

"I had to keep it on silent for a month."

"Face it, man. Even from beyond, Mike would be roasting your pressed khakis."Their laughter rises as sunlight glints off empty cups. The grief lingers, softened by memory.

Park leans back, drumming his fingers on the worn table. He eyes their usual spot, then grabs the unused steak knife beside his plate.

Zane watches as Park's hand moves with deliberate strokes, the metal tip scratching against the surface. The letters emerge one by one: C... B... C... K.

"What are you doing?" Zane frowns at the new etching among the scars and initials.

Park sets the knife down, admiring his handiwork with exaggerated pride. "Just giving you a head start on your next big marketing campaign."

"CBCK?"

"Crossroads Between Chaos and Kismet." Park's grin widens as he watches Zane's expression shift from confusion to disbelief. "Has a nice ring to it, don't you think? Very zen. Very now. The millennials will eat it up."

Zane stares at the crude letters, his marketing brain already picking apart the absurdity. "That's not even-"

"What? Too philosophical for the Johnson pitch?" Park's eyes sparkle as he teases. "Come on, it's better than your usual 'Synergy Through Innovation' corporate speak."

Zane glances at his watch. His stomach drops. "Shit. The Johnson meeting's in twenty."

"And there it is." Park shakes his head, gathering his jacket. "The corporate panic face. Like clockwork."

"Some of us care about being punctual." Zane stands and adjusts his tie. Morning light shows the creases in his shirt."

Hey." Park's hand catches his sleeve. "Before you sprint off to save the marketing world, you'll think about what I said?"

"About Emily?" Zane's fingers tap against his phone. "Yeah. Maybe I'll ask her about that gallery opening next weekend. The one with the weird light installations."

"Progress." Park releases his grip. "Small steps toward actual human interaction. I'm touched."

"And maybe..." Zane's lips quirk up. "We could discuss our future over overpriced wine and pretentious art descriptions."

"Now you're speaking her language." Park slides out of the booth. "Just don't lead with PowerPoint presentations about your five-year relationship roadmap."

"That was one time, and it was a very well-designed presentation."

"With transition effects and everything." Park claps him on the shoulder. " Go. Save Johnson from their marketing crisis. Just remember, Emily's not a quarterly target."

Zane nods and gathers his things. His fingers touch the new etching—CBCK—and he can't help but smile. "Thanks, Park. For everything."

"That's what best friends are for. Keeping you from drowning in spreadsheets and missed opportunities."

Park watches Zane move through the morning crowd, pressed shirt sharp against the sea of casual wear. His retreating form stirs both affection and concern.

"That man needs Emily more than he needs another promotion." Park's words vanish into his cooling coffee. He traces the new carving, feeling the grooves cut through years of layered stains.

Morning sun shifts, shadows falling across the wood. Around the fresh CBCK, the table tells other stories - initials enclosed in hearts, phone numbers long disconnected, fragments of poetry written in moments of inspiration or desperation. Someone's "Call Sam!" sits next to what looks like song lyrics. A crude sketch of a coffee cup overlaps with mathematical equations.

Maya appears at his elbow, coffee pot in hand. "Another round?"

"Nah, I should head out too." Park's hand lingers on the table. "You know, I've been coming here for years, and I never really looked at all these marks before."

She smiles at the carved mess. "Each one's a story. Sometimes customers point out their old messages: from first dates, breakups, job celebrations. It's like a diary written by everyone and no one."

Park nods. His etching already looks like it belongs. A thread in the wood's woven tapestry of New York moments.

"Your friend okay?" Maya gestures toward the door with her chin. "Seemed intense today."

"He will be." Park stands, adjusting his hoodie. "Just needs to remember what matters."

He glances back once more. The morning's carving blends into the chaos, the scratches catching light like a map of choices and connections.

Chapter 3

THE ELEVATOR DOORS PART with a soft chime, and Zane steps onto the thirty-second floor of Madison Square's glass tower. Chrome and white surfaces gleam under recessed lighting, while floor-to-ceiling windows frame Manhattan's urban sprawl.

A buzz of nervous energy fills the open office space. Jessica from Creative hunches over her tablet, furiously adjusting presentation slides. Two junior associates huddle around Mark's desk, papers scattered across the surface as they double-check their numbers.

"Morning everyone." Zane's footsteps echo against the polished concrete floor. His presence draws attention, shoulders relaxing as he passes.

"Thank god you're here." Tom, a fresh-faced junior associate, clutches a stack of reports. Sweat beads on his forehead. "The metrics from Q3 aren't matching up with the forecast."

"Deep breath, Tom." Zane places a steady hand on his shoulder. "Show me what you've got."

Tom spreads the reports across a desk, his fingers trembling as he points to the charts.

"See? The engagement rates don't align with our projected-"

"Because you're looking at raw data." Zane leans in, tapping a different column. "Factor in the seasonal adjustments. The story's right there."

Relief floods Tom's features. "I can't believe I missed that."

"First big presentation?" Zane straightens Tom's slightly crooked tie. "You've done the work. Trust it."

"But Johnson's reputation for being... difficult?"

"Just people, like us." Zane flashes a warm smile. "Looking for solutions to their problems. And guess what? We have those solutions."

Tom relaxes. Around them, the office regains its rhythm, feeding off Zane's calm.

"Now," Zane claps his hands together, "let's make this presentation sing."

Zane cycles through slides in the empty conference room. His reflection shows tired eyes, proof of another sleepless night.

He pulls up the competitor analysis. Graphs fill the screen—weeks of work. His hand brushes his scar as he studies each detail.

"Font's too small." He adjusts the text size, then readjusts it back. "No, original was better."

The door clicks open. Jessica pokes her head in, tablet pressed against her chest.

"Five minutes until Johnson arrives. Need anything?"

"Water. And maybe some aspirin."

She nods and disappears. Zane loosens his tie, then tightens it again. The presentation remote feels slick in his palm. He wipes his hand on his pants and checks his phone. There are no messages from Emily. The thought stirs unease, but he pushes it away.

The projector hums as it powers on. Zane clicks through the slides, silently rehearsing key phrases. His reflection in the window looks steady and composed, but his bouncing leg under the table tells another story.

Jessica returns with water and two white pills. "They're in the lobby."

"Thanks." He swallows the aspirin dry. "How's Tom holding up?"

"Still looks like he might throw up."

"Tell him to breathe. We've got this."

She leaves, and Zane straightens the materials in front of him: notes, research, backup charts. Each one exactly three inches from the edge. The ritual steadies his hands.

The distant ding of the elevator signals the clients' arrival. Zane takes a deep breath, squares his shoulders, and opens the first slide.

Zane's phone vibrates on the table. Emily's name lights the screen: "Knock them dead today. You've got this!"

A small smile breaks through. The message softens his chest, reminding him why he fell for her—her support, even when he didn't deserve it.

His thumbs hover over the keyboard. A dozen responses flash through his mind. An apology for breakfast, a promise to make it up to her, a heartfelt thank you for being there. Instead, he types "thanks" and hits send, the single word feeling inadequate even as it appears in their chat.

The phone screen dims. Zane sets it face-down on the table, pushing thoughts of Emily into a mental box labeled 'Later.' The presentation remote feels heavier in his hand as he refocuses on the task ahead. Numbers and charts are easier than emotions.

Voices approach. Zane straightens, boxing up Emily and the morning. The phone buzzes again, but this time he doesn't look. Some things have to wait.

The conference room door swings open. Johnson strides in, followed by his team of executives in crisp suits and power blazers. Zane rises to greet them, his handshake firm, his smile practiced.

"Let's talk about revolutionizing your market presence." Zane clicks the slide. Blue light floods the room. His voice is clear, every word calculated.

Charts roll by. Numbers dance, stories of growth and opportunity. Pens scratch notepads.

"But what about the Q4 projections?" Johnson interrupts, pointing to a graph. "These numbers seem optimistic."

"Actually..." Zane queues a prepared slide. The data flows. Johnson's doubt fades to interest.

Tom catches Zane's eye from across the table, a mix of awe and admiration on his face. This is success, Zane thinks. It's what he's supposed to want.

Yet as he walks through the market analysis, something feels hollow. The words echo, rehearsed. Praise rolls off him, weightless.

A memory flashes of Emily's face this morning, trying to connect. Here he stands, commanding attention, solving problems, but the victory feels mechanical. Like reading from a script he's performed too many times."

Impressive approach." Johnson nods, scribbling notes. "Very thorough."

Zane responds on autopilot, confidence on the outside while his mind drifts. When did success turn into box-checking?

He advances to the next slide, statistics and projections filling the screen. Everyone listens intently, yet a doubt lingers: Is this it?

The room empties in a blur of handshakes. Johnson pats his back, promising more work. The words "game-changer" and "breakthrough" float through the air like confetti. "Drinks tonight?" Jessica squeezes his arm. "This calls for celebration."

"Maybe." Zane gathers his materials, each page filed with precision.

Lights hum overhead as he passes rows of typing colleagues. Whispers follow him down the hallway, but the victory feels like sand slipping through his fingers, impossible to grasp, leaving only grit behind.

His office door shuts, muffling the champagne pop from the break room. Zane drops his presentation folder on the desk, the thud echoing in the quiet space. Outside his window, yellow cabs crawl through midday traffic like toys. People stream along sidewalks, each caught in their own rush toward something better, bigger, more.

He leans back in his chair, his reflection framed in the window: crisp suit, perfect tie, corporate polish. But his eyes hold something different. But his eyes hold something different, something that doesn't match the polished surface.

Messages light up his phone. The project's approved. More work. More empty wins.

Zane rubs his face. The city stretches endlessly before him, a maze of glass and steel reaching toward an overcast sky. Somewhere in those streets, life happens, real life, not this choreographed dance of meetings and metrics.

His desk calendar is packed with client names and deadlines for the week ahead. The future sits heavy on his chest.

Zane thumbs through a stream of congratulatory messages. "Crushed it!" "You're unstoppable!" "Legend!" The words blur together—loud and empty. He stops on Emily's text. One quiet line, heavier than the rest.

Zane traces the scar on his cheek, the skin still uneven. It's been years, but the crash with Mike hits just as hard. Twisted metal. Shattered glass. The promises made in those final moments about what really matters. Promises he lost somewhere on the way up.

In the corner of his desk sits a framed photo from his first big win three years ago. His smile back then was unguarded, real. Now, the victories feel hollow.

He reaches for his coffee. It's empty, like everything else. The folder that once felt urgent is now just numbers, stripped of meaning.

Zane's thumb hovers over Emily's message. Her words cut through the corporate fog: "Knock them dead today. You've got this." He barely acknowledged it.

He opens their text thread, "Thanks," "Running late," "In a meeting." When did he stop talking to her?

The calendar app draws his eye. No meetings after five. He taps his phone, an idea forming: that Italian place in the West Village. Emily said their tiramisu tasted like clouds.

He dials the restaurant, ducking behind his desk as colleagues pass by his office.

"Salvatore's? Yes, table for two tonight. Something quiet, by the window if possible."

The maître d' recognizes him. They used to be regulars before work took over. "Ah, Mr. Hart! For you and Miss Emily? Your usual table is available."

The corner spot where Emily would steal bites of his pasta, laughing that hers tasted better. Where she'd tell stories about her students with her eyes sparkling in the candlelight.

He books it for seven. Enough time to stop by that flower shop. The one with the name he always forgets, but they always have purple dahlias.

His fingers type out a message: "Don't make dinner plans tonight. I'm taking you somewhere special." He adds a heart emoji. It's something he hasn't done in weeks.

Emily's response comes quickly: "Oh? What's the occasion?"

"Just because." He smiles at his phone, warmth spreading through his chest. "Because you deserve it."

A knock breaks the moment. Jessica stands in the doorway, tablet hugged to her chest.

"Sorry to interrupt your victory moment, but the Peterson account needs immediate attention." She steps into his office. "Their CMO sent over some concerns about the digital strategy."

Zane sits straighter, professionalism snapping into place. "Walk me through it."

She shows him analytics. Red arrows. "Engagement's down fifteen percent since we rolled out changes."

"Let me see the demographic breakdown." Zane leans forward, his eyes scanning the numbers. The familiar rhythm of problem solving takes over. "

We're targeting too broad. Narrow it to twenty-five to forty, urban professionals. Adjust the ad copy accordingly."

"That's exactly what I was thinking but wanted your confirmation," Jessica says, making quick notes. "Should I schedule a call with their team?"

"Set it for tomorrow morning. I'll draft a revised strategy tonight."

Jessica nods and heads for the door, pausing briefly. "You really should celebrate today's win, you know."

The door shuts. Alone again, Zane slumps, fingers to his temples. A dull ache pulses in his head due to too many spreadsheets and not enough sleep. He exhales, the weight of tasks pressing down.

Emails blink, calendar pings. Peterson needs review. Calls stack up. Pressure rises again.

His typing echoes through the quiet office. The Peterson account needs attention, but Emily's face keeps floating into his thoughts. He straightens his posture, squaring his shoulders against the leather chair."

This is all for us," he whispers to the window. The city lights twinkle behind his silhouette, a constellation of possibilities. Every late night, every missed dinner, building for their future. A house in the suburbs, maybe. Kids running through a backyard. Emily's smile over morning coffee, without the worry lines he's noticed lately.

The thought steadies him. Numbers align into neat rows, each spreadsheet cell another brick in the foundation he's building.

He powers down, movements precise despite the exhaustion. The office has emptied, leaving him alone in the fluorescent glow.

Chapter 4

ZANE GUIDES EMILY THROUGH the entrance of Salvatore's, his hand resting on the small of her back. Crystal chandeliers cast a warm glow across exposed brick walls, and the host leads them to a corner table draped in crisp white linen. A single red rose stands in a slim vase between them, complementing the bouquet Zane presented to Emily earlier."

This is beautiful," Emily says. Candlelight catches in her eyes as she sits. Her auburn hair falls in soft waves, and she wears the black dress Zane always loved. Vintage, like old Hollywood.

The sommelier pours Cabernet into their glasses. The scent of blackberry and oak rises as it swirls. A jazz quartet plays softly under the clink of silverware and low conversation.

"I know we haven't had much time together lately." Zane's fingers brush against Emily's across the table. Her skin is warm against his. "I wanted tonight to be special."

Emily takes a sip of wine, leaving a faint lipstick mark on the glass. "It feels like ages since we've done something like this."

The candle flickers, shadows playing across their faces. A waiter passes, plates balanced, as the scent of bread and garlic drifts over.

"Remember our first date?" Zane leans forward, his voice soft. "That terrible Chinese place in the East Village?"

"Where the fortune cookies were all in Spanish?" Emily laughs, the sound mixing with the saxophone's melody. "And you tried so hard to translate them."

Their wine glasses catch the light, casting ruby shadows. For a moment, it's like before: the stories, the candlelight, the city beyond.

"You're setting a dangerous precedent here." Emily rubs her finger against the stem of her wine glass. "Next time I'll expect a private yacht or maybe our own island."

"I could probably expense the yacht as a team-building exercise." Zane's shoulders drop, the tension from his workday melting away. Emily takes another sip of wine. "

This is exactly what we needed. No emails, no lesson plans, just us."

"Remember that weekend in Vermont?" Zane's eyes light up. "When we got lost hiking and ended up at that maple syrup farm?"

"The one where you convinced the farmer to let us sample every single flavor?" Emily covers her mouth, stifling a laugh. "I couldn't look at pancakes for weeks after that."

"But you have to admit, the bourbon barrel-aged syrup was worth it."

"Worth the sugar crash that had you passed out in the car? Absolutely." Emily leans back. "Though I think my favorite part was when that goat started chasing you."

"He was not chasing me." Zane straightens his napkin. "We were playing tag."

"Is that what you call running and screaming?"

The jazz quartet slows into a softer tune. Zane taps to the rhythm, his phone forgotten in his jacket.

"Oh! And that tiny bed and breakfast," Emily says. "With the quilts that looked like they were from the 1800s?"

"And the owner who kept trying to set us up with her grandchildren, even though we were clearly there together."

Their laughter blends with the music and the soft murmur of nearby tables. Wine warms their cheeks. Stories flow like the Cabernet.

A waiter arrives with a crystal decanter. Zane nods, and deep red wine fills Emily's glass, then his.

"We'll take another bottle of the Cabernet." Zane spots the label as the waiter turns the bottle. "The 2018 vintage."

Emily traces the stem of her glass, her fingers moving in slow circles. Light hits her green eyes as she looks up at Zane. "You know what I love most about tonight? It's not the fancy restaurant or the wine. It's this: just us, really talking."

"I miss these moments." Emily's voice softens as the waiter steps away. "Remember when we used to do Sundays in bed, reading the paper and arguing over who'd make coffee?"

"The coffee maker misses your touch." Zane smiles over his glass.

"I'm serious." Emily leans forward, her auburn hair falling across one shoulder. "

These past few months, it feels like we're ships passing in the night. But tonight, tonight reminds me why we work so well together." She pauses, running her thumb along the edge of the table. "I want more of this, Zane. More moments where work stays at work, where we can just be us."

The quartet slows again. Emily's words linger. Her hand finds his, interlacing their fingers.

"I want a future full of Vermont weekends and Spanish fortune cookies. Of morning coffees and evening wines." Her voice carries a gentle strength. "I want that with you."

Zane's fingers tighten around Emily's, his thumb tracing the delicate bones of her wrist. Candlelight shadows his face as her words settle in his chest.

"You're right," he says, his voice soft. "I've been letting work consume everything. Even when I'm home, I'm not really there."

She squeezes his hand, and he notices the slight tremble in her fingers.

"Remember last month when you wanted to try that new breakfast place?" Zane shifts in his chair. "I checked emails throughout the entire meal. Didn't even taste the food."

"The pancakes were amazing, by the way," Emily whispers with a gentle smile.

"See? That's exactly what I mean." Zane sets his wine glass down. "I want to know how the pancakes taste. I want Sunday mornings and Vermont weekends. I want to be present for all of it."

Music surrounds them. Zane shifts in his seat, something inside him loosening, a wall giving way.

"You deserve better than half my attention." His free hand covers their already joined ones. "And I want to give you that. Not just tonight, but every day."

Her eyes shine in the dim light. She blinks fast, smile widening.

"I mean it, Em. No more working through breakfast. No more missed date nights." He leans closer, his voice dropping to match the intimate space between them. "I want all those moments with you too."

Dessert menus land. Zane barely notices. His fingers brush the velvet box in his pocket, heartbeat climbing. The weight of it feels strange yet familiar after carrying it for weeks, waiting for the right moment.

Emily studies the menu, her lips moving silently as she reads the descriptions. A strand of auburn hair falls across her face, and she tucks it behind her ear without looking up. The gesture is so quintessentially her that Zane's throat tightens.

His palm sweats around the box. The speech from that morning splinters in his mind. Wine does nothing to quiet his chest's thunder.

Emily glances up. "You okay? You look a bit flushed."

"Just the wine." The lie comes out higher than intended, and he clears his throat.

The box burns in his pocket. He traces its edges, every corner memorized. The music softens, freezing time.

"Actually..." Zane shifts, gripping his knee to still the bounce. The word lingers while his mind fumbles for his rehearsed opening.

Emily tilts her head, waiting. Zane's heart flips, somersaults, crashes.

The waiter delivers their desserts, placing a soufflé in front of Emily and crème brûlée in front of Zane. The steam from Emily's dish carries a deep chocolate scent across the table."

Remember when I burned that chocolate cake for your birthday?" Zane watches Emily break through her soufflé's crisp top. "You ate it anyway."

"Because you spent all day making it," Emily says, spoon dipping into the molten center. "Even called your mom for the recipe."

"You've always been there," he says, tapping his spoon against the caramel top. "Through every disaster, culinary and otherwise. "Emily looks up, her spoon pausing halfway to her mouth. "That's what we do."

"When I lost that account, you didn't let me spiral." His voice drops. "You brought takeout. Made me laugh."

"And you helped me grade papers until midnight when I had the flu." Emily reaches out, the soft touch of her fingers meeting his across the table. "We're good at being there for each other."

"That's just it, Em." He sets his spoon down. "I can't picture my life without you in it. Without your strength, your patience." He swallows hard. "Even lost in work, knowing you're there keeps me grounded."

The soufflé cools untouched. Emily's eyes stay on him, shining.

"These past few years with you, through the good days and the bad ones, they've shown me what matters." Zane's thumb traces her palm. "And what matters is us, together."

Zane's chair scrapes against the hardwood floor as he rises. His fingers tremble around the velvet box in his pocket, and his heart pounds so loud he's sure the entire restaurant can hear it. The jazz quartet's melody seems to fade into the background, leaving only the sound of his pulse in his ears.

Emily's eyes follow his movement, widening as he steps beside her chair. The candlelight catches the tears already forming at their corners. Zane drops to one knee, the polished floor cool through his pants.

The box opens with a soft click. A platinum ring reflects the light—just like the one she admired outside Tiffany's.

Her hands cover her mouth as she gasps. Hair falls forward. The sound carries across their corner of the restaurant, drawing subtle glances from nearby tables. Her eyes lock onto the ring, then lift to meet Zane's gaze.

"Emily," his voice cracks. He swallows. "Will you marry me?"

Emily's hands remain pressed against her lips, tears now flowing freely down her cheeks. The restaurant holds its breath.

"Yes," she breathes, then louder, "Yes, of course!"

Applause ripples as the word echoes. A couple nearby smiles. A waiter joins the moment mid-step.

Zane's hands shake as he slides the ring onto her finger. The platinum band reflects the ambient light, sending prisms dancing across the tablecloth. Emily flexes her fingers, watching the diamond sparkle, and tears roll down her cheeks.

She reaches for him, pulling him close. Their lips meet, and Emily tastes salt from her tears mixed with the lingering sweetness of wine. Zane's hand cups her face, his thumb brushing away the moisture on her cheek.

She rests her forehead to his. "I love you," she whispers, voice thick with feeling.

Zane helps her to her feet, and she wraps her arms around his neck. The jazz quartet shifts into "At Last," the melody wrapping around them like a soft embrace. Other diners raise their wine glasses in quiet celebration, and the maître d' appears with a bottle of champagne, courtesy of the house.

She keeps staring at the ring, as if it's always belonged. Her chest swells, and Zane's smile mirrors hers.

The waiter approaches, tray steady and flutes aglow. "Compliments of the house," he says, setting them down.

Zane lifts his glass, the bubbles racing to the surface. "To us," he says, his voice soft but sure. "To morning coffees and Vermont weekends."

"To Spanish fortune cookies." Emily's eyes shine. Her ring catches the light as their flutes meet.

Their glasses chime. Champagne fizz mirrors the joy inside her. It tastes like celebration.

Outside, the air wraps around them. Under a streetlight, she lifts her hand. The ring scatters rainbows.

"It's perfect." She wiggles her fingers, watching the sparkles. "Though we might need to warn the kids not to stare directly at it. Could cause permanent damage."

"Kids already?" He laughs, pulling her in. "Let's get through the wedding first."

"Speaking of which..." Emily loops her arm through his as they walk. "I'm thinking a fall ceremony. October, maybe. When the leaves are turning."

"As long as there's no maple syrup fountain at the reception."

"But think of the photos!" She bumps his shoulder with hers. "The bride and groom, covered in sticky sweetness..."

Their laughter echoes down the street. Her heels match his stride, city sounds blending behind them.

Zane's arm rests across Emily's shoulders, her body fitting perfectly against his side as they walk. The weight of her head on his shoulder anchors him to this moment, making the usual chaos of New York fade into background noise.

Emily hasn't stopped smiling since they left the restaurant, and Zane matches her expression without effort.

"Your mom is going to flip when we tell her," Emily says, her fingers intertwined with his.

"Dad too, in his own quiet way." Zane squeezes her hand. "Though he'll probably just grunt and say 'about time.'"

The cool scent of blossoms from a nearby park. For once, Zane's phone stays silent in his pocket. There's just Emily, the ring on her finger, and the steady rhythm of their footsteps.

Emily points out a couple walking their dog, reminiscing about the shelter puppy they'd bonded with last month. Zane listens, really hears her this time. He stores her words instead of letting them wash over him like noise.

This is balance, he realizes. This is what he's been missing while chasing deadlines and client approvals. Peace wraps around him as he pulls her close, step by step toward home.

Chapter 5

ZANE AND EMILY STUMBLE through their apartment door, giddy with champagne and happiness. The city lights twinkle through their windows, casting a soft glow across the living room. Emily kicks off her heels with a contented sigh, wiggling her toes against the hardwood floor.

"My feet are killing me, but I don't even care." She holds up her hand. "Tonight was perfect."

Zane drops his keys in the bowl by the door, the clink echoing in their cozy space. His hand brushes his back pocket, empty. The familiar leather shape of his wallet is missing. His stomach drops as he pats his other pockets.

"Damn. I left my wallet at the restaurant." His chest tightens. That worn leather fold holds more than cards and cash. There's his favorite photo of Emily from their trip to Vermont, her auburn hair crowned with snow, green eyes bright with laughter.

Emily's brow furrows. "Again? Are you sure? You and that wallet!"

"Yeah, I remember putting it on the table when I paid." Zane grabs his coat from the hook. "I'll run back before they close."

"Want me to come with you?" Emily steps toward him, but he can see the exhaustion in her shoulders.

"Stay here. Get comfortable. I'll be quick." He brushes a kiss across her forehead. "Besides, someone needs to start calling our parents with the good news."

Emily leans against the doorframe, her loose waves tumbling over one shoulder.

"Don't stay out too late, fiancé," she teases, stretching out the word like taffy, savoring its newness on her tongue.

Zane's chest warms. The word feels different from 'boyfriend' ever did. A promise packed in seven letters. He breathes in her perfume and kisses her temple.

His footsteps echo down the empty hallway as he heads for the elevator, Emily's words following him like a gentle breeze. The metal doors slide shut with a soft ding, and he leans back against the cool wall, touching the spot where his wallet should be. The memory of Emily in Vermont returns. Snowflakes in her hair. Laughter he can almost hear.

The thought pushes him forward, quickening his pace. He needs that wallet back, needs that moment preserved in worn leather and fading ink. Some memories are too precious to lose.

Zane slides into the driver's seat. The car's leather interior still holds warmth. He turns the key. The engine purrs.

Rain dots the windshield in abstract patterns. Wipers hum in rhythm with his pulse. A soft song fills the car, matching the mood.

Traffic has thinned to occasional passing cars, their headlights reflecting off the wet asphalt. The city feels different at this hour, transformed by rain and darkness into something gentler. Street lamps cast halos through the water-streaked glass, turning ordinary scenes into impressionist paintings.

He taps along with the music, one hand on the wheel. The ring box nudges against his side as he takes the turn, empty now except for the memory of Emily's answer. Her face flashes in his mind, her eyes bright before she even spoke.

The downpour grows heavier, its steady beat filling the silence. It creates a cocoon of sound around him. Through the cascade of water, the city lights blur and stretch, creating streaks of color against the dark canvas of night.

The traffic light ahead turns red, and Zane eases his foot onto the brake. His car settles into stillness as raindrops race down his windshield. The wipers sweep back and forth, clearing his view of the empty intersection.

In the quiet pause, his thoughts drift to Emily curled on the couch, phone in hand, her eyes stealing glances at the ring.

The light changes to green. Zane releases the brake, and his car glides forward. Through his side window, a delivery truck idles at the cross street, its headlights cutting through sheets of rain. The driver's face is hidden in shadow, head bent down, maybe checking a phone or delivery schedule.

In the opposite lane, a sedan creeps forward, tires splashing through puddles. Its engine revs, the sound muffled by the rain and Zane's closed windows. The car's paint gleams dull red under the streetlights, like old wine.

Zane's car crosses the middle of the intersection. The radio host's voice fades between songs, a soft murmur beneath the steady drum of rain. Water beads on his side mirrors, distorting the reflection of passing lights into starbursts.

Through the rain-streaked windshield, a flash of movement catches Zane's peripheral vision. His muscles tense before his mind can process what's happening. A black SUV hurtles through the red light, its chrome grill filling his driver's side window.

The radio host's words fade mid-sentence. Raindrops hang suspended in the air, caught in the glow of street lights. Zane's fingers clench the steering wheel, knuckles white against leather.

The crash hits like a thunderclap. Metal shrieks as the SUV slams him broadside. The steering wheel jerks violently from his grip. His body jolts, the belt digging into his chest. The world spins in a kaleidoscope of shattered glass and twisted steel.

The airbag explodes in his face with the force of a punch, filling his nostrils with chemical powder. His head snaps back, then forward. Pain shoots through his neck. The crunch of folding metal drowns out everything else, a symphony of destruction that vibrates through his bones.

Glass rains across his skin. The driver's side door caves inward, inches from his leg. His car skids sideways across wet asphalt, tires fighting for grip that isn't there. The seat beneath him shifts and buckles.

The world tilts. Street lights streak by like falling stars. Something warm trickles down his face. His ears ring with a high-pitched whine that drowns out even his own heartbeat.

His car spins once more before coming to rest. Steam rises from the twisted hood. Rain seeps through shattered glass, pooling with something darker on the dash.

He gasps, the taste of iron thick on his tongue.

Voices filter through the ringing in his ears, distant shouts that sound like they're coming from underwater. "Call 911!" echoes off the wreckage, warped and far away.

Soon red and blue lights slice the dark. They strobe in slow motion, each strobe reveals glass like diamonds, rising steam, and a crooked wheel.

His cracked phone glows face-down. Emily's contact photo pulses with a call. He tries to reach it—pain flares through his shoulder.

Sirens wail closer, their pitch warping and distorting like a record played at the wrong speed. More voices join the chaos outside. Footsteps splash through puddles. A face appears at his window, mouth moving, but the words scatter before reaching him.

An ambulance's lights paint everything in alternating crimson and sapphire. Each flash reveals a new snapshot: uniformed figures rushing toward him, bystanders with phones raised, and the black SUV's crushed front end. The images stack on top of each other, overlapping and bleeding together like wet watercolors.

Rain continues to fall, but Zane can't tell if the drops are hitting him or if he's watching them suspended in mid-air. The edges of his vision pulse with each heartbeat. Someone touches his neck, checking for a pulse. Their latex-covered fingers feel cold against his skin.

Through the confusion, one thought surfaces with crystal clarity: Emily is waiting for him at home. He needs to tell her he'll be late. The thought slips away as quickly as it formed, lost in the strobing lights and cacophony of urgent voices.

Through the pain and flashing lights, Emily's face swims into focus in Zane's mind. Not the worried expression she'll wear when she gets the call, but her radiant smile from just hours ago. The way her eyes crinkled at the corners when he slid the ring onto her finger. The soft brush of her hair against his cheek when she leaned in to kiss him.

His chest tightens. She's home, still telling their story. She'll look at her phone soon and wonder.

The paramedics' voices fade into white noise. Zane's grip on consciousness slips. He can't hold on.

"I can't leave her now," he thinks, the words looping in his mind as darkness closes in. The thought clings to him as he slips under, Emily's smile lingering in his vision before everything disappears.

Chaos dissolves into velvet dark. Sirens fade. The wreckage vanishes. He floats, weightless, untethered.

The taste of iron disappears from his tongue. The sting of rain on his face dulls to nothing. Even the stabbing pain in his chest evaporates like morning mist. In this space between consciousness and oblivion, his senses shut down one by one, leaving only the quiet thrum of his own existence.

Time loses meaning. Each heartbeat stretches into infinity, then contracts to less than a second. The darkness wraps around him like a cocoon, both suffocating and comforting. No up, no down. Just endless black in all directions.

His thoughts scatter like leaves in the wind. Memories flash by: Emily's laugh during dinner, the Johnson pitch, the green light at the intersection. They blur together, losing their edges until they're nothing but impressions, feelings without form.

In the void, the edges of who he is start to fade. Zane Hart. A marketing executive. Emily's fiancé. The words lose meaning, washing away until nothing is left but awareness adrift in the dark.

The last thread connecting him to consciousness grows thin, vibrating like a plucked string before snapping. Zane slips into the emptiness, letting it swallow him whole.

The darkness shifts, taking on texture and depth. Zane feels himself drifting through it, weightless as a fallen leaf caught in an invisible current. His body, if he still has one, moves without direction, carried by forces he can't see or control.

Colors bloom in the void, soft and uncertain. Blues and purples swirl together like oil on water, never quite settling into recognizable shapes. The boundaries between his thoughts and the space around him blur until he can't tell where he ends, and the darkness begins.

Time stretches. Each moment could be seconds or centuries. There's no way to measure its passage in this formless place. His memories of the crash feel distant, as though they happened to someone else in another life.

Sounds reach him, but they're wrong somehow. They come from everywhere and nowhere, reverberating through his consciousness rather than his ears. A distant humming grows and fades. Whispers in languages he doesn't recognize drift past like smoke.

His awareness expands and contracts. Sometimes he's nothing more than a point of consciousness floating in the void. Other times he feels vast, spreading out across the darkness like stars scattered through space. The sensation should be terrifying, but fear seems as distant as his physical form.

The darkness pulses with a rhythm that might be his heartbeat, or might be the breathing of the universe itself. Each wave carries him further from what he was, deeper into this in-between space where reality has no meaning.

The formless void gradually takes shape around Zane. Pinpricks of light pierce the darkness, coalescing into constellations. Not the familiar patterns he learned as a child, but new arrangements that pulse with colors no star should possess, emerald, amethyst, and gold.

The emptiness beneath him solidifies into sand, but not the dull tan of Earth's beaches. This sand shimmers with metallic hues, each grain catching and reflecting light like thousands of tiny mirrors. Silver and rose gold swirl together in patterns that shift with each ripple of wind.

Waves crash against the shore, their sound both familiar and alien. The water glows with bioluminescence, each wave crest trailing ribbons of light as it rolls toward the beach. The foam sparkles with rainbow fragments, like someone shattered a prism and scattered the pieces across the sea.

Multiple moons hang in the sky, their surfaces marbled with swirls of color. Planets float close, their rings and atmospheres visible to the naked eye. One celestial body bleeds into another, creating a kaleidoscope effect that bathes everything in the ever-changing light.

A silhouette emerges at the water's edge, framed by the soft, otherworldly glow. A woman, her silhouette dark against the luminescent waves. Her hair moves in a breeze Zane can't feel, but her face remains hidden, turned toward the bizarre horizon. She seems both solid and translucent, as if she might dissolve into sea spray at any moment.

Zane's feet move across the shimmering sand without conscious effort. Each step leaves no footprint, as if he's weightless in this strange dreamscape.

The woman's presence draws him forward like a magnet pulling iron filings.

The multicolored waves crash closer, foam stretching for his feet, but never making contact. The air smells like something between sea salt and starlight—if starlight had a smell.

She turns as he approaches, her movements fluid like water. Her face shifts and changes, features refusing to settle into any fixed arrangement. But something in the way she holds herself, the curve of her neck, the tilt of her head, it strikes a chord deep within him.

"I know you," Zane whispers, though no sound leaves his lips. The words flow between them, glowing and unsteady, like ripples on the water.

Her delicate blonde hair dances in the nonexistent breeze, strands catching the light from the moons overhead. For a moment, he catches a glimpse of green eyes that remind him of forest pools, deep and ancient. Then they shift to amber, then back again, never quite settling on a single color.

Recognition slams into him. Not just from this beach, he knows her. The memory floats just out of reach, like a word on the tip of his tongue.

She raises her hand toward him, fingers trailing streams of stardust. The gesture feels familiar, as if they've done this dance before in another reality, another time.

Zane reaches toward her outstretched hand, but his fingers pass through empty air. The stardust trailing from her fingertips scatters like fireflies caught in a gust of wind. Her form wavers, edges blurring into the phosphorescent waves behind her.

"Wait." The word forms in his mind but dissipates before reaching his lips. The ground shifts, the metallic sand turning to vapor beneath his feet. Overhead, the moons melt into the sky, their hues bleeding together in an unnatural smear.

Her beautiful eyes lock with his. Recognition sparks between them—a connection beyond this dissolving dreamscape. Her features run like watercolors in rain, golden hair unraveling into the air.

An invisible force tugs at Zane's consciousness, pulling him backward through space. The bizarre constellations spiral and twist, their colors fading to grey. The luminescent waves crash one final time, the sound stretching and distorting until it's unrecognizable.

Her silhouette fragments into drops of light, scattering across the vanishing beach like stars falling from the sky. The last thing Zane sees is her hand, still reaching toward him, before the light breaks apart into countless glowing particles.

The dreamscape collapses inward, folding in on itself like paper burning from the edges. Darkness rushes in from all sides, swallowing the remaining traces of light. Zane feels himself falling, or perhaps rising, as the last echoes of that strange reality fade away.

Beeping cuts through the void. Sharp, insistent, Each electronic pulse, dragging Zane further from the shimmering beach. The rhythmic sound anchors him, pulling his consciousness up through layers of darkness.

Pain blooms, dull at first, then sharp. His chest compresses. Fire races down his arm. Even shallow breaths stab.

Something cold touches his arm—jarring after the warmth of the beach. He tries to move, but his body won't respond.

More voices, closer now. A woman speaking in professional tones. The squeak of rubber-soled shoes on linoleum. The sharp antiseptic smell of hospital cleaners cuts through everything.

The dream fades, the metallic sand, shifting moons, the woman with changing eyes. He clings to them, but they slip away. Only the deep sense of connection lingers.

The beeping speeds up as awareness creeps in. His eyelids feel heavy. Light penetrates them anyway, harsh and white, nothing like the soft glow of bioluminescent waves. He manages to crack them open for a split second before squeezing them shut against the glare.

"Mr. Hart?" A voice breaks through clearer than the others. "Can you hear me?"

The fluorescent lights pierce Zane's retinas like needles, and his eyelids flutter, each movement requiring monumental effort. The world refuses to come into focus. It's just blobs of color swimming against institutional white.

A face hovers above him, features blurred but framed by dark hair pulled back tight. "Mr. Hart, try not to move. You've been in an accident."

The words trigger a cascade of fractured memories: headlights, shattering glass, the taste of blood. But they feel distant, less real than the strange beach with its metallic sand.

Pain radiates through his chest with each shallow breath. The beeping from the heart monitor spikes as panic sets in. Something's missing... someone's missing.

Emily.

The name cuts through the fog in his mind. Emily waiting at home. Emily showing off her ring. Emily's smile as she said yes.

"Emily," he tries to say, but his throat feels like sandpaper. The word comes out as a hoarse whisper. "Where's Emily?"

The nurse's face swims closer, concern etched in the lines he can almost make out. "Try to stay calm, Mr. Hart. We'll contact your family."

"No... Emily..." The effort of speaking sends fresh waves of pain through his chest. Black spots dance at the edges of his vision. "Need... Emily..."

Zane barely registers the nurse's call for help before the void swallows him again.

Chapter 6

DARKNESS WRAPS AROUND ZANE like a heavy blanket, muffling his senses. The hospital room dissolves, taking with it the sharp antiseptic smell and piercing fluorescent lights. Emily's name lingers on his lips, fading into the void along with everything else.

He drifts, untethered from his physical form. Time loses meaning in this space between. No up, no down, just the endless expanse of nothingness pressing in from all sides.

A sound breaks through the silence, distant at first, like a radio signal cutting through static. The soft rush of waves against shore. The rhythm pulls at him, drawing his consciousness toward it like a beacon in the dark.

A breeze touches him, carrying the tang of salt and something metallic. The void thins, darkness giving way to possibilities. The crash of the waves grows louder, pushing against the silence. Each crash sends ripples through the emptiness, creating patterns he can almost see.

The breeze strengthens, bringing fragments of sensation. Cool air brushes skin he doesn't quite have. Sand grits beneath feet that aren't fully solid. Reality rebuilds around him, piece by piece, like a puzzle assembling in reverse.

Zane condenses, consciousness forming a defined shape. The void clings, but the waves pull harder, drowning out the last hospital echoes.

Colors bloom in the dark—shades that shouldn't exist—swirling into forms beyond description. The breeze brings whispers in a language he nearly understands, words that slip away before he can hold them.

The void peels like tissue, revealing a shore beyond logic. Zane's feet sink into sand shifting from silver to molten gold, crystals scattering light from no obvious source.

Waves lap in electric-blue pulses, each crest trailing phosphorescent foam. The water generates light, rippling color across the surface like something alive. Every seventh wave breaks in a new neon shade, splashing the beach in fleeting purples, greens, and unnamed hues.

The sky stretches to infinity, a canvas of spiraling nebulae tinted in purples and burning oranges. Stars cluster in shifting patterns, stilling only in his periphery. Three moons cast overlapping geometric shadows across the shimmering sand.

The air breathes against his skin, warm as twilight turned sensation. Each inhale brings something sweeter than oxygen, lightening his head. The breeze smells of lilies, ozone, and unknown things.

Palm trees sway to an unseen rhythm, their leaves shifting from emerald to copper. Crystalline fruits fall and dissolve into sparkles before touching the ground.

Zane stands frozen, overwhelmed by the surrounding beauty. It doesn't feel like a dream—it feels sharper than anything he's known, like life before this was only a faded echo of something.

Zane flexes his fingers, trails of light following through the air, fading into the prismatic atmosphere. His body feels large and light, gravity loosened. Each motion glides with ease, responding to the smallest thought.

He lifts his arms into the shifting light. The accident scratches are gone, replaced by glowing, flawless skin. His clothes flow with color, iridescent and ever-changing.

"This can't be real," he whispers, but the words carry a weight that feels more authentic than any he's spoken in the waking world. The sound ripples outward, creating patterns in the sand at his feet.

Taking an experimental step forward, Zane finds movement here obeys new rules. Each footfall ripples energy like pebbles in a pond, as if he's swimming through air.

Everything holds steady. His thoughts stay clear, the world stable. He sees grains of sand, traces stars, and watches waves break in rhythm.

This place clicks with something hidden inside him, like discovering a piece he didn't know was missing.

Zane slowly turns, scanning the strange beach. Multiple moons cast layered shadows, each a different hue. He touches one and watches color ripple through the air.

Through the haze, a silhouette draws his focus. At the water's edge, where neon waves meet golden sand, a lone figure stands. Her form appears translucent, like watercolor fading into light.

The woman's hair drifts in the breeze, catching moonlight in every strand. She faces the horizon, calm, feet sunk into the sand. Her dress shimmers like starlight, blending into the landscape.

Zane blinks, expecting the apparition to vanish like a dream. But she remains, more solid than anything else in this surreal dreamscape. Something about her presence feels significant.

Her moon-cast shadows stretch like a sundial across the sand. Each shadow points in a different direction, yet they all seem to lead back to her. The waves break in sync at her feet, as if the ocean itself responds to her presence.

A melody floats through the space between them. As he walks, the sand hums beneath him, crystals pulsing with every note.

The pull toward the figure hits Zane like a physical force, magnetic and undeniable. Each step forward feels inevitable, as though invisible threads connect him to her presence. The sand gives underfoot.

His heart pounds with a clarity that shouldn't exist in a dream. The sensation unsettles him. He can feel individual muscles moving as he walks, count each breath that fills his lungs with star-scented air. The moons cast his shadow in three directions, but they all point toward her like compass needles finding true north.

The distance warps with every step—close, then distant—but the pull never fades. Crystals chime beneath him, each note joining the melody in the air.

His mind searches for logic, to file it away as a vivid dream or medication-induced hallucination. But the weight of reality presses in from all sides. The way his toes curl against the sand, the salt spray cooling his skin, even the slight resistance of the air as he moves through it.

The woman's presence grows stronger as he approaches, like a radio signal coming into focus. The air vibrates with possibility, drawing him forward with an urgency he can't explain. Each step closer makes the rest of this world fade further into the background until she becomes the only solid point in a universe of shifting light and color.

She turns, and Zane's world tilts on its axis. Recognition hits him, stopping him mid-stride. Dark blonde hair frames a face he hasn't seen in years, yet one that sparks an instant connection in his memory.

He opens his mouth. The words slip out before he can stop them. "Do I... know you?"

The thought that follows isn't clear. There's no name. Just a pull. Her face feels familiar, but not explainable. Maybe he saw someone like her once. Maybe not. The feeling runs deeper than memory, like source-less déjà vu.

She watches with the same uncertainty. She seems older than someone he should know, but something about her lingers in him. Her eyes shimmer under the moons. The sand stirs beneath her like it responds.

His heart pounds. The dream shrinks until only she remains. Not someone he remembers. Just someone who feels important.

The air between them crackles like the moment before a lightning strike. Each breath fills him with star-scented air, dizzying in its blend of familiarity and strangeness.

Her voice sends ripples through the glowing air, every word heavier than its meaning. The accent is soft, maybe Canadian, but touched by something that belongs here.

Zane's mind reels. Her calm tone hints she might know him, but he can't place it. She feels important. He steps back without realizing.

"You... know me?" he asks, the words catching on the star-laden air.

Her smile deepens, creasing at the corners. Moonlight layers her face in shadows, making her seem ancient and new. Her emerald eyes mirror the sky.

"I'm not sure," she says, voice quiet, uncertain. The waves behind her pulse in time with the space between her words, their electric blue crests rising and falling like a slow breath.

Something unspoken crackles between them. Zane studies her—so grounded, yet unreal. Starlight clings to her hair, each strand holding fragments of constellation like a half-formed memory.

She watches him and says, "Are you real?"

Her words ripple through the sand, soft and uncertain, as if surprised to speak them. Her voice settles into the air like a question unfinished.

Zane swallows. "Who are you?" His voice shakes a little as it moves across the glowing waves. "Do I know you? Because this—" He glances around at the shifting beach and the sky painted in motion. "This feels like a memory."

She steps forward. Bare feet leave glowing prints that fade. Ripples of color spread like light through water. The moons stretch her shadow toward him from every angle.

"I don't know," she says, eyes lifted to the stars. "But this place... it's been reaching for you, hasn't it? Even before tonight?"

Zane struggles for breath. Memories surface like static—flashes of dreams he once ignored. Sand underfoot. Waves brushing his ankles. Mornings with stardust on his tongue and no way to explain it.

"How is this even happening?" The words come out quiet, but in this place they land with weight.

Her unreadable smile holds both wonder and restraint. "Some things connect without reason," she says. Her accent folds into the surf like a second tide. "Maybe we're just pulled here. Maybe it's not about understanding."

The surf crashes behind her, as if answering her voice. The space between them thickens, charged with something waiting.

Questions flood Zane's mind, all pressing at once. He steps closer. The sand shifts beneath him, soft and unstable. His shadow stretches three ways under the moons.

Her face dims, shadowed like clouds moving across a cosmic sky. "This isn't how it was supposed to happen." Her voice falls. The waves soften. The blue dims.

Zane blinks, caught between her words and the weight of everything he feels.

"Am I dead?" he asks, the question spilling out before he can stop it. "Is this... heaven?"

She doesn't answer. She just looks at him.

She steps forward. Her hand lifts, slow and cautious, like she's unsure whether to follow through. Her fingers brush his arm. Peace spreads from her touch like a tide. His thoughts quiet, one by one, until only she remains. The sand firms. The sky steadies.

It isn't comfort, it's recognition without explanation. Like something vital has locked into place.

The connection pulses, more rhythm than sensation. Zane nearly sees it—threads of light from her hand to his chest. Their shadows tangle across the sand like the start of a shared story.

The thought of Emily flickers, just a ripple in the stillness. It doesn't reach far. It can't touch what he feels now. This is something deeper than he's ever let himself believe in.

The world around him begins to shift.

The beach flickers like a failing image. Colors drain. Electric-blue waves fade to gray. The moons dim, their glow sputtering like dying stars. The shimmering sand becomes coarse beneath his feet.

"No, no, no." Panic claws at him. The moment slips away. The connection thins. That unknown sense of wholeness vanishes like mist in sunlight.

She begins to fade.

She fades like smoke against the dark sky. Only her emerald eyes remain, locked on him, glowing with an unnamed color.

Zane lunges to grab her, but his hand meets empty space. She's gone.

"Wait! Don't go!"

"Find me," she whispers, her voice rippling through the air until it fades.

The beach collapses like wet sand. Darkness rushes in. Her form scatters like stardust, her eyes still glowing green, fixed on him as if holding a truth he can't name.

"Please!" he shouts into the collapse. His hands close on nothing but fading light, like smoke, like memory—something never meant to stay.

The moons shatter, their pieces falling like sparks that vanish. Panic hits harder than any wave. The connection tears loose, leaving a hollow ache in his chest.

His legs give out, knees hitting sand that no longer feels solid. The darkness creeps in from all sides, devouring the cosmic colors that had made this place so vibrant.

Her touch lingers like a ghost, fading by the second. He presses his palms against his temples, trying to burn every detail into his mind, her eyes, her hair, the Canadian lilt in her voice.

"Please," he begs. "Just a little longer," but the darkness takes everything. The light, the belonging, gone. He's left hollow, the loss knocking the air from his lungs.

Zane curls into himself as the dream collapses. "Find me" echoes one last time, then fades. The void takes everything, leaving him in darkness, clinging to what felt like home.

The void breaks into sensation. Sharp beeping cuts through the dark. His fingers twitch against cool sheets, rough compared to the sand.

Voices reach him, warped like they're underwater. "...stable now..." "...response to stimuli..." They drift past, meaningless beside the echo of her last words.

Pain creeps back into his awareness. His ribs protest with each breath, and a dull throb pulses through his head. The dream's scent is gone, replaced by sterile hospital air that turns his stomach.

Light burns through his eyelids, harsh and cold. The dream slips with each breath—the beach, the waves, her green eyes. Only scraps remain: her voice, her hair, the sense that she mattered.

A door opens. Footsteps draw near. Someone, maybe a nurse, adjusts something by his head. The monitor's beeping skips, then settles back into rhythm.

"Mr. Hart?" a voice says. Calm. Professional. Distant. Nothing like hers. "Can you hear me?"

He tries to answer, but his throat burns. Maybe he has been screaming. His tongue won't move. A groan escapes.

More footsteps. Hushed voices. "Concussion." "Observation." The dream recedes further with each intrusion of reality, leaving him grasping at disappearing pieces.

Zane's eyelids flutter open, immediately assaulted by the harsh lights above. The white ceiling swims. His body feels heavy, every movement resisted.

The steady beep of monitors cuts through his fog. An I.V. line snakes from his arm, and the pressure of bandages wraps tight around his ribs. The accident comes back in fragments, shattered glass, screeching metal, the violent jolt of impact.

The crash fades next to the dream still pulsing inside him. Sand under his toes. Electric waves. Her green eyes, holding constellations he might never find again.

His lips part, voice rough from disuse. "Who are you?" he whispers, the sound barely louder than the beeping machines around him.

A nurse appears at his bedside, checking monitors. "Mr. Hart, try not to speak too much right now. You've been through quite an ordeal."

Zane barely hears. His mind spins with her voice, her presence, the feeling that nothing else had ever been more real. He tries to hold on to the details, but they slip through him like sand. Except one thing.

"Find me."

Those two words echo louder than the rest, planted deep where nothing else can reach.

He doesn't know her name. He doesn't know where to start.
But he's going to find her.
Whatever it takes.

Chapter 7

THE FLUORESCENT LIGHTS BLUR into halos above Zane's head, pulsing in rhythm with the monitors. His eyelids feel weighted, refusing to open fully against the harsh glare. Each breath sends daggers through his ribcage, and the tang of antiseptic burns his nostrils.

The steady beep... beep... beep anchors him to consciousness, though his mind drifts between clarity and fog. His tongue feels thick, stuck to the roof of his mouth. An I.V. line pulls at his arm when he shifts, the tape tugging at his skin.

Fragments of sensation filter through: the scratch of hospital sheets against his legs, a blood pressure cuff inflating around his bicep, voices murmuring in the hallway beyond his room. The pain sharpens his awareness with each passing moment, radiating from points he can't quite pinpoint.

His fingers twitch, sending sparks of pain up his arm. The world spins when he moves, so he stays still, watching ceiling tiles swim.

His heart rate climbs with a growing awareness of pain. A dull throb pulses behind his eyes, echoing the beeping monitor.

Consciousness rolls in waves, clearer, heavier, more painful. Breathing takes effort. Bandages tighten his chest.

The world gradually solidifies around him - the outline of medical equipment, the shadow of a privacy curtain, the muted sounds of a hospital in motion beyond his room. Reality crashes in with brutal force, leaving him no choice but to accept his broken state.

A flutter of movement catches the corner of Zane's eye. The shape resolves into Emily, slumped in a chair beside his bed. Dark circles hollow her gaze, and her hair, usually neat, hangs in unkempt waves. Her blouse is wrinkled, as if she's been wearing it for days.

His fingers twitch, and she bolts upright. Their eyes lock. The ring on her finger. The one he gave her hours... or days ago. Time blurs.

She leans in, brushing his hair with a trembling hand. Her light touch avoids the bandages. Her perfume cuts through the smell of antiseptic.

"You're awake. Thank God." Her voice cracks on the words, tears spilling down her cheeks. She presses her lips together, fighting for composure as she strokes his hair.

The simple gesture of comfort makes his throat tight. He tries to speak, but his mouth is too dry, his tongue refusing to form words. Emily seems to understand, reaching for a cup of water with a straw. Her hands steady as she helps him take small sips.

The water soothes his throat, but a memory lingers of green eyes, a soft accent, and the dream's pull. Gratitude and guilt mix. The glowing beach and the woman from his dream press against the tear-stained reality of his fiancée's face, like two worlds trying to occupy the same space.

The air between Zane and Emily hums with words left unsaid—then the door bursts open. Park strides in, flashing his signature grin as he expertly balances a coffee cup in one hand.

"Look who decided to join the land of the living! You know, there are easier ways to get out of work than totaling your car." Park plops into the empty chair, his casual demeanor cutting through the heavy atmosphere.

Zane's lips twitch despite the pain. Trust Park to make light of near-death experiences.

"I mean, you could've just called in sick like a normal person." Park takes a loud slurp of coffee. "But no, you had to go full drama queen on us. Classic Zane Hart move."

Emily dabs at her eyes, a small laugh escaping. "James, this isn't funny."

"Oh, come on, Em. Look at him - he's already plotting his next marketing pitch. 'Near-death experience? Try our new energy drink instead!'" Park winks at Zane. "I bet you're composing taglines in your head right now."

Their banter steadies Zane. Park's irreverent humor grounds him better than silence or sympathy.

"Though I gotta say," Park continues, gesturing with his coffee cup, "if you wanted attention, you could've just dyed your hair blue or gotten a tattoo. I could have carved some meaningful acronym on your arm for you, like CBCK. This whole 'surviving a car crash' thing is a bit extra, don't you think?"

Zane's throat tightens as he looks between Emily and Park, their presence anchoring him to reality. "I'm sorry I scared you both," he rasps.

Emily grips his hand. The ring flashes under the lights—a reminder of what nearly slipped away. "Don't apologize. You're here and that's all that matters."

"Yeah, what she said." Park sets his cup down, smirk softening. "Emily called me at 3 AM. I broke every traffic law getting here."

"I didn't know who else to call," Emily's voice wavers. "When they brought you in..." She stops, collecting herself. "The doctors weren't sure when you'd wake up."

Zane tries to squeeze her hand, but his muscles refuse to cooperate fully. "How long?"

"Two days," Park answers. "Emily hasn't left your side. Had to practically force her to eat something besides vending machine crackers."

"You didn't have to stay." Zane's eyes meet Emily's, seeing the exhaustion etched in her features.

"Of course I did." She brushes her thumb across his knuckles. "I couldn't bear the thought of you waking up alone."

The words hit harder than the morphine coursing through his veins. "Thank you. Both of you."

Park clears his throat, shifting in his seat. "Hey, what are friends for? Besides, someone had to keep Emily company while you took your beauty nap."

Zane's head throbs as he tries to piece together the fragments of that night. The last clear memory was proposing to Emily, walking to his car, the rain-slicked streets. Everything after exists in shattered pieces.

"What exactly happened?" His voice comes out rougher than intended.

Emily's fingers tighten around his. "A drunk driver ran the red light. Hit your driver's side going way over the speed limit." She swallows hard. "The police said he was doing at least sixty in a thirty."

"Your car..." Park shakes his head. "Man, I saw it being towed. It's a miracle you made it out alive. The entire driver's side was totally crushed in."

The clinical details wash over Zane. Spinal contusions, a collapsed lung, internal bleeding that required emergency surgery. Each injury Park lists makes Emily flinch, her grip on Zane's hand growing tighter.

"The first responders had to cut you out of the wreckage." Emily's voice wavers. "When they brought you in, there was so much blood. They rushed you straight into surgery."

"The drunk driver?" Zane asks.

"Walked away with barely a scratch," Park says. "Already out on bail."

He closes his eyes, trying to process it all. Everything blurs but one thing stays sharp: the beach, the woman, "Find me."

"You kept saying something in your sleep," Emily mentions, pulling him back to the present. "The nurses said it's normal with head trauma, but you seemed... distressed."

Zane's heart rate picks up slightly, registering on the monitor. "What was I saying?"

"Mostly gibberish," she says, smoothing his hair. "But you did keep mentioning something about a beach."

Zane's throat pulses as her words echo. The lights buzz while he debates sharing the dream that feels like a memory.

"There was this beach," he says. "But not like any beach I've ever seen. The waves... they glowed. Like someone had poured liquid neon into the ocean."

Park leans forward in his chair, coffee forgotten. Emily's hand stills in Zane's hair.

"The sand wasn't normal either. It shimmered gold and silver." Zane pauses, struggling to translate the vivid imagery into words. "The sky kept shifting colors, like an aurora but more intense. More alive."

His heart monitor picks up speed as the memory crystallizes. "And there was someone there. A woman standing at the water's edge. When she turned around, it felt like..." He stops, conscious of Emily's presence. "Like I knew her somehow. She told me to find her."

The words hang in the sterile air. Park glances at Emily, concern replacing his grin.

"It wasn't just a dream," Zane says, fighting against the heaviness of his medication. "I still feel the sand. The waves didn't sound normal."

Emily's fingers squeeze his hand. "The doctors said vivid dreams are common with head trauma."

"No, this was different," he says. "Like something pulled me there. To her."

Emily shifts in her chair, her fingers twisting the engagement ring on her finger. "The medications they have you on are pretty strong, Zane. Dr. Marshall said they can cause intense dreams."

Her dismissal is soft but sharp. The monitor beeps faster with his growing frustration.

"I get how that sounds, but this didn't feel like any dream I've had before." His voice strains against the dryness in his throat. "The light, the sand—"

"Honey," she says, voice gentle and practiced. "You've been through trauma. These dreams are normal." She smooths the blanket, careful not to touch any injuries.

The patronizing undertone in her voice makes his jaw clench. Even Park goes quiet, watching with uncharacteristic seriousness.

"Focus on healing," she says, smiling firmly. "Not some dream woman on a glowing beach." She pats his hand. "Rest is what matters."

Zane sinks back, drained. The dream's certainty crashes against Emily's logic. But arguing feels pointless when she's already decided to attribute everything to trauma and medication.

The lights glare. The room feels smaller. Emily hums, stroking his hair like he's one of her students after a nightmare.

Park shifts in his chair, the plastic squeaking beneath him. He takes an exaggerated sip of his coffee, eyebrows raised over the rim of the cup.

"So let me get this straight. You're telling me there's some dream girl waiting for you on a beach that looks like a Pink Floyd light show?" He sets the cup down with a dramatic flourish. "Did she happen to mention if she likes long walks on these glow-in-the-dark beaches?"

Zane flinches. Park barrels ahead. "Most guys use dating apps. You go full mystical beach babe in a coma."

"It wasn't like that," Zane protests, wincing as he tries to adjust his position.

"Oh, I'm sure it wasn't." Park winks at Emily. "Just a totally normal, completely realistic dream about a mysterious woman telling you to find her. Happens to me all the time. Usually after too many tacos."

"Though I gotta say, buddy, if you're going to have a near-death hallucination, you could've at least dreamed up something more original. Mystery woman on a beach? That's straight out of every Hallmark movie ever made."

The monitor betrays Zane's rising irritation with quickened beeps. Park's expression softens slightly, though his tone stays light.

"Look, I'm just saying - maybe cool it with the mystical dream talk until the morphine wears off?" He gestures at the I.V. drip. "That's some pretty good stuff they've got you on. Last time I had it, I thought my nurse was secretly a mermaid."

The monitor ticks faster. Zane shifts against scratchy sheets, ignoring the jolt in his ribs.

"You don't get it," he says. "The colors moved. They pulsed. The waves sang. And that woman..."

Emily's hand tightens around his, but he pulls away, needing space to articulate what burns in his mind.

"She knew me," he says. "Like we always had." The words spill, voice stronger. "I still see her face. Her eyes."

"Zane—" Park starts, but Zane cuts him off.

"No, listen. When I dream normally, everything's fuzzy, disconnected. This one wasn't. I felt the sand. I smelled the air—it was like ozone and starlight."

The monitor speeds up as Zane leans in, ignoring Emily's soft hand trying to hold him steady.

"I've had morphine dreams before, after my appendix surgery. This wasn't the same. This was as real as this room, as real as you both sitting here." His eyes lock onto Park's, challenging the skepticism he sees there. "I need you to believe me. Something happened on that beach. Something important."

Emily leans forward, her chair scraping against the linoleum floor. "Hey, let's talk about getting you home instead. The doctor mentioned you might be released in a few days if your vitals stay stable."

Her fingers brush against the bandage on his arm, her touch feather-light. "I've already arranged time off work. The kids will survive without me for a week or two."

Zane stares at the rain-blurred window. The beach fades but doesn't vanish.

"I've been thinking we could move the bed to the living room," Emily says, voice shifting to problem-solving cheer. "Easier for you to rest and watch TV while you recover."

She unlocks her phone and skims through her notes. "I found a few great physical therapists nearby. Dr. Marshall said it's best to start rehab as soon as possible."

Each plan widens the gap. Her world of checklists and logic leaves no room for glowing waves or mystery.

"That sounds..." Zane swallows hard, tasting the lie. "Great. Thanks."

Emily beams, assuming his silence means agreement. "We'll get through this together. One day at a time."

She keeps talking, but Zane drifts. Her voice becomes background noise to the memory of that other voice, the one that whispered "Find me" with such urgency. The voice that somehow knows him better than the woman who wears his ring.

Park downs his coffee, studying Zane over the rim of the paper cup. Something's different in his friend's eyes. Emily chatters about recovery plans and physical therapy, but Zane's answers are hollow. His eyes keep drifting to the window.

The change is subtle. Most wouldn't notice it. But Park has known Zane since middle school. He's seen Zane retreat before. Through breakups and car accidents that seem to plague Zane. Especially that horrible night they lost their friend Mike in a similar accident.

She touches Zane's arm, pointing at something on her phone. Zane nods and mumbles the usual encouraging sounds, but his fingers drum the hospital blanket in the pattern he uses when he's only half-listening.

Park crumples his empty cup, the sound drawing Zane's attention for a moment. Their eyes meet, and Park catches a flash of something beneath the polite mask Zane's wearing. Frustration, maybe. Or desperation. Something trying to break through.

Emily gestures, her ring flashing. Park notices Zane's eyes skip past it, as if he's avoiding it on purpose. The same way he used to avoid looking at Mike's empty chair after the accident. Different street. Different year. Same hollow feeling.

Zane lets Emily's and Park's voices fade into the background hum of medical equipment. The beach wasn't just a product of trauma or medication. The woman's voice still echoes in his mind, carrying weight and purpose beyond mere hallucination.

His fingers trace invisible patterns on the hospital blanket, matching the rhythm of those glowing waves. He needs to record it all, the colors of the sky, the texture of the sand, the way her voice seemed to bypass his ears and speak directly to his soul.

Emily's hand grazes his cheek, drawing him back to the sterile hospital room. "You look tired, honey. We should let you rest."

She tucks the blanket gently. Guilt twists in his gut. Here she is, doing everything right, while his mind wanders to a woman who might not even exist.

"Try to get some sleep, okay?" Emily's lips press against his forehead, lingering a moment longer than usual. When she pulls back, a smile flickers across her face. "No more glowing beaches."

She meant it as a joke, but Zane catches the worry beneath her light tone. It's the same concern she's shown when he's pushed himself too hard at work or stayed up too late obsessing over projects. But this time, it feels different.

Emily squeezes his hand one last time, gentle but uncertain. Like she feels the distance too and doesn't know how to cross it.

The door clicks shut, leaving Zane alone with the steady rhythm of medical equipment. Shadows stretch across the ceiling as evening settles in. The dream glows behind his eyelids, brighter than anything in this room.

He shifts, wincing at the pull of stitches. The pain feels small compared to the tightness in his chest, the urgent need to understand what happened on that otherworldly shore. The woman's face lingers in his memory, each feature clear and familiar.

Emily's plans and Park's jokes echo, their doubt raw against his certainty. They didn't feel it. That place made sense. Her presence wasn't new, it felt remembered.

"I'll find you," he whispers into the dark.

Chapter 8

THE HOSPITAL DISCHARGED HIM three days ago, but rest didn't come easy. Especially not with dreams like his.

Nights passed in a haze of painkillers and half-formed memories. Now, back in his apartment, reality feels fragile and insubstantial.

Zane sinks into his couch, the cushions familiar yet somehow different after weeks away. His ribs protest at the movement. Physical therapy pamphlets and prescription bottles crowd his coffee table, their labels a blur of medical terminology and warnings.

Emily's touch lingers in the space—fresh flowers by the window, organized pill schedules on the fridge, a stack of magazines within easy reach.

He picks up a get-well card from Park, adorned with a terrible pun about car accidents. The sight of "CBCK" scrawled inside makes him pause. The letters trigger something—a flash of golden sand, the rhythm of waves that didn't belong to any normal sea.

A half-empty water bottle tips as he reaches for his phone. Three missed calls from Emily blink on the screen, but he sets it aside. The walls feel closer than before, decorated with photos of their life together that now seem like snapshots from someone else's story.

His laptop waits on the desk, surrounded by sticky notes of meds and doctor times. The screen reflects his tired face, the healing cuts still visible. But beneath the physical exhaustion burns urgency, rooted not in recovery, but in the woman on the dream beach.

Golden light spills across the floor. A delivery confirmation email chimes—more books on dream interpretation arriving tomorrow. Emily won't approve, but he needs answers.

Zane pushes himself off the couch, wincing at the pain in his body. The laptop calls from the desk like a beacon of potential answers in this fog of uncertainty. Each step across the room feels like a mile, each step slow but certain.

He props the laptop on his knees. The screen lights up dozens of tabs—dream forums, near-death essays, trauma theory. None of it matches what he experienced.

His head throbs. He skims another useless article. The words blur together: "subconscious manifestations," "trauma response," "coping mechanisms." Clinical terms that reduce his experience to footnotes in a medical journal.

A forum thread catches his eye: "Meeting Someone in Dreams." He clicks through pages of responses, each one more disappointing than the last. Stories of forgotten faces, vague encounters, nothing concrete. Nothing like the silver-gold. Nothing like her.

He hovers over another near-death link. Fingers twitch. It's all tunnels and light. Theories. But the woman wasn't a hallucination or a random synapse firing in his injured brain. She was real.

He skims symbolism sites. Nothing fits. Water, emotion. Women, unconscious desire. It all feels shallow.

Zane closes his laptop, a nagging sensation tugging at his mind. He remembers her face, not from the dream beach, but from somewhere else. Her smile and the way her eyes looked feel tied to wooden desks and locker-lined hallways.

He stands, pain flaring. The hall closet beckons. Past Emily's neat rows of shoes sits a box marked "School Stuff" in faded marker. Emily labeled it when they moved in together, insisting they keep everything, even the junk from his teenage years.

He pulls it out and sets it on the bed. The cardboard is soft at the edges, the lid slightly torn. Dust rises as he lifts it. Inside are fragments of a life he barely thinks about—old notebooks, a student ID, a cracked CD case. The scent of aged paper and forgotten memories wafts up. He pulls out his senior yearbook, its blue cover scratched and worn.

Page after page of faces blur past. Each photo holds the potential of recognition, of confirmation that the mysterious woman exists beyond that dreamy beach. His finger traces down columns of names—Andrews, Baker, Collins.

Beneath the yearbook lies a stack of the original photos that had made it in the yearbook. Faces he hasn't seen in years. He lays them out on the bedspread, scanning for something familiar.

One photo catches his eye. A group of students gathered on the library steps, books and backpacks scattered around. At the edge of the frame, a girl sits cross-legged. She's turned toward someone out of frame, caught mid-laugh.

He freezes.

The way her hair falls. The shape of her smile. The same dimple he saw in the dream.

He flips the photo over, but there's nothing written on the back. Just a line that reads "Study Group, Spring."

His pulse climbs when discovers the photo had made it into the yearbook. She's there, clear as day, but no one bothered to label her. No senior portrait. No mention on the index page. She must have started late that year.

Zane studies her face like a map. The navy blue dress. A pen tucked behind her ear. That same look of knowing from the beach. She wasn't imagined. She wasn't made up by medication or trauma.

She exists.

"It's you," he says, barely a whisper, but the truth of it fills the room like oxygen.

Zane traces her face in the photo, his fingertip lingering on the minor details. The slight tilt of her head. The way her wavy hair falls across her cheek. Even in this still image, her presence feels familiar, like a memory that's been waiting just out of reach.

The medical papers scattered across his bed insist his experience was trauma-induced. His brain creating comfort during crisis. But that doesn't explain how he remembered someone like this. Someone he hasn't thought about in years, yet now sees with such clarity.

He closes his eyes. The dream rushes back. The woman's voice had a lilt he starts to remember, soft and steady, from a seat two rows from his in school.

He opens his eyes and looks again. A small pendant rests just below her collarbone. A silver compass. It's the same one she wore in the dream. He saw it glint in the moonlight as she stepped toward him.

This isn't random. This isn't some projection from his subconscious. She wasn't invented by his mind. She was there. And somehow, still is.

A chill cuts through him. Her face isn't abstract. She's reaching across something vast, trying to say what he still can't grasp.

The door clicks open. Emily steps in, juggling grocery bags. Her face brightens when she sees Zane up from bed, but her smile falters as she notices the scattered papers and open yearbook across the table.

"What's all this?" she asks, setting the bags on the kitchen counter. She moves closer, eyeing the mess.

Zane's hands shake as he lifts the photo. "I found her, Em. The girl from the dream. I think this is her." He taps the image with his finger, heart pounding. "She went to my school."

Emily's expression shifts, concern taking hold. "Honey, you've been through a lot. It's normal for your mind to—"

"Look at the necklace she's wearing." Zane leans forward, ignoring the pull in his ribs. "It's the same one from the dream. And her posture, the way she smiles—it's all exactly the same."

Emily perches on the armrest beside him, her hand settling on his shoulder. "Maybe you remembered her subconsciously. The brain does strange things during trauma."

"No, you don't understand." Zane's voice tenses. "She was there. I felt it. This wasn't just a memory surfacing. She knew me too."

Emily picks up a medical paper, pressing her lips into a thin line. "The doctors said dreams are common with your meds. You need rest. Not..." She gestures at the mess. "Not this."

Her fingers tap the paper. "Or maybe the research helps. Gives you something to focus on." Her voice is careful.

"You don't believe me."

"It's not that," she says. "Dreams can feel incredibly real, especially after what you've been through. And finding someone from your past in that yearbook... maybe it's a strange coincidence."

The word feels like a slap. Zane pulls the yearbook toward him, shielding the photo. "This isn't random. She spoke to me. She knew things."

"Of course it felt real." Emily rests a hand on his shoulder again. "Your brain was processing trauma. Maybe it pulled her from a buried memory. It's not uncommon."

"Stop." He pulls away. "Stop trying to make it logical. I know what I felt."

Emily walks to unpack the groceries. The crinkle of paper bags fills the silence. When she speaks again, her voice softens to the tone she uses when trying to calm her students. "I just don't want you getting too invested in something that might not be what you think it is."

His grip tightens on the yearbook. "You think I'm delusional. Like I can't tell the difference." The rest fades. She won't feel what he felt. But he knows.

"I'm treating you like someone who nearly died." she says, slamming a can onto the counter. "Someone who's on heavy medication and needs to focus on getting better."

"This is different." Heat rises in his chest, making his ribs ache. "When she looked at me, when she spoke—it wasn't just some drug-induced hallucination. She knew things, Em. Things about me, about..."

"About what?" Emily turns, arms crossed. "What could this girl you haven't seen since, who knows when, possibly know?"

"I can't explain it!" His voice cracks. "But dismissing it as trauma or medication is easier than considering something bigger might be happening."

She crosses to the couch, kneeling in front of him. "Listen to me. You survived something terrible. We're supposed to be planning our wedding, building our future. Instead..." She waves at the scattered papers. "You're chasing ghosts."

"They're not ghosts." He holds her gaze.

Emily stands, palms to her eyes. Her voice is steady. "You need rest. You need therapy. You need to work on healing and coming back to reality."

Zane clutches the yearbook, his knuckles white against its worn edges. The pain in his ribs sharpens, but the discomfort only fuels his resolve. "I have to do this, Em. Something happened on that beach."

"Fine." Her voice is flat. She collects the papers in sharp, neat stacks. The pages rustle softly as she aligns them.

He watches her movements, recognizing the careful way she avoids his gaze. The familiar warmth of their earlier moments has frozen over, replaced by a chill that seeps through the room.

Her hand pauses on a shared-dream printout. She says nothing, just adds it to the stack. Her soft footsteps fill the silence. She straightens pillows and adjusts frames that don't need fixing.

Zane turns back to the yearbook photo, eyes fixed on the girl at the edge of the frame. The pull he feels toward her grows sharper, cutting through the noise in his head. He spreads more old photos across his lap, hunting for another glimpse. Some sign. Anything.

Emily's movements echo from the kitchen. Cabinet doors, water, dishes. Sounds that once comforted now feel like quiet judgment.

He should say something. Acknowledge her. Reach across the space stretching wider between them. Instead, he pulls the laptop onto his knees and opens a new tab. His fingers hover over the keys, then begin to type a name. He doesn't know for sure if it's hers, but it feels like it is. Each keystroke pulls him further from the kitchen. Further from the life he's meant to reclaim. Closer to the one he can't ignore.

The blue light from the laptop spills across the cluttered table, casting shadows over yearbook photos and scrawled notes. The clock flashes 2:17 AM. His eyes burn from scrolling.

The search yields nothing but dead ends. No familiar face on social media. No mention in alumni sites. Irrelevant names and useless links. A cold mug leaves condensation rings over his scribbled guesses.

The yearbook stays open beside him. That image draws him in again. The necklace. That strange, familiar smile that seems to belong both to his past and something far beyond it.

A floorboard creaks from the bedroom. Guilt stirs, but his hands keep moving. He types again. Different spellings. Alternate initials. What if the name changed? What if she moved?

She existed. He knows it. So why did the world erase her like she never was?

He rubs his eyes, dragging fatigue across his face. His medications sit untouched on the counter. He needs clarity, not fog. Every dead-end search only deepens his conviction. She exists. Somewhere out there. And somehow, through that dream, she reached him.

His head pounds, but the yearbook stays open. That photo draws him back again and again, like a compass trying to find north.

His finger drifts along the edge of her face in the photo. The same curve of her mouth. The same quiet pull in her eyes. Like she'd been waiting.

Light cuts across the mess on the table. Most of it feels meaningless now, just notes and guesses that lead nowhere. But that photo stays clear. It's the only thing tangible.

"I'll find you," he says, voice low. The promise hangs in the silence, steady and sure.

Chapter 9

CLAIRE JOLTS AWAKE, HER chest heaving as if she's run for miles. Her heart pounds while fragments of the dream flash through her mind. The silver sand between her toes, waves that glow like liquid moonlight, and a man's face she can't quite grasp linger in her mind.

The red numbers on her bedside clock blur into focus: 3:47 AM. Her apartment sits quiet except for the steady drum of Seattle rain against the windows. She sits up, wincing as the ache in her spine flares. The dream lingers, stubborn and sharp, unwilling to fade like dreams should.

She stretches out a shaky hand toward the prescription bottle beside her bed. The label warns against mixing with alcohol, but the empty wine glass beside it tells its own story. She hesitates, then draws back.

That beach. Those breathtaking colors. She's never seen anything like it. The man's presence lingers like a phantom touch on her skin. She knows him, somehow. Knows him deeper than memory should allow.

Claire presses her palms against her eyes until spots dance in the darkness. These dreams have been getting stronger, more insistent. They're different from her usual pain-induced fantasies.

The rain intensifies, rattling against the glass. She hugs herself, chasing the dream's warmth. But reality seeps back in. The constant ache in her body, the lonely echo of her apartment, the growing fear that she's finally losing her grip on sanity.

Claire stumbles to her bathroom, each step a negotiation with her rebellious back and hips. The man's face from her dream burns bright in her mind. The deep brown eyes, a faint scar on his cheek, and a presence that felt comforting. But his name dances just beyond her reach, a word stuck on the tip of her tongue.

Holding onto the sink, she studies her face in the mirror. Her eyes are tired, her blonde hair dull and unkempt.

The bathroom cabinet creaks as she opens it. Orange bottles line the shelf in neat rows, their white caps accusing her of dependence. She counts them—muscle relaxants, anti-inflammatories, pain meds. The wine bottles in her bedroom complete the picture of her nightly ritual.

She massages her neck, working out the knots that form during sleep. The morning stretch routine begins: shoulders first, then spine, hips last. Each movement comes with its own special brand of discomfort. Every movement stings as she stretches her arms upward, but she refuses to stop. The words of her therapist resurface. "Motion is lotion."

The dream man's face flashes again, stronger this time. Something about him feels deeply familiar, like a childhood friend she's forgotten. But that can't be right. She'd remember someone who made her feel this way, wouldn't she? The certainty of his existence clashes with logic.

She catches herself reaching for the pain meds, an automatic gesture born from years of morning agony. Her hand hovers over the bottle. Faint traces of the dream remain, dulling the edges of her pain.

She drifts through her studio apartment like a ghost, her bare feet silent on the hardwood floor. The desk by the window draws her in, her sanctuary of order amid chaos. Her laptop sits closed next to neat stacks of notebooks, each filled with travel stories she hasn't submitted. A half-empty wine glass leaves a ring on her latest draft.

Beyond this careful corner, disorder reigns. Clothes spill from her hamper, forming dark islands on the floor. Empty takeout containers crowd her kitchen counter. The recycling bin overflows with wine bottles.

She traces her fingers along the typewriter keys, a gift from Sarah, meant to inspire her writing. Dust has settled between the letters. Her latest assignment sits untouched: "Top 10 Hidden Gems of the Pacific Northwest." The irony doesn't escape her, she hasn't left her apartment in days.

Rain streaks down the glass, turning the skyline into a shifting blur. Her desk faces this view, positioned to watch storms roll in from the Puget Sound. Today's weather matches her mood: heavy, persistent, refusing to break.

A stack of unopened mail teeters on her coffee table, medical bills mixed with rejection letters from publishers. Her orthopedic surgeon's card sits on top, a reminder of next week's appointment. She should call to cancel. She's not ready to discuss a potential spine surgery.

The contrast between her workspace and living space mirrors her internal struggle. Her desk represents the writer she wants to be: organized, productive, in control. The rest of the apartment reflects her reality: messy, complicated, overwhelming. She's caught between who she wants to be and who she has become.

The front door slams with enough force to rattle Claire's wine glass. She flinches, her pen skidding across the journal page, leaving an ugly black line through her dream description.Liam's heavy footsteps echo through the apartment. "Place looks like shit." He drops his keys on the counter with a metallic clang. "You been writing all day?"

Claire closes her journal, sliding it under a stack of papers. The dream beach fades from her mind, replaced by the sharp edges of reality. "I was just—"

"Just what? Wasting time?" He moves through the room, picking up empty wine bottles, counting them with his eyes. "Three bottles since Tuesday?"

The muscle in his cheek twitches, the tell she's learned to watch for. She folds into herself. "I had a rough night."

"You always have rough nights." He yanks open her fridge, scowls at the sparse contents. "When's the last time you went grocery shopping? Or cleaned? Or did anything productive?"

The morning's peaceful solitude evaporates under his scrutiny. She watches him stalk through her apartment, touching her things, moving them, judging each item he finds out of place.

"I brought lunch," he says, tone sharp under the offer. "Though maybe you don't deserve it, sitting around like this."

The smell of Thai food fills the apartment, her favorite, but her stomach twists. This is how it always goes: criticism wrapped in care, control disguised as concern. She forces a smile, knowing it's easier than resistance. "Thank you. That's thoughtful."

He circles like a prowling cat, checking for weakness. "When did you last clean? The dust is thick enough to write in." He pauses at her desk, picking up her pill bottles one by one.

Her shoulders tense as he invades her space. The lingering peace crumbles under his inspection. Her medication schedule is none of his business, but she knows better than to say that aloud.

He opens her kitchen cabinets, clicking his tongue at the empty spaces. "How are you supposed to get better if you don't take care of yourself?" His voice softens to that honeyed tone she's learned to dread. "I worry about you, you know. Sitting here alone all day, drinking wine, not following your doctor's orders."

Claire's throat tenses as he moves behind her chair, his hands settling on her shoulders. The gentle pressure feels like a trap.

"I should start coming by more often. Help you stay on track." His thumbs dig into her neck muscles. "You need structure, Claire. Routine. Someone to keep an eye on you."

She stares at her reflection until his shadow swallows it. Outside, rain turns the world into blurred shapes that resemble her thoughts.

"I know what's best for you," he continues, squeezing her shoulders. "You just need to trust me."

She tucks the journal deeper beneath the papers, her fingers lingering on its worn cover. She rises from her chair, each movement careful and measured, like a deer avoiding a predator's attention.

Empty takeout containers clatter as she clears the table, creating space for the Thai food that now feels more like a collar than a gift. She tosses the containers into the overflowing trash.

Her back flares as she wipes the table, erasing the wine rings. She feels Liam's eyes tracking her movements, assessing her performance of domesticity.

Tucked beneath the papers, her journal guards the only part of her he cannot touch, her dreams, her secrets, the bond she refuses to question. She squares the stack, corners aligned.

She continues her quiet ritual of cleaning, letting the mechanical actions shield her from his scrutiny. She knows this dance. How to bend without breaking, how to yield without surrendering completely.

The bathroom door shuts, and Claire's shoulders drop with relief at Liam's temporary absence. Water runs through old pipes as he showers. Her window of freedom shrinks with each passing second.

She pulls her journal from beneath the pile, her fingers unsteady against the worn leather. The pages fall open to her latest entry, and she writes furiously, trying to pin every detail before they fade like water slipping through her hands.

The man's face emerges in her memory, warm eyes that crinkle at the corners, a slight scar near his cheek. She sketches his features in hurried strokes, chasing the feeling of knowing him.

The beach comes next with colors bleeding across her page. Silver sand that sparkled like crushed starlight between her toes. Waves that glowed with their own inner light, rolling in endless patterns beneath a sky that couldn't exist in nature.

Claire's hand cramps as she captures the warmth, the sense of belonging that wrapped around her like a blanket in his presence. No wine-induced haze or painkiller fog had ever felt like this. The connection pulses in her chest even now, hours later, like a second heartbeat.

She pauses at the end of the page, pen hovering over paper. How to describe the recognition? Even though she's never seen his face in waking life. Her words feel inadequate, but she writes them anyway, racing against the sound of the shower slowing to a drip.

Her fingers brush the orange bottle without looking. She twists the cap, pops a pill, and chases it with a sip from the glass of flat wine beside her.

Her journal lies open before her, the fresh ink still drying on its pages. The man's face emerges from her hurried lines, with eyes that seem to see right through her and a scar that somehow feels significant. Her fingertips trace the rough sketch, following the curve of his jaw, the slight upturn of his lips.

Something about him tugs at her memory. She's drawn him three times now, each attempt bringing his features into sharper focus. The certainty that she knows him, has always known him, burns stronger with each passing hour.

Water drips from Liam's hair as he emerges from the bathroom, a towel slung around his shoulders. Claire's fingers freeze on the journal pages, but she's not quick enough to hide it.

"Still scribbling in that thing?" Liam snatches the journal from her hands. His eyes scan the fresh ink, brows furrowing at her sketches. "Weird little hobbies you've got. Drawing strange men now?"

Claire reaches for the journal. "It's private."

"Private?" he mocks, droplets of water falling onto her careful words. "From your boyfriend? Come on, Claire. What's with all this nonsense?" He laughs as he tosses the journal back along with his towel, pages crumpling under the impact.

"I said it's private." Her voice comes out smaller than intended.

"Whatever. At least it keeps you busy while you're hiding in here all day." He grabs his keys from the counter. "I've got to head back to the shop. Try to do something productive today, okay?"

The door closes behind him. Claire sits motionless, holding her journal. The unknown man's face stares up at her from the wrinkled pages, water spots blurring his features.

She smooths the crumpled paper, anger burning behind her eyes. Every day, the same dismissal, the same casual cruelty wrapped in concern. The dream tugs at her consciousness, a reminder that somewhere, somehow, there's more than this suffocating routine.

She traces the man's sketched features, remembering the peace she felt on that beach. The contrast between that connection and Liam's controlling presence grows sharper by the hour.

Later that evening, the TV screen flickers across Claire's shadowy den. She melts deeper into the worn cushions, balancing her notebook on her legs. As the evening news drones on about traffic and weather, her attention drifts to the sketch lying open before her. Her nightly medications make her eyelids heavy, but she fights the drowsiness, not wanting to lose this moment of quiet contemplation.

The sketch seems to come alive in the television's blue glow. Her head nods forward, jerking back up as she catches herself drifting. The news anchor's voice fades to a distant murmur. In this twilight state between waking and sleeping, the man's face seems to shift and breathe.

"Why do I know you?" she whispers, tracing the outline of his face with a mix of longing and confusion in her eyes.

Chapter 10

Zane's fingers tap against the desk, the only light in the room coming from his laptop screen. The rest of the apartment is silent. No footsteps in the hall, no quiet voice asking him to come to bed.

A new lucid dreaming forum loads, bathing his face in cold blue light. His notebook pages are filled with loops of ink and frantic corrections. His handwriting has grown sloppy, rushed. The same mantras repeat: "Reality checks every hour. Set intention before sleep. Visualize the beach."

"Dream signs, dream signs," he mutters, flipping back and forth. His eyes scan each phrase like he's trying to force something loose.

The latest post catches his attention. Shared dreaming experiences and how to trigger them.

Zane clicks. His breath slows as he scrolls. He copies notes, underlines methods. Some users suggest supplements or sound frequencies. Others talk about synchronicity, belief, emotion.

He rubs his temples. The beach is still sharp in his mind with gold sand and waves glowing like they swallowed starlight. But each time he dreams, it falls apart. She fades too quickly. Her voice never quite reaches him.

He flips to a fresh page. The words "Find her" are already written in the center, underlined, circled. They blur under his stare. He doesn't remember writing it, but it feels like a plea. The apartment creaks softly behind him. Still no sign of Emily. He exhales and closes the notebook.

The lights go off. His phone goes dark. He stands in silence for a long moment before finally walking to the bedroom, tension vibrating under his skin.

Zane rakes a hand through his messy hair. "You wouldn't understand."

Zane moves through the dim hallway, stepping over the scattered notes. The air is stale with forgotten coffee and closed windows. A blanket still drapes the couch where someone once curled up regularly to read or doze. Tonight, it's undisturbed.

He stops at the bedroom doorway. The lamp glows beside the bed, casting shadows across the floor. One side of the comforter remains untouched. No shoes by the door. No light under the bathroom door.

Zane peels off his shirt, lets it drop where it lands, and climbs into the bed. The sheets are cool against his skin. He lies back and exhales through his nose, fingers folding across his chest. His mind, despite the exhaustion, refuses to slow.

He closes his eyes and begins the steps, the ritual now etched into muscle memory.

Reality checks.
Set the intention.
Visualize the beach.

He focuses on the image: shimmering sand, surf pulsing like breath, the woman who never stays. She never speaks. Always turns away.

Tonight, he whispers the words aloud."

I will become aware in my dreams. I will find the beach. I will find her."

He breathes slower. Then deeper. Sleep doesn't crash over him. It drags him down in gentle layers, like sinking through warm water. The bed dissolves. The light disappears.

And then, it begins.

The beach begins to form.

The sky pulses above, violet fading to electric blue. Zane stands ankle-deep in warm sand, the wind thick with salt and something sweet.

He knows he's dreaming. And this time, it holds.

"Hello?"

His voice echoes oddly, stretched and warped, like shouting through water.

The beach stretches too far in both directions. The horizon folds inward. His legs fight each step, like wading through syrup. His breath shortens. The sky tilts. Light bends.

Then—there.

She stands at the tide's edge.

She stands at the tide's edge. No blur. No distortion. She's clear.

Green eyes meet his.

Recognition hits like a wave, deeper than memory or logic. Her mouth opens, startled.

"Wait—"

The dream shatters.

Light collapses. The sand melts into white static. Her outline flickers twice, then vanishes.

Zane bolts upright, lungs tight. His shirt clings to him, soaked through. The room is dark. The apartment still.

The clock reads 3:24 a.m.

The numbers sear into his brain. He doesn't know why it feels important. It just is.

He scrambles for his journal. His hands shake as he sketches her jawline, the tilt of her head. He saw her. She was there. Not imagined.

***

At that exact moment, across the country, Claire jolts awake.

Her eyes shoot to the clock beside her bed. 12:24 a.m.

The numbers glare back in red, sharp against the dark. She blinks, but they stay the same.

12:24.

She doesn't know why, but it plants itself in her chest like a warning or a whisper.

She fumbles for her journal, scribbling the time in the margin. Just in case.

Her heart pounds. The room feels too close. The air is heavy as she grips the sheets, trying to catch her breath.

Rain taps the window in a steady rhythm. Lights from the street smear across the ceiling.

It's too early to be awake, too late to fall back asleep.

She reaches for her journal, the pencil already in her hand. The man's face appears easily with every line, every shadow falling into place. The scar near his cheekbone. The way his mouth moved when he tried to speak. The warmth in his eyes, as if he already knew her.

Her spine flares with pain as she shifts, but she barely registers it. "Just a dream," she whispers.

But the way her hand won't stop sketching says otherwise.

Claire's hand moves quickly across the page, the dream humming beneath her skin as if it still clings to her.

She taps the pen against the margin, searching for something that can capture the feeling that passed between them. That moment their eyes met. It wasn't just a look. It was electricity, alive and aware.

She writes:

Different.
Underlines it.
Then crosses it out.
Not because it's wrong.
Because it's not enough.

Each sketch shows the same beach, the same man. And with each one, the detail sharpens. Normal dreams don't do this. They fade. Twist. Rearrange.

These don't.

She starts a new list in the margin: same man, same beach, increasing detail, unchanged location. And always, that strong emotional connection.

She stares at the last point.

It's that feeling, the strange sense she knows him somehow. But from where? It doesn't make sense.

"Stop it," she whispers, but even she doesn't believe it. The dreams are building toward something. She can feel it. Like they're leaving breadcrumbs.

She sets the journal aside but doesn't close it. The sketch stares up from the page, watching her the same way he did. She lies back with her eyes open in the dark.

Sleep never comes.

Chapter 11

ZANE SLUMPS AT HIS desk, the apartment dim despite the hour. Emily's absence fills the apartment, a heavy silence settling in. Her coffee mug still sits unwashed in the sink, a quiet reminder of their argument and her hasty departure.

His gaze drifts to the notebook across the room. Its pages are filled with sketches of the woman from his dreams.

His phone buzzes. Park's name lights up the screen.

"Hey man, you holding up?"

"Been better." Zane rubs his eyes.

"Listen, I snuck out pretty quick after... you know. That fight looked rough." Park clears his throat. "Mind if I stop by tonight?"

"Yeah, come over." Zane straightens in his chair. "Emily's staying at her sister's."

"Look, I get it. This dream thing... it means something to you. But be careful, alright? You're pushing away people who actually care about you for something that might not even be real."

"It's real, Park. I know how it sounds—"

"Hey, I'm not judging. Just saying... don't lose yourself in this anymore than you already have." Park's voice softens. "But whatever happens, I've got your back. I'll bring dinner, how about that Vietnamese place you like?"

"Thanks, Park." Zane exhales, his posture loosening just a little. "Really."

Zane's fingers trace over an old yearbook photo. Her smile triggers long-forgotten memories. They rush back, not just from the dreams, but from his senior year in high school. She'd sat right in front of him in one of his classes, her blonde hair always falling over his desk.

He grabs his notebook, scribbling frantically. She was in a dance club. He used to watch her practice in the auditorium after class, always from the hallway. He'd watch as he passed by, too nervous to make contact.

His hand trembles as he writes about the way she flicked her hair. How she'd lean back in her chair, her hair spilling onto his desk. He'd always thought it was deliberate, the way she'd do it right before turning to ask him for a pen.

Once, she'd caught him—turned around suddenly while his fingers were still twirling her hair. But instead of being angry, she'd just smiled and turned back around.

How had he forgotten all this? The quiet crush he'd nursed all year, never brave enough to act on it. Now her face haunts his dreams, and he wonders if maybe there had always been something pulling them together, even back then.

The doorbell rings just as Zane finishes organizing his notes into neat piles. He opens the door to find Park standing there, arms full of Vietnamese takeout bags, the familiar aroma wafting through the hall.

"Holy shit," Park says, stepping inside. He freezes mid-stride, scanning the chaos. Books and papers coat the floor. Sticky notes everywhere. "Getting some real *Beautiful Mind* vibes here, minus the whole genius mathematician thing."

"Thanks for the vote of confidence." Zane takes one coffee from the tray.

Park drops onto the couch. He picks up a book from the coffee table, raising his eyebrows as he reads the title. *The Art of Lucid Dreaming: Gateway to the Subconscious.* He flips through the pages, pausing at Zane's scribbled notes in the margins.

"Man, when you fall down a rabbit hole, you really commit."

"It's not—"

"A rabbit hole?" Park cuts him off. "Dude, your apartment looks like a conspiracy theorist's Pinterest board."

Zane sinks into the chair across from him, dragging a hand through his messy hair. "You wouldn't understand."

"Try me." Park tosses the book aside and leans forward. "I mean, yeah, this looks certifiable, but you're the most rational person I know. Or you were, before this."

"The beach was undeniable, Park. The colors—I've never seen anything like it. Silver sand, waves that glowed like neon. And her..." Zane's voice softens. "When our eyes met, it felt like... like finding something I didn't know I'd lost."

"Wow." Park's brow lifts, surprised. "That's some Nicholas Sparks level romance right there."

"I know how it sounds."

"Actually, I was gonna say it sounds important." Park's teasing fades into something quieter. "Look, you're clearly not letting this go. And yeah, maybe it's crazy, but... you need this. Whatever this is."

Zane blinks. "You believe me?"

"I believe you believe it. And that's enough." Park sets the food down, pulling out containers. "So, what's the game plan?"

Park eyes the mess again. "Grilled pork Banh Mi, just like you like it. And damn, this place? You just need some red string and a corkboard."

Zane pulls a photo from his notebook and lays it on the table between them.

"Funny." He clears space for their dinner. "But I remembered something today. This woman, a girl then, was in some of my classes in school."

Park leans over, squinting at the picture. "Oh yeah?" He drops into a chair, chopsticks poised. "Let me guess, you were secretly in love with her but too scared to ask her out?"

Zane's face flushes. "It wasn't like that. We barely talked, but—"

"But you played with her hair to... get her attention?" Park grins at Zane's startled expression. "Dude, I sat behind you in that class. Watched you pine over her for months." "Why didn't you ever say anything?"

"And mess with your adorable little crush?" Park shovels noodles into his mouth. "Besides, you were too busy pretending to be cool and mysterious."

"Do you even remember her name?" Park asks, leaning forward.

Zane shakes his head. "No. It's been too long. I just remember how she looked... how it felt being near her."

Zane pushes his food around. "The dreams are getting clearer. It's like—"

"Like destiny?" Park raises an eyebrow. "Come on, man. You really think the universe is sending you dream messages about some girl from so long ago?"

Zane sets his chopsticks down, the pork Banh Mi barely touched. "You don't understand, Park. These aren't just random dreams. When I see her there, it's like... like I've known her my whole life. It's like we talk for hours on that beach."

"Hours of dream time or real time?" Park dabs his mouth with his napkin. "Because that's the thing about dreams, man. They mess with your perception."

"Both. Neither. I don't know," Zane says, pacing the small space between kitchen and living room. "But it's like she knows things about me. True things. Last night she mentioned the scar on my knee."

"Or maybe your brain filled in details from memories you already had. That's what dreams do. They remix what's already in your head."

"I don't know, it's different." Zane stops at the window, staring at the city lights below. "When I'm with her, everything makes sense. The accident, the emptiness I've been feeling—"

"Hey." Park's chair scrapes against the floor as he stands. "You almost died... That kind of thing messes with your head. It's normal to look for meaning, but maybe..." He places a hand on Zane's shoulder. "Maybe it's okay to let it go, man."

Zane shrugs off Park's hand. "I can't. Not when I know she's real. Not when—"

"When what? When you're throwing away everything in your life for some dream?" Park's voice softens. "Emily loves you. She's here, and she's worried sick about you."

"I know." Zane slumps against the window frame. "But what if this is more than just dreams? What if this is where I'm supposed to be?"

Zane turns from the window, his jaw set with determination. "You don't get it. These dreams are different. It can't be a coincidence."

"Come on, man. Your brain could just be—"

"No." Zane's voice rises. "I remember her now. We had brief experiences back in the day. There's a connection here that goes deeper than random memories getting mixed up in my head."

Park raises his hands in surrender, but concern creases his forehead. "Okay, okay. Just trying to look out for you."

"I know you are." Zane softens slightly, but his eyes drift to the yearbook photo. "But I need you to trust that I know what I'm doing. This isn't some trauma response or whatever Emily thinks it is."

"Right." Park lets out a long breath, then cracks a smile. "Well, if you find her, let me know—I'll help you write the rom-com. *Dream Girl: A Love Story That'll Keep You Up At Night.*"

Zane shoots him an irritated look, but Park just chuckles and starts clearing the takeout containers.

The apartment door opens. Emily steps inside, her teaching bag heavy on her shoulder. The scent of Vietnamese takeout mingles with stale coffee and paper. Zane and Park look up from their huddle at the table, surrounded by scattered notes.

"Hey guys." Emily's smile brightens the room as she sets down her bag. "Smells like Pho Queen in here."

"There's still some left if you're hungry." Park pushes back from the table, offering her space.

Emily's eyes drift over the clutter of sticky notes, dream journal entries, old high school photos. Her smile wavers.

"I see you've been... busy."

She moves to the kitchen, busying herself with making tea. The ceramic mug clinks against the counter as she works up her courage.

"I was thinking, maybe we could do something this weekend? Just us?"

Zane glances up from his notes, catching Emily's hurt expression.

"There's that new restaurant in Brooklyn you mentioned." Emily leans against the counter, cradling her mug. "Or we could drive up to that bed-and-breakfast in the Catskills. You know, the one with the amazing breakfast spread you loved?"

Park clears his throat.

"Actually," Emily adds, her voice tight but hopeful, "my sister gave me tickets to that jazz show you wanted to see. Thursday night at Blue Note."

Zane finally looks up. Guilt flickers across his face as he meets her gaze. Papers rustle under his fingers as he fidgets with his notes.

"Thursday might be tough. I've been making progress with my research, and the timing needs to be—"

"Right." Emily's fingers tighten around her mug. "Of course."

Zane glances up from his notes, catching Emily's hurt expression. His stomach twists with guilt, but the pull of his research proves stronger.

"Em, I know you're worried, but look at this." He grabs a page covered in his cramped handwriting. "The woman. She was in some of my classes. She sat right in front of me."

Park stands, gathering his jacket. "Think that's my cue to head out."

"The timing can't be random." Zane spreads more papers across the table, oblivious to Park's departure. "She moved away before graduation, but now these dreams feel like we're continuing something that never had the chance to start."

Emily walks Park to the door. "Thanks for coming by."

"And last night's dream was even clearer." Zane's voice rises with excitement, following them without pause. "She always orders herbal tea with honey. The way she says it, 'HER-bal,' like she's

British or something." It has to mean something, right? The universe doesn't just give you these kinds of details without—"

The door shuts behind Park, cutting Zane off mid-sentence.

Emily stands with her hand on the doorknob, her back to Zane as his voice fills the apartment, rambling about symbolism and cosmic threads.

"Stop." Her voice is soft and controlled, the last thread holding.

Zane doesn't hear it. He keeps shuffling through pages. "And the way the light hits the water in the dreams—it's exactly like—"

"I said stop!"

Emily whirls around, eyes glassy, chest rising fast.

"Do you even hear yourself anymore?" Her voice trembles. "Do you have any idea what this is doing to us?"

"Em—"

"No. You need to listen." She takes a step closer, tears brimming. "I'm losing you. Every day, you slip further into this... fantasy. It's like I'm competing with a ghost. A dream version of some girl you barely even knew."

"That's not what this is." Zane sets his papers down. "You don't understand—"

"Then help me understand!" Her hands sweep toward the mess surrounding them. "Because from where I'm standing, my fiancé is chasing dreams instead of building a life with me."

"This isn't about replacing you," Zane says. "It's not just in my head. I can feel it. And if you'd just—"

"Just what? Accept that you'd rather be there than here?"

She stares at him, jaw clenched. "You barely even look at me unless I'm standing between you and your notes."

Zane's voice hardens. "I need to figure this out. If you could experience what I'm experiencing, you'd understand why it matters."

"What matters is *us*, Zane. Remember us? The life we were building?"

Emily's tears finally spill. "But I guess that's not enough anymore, is it?"

The bedroom door slams shut.

Zane stands frozen. Notes lie scattered across the table. The faint smell of takeout hangs in the air. Somewhere behind the wall, Emily's sobs push through the silence.

He slumps back into his chair. The leather creaks under him.

His fingers drift to the yearbook photo and the girl in the background, half-turned, her expression familiar in a way that cuts.

The city lights flicker through the window, painting shifting shapes across the chaos.

Park's voice echoes like a whisper.

"Just don't lose yourself, man."

Zane's hand trembles as he traces her face. The beach. The sky. The way her voice cut through that world.

But Emily's tears were real.

The ring on her finger is real.

The life they had built together was real.

He rubs his eyes. Exhaustion tugs at every part of him. The apartment feels too quiet despite Emily being just one room away.

His gaze shifts between the open notebook and the closed bedroom door.

The distance between them feels wider than any dream could ever bridge.

"Just don't lose yourself, man."

Chapter 12

CLAIRE MEASURES COFFEE GROUNDS with trembling hands as morning light stretches across her cramped Seattle kitchen. Each movement aches and reminds her of another restless night haunted by fading dreams.

Liam peers over her shoulder. "You're using too many grounds again." He reaches past her to grab the spoon, his chest pressing against her back. "Let me show you the right way. You always make it too strong."

The spoon scrapes against the filter, and he removes half the grounds. Claire's fingers curl against the counter edge, her shoulders tensing.

"There." Liam dumps the excess grounds in the trash. "That's how you make proper coffee. Don't want to waste the good beans I bought, right?" His smile doesn't reach his eyes as he adjusts the filter. "You'd think after all this time, you'd remember how I like it."

Claire watches the water drip through the thinner layer of grounds, the resulting brew paler than she prefers. Her throat tightens as Liam hovers beside her, monitoring her reaction.

"Thanks for fixing it," she manages, the words tasting bitter on her tongue.

Claire pours the coffee into Liam's favorite camping store mug. The ceramic is still hot against her fingers."

Here." She slides the mug across the counter.

Liam takes a sip, nodding in approval. "Much better." He settles into his usual spot at the kitchen table, phone already in hand, scrolling through emails.

Claire stares into her weak coffee, and suddenly she's sixteen again. The kitchen transforms into her childhood home with dishes piled in the sink, takeout containers littering the counter, and the sharp bite of her father's whiskey.

She stands at the stove, stirring boxed mac and cheese. Her stomach growls. The front door creaks open, and her father stumbles in, tie loose around his neck.

"Dad? I made dinner."

He walks past without acknowledgment, collapsing into his armchair. The TV blares with another hockey game. Empty bottles clink as he sets down a fresh one.

Claire serves herself a small portion, leaving the rest for him. She eats alone at the kitchen table, homework spread before her. The phone rings. It's Richard. Her heart pounds as she listens to him on the other end.

"Where were you after school?"

She'd hidden in the library until she was sure he'd left. Her wrist still aches from where he had grabbed her yesterday, insisting she skip study hall to be with him.

"Don't ignore me."

Claire immediately hangs up.

Claire glances at her father, wishing he'd notice, ask about her day, and see the bruises she's hiding under long sleeves. But he stays fixed on the game, muttering about missed shots.

The mac and cheese turns to paste in her mouth. The phone rings again, but goes unanswered this time. Her father cheers at the TV, lost in his own world. Claire hugs herself tightly, as if holding together the fragments of a girl the world refuses to notice.

Her memory shifts. She's at her locker as Richard approaches, his eyes sharp with control.

"Where were you at lunch?" He leans close, blocking her view of the hallway.

"I had to finish my English essay in the library." Claire's fingers fumble with her combination lock.

Richard's hand slams against the locker. "You're lying. Brandon said he saw you talking with Jack in the cafeteria."

"He just asked about homework—"

"Don't." Richard grabs her wrist, squeezing until she winces. "You know how it makes me feel when you talk to other guys."

Claire's throat tightens. "I'm sorry."

"You should be." His grip loosens, but his thumb traces circles on her skin—a gesture that once felt romantic, now a reminder of his control. "I just love you so much. I can't stand seeing you with anyone else."

The words twist in her chest. Love. That's what this is, right? That's what he tells her when he checks her bag, when he decides what she wears, when he spies on her every move. "Come over after school," Richard says. It's not a request.

"I have to study—"

"You study too much." His fingers dig into her arm. "Don't you want to spend time with me? Or is Jack more important?"

Claire sees other students passing by, their eyes sliding away from the scene. Nobody stops. Nobody asks if she's okay. Just like at home.

"I'll come over," she whispers.

Richard's face brightens. He kisses her forehead, and for a moment, she almost believes this is normal. That this is what love feels like—this constant fear of doing something wrong, of being too much or not enough.

"That's what I thought." He takes her books, an act of possessiveness masked as chivalry. "I'll walk you to class."

Claire follows, her wrist throbbing from the mark his fingers left behind. She's learning the lesson that will shape her future relationships: love hurts, and she deserves the pain.

The memory hits her: she stands before her father, clutching her acceptance letter to UBC. His bloodshot eyes scan the scholarship offer before he crumples it, tossing it aside like yesterday's racing form.

"We're moving to Seattle. I got a job there." He doesn't look at her. "Pack your things."

"But I'm three months from graduating—"

"You think I care about that?" He stumbles toward the kitchen, reaching for another beer. "We go where the money is."

She remembers the hollow feeling as she packed up her books, the careful notes she'd taken, the practice SATs she'd aced. All meaningless now. Even her perfect GPA couldn't save her from being uprooted.

Seattle brought minimum wage jobs: waitressing, retail, anything to help pay rent while her father drank away his paychecks. Each rejection from community colleges stung less than the last until she stopped applying altogether.

Some nights she pulled out her old calculus notebook, solving equations no one would grade. The familiar rhythm of numbers offered a comfort people never did. Math problems had obvious solutions and definite answers. They didn't leave without warning or use love as a weapon.

Claire watches Liam's reflection in the kitchen window. That strong jawline and rugged look were what first caught her eye that rainy afternoon at his shop.

She'd wandered in seeking shelter from the downpour, dripping onto the polished wooden floors. Instead of shooing her away, Liam offered her coffee from his personal thermos, asked about her writing, and seemed genuinely interested in her answers. His confidence filled the space around her, made her feel less alone.

The first few months blazed. Surprise deliveries of her favorite tea at work. Late-night conversations about dreams and fears. He called her beautiful, held her through panic, and promised she'd never face the world alone.

But promises shifted to expectations. Suggestions became commands. That same confidence that once sheltered her now casts a shadow over every choice she makes.

"Your coffee's getting cold." Liam's voice cuts through her thoughts. "You should drink it while it's hot. You know how I hate waste."

Claire lifts the mug to her lips, the weak coffee barely masking the bitter taste of words unsaid. She remembers the first time he "fixed" her coffee, explaining how she'd been making it wrong all along. Just like he fixed her wardrobe, her friend circle, her writing schedule, each correction was delivered with a smile that never quite reached his eyes.

His hand slides across the table, fingers wrapping around her wrist. The touch is gentle but firm, a reminder of his constant presence. "You seem distracted today. Everything okay?"

The question sounds caring, but Claire recognizes the undertone of suspicion. She forces a smile, the same one she's perfected over months of walking this tightrope. "Just tired. Didn't sleep well."

Liam sets down his phone, his gaze settling on Claire with practiced intensity. "So what's on the agenda today?"

Claire shifts in her chair, fingers tracing the rim of her coffee mug. "I need to finish that travel piece about Vancouver. And I wanted to work on my journal—"

Liam laughs. "Still wasting time with that, huh?" He stands, moving behind her chair. His hands rest on her shoulders, thumbs pressing into the knots of tension. "The apartment's a mess. Look at these dishes. When's the last time you vacuumed?"

Claire stares at her half-empty mug, her shoulders rigid under his touch. "The deadline for the article is—"

"That little blog barely pays anything." His grip tightens. "You need to focus on priorities. The living room's a disaster. Don't get me started on the bathroom." He nods at her notebook. "Your writing can wait. It's not like you're working on the next great American novel."

The familiar weight of shame settles in Claire's chest. Her gaze drifts to the pile of dishes, dust collecting on the windowsill, the scattered papers she'd meant to organize. Each imperfection magnified under Liam's scrutiny.

"I'll clean today," she breathes, the words tasting like surrender.

"That's my girl." Liam kisses the top of her head. "You'll feel better once everything's in order. You know how scattered you get when things are messy." He takes out his phone, scrolling through his messages. "I made a list of everything that needs to be done. I'll send it to you."

Her phone buzzes with a detailed breakdown of chores, organized by room. Her article deadline looms in her mind, but she closes the notebook, tucking away her writing along with her protests.

The kitchen faucet drips in a steady rhythm as she stands, gathering cleaning supplies. She tucks her notebook under the sink, behind the extra paper towels where Liam never looks. A minor rebellion, but her heart pounds anyway.

"Starting with the living room," she calls out, loud enough for him to hear. The vacuum roars to life, masking the quiet sound of her retrieving the notebook. She props it on the windowsill, just out of sight.

Between cleaning bursts, Claire steals seconds to write.

The vacuum falls silent. "Looking better already," Liam shouts from the bedroom.

Claire's hand doesn't pause on the page. "Just being thorough," she replies, adding another line to her entry. The small act of writing fills her chest with warmth. It's a quiet defiance that's entirely her own.

Claire collapses into bed that night, her muscles aching from scrubbing floors and reorganizing shelves. Liam snores beside her as she stares at the ceiling, thinking of the scraps of writing she managed to save.

Sleep takes her, and suddenly sand sparkles beneath her feet, and waves of liquid gold crash against the shore. The air shimmers with an otherworldly glow that makes her forget about the day's exhaustion.

He waits at the shore, his form unmistakable against the vast celestial sky. Claire approaches, drawn by an inexplicable certainty. He turns, and his gentle smile reaches his eyes which is so different from Liam's calculated expressions.

"You found your way back," he says, his voice carrying none of the judgment she's grown accustomed to.

Claire wraps her arms around herself, an old habit. "I don't understand why I know you."

He doesn't press for answers or demand explanations. Instead, he sits in the sand, leaving space beside him. Claire settles there, surprised by how natural it feels.

"Sometimes knowing isn't what matters," he says, watching the surreal waves dance before them.

The silence between them feels different. It's not loaded with expectations or underlying tensions. His presence radiates a quiet strength that makes her feel seen rather than scrutinized.

"I spent all day cleaning," she finds herself saying. "Making everything perfect for someone else."

He nods, understanding in his eyes. "And what do you wish you had done instead?"

The question catches her off guard. No one has asked her that in years.

"Write," she whispers. "I'd have written until my hand cramped."

His smile grows warmer. "Then that's what matters."

Claire jerks awake, her heart racing not from fear but from something unfamiliar—peace. Moonlight spills across Liam's form. Her cheeks are warm, as if touched by the sun.

The man's face lingers in her mind with startling clarity, his kind brown eyes and gentle smile reaching past her defenses. She still feels the texture of the sand beneath her fingers and hears the melodic crash of waves.

Careful not to disturb Liam, Claire slides out of bed. Her bare feet make no sound as she retrieves her journal from its hiding spot behind the loose baseboard in the hallway. She settles at the kitchen counter, the streetlight casting just enough glow to write.

Her pen glides across the page with urgency. She sketches his features, including the way his hair fell across his forehead. Each detail feels precious, like capturing a rare butterfly before it can flutter away.

She writes, 'He didn't try to fix me,' the words spilling out. 'He just listened. Asked what I wanted. No one asks that anymore.'

Claire stills, her palm resting on the page. The dream man's question lingers in her mind. "What would you rather have done?" It's a simple question, yet it unravels something deep within her.

She recounts the beach, but what stays with her most is the feeling. It was a quiet certainty of safety, of being understood without the need for words.

'Why do I know him?' she writes, underlining the words twice. 'Why does this feel more solid than my own life?'

A floorboard creaks behind Claire, and her pen freezes mid-sentence. Liam's shadow falls across her journal.

"What are you doing up?" His voice carries that familiar edge of control masked as concern.

Claire's fingers curl around her pen. "Couldn't sleep. Just writing down some thoughts."

"Thoughts?" Liam reaches over her shoulder, flipping through the pages. His thumb smudges the fresh ink of her dream sketch. "More of this dream nonsense? Focus on things like that mess you left in the guest room."

"I cleaned all day—"

"And there's still work to do." He closes her journal with a snap. "You waste so much energy on these fantasies. No wonder you're always tired."

Claire stares at her closed notebook, at Liam's hand resting heavily on its cover. The dream beach's warmth fades, replaced by the familiar chill of his disapproval.

"Come back to bed," he says, but it's not a request. "You need proper sleep if you're going to be productive tomorrow."

Claire waits until he's gone. Her fingers trace the spine of the journal, the man's question still echoing. The contrast between acceptance and control leaves her twisted inside.

She clutches the notebook close, its pages holding the only piece of herself that still feels real. "Who are you?" she whispers into the darkness, before following Liam back to bed.

Chapter 13

ZANE KNEELS ON HIS meditation cushion, breath steady as moonlight spills through the apartment. He sets his phone alarm for three hours, aiming for prime REM.

He closes his eyes, counting backward from one hundred. Each number brings a deeper state of relaxation. His muscles unwind. His thoughts quiet down. The distant sounds of New York traffic fade.

"I will know when I'm dreaming," he repeats in his mind. "I will find her."

Sleep takes him. His mind drifts. When his eyes open, he's on familiar sand. The beach stretches endlessly, waves glowing as they roll in. Above, The sky shifts from purple to orange, then back again.

He lifts his hand, studying it. Five fingers. Then six. The extra digit confirms it. He's dreaming. And this time, he's in control.

"Are you here?" His voice carries.

The waves whisper back, tugging at his feet. Each pulse draws him forward. The sky shifts overhead, reacting to his presence.

He walks the shoreline, leaving no footprints. Each step feels as natural as waking life. This is where he's meant to be. Where she is.

"I'm here," he calls out again. "I found my way back."

A figure materializes near the water's edge. It's a woman with wavy blonde hair falling loose past her shoulders. Even from behind, Zane knows it's her. His pulse quickens. She stares at the waves, posture both familiar and strange.

He steps forward, the sand rippling in silver and gold. With each step, she becomes more than a sketch or a memory. She is present.

She turns before he reaches her. Her emerald eyes meet his, carrying that same haunted look from the photo, but softer here.

Recognition flickers in her expression, quickly followed by caution. A barrier rises, even as curiosity keeps her from looking away.

She wraps her oversized sweater tighter around herself, a defensive gesture that makes her seem more substantial, more human than any dream figure could be. The waves behind her pulse brighter, casting shifting light.

"You found your way back," she says, her voice carrying a slight Canadian lilt that surprises him. He remembers it now—soft and precise, just like when she spoke in school.

Zane stops a few feet away, afraid to break the moment. The dream feels more stable, colors vivid, her presence solid. He smells salt and something like paper and coffee, as if she had just been writing.

"I'm Zane," he says softly, keeping his distance as the waves pulse behind them. "From New York."

A beat of silence follows. Then she answers, voice quieter but steady:

"I'm Claire."

Claire shifts her weight as the sand swirls in patterns beneath her feet. "This doesn't feel like a dream, not the way it should."

"No," Zane says, stepping closer, careful not to break the moment. "But it feels good."

The sky pulses with shifting colors, deep blues bleeding into violet. Claire glances up, her brow furrowed. The waves behind her darken slightly, as if mirroring the uncertainty rising between them.

Zane keeps his voice low, steady. "I just wanted you to know you're not alone in this. Whatever this is."

She studies him, eyes sharp and searching. "Why are you here?"

"I've been trying to find you. Every time I wake up, I'm trying to get back here. To this place. To you."

Claire hugs herself tighter. The wind tugs her hair into her face, but she doesn't brush it away. The glow of the waves softens, steadies.

"I thought maybe I was going crazy," she says, barely above a whisper.

"You're not." Zane nods, sure of this. "I'm here. I feel you here. And this—" He gestures to the sand, the sky, the space between them. "It has to mean something."

Claire takes a step back, the waves behind her pulsing in sync with her unease. She studies Zane's face, her fingers digging deeper into her sleeves. "I've seen you before... but I don't know how. That part of my life is just... gone."

The sky deepens into bruised purples, casting shadows that stretch like ink across the sand. The waves churn darker, streaked with hints of green and violet, reacting to the shift between them.

"We had classes together," Zane says gently. "Senior year. You used to flick your hair back over my desk. I always wondered if it was on purpose."

Claire furrows her brow. "I wish I could remember." Her voice is quiet, the Canadian accent more distinct now. "It's like there's static in my head whenever I try to reach for anything from back then."

Zane stays still. The dream feels reactive to every movement. The sand between them glitches—shimmering, freezing, rippling again.

"Since my accident... finding you here," he says, keeping his voice low, "has made everything else feel like noise."

Claire's defensive posture softens slightly. The waves behind her begin to steady, the light shifting to a warmer tone. "I shouldn't trust this," she says, barely above a whisper. "But when I'm here... with you..." Her fingers unclench from the hem of her sweater. "The noise in my head gets quieter."

The words hover between them. They are more than just sound. The sky above continues its shifting color cycle, casting flickers of lavender and gold across her face. Zane watches the way the light settles in her eyes, giving them that familiar shimmer that never fades in his memory.

Something glints near her feet. Zane steps closer, drawn to a soft glow beneath the sand, a spiral shell pulsing faintly with the waves.

He crouches to pick it up. The shell is smooth, and tiny patterns move across its surface like shifting constellations.

"Here." He offers it to her without knowing why. The gesture feels sacred, like something they've done before but forgotten.

She studies the shell, not him. The glow reflects in her eyes. Their fingers meet, and a pulse shudders through the air. Light trembles across the ground.

The sand ripples beneath their feet, lines of gold and silver crisscrossing between them.

She turns the shell over. A soft smile forms as the light within it warms to her touch and glows gold. Wonder smooths her Canadian accent as she murmurs, "It's beautiful."

The shell bridges the space between them. Claire holds it to her chest. Her guardedness slips away.

The glow dims, and a weight settles in Zane's gut. The dream begins to blur, colors running like ink on wet paper.

"No, not yet." He reaches for Claire, but his hand passes through the space where she stands. The silver-gold sand beneath his feet loses substance, becoming mist that swirls around his ankles.

Claire's eyes widen with recognition of what's happening. The shell in her hands grows transparent, its light fading to a mere whisper. "Zane?" Her voice echoes from far away, her accent stretched thin like pulled taffy.

The waves behind her collapse into formless light, their rhythmic pulse growing erratic. The celestial sky above bleeds its colors together, purples and blues swirling into a void. Claire's form wavers, becoming translucent at the edges.

She looks at him with an expression that tightens something deep in his chest—desire to stay pulled against the quiet resignation that this moment, like all the others, is slipping away. Her emerald eyes shine with something raw. The collapse of the dream feels like a loss.

"Wait," Zane says, his voice too thin for the crumbling air around them. "How do I find you again?"

Claire's mouth moves, maybe to answer, but no sound reaches him. The dream fractures like glass struck at the center. Her figure splits into shards of light, the shell vanishes from her hand while the beach unravels.

Darkness rushes in, pulling everything into silence. Claire's face is the last thing to remain, confusion and yearning suspended in the void, then gone.

Zane jolts upright, drenched in sweat. The room is too quiet. Saltwater, or her perfume, lingers. He knocks over a glass reaching for his journal.

His hands shake as he writes, chasing the details before they vanish. He sketches the shell's spiral glow. Her eyes. Her accent. The sweater she wore like armor.

The silver-gold sand. The waves that rose and fell in sync with their connection, he writes it all down, his pen moving faster than his thoughts. But it's the feeling that's hardest to put into words. That moment when she looked at him and the entire dream clicked into something deeper.

Zane stops, raking a hand through his hair. This dream was clearer. Claire was no longer a blur. She pulled back at the mention of high school. The waves darkened with her hesitation.

He circles these thoughts, connecting lines across his notebook. The dreamscape reacting to emotion. The shell's arrival. Claire's guarded responses. The missing memories. None of it feels random anymore.

His hand cramps, but he refuses to stop. The encounter wasn't just important, it was proof.

***

Claire's eyes snap open, her fingers digging into her pillow. The soft glow of Seattle's perpetual rain filters through her curtains, but her mind remains anchored to the surreal beach. Zane's face burns clear in her memory—not the usual dream-fog that dissipates upon waking, but sharp details. The kindness in his brown eyes. The careful way he'd kept his distance, respecting her space.

She sits up slowly, her body aching. She can still feel the shell's weight in her hands. Her fingers flex, searching for something that isn't there.

She perches on the edge of her mattress, bare feet pressing against the cold floor. His voice echoes in her mind, carrying fragments of their conversation. High school. New York. The accident he'd mentioned. Each detail feels too specific, too grounded to be mere imagination.

"This is ridiculous," she whispers to her empty room, her accent thick with exhaustion. Dreams are dreams. Her therapist had been clear about that. Just the mind processing daily stress, nothing more.

The memory of Zane tugs at her. The waves responding to her emotions, the shifting sand—everything had felt natural. Good.

Claire rubs her temples, trying to separate fantasy from reality. She's had vivid dreams before, especially when her pain medication doses change. This has to be another side effect, another trick of her tired mind.

She reaches for a pill bottle, then pauses. She tips it, counting the remaining tablets, which is more than she'd expect for this time of the month. Her brow furrows as she tries to recall her last dose.

The realization hits her: she hasn't needed as many pills since the dreams began. Lingering back pain still bothers her, but it doesn't preoccupy her mind like before. The fog in her mind feels thinner and clearer.

She sets the bottle down, studying its reflection in the light filtering through her window. The label stares back at her, a reminder of years spent managing pain with increasing doses. But now...

Her fingers trace the plastic, recalling the shell from her dream, how it had felt in her hands.

"What are you doing to me?" she whispers, thinking of Zane and their shared dreamscape. The pain still exists, but somehow, in the space between their encounters, it feels more manageable.

Doubt lingers like mist. The shell's warmth, silver-gold sand, and his voice saying her name refuse to fade. They won't be dismissed as imagination.

Claire's fingers tremble as she opens her leather-bound journal, its pages worn from years of late-night confessions. The pen hovers over blank paper before she begins to write:

Last night's dream lingers like a shadow I can't shake. The beach again. The colors painting the sky, waves that moved with my thoughts. But this time, he had a name. Zane. His eyes held such kindness, such patience. No judgment when I couldn't remember high school.

The shell he gave me pulsed with light, warm against my skin. For those few moments, my pain faded to background noise. How can a dream do that? The waves matched my heartbeat. The sand shifted beneath us like stardust.

He kept his distance, understood without words. No one does that. Not Liam, not my family—they push and prod and demand. But Zane... he just waited. Let me decide.

The accent in my voice came out stronger there. I haven't let that happen since moving to Seattle. Something about his presence made me forget to hide it.

What about the meds? Coincidence, probably.

She studies the words, their slanted strokes betraying the emotion she tried to suppress. Her mind snaps to attention, defenses rising fast.

"It's just a dream," she whispers, snapping the journal shut. Her fingers trace the cover. Fantasies are just her mind's way of escaping Liam and the pain.

She slides the journal under her pillow, ignoring the urge to reopen it. Morning light streams in, grounding her in a world where connection is never that simple.

Chapter 14

THE LAPTOP'S BLUE GLOW casts shadows across Zane's face as he types. Stacks of lucid dreaming books tower beside him, pages marked with sticky notes. His coffee sits cold, forgotten since he found a promising forum thread on dream anchors.

He scrolls through another page, adding to his overflowing journal. The technique sounds promising: focus on a physical object before sleep, then find it in the dream. He brushes the shell he sketched earlier. Its spiral is burned into memory.

A notification appears on his phone. It's Emily's third missed call. He closes it without hesitation, diving into an article on maintaining dream consciousness. Exhaustion creeps in, but he forces his eyes open. Each piece of information might be the key to reaching Claire.

His desk calendar is filled with missed meetings and crossed-out appointments. Margins brim with notes about Claire along with fragments of conversations, beach details, connection theories. Her photo in the yearbook stays close. It's a constant reminder.

A forum post grabs him where someone describes shared dreams with uncanny accuracy. Zane leans in, heart racing. The lighting, merged awareness, lingering memory all match. He adds the post to his growing pile of proof.

Outside, the city flows through its rhythm. Zane doesn't move, anchored to his chair. The line between obsession and dedication fades, each new discovery pulling him deeper.

Emily shoulders her way through the apartment door. Her teacher's tote bag is heavy with ungraded papers. Their once-tidy space has transformed into a research den, with printouts of dream theories plastered across the walls.

"Hey, babe." She drops her keys in the bowl and winces at the clatter. "I brought that pasta you like from Tony's."

Zane mumbles a reply, fingers still tapping. He hunches over his makeshift command center of monitors and notebooks. Three coffee cups crowd the desk, staining papers.

Emily notices a new detail on his wall, a map drawn by hand, its coastline lined with strange symbols. She sets the takeout bag down, sliding a stack of dream books out of the way.

"Thought we could eat together." She keeps her voice light, masking the weight in her chest. "Maybe watch that show we started?"

"Mm." Zane highlights something on his screen, scribbling in his journal. "Just give me a minute. I think I found something about shared consciousness during REM sleep."

Emily stares at the back of his head, his hair sticking up from too many frustrated hand passes. She fidgets with her ring, twisting it in the dim lamplight.

She opens her mouth, but nothing comes out. She turns her attention to unpacking the food, letting the sound of plates fill the silence.

Emily drops her bag with a thud, planting herself between Zane and his laptop. Her shadow falls across his notes, forcing him to look up.

"What are you doing?" He leans slightly, fingers poised over the keyboard, trying to see past her.

"No. You're going to look at me." Emily's voice trembles. "Really look at me, Zane. When did you do that last?"

He leans back, running a hand through his disheveled hair. "I'm just in the middle of—"

"Of what? Chasing someone who doesn't exist?" She grabs one of his notebooks, flipping through pages of dream descriptions. "Look at this. Pages and pages about her. About this, Claire. But what about us? What about our engagement?"

"You don't understand." Zane reaches for the notebook, but Emily pulls it away. "These dreams mean something."

"And what do I mean?" Emily's eyes glisten. "Because right now, it feels like I'm competing with memory. Someone you made up in your head."

"I didn't make her up." Zane stands, his chair rolling back. "She's... I knew her. And these dreams—"

"These dreams are destroying us!" Emily slams the notebook down. "You barely sleep. You skip work. You haven't touched me in weeks. And for what? Some girl you think you remember from high school?"

"It's not that simple."

"Then explain it to me." Emily's voice cracks. "Help me understand why you're willing to throw away everything we built for someone who only lives in your dreams."

Zane paces behind his desk, his hands gesturing in frantic patterns as he tries to gather his scattered thoughts.

"You have to trust me on this." His voice rises, defensive. "These aren't just regular dreams. There's something deeper happening here."

Emily's hurt expression barely registers as he grabs his journal, flipping through pages of hastily scrawled notes. "Look at the patterns, the consistency. The way the beach changes with our emotions. The way she—"

"The way she what, Zane?" Emily's words cut through his rambling. "The way this dream version of someone you barely knew somehow matters more than your fiancée?"

"That's not—" He drags a hand through his unruly hair. "You're making this about us when it's about something bigger. These dreams are saying something important."

"And what am I trying to tell you?" Emily steps closer, but Zane turns back to his desk, shuffling through papers.

"I just need more time to figure this out." His voice drops. "If you'd just listen instead of dismissing everything—"

"Like you're dismissing me right now?"

Zane's shoulders tense. "You don't understand. You can't understand because you're not experiencing it."

Emily's hands shake as she grips the edge of Zane's desk. "Real? You want to talk about what's real?" Her voice cracks. "What's real is I've spent weeks watching you slip away. What's real is coming home every night to find you lost in this... this fucking fantasy!"

Zane's head snaps up, startled by her outburst, but Emily continues, tears streaming down her face. "What's real is that I've been sleeping alone while you chase some dream girl who probably doesn't even remember you exist!"

She storms into their bedroom and emerges with an overnight bag Zane hadn't noticed before. His stomach drops at the sight of it.

"Emily, wait—"

"No." She wipes her eyes. "I'm done waiting. I'm done competing with a goddamn ghost. I can't—" Her voice breaks. "I can't keep pretending this is normal anymore."

"Please, just let me explain—"

"Explain what?" She spins to face him. "That you'd rather live in your dreams than in reality? That you'd rather obsess over some girl from years ago than build a life with me?"

Zane reaches for her, but she steps back, shaking her head. "I can't do this anymore," she whispers. She grabs a bag and moves toward the door.

The slam echoes through the apartment, leaving Zane alone with his research and the lingering scent of her perfume.

Zane stares at the closed door, Emily's words still ringing in his ears. The apartment feels stripped of something, hollow in a way it wasn't before. His hand trembles as he lifts his coffee mug, only to find it empty.

He should feel devastated. He should be running after her. Instead, his eyes drift back to his research, to Claire's photo. "I can't stop now," he mutters, fingers drumming against his desk. "I'm too close."

A knock cuts through his thoughts. Before he can respond, the door swings open. Park stands there with two coffees and that look that says he already knows everything's gone sideways.

"I figured you could use a wingman." Park steps inside, kicking the door shut behind him. He surveys the clutter of journals and loose pages, taking in the depth of Zane's obsession.

"Also," Park adds, setting the coffee down, "pretty sure I just passed Emily in the lobby. Said hi. She blew past me like I was a ghost."

Park sets a coffee in front of Zane as he circles the desk, whistling low at the explosion of papers and coffee cups. "So this is what a beautiful mind looks like. Though I gotta say, Russell Crowe had better handwriting."

Zane barely looks up. His fingers keep moving. Empty energy drink cans form a wall around his laptop, Post-its fluttering from the desk fan's breeze.

"You know," Park continues, picking up a crumpled paper covered in spiraling notes, "when I said you needed a hobby, I was thinking more along the lines of fantasy football." He squints at the scribbled writing. "Though I guess dream journaling is basically fantasy sleeping, so..."

Park's eyes catch Emily's coffee mug, lipstick stain still visible. The silence in the apartment speaks volumes, but Park keeps his tone light as he clears a space on the desk.

"Your cleaning lady quit?" He nudges an empty pizza box with his foot. "Or did she get lost in this labyrinth of lucid dreaming literature?"

Post-its blanket the wall in a chaotic web, like a crime scene board. Park tilts his head, reading: "Metallic grains?" "Temporal sync patterns?" "Group mindscape catalysts?"

"Come on, dude," Park laughs, "just add a bulletin board and you'll hit peak conspiracy nut. Throw on some aluminum headgear and—" His words die as he notices Emily's framed photos are missing from the shelves.

Park drops onto the couch, brushing aside a stack of papers to make room. "Alright, spill it. What happened with Emily?"

Zane slumps into his chair and spins to face Park. He taps the armrest with his fingers in a nervous rhythm. The words won't come.

"She left." The words hang heavy in the air. "Said she couldn't compete with..." He gestures vaguely at his research-covered walls.

"With your dream girl." Park's usual smirk fades. "Claire."

"You don't get it." Zane leans forward, running his hands through his hair. "These dreams aren't like the others. When I'm with her, it feels stronger, like I'm actually there."

"More than Emily?"

Zane winces at the question. "It's not about replacing her. These dreams, they're trying to tell me something. Claire and I, we shared moments in the past. What if this connection means something?"

Park scans the chaos—the messy notes, Zane's twitchy energy, the exhaustion in his eyes. "Look, man, I've known you since we were kids. I've seen you hyper-focused before, but this..." He picks up a dream journal, thick with post-its and coffee stains. "This is different."

"Because it is different." Zane's voice cracks with desperation. "Every night, same beach. And Claire, she remembers the dreams too."

Park sets the journal down, leaning forward. His usual jokes and quips fade away, replaced by genuine concern. "And Emily? Was she not enough?"

Park sets his coffee down with a sharp click. "When's the last time you left this apartment?"

Zane blinks. He draws a blank. The cluttered walls blur.

"That's what I thought." Park stands, his shadow falling across Zane's desk. "Look at yourself, man. When did you last shower? Eat something besides takeout?" He gestures at the empty containers littering the floor. "You're not just chasing dreams anymore. You're drowning in them."

Zane's fingers twitch toward his keyboard, but Park steps between him and the screen. "The dreams will still be there tomorrow.

Claire will still be there. But you?" He taps Zane's chest. "You're disappearing."

"I can't stop now." Zane's voice cracks. "I'm so close to understanding—"

"Understanding what? That you've turned your life into this?" Park sweeps his arm across the papers and books. "The Zane I know wouldn't lose himself like this. He wouldn't throw away everything for some... connection that only exists when you're unconscious."

Zane slumps in his chair. His greasy hair, coffee-stained shirt, and messy apartment reflect his spiral.

"Take a walk with me." Park grabs Zane's keys from where they're buried under a stack of papers. "Get some air. Remember what the sun feels like." He tosses the keys to Zane. "The dreams aren't going anywhere. But your life?" He points to the area where Emily's photos used to hang. "That's slipping away while you're lost in your head."

The air outside feels strange against Zane's skin, a sharp contrast to the days spent buried in his apartment. Park walks beside him, matching his slow pace.

Zane's hands feel empty without his notebook. His mind slips to the unfinished theories waiting at his desk until Park nudges him back.

"You're doing it again." Park guides him around a street vendor. "That thing where you check out mentally and probably dream about your dream girl."

The coffee shop's worn brick exterior comes into view. Its faded awning flutters in the breeze. The bell chimes as they enter, and the rich aroma of coffee beans wraps around Zane like an old friend, and his shoulders ease.

Their usual table waits for them. Zane notices the CBCK initials Park carved. The steam wands hiss in the background.

Park calls to Maya behind the counter, who responds with a knowing nod. She's been serving them their morning coffee for years, though Zane realizes he hasn't seen her in quite some time.

"When did they change the artwork?" Zane asks, noticing different local photographs on the walls.

"Dude, that was a while ago." Park raises an eyebrow. "You really have been gone, haven't you?"

Sitting here with Park feels strange but comforting.

"Thanks for dragging me out," Zane admits, taking a sip of his coffee. The taste reminds him of mornings before the dreams, before Claire, before everything got so complicated.

The familiar buzz of the café feels surreal. Zane watches the foam swirl like waves.

"What if..." Park leans forward, his coffee untouched. "What if you find her, and she's just a normal person living a normal life? What if these dreams don't mean what you think they mean?"

"I have to know," he says, but his voice lacks its usual conviction.

"Know what exactly?" Park's eyes fix on him with uncomfortable intensity. "That you're not crazy? Or is it something else?"

Zane opens his mouth to defend himself, but the words never make it out. The truth is, he hasn't really asked himself why. Why Claire? Why these dreams? Why this obsession?

"Maybe..." Park's voice softens. "Maybe this isn't about Claire at all. Think about it. When did these dreams start? Right after the accident. Right when everything in your life was perfect but felt..."

"Empty," Zane whispers, the realization settling like a weight in his chest.

"You had everything you thought you wanted, the job, the girlfriend, the perfect life. But something was missing, wasn't it?"

Zane sets the cup down. The walls press in as memories flood back with endless meetings, routine kisses, a life lived on autopilot.

"What if Claire isn't the answer?" Park asks. "What if she's just your mind's way of telling you something isn't right? Something that was broken long before these dreams started?"

Zane runs his finger along the rim of his coffee cup. His reflection wavers in the deep black surface. "I don't know what I'm searching for anymore," he admits. "Maybe you're right about the accident changing things. But these dreams..." He looks up at Park, his eyes haunted. "They're the only thing that make me feel alive anymore."

Park takes a sip, studying his friend over the rim. "You know this could all lead nowhere. Or somewhere you don't want to go."

"I know." Zane taps each letter in CBCK. "I can't ignore it. She's always there. The beach, her voice, the colors. It's a puzzle I need to solve."

"Then solve it." Park sets down his cup with a decisive click. "If you're going down this rabbit hole, I'm coming with you." He leans back. "But speaking of reality, when are you coming back to work? Thompson's been asking about you."

Zane winces, suddenly remembering the pile of unread emails in his inbox. "I should probably head back soon. My leave is almost up, anyway."

"Good." Park nods. "Because if you're going to chase dream girls, you might as well have a paycheck while doing it."

The breeze trails them as they leave. Zane's steps are steadier, his mind sharper from fresh air and caffeine.

"I found a technique," Zane says, matching Park's pace. "You anchor yourself in the dream by focusing on physical sensations."

Park snorts. "So basically, you're becoming a professional napper?"

Zane gestures as he speaks, energy returning. "If I stay aware while falling asleep, I might control when I see her."

"Just promise me one thing?" Park stops at the corner where they usually part ways. "Promise you'll come up for air. I'm not above breaking into your apartment and dragging you out for coffee again."

"Yeah, yeah." Zane rolls his eyes. Warmth spreads through his chest at his friend's concern. "Thanks for today, man. Really."

Zane steps into his apartment. The silence feels less suffocating now. He touches his dream journal, settles into his chair, and opens his laptop.

Chapter 15

CLAIRE STUDIES THE FRESH ink in her journal, Zane's face still vivid from the dream. Silver-gold sand, colorful waves, and his steady presence felt more solid than her Seattle apartment. She's been writing since dawn.

Heavy footsteps break her concentration. The floorboards creak behind her, and Claire's shoulders tense instinctively. She knows that deliberate pace, the way Liam likes to announce his presence without saying a word.

"Still writing in your little diary?" His voice drips with mockery as he leans against the doorframe. "What are you, twelve?"

Claire's grip tightens on her pen, but she doesn't stop. The dream was too clear, too important. She won't let him take it away from her.

"You know, some people wake up and do something with their lives," Liam says, stepping into the room. "But I guess that doesn't apply to you."

His shadow falls over her pages. Claire resists the urge to close the journal, refusing to hide what matters from someone who never understands.

Claire sets her pen down carefully, keeping her breath even. "Journaling helps me process things. My therapist suggested it, remember?" Her voice remains soft, neutral, and controlled.

Liam grabs the journal without warning, flipping through it with careless hands. Pages bend, corners crumple. "Process what exactly? These strange dreams you keep having?" His jaw tightens as he scans the handwriting. "You barely say two words to me anymore, but you've got time to write pages about some guy in your head?"

"It's not like that." Claire's fingers curl into fists beneath the desk. "Writing helps with my pain management too."

"Pain management?" Liam throws the journal down, the slap of it hitting the desk making her flinch. "I'm the one managing your pain. Who carries you when you're hurting? Who keeps the lights on around here?" He starts pacing, footsteps loud and deliberate. "And you repay that by checking out every time you close your eyes?"

Claire looks down at her hands and wills herself not to shake. "I'm grateful for what you do—"

"Doesn't sound like it." He stops behind her, both palms pressing into the back of her chair. "You're always in that journal or chasing sleep. Like you're hiding from me."

The chair groans under the weight of his grip. Claire sits frozen between his arms, her shoulders curling inward. "I'm not hiding."

"Then what is this?" His voice rises, sharper now. "You think I don't see what's going on? Replacing me with some fantasy man in your dreams?"

Her journal closes with a quiet snap. Something in her spine locks into place. She stands, forcing him to take a step back.

"Stop it." Her voice comes out stronger than she expected. "Just stop."

Liam's eyebrows shoot up, his mouth curling into a sneer. "Excuse me?"

"Everything I do is wrong to you." The words pour out, years of silence breaking like a dam. "The coffee's never hot enough. The apartment's never clean enough. My writing's childish, my dreams are stupid. I can't breathe without disappointing you."

"I'm looking out for you—"

"No." Her palm hits the desk with a crack. "You're controlling me. That's not the same thing." Her chest rises and falls with sharp breaths. "You act like you're doing me some huge favor just by staying."

Liam's face darkens. "After everything I've done for you—"

"What have you done?" Claire's voice climbs, her body trembling but unmoving. "Humiliated me? Questioned my every thought? Mocked everything that brings me peace?" She grabs her journal, clutching it to her chest like armor. "I'm tired of shrinking myself just to survive your moods."

"You're being dramatic."

"I'm being honest!" she shouts, the words ragged. "This is the first time I've said what I actually feel. And you still won't listen." Her eyes shine, but the fire in them doesn't dim. "You've chipped away at me piece by piece until I barely recognize who I am. And I'm done pretending that's love."

Liam lunges forward, yanking the journal from her hands. Pages scatter like startled birds as he flips through it, grip tight around the binding.

"Let's see what's so important in here." His voice drops to a mocking whisper. "Oh, this is rich. 'His presence feels like safety.' 'The beach glows with amazing colors.'" He barks out a harsh laugh. "You're living in a fantasy world, Claire."

Claire reaches for the journal, but Liam steps back, flipping another page like he's onstage. "'He understands me without words.' Really? Some made-up guy in your head understands you better than I do?"

"Stop it." Her voice wavers, but she holds her stance. "Those are private."

"Private? From me?" His eyes narrow as they skim the page. "I'm your boyfriend. I put up with everything. Your pain, your moods, your silence. And this is what I get? A notebook of fantasies?"

He jabs at a passage, spitting each word like venom. "And this? This crap about some dream guy named—" Liam stops, brow tightening. His mouth opens again, but the name doesn't come out. Just static. A brief, unnatural stutter in his voice like a skipped beat on a scratched record. "Zuh—"

Claire's eyes widen. "What did you say?"

Liam blinks, confused. "I—" He looks back at the page. The name is gone. Smudged ink. Blank space. "What the hell?"

Claire stares at him, blood draining from her face. "You shouldn't know that name," she whispers. "I've never written it down."

The silence that follows is thick, unnatural. Even the city outside seems to pause.

Liam clocks her reaction, eyes narrowing. "What, surprised I found his name buried in here?" He waves the journal in her face. "It's scribbled everywhere. You're seriously delusional. Some made-up dream man giving you more than I ever could?"

He rips a page from the journal, the sound sharp and final. "Maybe this will snap you out of it."

Claire holds her breath. The page crumples in his fist. He rips another, and another. Each tear lands like a slap to her chest.

"Please stop." Her voice is barely audible.

Liam doesn't hear—or doesn't care. "This is garbage. Every word. These dreams, this fantasy..." He tears more pages, the shreds falling like dead leaves. "You think this will save you? You think he's real? You need professional help..."

He tears until the journal is a mangled wreck, flinging the half-destroyed cover across the room. It slams into the wall with a flat, heavy thud, landing face-down in a sprawl of ruined pages.

Claire flinches, instinct curling her inward on itself. The scattered pieces of her mind, her space to breathe, to hope, now lie torn at her feet. Her arms wrap around her middle, trying to hold something together.

And something inside her... shifts.

Liam stalks through the paper debris, crushing the pages under his boots. "There. Now maybe you'll focus on what's important instead of living in some dream world."

The crunch of paper under his feet echoes in Claire's ears. Each step grinds her words deeper into the floor, a physical demonstration of how he's always trampled her spirit.

Claire stands still amid the wreckage, each torn page a quiet testament to Liam's cruelty. Tears threaten, but she forces them down.

The violation cuts deeper than any physical pain she's endured. These weren't just words. They were pieces of herself she had dared to express. Liam destroyed them with the same casual cruelty he used to wear down her confidence.

Her hands tremble but not from fear. Something shifts inside her, like a key turning in a rusted lock. The tears harden into resolve. Her jaw sets, and she lifts her chin to meet Liam's glare with steel.

This isn't just about the journal anymore. It's about every dismissive comment, every mocking laugh, every moment he made her feel small. Her face hardens as clarity strikes - she sees him now, truly sees the pattern of control and cruelty she's endured.

Claire's fingers curl into fists, nails pressing into her palms. The usual ache fades, replaced by something stronger. Resolve burns through her like wildfire.

Liam's expression softens, a calculated shift from rage to concern. He steps toward Claire, crunching torn paper beneath his feet. "Baby, I'm only trying to help you." His voice drips with honey over poison. "These dreams, this writing - it's not healthy. You're losing touch with what matters."

He reaches for her arm, but Claire steps back, her shoulders pressed against the wall. "Look at you, living in this fantasy world while I'm here, taking care of you." His fingers brush against her cheek. "Who else would put up with you?"

Claire's stomach churns at his touch. "Remember last month when your pain was so bad you couldn't get out of bed? Who brought you food? Who picked up your prescriptions?" He gestures around the apartment. "Who pays most of the rent so you can keep pursuing this writing hobby?"

His eyes find hers, practiced sincerity replacing the earlier rage. "I do these things because I care about you, Claire. Because I want what's best for you." He kneels and gathers some torn pages with exaggerated gentleness. "Sometimes that means being tough, showing you when you're going down the wrong path."

"You need me," he whispers, moving closer. "Who else understands what you're going through? Who else would stay?" His hand finds her shoulder, squeezing just tight enough to remind her of his presence. "I'm just trying to keep you grounded in reality. These dreams, this Zane person - they're not here. I am."

Claire kneels and gathers torn pages with trembling hands. Each one holds fragments of dreams, thoughts, and her connection to

Zane, pieces Liam tried to erase. She holds the papers to her chest, ignoring his looming presence. Pain pulses up her spine, but she welcomes it. It's proof she's still here, still capable.

Liam's voice drones on above her, a litany of manipulation she knows by heart. "You're not even listening to me, are you?" His boot nudges her knee, but she doesn't flinch.

Claire smooths a wrinkled page, tracing her words. Descriptions of silver-gold sand, feeling understood, peace in dreams. Not delusions. Lifelines.

She rises slowly with the papers clutched to her chest and meets Liam's gaze. Where he expects submission or tears, he finds only quiet resolve. His practiced concern falters under her silence.

"Say something," he demands, his facade cracking.

Claire stays silent. She doesn't need words. Every torn page tells the story of his control, his jealousy, his need to break what gives her strength. She sees it now. She lifts her chin, her voice steady despite her racing heart. "Get out."

Liam's eyebrows shoot up. "Excuse me?"

"I said get out." She clutches the torn pages closer. "I need space."

"Space?" His laugh comes sharp and bitter. "From what? Reality?"

"From you." The words feel like freedom on her tongue. "Just go, Liam."

He steps toward her, but Claire holds her ground. His mouth opens, closes, twists into a sneer. "Fine. Call me when you're done with this little tantrum." The door slams behind him, rattling the windows.

Claire drops to the floor, her legs giving out as adrenaline drains. She spreads the pages, trying to piece them back together.

Hours pass in a blur of tears and scattered paper. The afternoon sun casts long shadows across the floor when three sharp knocks break the silence.

"Claire? It's Sarah."

Relief floods through her as she hears her best friend's voice. "It's open."

Sarah enters and stops, taking in Claire cross-legged on the floor, tears dry on her face, journal in shreds.

"Oh, honey." Sarah drops her purse and kneels beside her. "What happened?"

Claire looks up through tear-stained eyes, explaining Liam's explosion over her journal. Sarah's face hardens with each word, her hands balling into fists.

The door bursts open. Liam strides in, freezing when he spots Sarah standing protectively near Claire.

"What are you doing here?" His voice carries a dangerous edge.

Sarah steps forward, positioning herself between Claire and Liam. "I could ask you the same thing. Wasn't destroying her journal enough for one day?"

"This is between me and Claire."

"No. It stopped being just between you two when you decided to tear apart someone I care about." Sarah's eyes flash with anger. "You think I haven't noticed the changes in her? How she second-guesses everything? How she's stopped writing?"

Liam scoffs. "You don't know what you're talking about."

"I know exactly what I'm talking about." Sarah takes another step forward. "I know about the criticism, the control, the way you use her pain against her. Claire deserves someone who builds her up, not tears her down."

"I take care of her—"

"You manipulate her." Sarah's voice cuts like steel. "There's a difference. And I'm done watching you hurt my friend."

Liam's face flushes red. "This isn't your business—"

"Claire is my business." Sarah stands her ground. "And if you think I'll let you keep treating her like this, you're wrong."

Sarah locks the door after Liam's retreat, her hands shaking with residual anger. She turns to find Claire still on the floor, gathering torn pages with methodical care.

"Leave those for now." Sarah's voice softens as she sits cross-legged beside her. "We need to talk."

Claire's fingers still hover over a crumpled sheet. "I know what you're going to say."

"Good. Then you know I'm right." Sarah pries the page gently from Claire's grip. "You can't stay with him."

"It's not that simple." Claire pulls her arms close and holds herself. "The apartment's in his name. The bills—"

"Stop." Sarah takes her hands. "We can handle logistics. What we can't fix is what happens if you let him keep grinding you down."

Claire's lower lip trembles. "What if I can't do it?"

"You already did the hardest part." Sarah squeezes her hands. "You stood up to him. You told him to leave. That took incredible strength."

Tears spill down Claire's cheeks. "I'm scared."

"Of course you are. But you don't have to do this alone." Sarah pulls her into a tight hug. "My place is yours for as long as you need. We'll get your prescriptions transferred. I'll help you find a new place when you're ready."

Claire buries her face in Sarah's shoulder while her body shakes. "I don't deserve—"

"Stop right there." Sarah pulls back, holding her at arm's length. "You deserve everything. Friends who support you. Space to write. Freedom to dream." She wipes a tear from Claire's cheek.

Claire's shoulders tremble as Sarah's words pierce years of carefully constructed walls. The afternoon light casts long shadows across the torn pages of her journal, each scattered piece a reminder of Liam's control.

"I don't know if I can." She grips Sarah's sweater, anchoring herself to this moment of honesty. The familiar ache in her back intensifies, but she forces herself to stay present.

Sarah's arms tighten around her. "You already are. Look what you did today. You stood up to him. The old Claire would've apologized. Would've blamed herself."

Claire pulls back, wiping her eyes with the heel of her hand. Her gaze drops to a torn page where Zane's name remains visible. Something shifts in her chest. It's not quite hope, but its distant cousin.

"But everything's tied to him." She picks up the page, smoothing the crumpled edge. "He made sure of that."

"That's what abusers do." Sarah's voice holds no judgment. "They build cages so slowly you don't even see the bars."

Claire's fingers trace Zane's name. In her dreams, she feels whole. Strong. Here, surrounded by the wreckage of her journal, that strength feels impossibly far away.

"I keep thinking about all the times he was there for me." Her voice shrinks. "When the pain was bad, when I couldn't work..."

"Being helpful doesn't erase being harmful." Sarah reaches for her hand, squeezing gently. "You don't owe him your life because he did the bare minimum sometimes."

Claire leans into Sarah's shoulder, her body heavy. "I don't know if I can," she says again, but now it feels like the start of something instead of the end. She surveys the wreckage, pages catching fading light.

She shifts, surprised that her back aches less than usual. The pain feels lighter now, as if the dreams are bleeding into the living world.

She picks up another page. Her handwriting describes the colors and a wordless sense of understanding. The memory brings warmth to her chest, pushing back years of doubt.

Sarah's steady presence feels like an anchor. Claire realizes how much of herself she's surrendered to Liam's care. The prescriptions he managed, the bills he paid, the life he claimed to provide. They weren't gifts. They were chains.

Her fingers trace a line about Zane's kind eyes. Something clicks. The dreams aren't an escape anymore. They're proof another way exists, one where she isn't defined by pain or trapped in someone else's idea of love.

Claire turns to Sarah, her voice barely above a whisper but steady with newfound clarity. "I can't live like this anymore."

Chapter 16

SUNLIGHT GLINTS OFF GLASS towers as Zane moves through Manhattan's morning crowd. The city pulses with sound: car horns, voices, footsteps. Everything feels more vivid since the dreams began. He pauses at a crosswalk, watching pigeons scatter as a taxi passes. The usual walk to the coffee shop feels different now. Every stranger's face catches his attention. Maybe one of them connects to Claire.

He rounds the corner, sidestepping a bike messenger. The coffee shop's worn brick facade comes into view, their regular table visible through the window. Park isn't there yet, but Zane spots the etched "CBCK" on their table. Crossroads Between Chaos and Kismet. The words feel heavier now.

The bell chimes as he enters. The barista nods and starts his usual. Zane sits at their table, tracing Park's carving with his fingers. Each person who walks in catches his eye. He watches, always wondering if someone is linked to Claire.

He opens his journal to a blank page. The dreams give him direction, something to solve. The city feels like a puzzle, every detail a possible clue.

The bell rings as Park walks in, and his confident smile slips when he sees Zane. The tired eyes are still there, but so is something new. A spark, a focused energy he hasn't seen in weeks.

"You look suspiciously chipper for someone who's barely sleeping." Park slides into his seat, eyeing the open journal.

"The dreams are getting clearer." Zane leans forward, lowering his voice. "Last night, we actually talked. Like an actual conversation."

"We?" Park raises an eyebrow, wrapping his hands around his coffee mug. "Your dream girl has a voice now?"

"It's not just fragments anymore. The beach, the way the waves glow - it all feels solid, permanent. And Claire..." Zane pauses, collecting his thoughts. "She feels genuine, Park."

Park watches him, noting the way Zane's hands move faster, how his eyes light up. This is the most present he's been since the accident.

"She said things that surprised me," Zane continues. "Things I couldn't have made up. We connected on this deep level that I can't explain."

"And you're sure these aren't just really vivid dreams?" Park keeps his tone gentle, careful.

Zane runs a hand through his hair. "But there's something different about them."

Park sips his coffee slowly. Zane's voice holds something sincere, something that gives him pause. Zane flips through his journal, lost in a search no one else seems to see.

"Look at this." Zane points to a sketch. "The waves glow silver, and the sand changes color where you step."

"You've gotten better at drawing." Park leans closer, examining the intricate details. His usual skepticism wavers at the conviction in Zane's voice.

"And here," Zane turns to another page filled with notes. "Claire mentioned growing up near Edmonton. I couldn't have known that."

Park lowers his cup. Zane's excitement reminds him of college, back when new ideas used to light him up.

"You know what?" Park straightens in his chair. "If it's making you this happy, why not see where it leads?" He grins, adding, "Just promise me you won't turn into a weirdo dream guru."

Zane looks up, surprised by the sudden support. "You're not going to tell me I'm losing it?"

"Hey, I still think it's bizarre." Park shrugs. "But I haven't seen you this passionate about anything since before the accident. Maybe there's something to it."

Zane puts the journal away, feeling lighter. Park's support eases the weight.

"Thanks for not thinking I'm completely insane," Zane says, shouldering his bag.

"Oh, I definitely think you're insane." Park holds the door open. "Just the good kind of insane."

They step into the street, weaving around tourists. The city feels lighter now, filled with something new. Zane breathes it in and lets his mind be still.

At work, Zane moves through meetings with ease. The urgency to analyze every detail fades. He smiles more, enough that coworkers take notice.

Evening comes, light slanting through the windows. Zane packs up, leaving the journal untouched. For once, he doesn't feel the need to write or analyze.

Walking home, he passes the coffee shop again. The "CBCK" etching catches the setting sun. He doesn't overthink it this time. Whatever this is with Claire, he'll let it come on its own.

***

That night, Claire falls into sleep, her body relaxing after another tense day with Liam. Instead of the usual fog, the dream comes softly, like stepping through light.

The beach she expects is gone. Instead, emerald grass and shimmering flowers stretch beneath tall oaks, their shadows swaying in slow, fluid motion.

Distant laughter floats on the breeze, reminding her of childhood summers, though she can't place the specific memory. The sound brings comfort rather than the usual anxiety that accompanies crowds.

She spots Zane sitting on a wooden bench near a bubbling fountain. Sunlight casts warm colors over the scene. Her body moves toward him before her mind catches up.

"This is different," Claire says as she sits beside him. The bench feels stable, not like the usual dream furniture that fades or flickers.

Zane turns to her, his presence calm and anchoring. Sunlight touches his eyes, and Claire sees amber flecks she hadn't noticed.

Children's laughter drifts from beyond the trees, but Claire stays focused on Zane. In this dream, she doesn't feel the need to hide or choose her words carefully. The weight of Liam's judgment fades, replaced by quiet certainty.

The air feels charged, time slipping by in a gentler rhythm. Each breath fills her with grass and sun, too vivid to be a typical dream.

Claire watches Zane's hands as he talks, his movements deliberate, tracing shapes in the air. He reminds her of her favorite English teacher, animated but calm.

"I used to hate marketing, if you can believe it," Zane says, leaning back against the bench. "Thought it was all manipulation and false promises."

"What changed?" The words flow easily from Claire's lips, none of her usual hesitation present.

"I realized it could be about connecting people to things that actually help them. Making the important stuff visible." He turns toward her, one arm resting on the bench back. "Kind of like writing, in a way."

Claire raises her eyebrows. "How did you know I write?"

"Just seemed right somehow." He shrugs, his smile genuine. "You have that observer's way of listening."

The fountain bubbles nearby, blending with birdsong. Claire pulls her legs up onto the bench without pain. Her body remembers ease, if only here.

"I mostly write travel pieces," she says, surprised by her own openness. "Small stories about hidden places."

"Making the important stuff visible," Zane echoes, and they share a laugh that feels as natural as breathing.

The dream holds steady, slower than usual. Patterns of sunlight flicker through the leaves. The scent of flowers lingers. Everything feels softer, like the world has been lowered to a quieter setting.

"It's strange," Claire says, "talking like this feels..."

"Like we've known each other forever?" Zane finishes.

She nods, relieved he understands without explanation. Here, speaking feels easier. The usual tension in her shoulders is gone, replaced by a calm awareness.

A breeze carries the scent of flowers as Claire shifts, her fingers moving along the wood grain. Zane's quiet question lingers, unspoken but waiting.

"I write from home mostly," she says, voice quiet but firm. The truth feels heavy, but here, she can carry it.

Zane nods, his presence steady beside her. "Sounds peaceful."

"Sometimes." She watches a golden leaf fall from the surreal trees. "When writing flows. When the pain eases." The words escape before she can stop them, and her body tightens.

"Physical pain?" His voice carries no pity, just gentle understanding.

Claire crosses her arms, a reflex she knows too well. "Chronic. It complicates everything." She says nothing about Liam, but her eyes shift.

"Writing helps though?" Zane asks, giving her space to retreat if she needs to.

"It's an escape." Claire smiles, just slightly. "Like these dreams." She looks at her hands, surprised by how easily the truth comes. "Sometimes, it's all I have that's mine."

The fountain murmurs between them. Claire feels the usual pull to retreat, to shield herself, but Zane's steady attention makes her want to stay.

"I have good days and bad days," she says, choosing each word with care. "Today was harder." She leaves the rest unsaid, but even this feels like a win.

Zane shifts slightly, keeping a respectful space between them. The soft light outlines the tight line of Claire's jaw as she weighs what to share.

"You don't have to tell me now," he says. The words drift between them and settle gently. "Just know that I'm here."

Her shoulders ease, spine no longer rigid. In this dream, where things feel both distant and close, his quiet acceptance holds her. She doesn't have to explain or defend anything.

The fountain murmurs on. Claire feels the rare calm of being seen without pressure. Zane's presence stays steady with no questions or demands.

His words echo in the peaceful silence, "I'm here," and for once, those words don't feel like a threat. They just exist, like the bench or the sunlight above, solid and without strings.

Claire watches Zane's face in the soft light, his smile quiet and kind. Here, she doesn't have to measure words or brace for judgment. The fountain and birdsong wrap them in calm.

"Sometimes I forget what it's like," she says, "to just... be heard."

Zane turns, focused but gentle. His way of listening reminds her of waves on the shore, steady, patient, without interruption. Not like Liam.

"It's different here," Claire continues, her voice growing stronger. "I don't feel like I have to..." She gestures vaguely, searching for words.

"Hide?" Zane offers softly.

The simple word strikes a chord. Claire feels tears prick at her eyes, but they don't carry their usual sting of shame. In this dream, with someone who truly sees her, even her rawest feelings feel allowed.

"Yes," she whispers, "hide." She allows herself to fully inhabit this moment, to accept the gift of being truly seen.

Claire suddenly wakes to the sound of Liam's shower running, her body tense despite the warmth of the dream. She smothers her face into the pillow, trying to hold on to the feeling of safety she felt with Zane.

The mattress creaks as she sits up, her pain flaring as reality sets back in. Her journal waits on the nightstand, but she hesitates. Writing about Zane feels risky, like naming something she shouldn't.

She runs her fingers through her hair and tells herself the dreams are just her mind's escape from Liam. Zane's quiet attention, the peaceful garden, it was too ideal to be true.

The shower stops. Claire quickly smooths the bedsheets, erasing any evidence of her restless night. She tells herself that Zane is just a figment of her imagination, a composite of qualities she wishes existed in her life. The connection she felt, the understanding in his eyes, it's safer to dismiss it all as fantasy.

Her hands tremble while she smooths the bed. In the dream, words came easily. Here, they cost too much. Vulnerability isn't safe.

Steam spills into the room when the bathroom door opens. Claire buries her thoughts in the back of her mind. She forces herself back into routine, even if reality stings.

"Just a dream," she murmurs, but she doesn't believe it. "Why do I feel like I know you?"

***

Zane's eyes open to sunlight. He doesn't reach for his journal like usual. Instead, he lies still, smiling as the memory of Claire's warmth lingers. He stretches, surprised by how light he feels. No tension, just quiet calm. In the mirror, his face seems softer, eyes clearer.

He hums while he makes coffee. The scent grounds him. The dream's calm lingers. No frantic scribbling or searching, just quiet appreciation for the way the light hits his mug.

His phone buzzes with work messages, but they don't trigger the usual spike of anxiety. He responds with the same patient attention he felt in the dream. Each interaction feels more genuine, more present.

As he packs for work, Zane pauses at his desk. The dream journal stays closed. He doesn't need to decode it. He just feels sure.

The deli hums with midday noise as Zane slides into the booth. Park wipes his mouth mid-bite, crumbs flying.

"There's that dopey smile again." Park gestures with his pickle spear at Zane. "Let me guess. Another midnight rendezvous with dream girl?"

Zane unwraps his sandwich, unable to suppress his grin. "Her name is Claire."

"Oh, we're on a first-name basis now?" Park's eyes crinkle with amusement. "Must have been some dream."

"It felt different this time." Zane bites into his sandwich, slower than usual. "We just talked."

Park studies him, his teasing expression softening. "You know what's weird? You actually look rested for once."

"Feel rested too." Zane shrugs, surprised by how light his shoulders feel. "It's like... I don't know, man. Everything's clearer somehow."

"Well, well." Park leans back. "Never thought I'd say this about your dream obsession, but it's nice to see you actually enjoying life again." He kicks Zane's foot under the table. "Keep chasing it, man."

Zane blinks, surprised. He expected skepticism, not support. Park's words settle deep, filling him with quiet resolve.

Hours later, with the city moving around him, Zane slows at a wooden bench beneath blooming trees. Sunlight filters through the branches, shadows matching the ones in the dream. He brushes his fingers over the grain. It feels just like the one from the garden.

A breeze carries floral scents, and for a moment, the world tilts. He closes his eyes, waiting for the sound of the fountain.

His phone shuffles to a new song as he walks, and the lyrics stop him cold: "Making the important stuff visible." It's the exact phrase he spoke to Claire about marketing. He pulls out his phone, checking the artist and song title, hands shaking slightly as he types the details into his notes.

A woman's laugh carries across the street, sounding just like Claire's. Zane turns, heart racing, but it's just a stranger. Still, the coincidence adds to the growing list of overlaps between his dreams and daily life.

At a newsstand, a travel magazine lies open. The page shows a Seattle garden with a fountain almost identical to the one in his dream. His breath hangs tight.

Each echo of the dream world feels like a breadcrumb, leading him toward something. These aren't just random coincidences anymore. They're confirmations, tiny proofs that Claire could really exist beyond his dreams.

Zane walks through crowded streets, his steps light despite the day. The sunset warms the city in amber, echoing the dream. A nearby melody drifts past. He drops a few bills in the case and keeps moving.

Rush hour moves around him, but it feels distant. Something steady grows inside him with each step home. Each step closer to sleep. Closer to her.

Chapter 17

CLAIRE'S FINGERS HOVER OVER the keyboard. The cursor blinks as she writes about bed-and-breakfasts along the Oregon coast. Heavy footsteps approach, tightening her shoulders.

Liam bursts through the door, his jaw clenched. "You didn't answer my texts."

She keeps typing, trying to maintain her focus. "I was working. Deadline's tomorrow."

"Working?" He stalks closer, planting his hands on her desk. "That's what you call avoiding me? I made dinner reservations. You knew that."

"I never agreed to—"

"You're always writing these days. Living in your head instead of the real world." His voice rises, sharp edges cutting through the quiet apartment. "After everything I do for you, this is how you show gratitude?"

Claire keeps her hands still, eyes fixed on the screen. The words blur: coastal views, morning fog.

"Look at me when I'm talking to you." Liam slams his palm against the desk, making her jump. "God, you're pathetic. Can't even handle a simple conversation without shutting down."

The words hit their mark, each one precise and practiced. Claire forces composure, clinging to the fantasy of escape.

"Is this about those dreams again?" He snatches her journal from the corner of her desk. "Still writing about your imaginary friend?"

Claire's hands tremble as she minimizes her travel blog draft. The half-finished article about seaside inns feels unreachable.

"I pay the bills while you play make-believe." Liam flips through her journal, his lip curling. "Writing about dreams and fairy tales instead of doing something useful."

The leather binding creaks as he bends the journal's spine backward. Claire flinches at the sound, her chest tight.

"You think anyone cares about your little stories? About where to find the best coffee in Portland?" He tosses the journal onto her desk. "Wake up, Claire. You're living in a fantasy."

She digs her fingernails into her palms under the desk. "My blog has subscribers. The affiliate links—"

"Pocket change." He leans closer, his cologne overwhelming. "You'd be nothing without me. No apartment, no fancy laptop." He brushes his fingers across her screen. "Remember where I found you? That dump in Edmonton?"

Claire stares at her hands. The words she wants to say stick like glass in her throat.

"And now look at you wasting time with these dreams instead of appreciating what's here and now." He grabs her chin, forcing her to meet his gaze. "I'm here, Claire. Not whatever fantasy man you're scribbling about."

Panic surges through her as she tries to break away, but his hold clamps down harder. "You're hurting me."

"I'm helping you," he snarls. "Someone has to keep you grounded. God knows you can't do it yourself."

Liam's fist crashes against the desk, sending Claire's coffee mug teetering. "Look what you made me do!"

Coffee seeps between the keys. Her hours of work blink once, then vanish.

"This is what happens when you live in dreamland." Liam towers over her, his shadow falling across her face. "When you forget who takes care of you."

The familiar spiral of fear and guilt rises in Claire, but something else cuts through it—clarity. She sees the pattern now. The constant criticism. The constant blame. The control. The isolation. The way he twists everything to be her fault.

Her hands steady as she unplugs the laptop and sets it aside. "I need to clean this up."

"Don't you dare walk away from me." He blocks her path, chest heaving. "We're not finished."

Claire meets his gaze, her voice quiet but firm. "Move."

"What did you say to me?" His face contorts, a vein pulsing in his neck.

"I said move." The words come out stronger this time. Her legs shake as she stands, but she doesn't back down.

Liam's nostrils flare as he steps closer, using his height to intimidate. "You ungrateful little—"

"Get out of my way." Claire's heart pounds, but her voice remains steady. Each second she holds her ground feels like an eternity, but she refuses to shrink back.

His fist slams the desk again, harder. The impact knocks over a framed photo—the glass shatters on the floor between them.

Claire steps around the shattered glass. Her movements are precise and controlled. The broken frame crunches under her shoes as she walks to the bedroom closet, leaving Liam's stunned silence behind her.

Her hands find the small navy suitcase tucked behind winter coats. The zipper sounds extra loud as she pulls it open, laying it flat on the bed.

"What do you think you're doing?" Liam's voice follows her, thick with warning.

Claire doesn't answer. She pulls open drawers, selecting clothes with practiced efficiency—jeans, sweaters, the basics she'll need. Each item folds neatly into the case, creating order amid chaos.

"You're being ridiculous." His tone shifts, softer now, manipulative. "Let's talk about this."

Her fingers brush against the soft wool of her favorite green cardigan—the one Sarah gave her for Christmas. Into the suitcase it goes, along with her laptop charger and phone cord.

Liam paces behind her. "Where are you going to go? You have nothing without me."

She pulls her passport and birth certificate from under the bed, tucking them into the suitcase. Liam's breathing grows louder.

"Stop packing." His voice cracks like a whip. "I said stop!"

She collects her toiletries, zips the bag, and adds it to the suitcase. Liam's anger rises, but she keeps going. The journal goes in last, the torn pages a reminder of why she's leaving. She shuts the suitcase.

She grabs her phone charger from the nightstand, wrapping it quickly around her hand before stuffing it into her purse. Her heart pounds as she scans the room for anything essential she might have missed. Passport, documents, laptop—all safely packed. The medication bottles rattle as she puts them into a zippered pouch.

"You're being hysterical." Liam's voice follows her movements. "Think about what you're throwing away."

She ignores him and checks her suitcase again.

"Claire, please." His tone shifts, softening into something that once would have made her pause. "I didn't mean to lose my temper. You know how I get when I'm worried about you."

She zips the suitcase, the sound slicing through his plea. When she grabs the handle, Liam steps in front of the door.

"Baby, wait." He spreads his arms wide, blocking the exit. "I'll do better. We can work this out." His eyes shine with manufactured tears. "Remember how good we were in the beginning? We can have that again."

Claire tightens her grip on the suitcase handle. The same promises, this time coated in desperation instead of charm.

"I'll go to therapy." His voice cracks. "I'll give you space to write. Whatever you want." He reaches for her free hand. "Just don't leave like this."

The tremor sounds rehearsed. She sees it clearly now, the slump, the practiced lip quiver.

"Move." She roared.

"You're making a mistake." His mask slips, anger flashing beneath the tears. "You'll never make it without me."

"I can't do this anymore." Claire says, cutting through years of doubt and fear. "I deserve better."

His face contorts as she steps around him. The suitcase bumps the carpet, but she keeps going. The living room shrinks around her, full of forced smiles and silenced thoughts.

Claire grabs the doorknob. Behind her, Liam's breathing deepens, thick with danger. She doesn't look back.

She pulls the door open, stepping into the hallway. The lights buzz overhead as she walks past the cheerful welcome mats of neighbors who never questioned the sounds from their apartment.

A cab waits at the curb, its engine humming low. She hadn't called one. It's just there, like it knew she'd need it. Claire climbs in without a word.

Twenty minutes later, Sarah opens the door to find Claire standing there, suitcase handle gripped in white-knuckled fingers. Without a word, she pulls her inside, wrapping her in a fierce embrace. Claire stiffens, her body still rigid from years of control, but Sarah's arms stay firm, asking nothing.

"I left him." Claire's voice cracks, barely a whisper against Sarah's shoulder.

"I know, honey. I know." Sarah rubs her back, cracking through the walls Claire spent years building.

A sob tears from Claire's throat, unexpected and raw. Sarah holds her tighter, guiding her to the couch.

"You're safe now." Sarah's voice is soft but firm. "Let it out."

Claire shakes while years of tears flood out. She clutches Sarah's sweater, sobbing out every word she couldn't say. Sarah rocks her, murmuring softly.

"I should have left sooner." Claire's words come between gasping breaths. "I was so stupid—"

"No." Sarah pulls back just enough to meet Claire's eyes. "You left when you were ready. That's what matters."

Claire collapses back into Sarah's embrace, her tears soaking through the soft fabric of Sarah's shirt. The safety of her best friend's arms allows her to finally release everything she's been holding inside. All the fear, the shame, the relief of escape.

Sarah just holds her, being the anchor Claire needs as waves of emotion wash over her. No judgment, no questions, just unconditional support as Claire's carefully built facade finally breaks apart.

Sarah leads Claire down the narrow hallway, past walls adorned with vintage travel posters and candid photos.

"It's not much." Sarah sets Claire's suitcase beside a wooden dresser, its surface decorated with small potted succulents.

Claire settles on the quilted bed and traces the stitching. The fabric, soft and warm, is nothing like the cold, sterile bedding Liam preferred.

A string of fairy lights casts a gentle glow across weathered hardwood floors. On the nightstand, a ceramic mug sits beside a stack of well-loved paperbacks.

Sarah opens a drawer, pulling out fresh towels. "I'll clear some space in the bathroom for your things." The drawer opens easily. Space inside waits to be claimed.

A small cat, Sarah's rescue, Milo, pads into the room, rubbing against Claire's legs. The soft purring fills the quiet space, grounding her in this moment of sanctuary.

"Thank you," Claire whispers, the words catching in her throat. Sarah just smiles, understanding everything left unsaid.

Claire stands in the doorway of Sarah's bedroom. After weeks of shrinking herself to fit Liam's moods, the room feels enormous.

"I don't mind the couch," Claire says softly. "You've done more than enough."

Sarah looks up from arranging the pillows, her expression soft but determined. "Don't be ridiculous. This bed is enormous, and you need actual rest." She pats the spot beside her. "You're not alone anymore."

Claire's throat tightens at the simple kindness. After years of calculated affection, Liam's love always came with conditions and costs. Sarah's straightforward care feels almost overwhelming.

She changes in the bathroom and avoids her reflection. Her hands shake less now as she buttons her flannel top, but exhaustion weighs heavy in her bones. When she returns, Sarah has already turned down the covers on both sides.

The mattress dips as Claire slides between cool sheets, keeping to the edge as if afraid to take up space. Sarah reaches over and squeezes her hand. It's a gentle anchor in the storm of emotions threatening to overwhelm her.

"Thank you," Claire whispers into the darkness, meaning so much more than just the bed.

Sarah's quiet response of "Always" fills the space between them, steady and sure as a heartbeat.

Moonlight drapes the bed in soft silver. Claire lies still, fingers trailing the quilt's edge, eyes on the ceiling.

"He wasn't always..." Claire's voice catches. "In the beginning, he made me feel special. Protected."

Sarah shifts beside her, a quiet presence in the darkness.

"The criticism started small. My clothes. My writing." Claire's words come faster now, like a dam breaking. "He'd say he was helping me improve. That no one else cared enough to be honest with me."

Sarah's hand finds Claire's, squeezing gently.

"Then it was my friends. My family." Claire's voice drops to a whisper. "He said they were jealous of what we had. That they didn't understand our love."

Tears slip silently down Claire's cheeks. "I started doubting everything. My memories. My feelings." Her breath hitches. "He'd do something cruel, then convince me I was overreacting. That I was too sensitive."

Sarah's thumb traces small circles on Claire's palm, grounding her in the present.

"The dreams were my escape." Claire turns her head, meeting Sarah's eyes in the dim light. "The only place he couldn't control. But he tried to take those too, calling them childish fantasies."

Sarah squeezes her hand again, and Claire draws strength from the simple gesture.

"I lost myself, piece by piece." Claire's free hand clutches the quilt. "Until I couldn't recognize who I was anymore."

The confession weighs down the moment. Sarah holds Claire's hand tighter, her presence a silent promise that Claire isn't alone anymore.

Claire shifts under the covers, her voice growing hesitant. "There's something else. Something I haven't told anyone."

Sarah waits, patient and steady beside her.

"I keep having these dreams." Claire's fingers pick at the fabric of her sleeve. "Not nightmares. They're... different. There's this beach and there's always this man there."

She steals a glance at Sarah, searching for signs of judgment or concern, but finds only gentle curiosity.

"He feels familiar somehow. Safe." Claire's voice softens. "Not like Liam's version of safe where protection comes with a price. This is... pure. Like remembering something I've forgotten."

Sarah props herself up on one elbow, facing Claire. "What happens in these dreams? Are they... you know."

"We talk. Sometimes we just sit together." Claire's tension eases as she describes it. "The strange thing is, it doesn't feel like a regular dream. Everything's vivid and clear. I can remember every detail when I wake up."

"Have you written about them?" Sarah asks.

Claire nods. "I started to, but Liam..." Her voice catches. "He found the entries. Said I was using them to escape reality. That I needed to focus on our relationship instead of living in fantasies."

"Hey." Sarah's voice is gentle but firm. "Your dreams belong to you. No one gets to tell you what they mean or how to feel about them."

The simple validation brings fresh tears to Claire's eyes. For the first time, she feels safe enough to embrace these dreams without shame or fear.

Sarah shifts to face Claire, her expression thoughtful in the dim light. "Dreams aren't just random images, you know..." Claire pulls the blanket closer, considering. "But these feel different from regular dreams."

"Maybe that's exactly why they matter." Sarah's voice carries no judgment, only gentle curiosity. "When was the last time you felt truly safe before these dreams?"

Claire opens her mouth to answer but closes it again. The silence speaks volumes.

"Listen." Sarah props herself up on her elbow. "Whatever these dreams mean, whether they're your subconscious working through trauma or something else entirely, they're valid. They matter because they matter to you."

Tears well up in Claire's eyes at the simple acceptance.

"And if you want to explore them, write about them, or just talk about them..." Sarah squeezes Claire's hand. "I'm here. No judgment, no trying to explain them away. Sometimes we need to trust what our heart is telling us, even if it doesn't make logical sense."

Claire lets out a shaky breath, years of tension releasing with Sarah's words. "Liam always said I was living in a fantasy world."

"Liam doesn't get to define your reality anymore." Sarah's voice is firm but kind. "Your experiences are yours. And if these dreams are helping you feel safe and whole again, then they're exactly what you need right now."

Claire sinks deeper into the bedding, her body loosening for the first time in weeks. Sarah's breathing beside her creates a peaceful rhythm against the soft hum of the city.

The bed feels warmer and safer. No need to lie still, braced for mood swings or silence. Sarah shifts and mumbles in her sleep, and the small, unguarded moment brings tears to Claire's eyes. When was the last time she'd shared space with someone who expected nothing in return?

Moonlight paints soft shapes across the ceiling. The day's weight lingers, but it feels lighter now. Claire doesn't fight the drowsiness. She turns toward Sarah, overwhelmed by the quiet acceptance beside her.

"Thank you, Sarah," she says, her voice thick with gratitude and hope. The words float into the quiet darkness as Claire drifts off, finally at peace.

Chapter 18

ZANE SETTLES INTO HIS evening ritual, the familiar steps grounding him after weeks of chaotic searching. Steam rises from a cup of chamomile tea as he dims the lights in his apartment. The usual city noise fades to a distant hum behind closed windows.

He arranges his dream journal and pen on the nightstand, running his fingertips over the worn leather cover. Park's earlier words echo in his mind: "If it makes you happy, chase it." A quiet smirk appears as he thinks of his friend's reluctant backing.

The meditation app on his phone casts a soft blue glow. Zane settles into position, his breath steady as the guided visualization begins to wash over him. Each exhale releases another layer of tension, each inhale draws him closer to that space between waking and dreaming.

He pictures the beach where he meets Claire, visualizing the sand, the sky, the glowing waves. The imagery feels sharper tonight, easier to reach.

Zane lies back, keeping his mind alert as his body unwinds.

Light shifts across the ceiling as Zane balances between sleep and awareness. His breathing deepens. The line between dream and waking blurs.

Just before drifting off, he holds Claire's image in his mind, not forcing it, just letting it float there like a leaf on the water. His last conscious thought is of the peace he feels in these moments, free from doubt and second-guessing. Sleep approaches like a gentle tide, and Zane surrenders to it willingly.

The world shifts and blurs around Zane, colors bleeding into one another until they reform into an unfamiliar space. He blinks, adjusting to the new dreamscape. A small living room materializes, not the usual ethereal beach, but somewhere more intimate, more lived-in.

A desk lamp glows over scattered papers and worn books. Zane brushes a shelf, the titles shifting like watercolors.

Outside, the city looks like an impressionist painting. Rain smears the skyline and drops tap the glass with unnatural rhythm.

A mug of coffee steams beside the desk. Zane reaches for it, but his hand slips through vapor.

He notices small details that feel significant somehow. A journal bound in purple leather, a collection of smooth stones arranged in a circle, and dried flowers hanging from twine. Though he's never been here before, the space carries Claire's presence, unmistakable and familiar.

The room pulses with a gentle energy, like a heartbeat just beneath the surface of reality. Shadows bend and pulse, and time flows in soft ripples instead of steady beats.

Claire appears in the doorway. Her posture is lighter, and her sweater soft rather than protective as she moves toward him.

"This feels different," she says, gliding her hand along the desk's edge. The dream reacts, colors sharpening beneath her touch.

Zane watches her explore the space, struck by the change in her. The guarded edge that usually surrounds her has softened, like a tightly wound spring finally allowed to relax. She meets his gaze without flinching away, a small smile forming.

"I left him." She lowers herself into the chair, her voice steady but the meaning clear. "I'm staying with my friend."

The dream room shifts subtly, the shadows receding as if responding to her confession. Claire leans back, her movements free and unrestrained for the first time since they've met in these shared dreams. She picks up one of the smooth stones from the desk, rolling it between her palms with quiet fascination.

"I feel like I can breathe again," she admits, her voice steady and clear. The stone in her hand throws rainbow patterns across her face.

Zane sits across from her. The dream breathes with their words, its color rising and falling with their rhythm.

"Some days the pain is so bad I can barely move," Claire says, touching her lower back. "The doctors can't figure out what's wrong. They just keep prescribing more pills."

The room dims with her words. Claire hugs her knees, the sweater bunching as she curls inward. "The painkillers helped at first, but then they became another prison. Just like Liam."

She meets Zane's eyes, her guard dropping for the first time. "I used to write travel pieces. I'd spend weeks exploring cities, finding hidden corners tourists never see." The smile fades. "These days, I can barely leave home."

The dream responds to her words, the walls seeming to breathe with each confession. Books flutter on the shelf, their pages lifting like birds in motion."

But leaving him..." Claire sits taller. "It feels like the first actual choice I've made in years. Sarah, my friend, she's helping me figure out what comes next." She releases a breath, and the dream room brightens slightly. "I think I'm ready to start over."

Zane leans forward in the dream chair, his presence steady as Claire's words fill the shifting space between them. The room's colors pulse gentler now, matching the quiet intimacy of their conversation.

"I kept telling myself it wasn't that bad," Claire says. "He'd criticize my writing, my dreams, even how I made coffee. But then he'd switch - become this perfect, caring boyfriend. It made me doubt everything."

Zane remains silent, giving her space to continue at her own pace. His stillness seems to anchor the ever-shifting dreamscape around them.

"Sarah saw through it all," Claire continues, a small smile touching her lips. "She kept telling me I deserved better, but I couldn't hear it then. Not until..." She pauses, taking a deep breath. "He tore up my journal. My writing was the one thing I had left that was just mine."

The room darkens momentarily with the memory, but Claire straightens her shoulders, and the shadows retreat. "That's when I knew. I packed a bag and walked out." Her voice grows stronger with each word. "Sarah took me in without hesitation."

Zane nods, understanding without need for words. The dream space wraps around them, creating a bubble of safety that allows Claire's walls to come down further.

"It's strange," she says, meeting his gaze directly. "I've never told anyone this much before. But here, with you..." She gestures at the room surrounding them. "It feels right somehow."

On a nearby table, three leather journals catch his eye. Each one displays different stages of wear. Sticky notes peek out from between pages, covered in what must be Claire's handwriting. The handwriting changes from neat to rushed across different notes, telling its own story.

A collection of smooth river stones lines the windowsill, arranged by size and color. One deep blue stone with a white streak sits apart beside a thriving succulent.

These objects feel too specific, too lived-in to be mere dream constructions. A stained coaster shows overlapping rings. A half-empty mug still steams, ignoring dream logic.

Everything in the room feels like her. A frayed blanket, creased travel magazines, faded postcards pinned to a corkboard.

These aren't shifting dream fragments. They feel rooted, specific. Zane's heart quickens. This might be her true space.

"I keep waiting for the other shoe to drop," she murmurs, her voice barely audible. "Like maybe I made a mistake, or I'm not strong enough to start over." Her fingers move in a slow, absent pattern along the chair's arm. "Sarah says I'm doing the right thing, but sometimes when I wake up..."

She trails off, looking out the dream window where beautiful colors swirl in the rain. The room's warm glow dims slightly, matching her uncertainty. "Everything feels so fragile. Like I could lose my grip on this newfound freedom at any moment."

Zane leans in, solid and unmoving as the dreamscape swirls around him. "You're stronger than you think," he says, with a gentle certainty that makes Claire look up. "It's okay to take things one step at a time."

The simple truth in his words settles over her like a warm blanket.

"I haven't felt safe in so long," she admits, surprising herself with her honesty. "But here, talking to you..." She gestures at the dream space around them, where the walls pulse gently with their shared energy. "It feels different. Like I can finally breathe."

Zane glances at the dream-coffee on Claire's desk, its steam forming spirals in the air. "You know what's funny? We're having the deepest conversation of my life, and I can't even offer you a proper cup of coffee."

Claire's laugh catches them both by surprise, like wind chimes in a gentle breeze. The sound transforms her entire presence, erasing years of tension from her face. The dream shifts with it, her face brightening as color blooms around them.

"The coffee here probably tastes better anyway," she says, her eyes crinkling at the corners. "No burnt beans or forgotten sugar." She reaches for the mug, her hand passing through it like smoke. "Though I guess we'll never know."

Zane finds himself chuckling along with her, struck by the absurdity of their situation. Here they are, two strangers sharing secrets in a dream-constructed room, unable to even share a simple cup of coffee. The laughter feels healing somehow, breaking down walls that words alone couldn't touch.

Claire wipes at her eyes, still smiling. "I can't remember the last time I laughed like this," she admits, her voice lighter than he's ever heard it.

The comfortable silence between them breaks as Zane's attention catches on a window behind Claire. The cityscape outside shifts like a living painting. One moment it's clearly Seattle's Space Needle piercing a cloudy sky, the next it morphs into New York's familiar skyline. The transition happens so smoothly that he almost misses it, but once noticed, he can't unsee the constant flux.

A nearby clock spins wildly. Its hands circling forward, backward, splitting apart. The numbers shift and rearrange, dizzying if he stares too long. But each sequence is always three hours apart.

Claire's bookshelf behind her keeps changing too. Books appear and disappear, their titles blurring together like watercolors. Only one stays fixed: a purple spine with gold text, "Crossroads Between Chaos and Kismet."

Shadows don't match their sources. The mug's shadow stretches like a cat. The plant casts none. Rain slides upward, then sideways.

"What is it?" Claire asks, noticing his distraction.

Zane blinks, trying to focus on her face instead of the surreal elements around them. "Just remembering this isn't real," he says, gesturing to the window where Seattle and New York continue their endless dance. "Well, not real in the conventional sense."

The room pulses, walls rising and falling like a sleeping breath. Claire stays constant, the only stable thing in the shifting dream.

Claire fidgets with a thread, the question rising from deep inside. "Why do you seem so familiar?"

"I think we went to high school together," he says, his voice gentle but certain.

Claire frowns. The room's glow dims with her uncertainty. She studies Zane, searching for a memory just out of reach.

"High school?" she chuckles. Her fingers trace slow patterns on the chair's arm. The answer adds to the mystery instead of solving it.

Zane watches her reaction carefully, resisting the urge to fill the silence with explanations or memories. The dream room pulses gently around them, matching the rhythm of their shared contemplation.

"That makes sense," she says, though her voice lacks conviction. "And yet..." The truth feels both right and wrong.

The question lingers in the dream space, unanswered but acknowledged, adding another thread to the tapestry of their growing connection.

Zane shifts, watching the colors swirl faster. His earlier certainty begins to blur, like the shadows crawling across the walls.

"Maybe we were always meant to find each other," he says, his voice sincere. The words feel right as they leave his lips, yet the shifting dreamscape makes him question everything he thought he knew.

The bookshelf behind Claire shifts again, titles blending together like watercolors. The purple spine he noticed earlier, "Crossroads Between Chaos and Kismet," flickers and vanishes, replaced by blank covers that pulse with inner light.

His memory of Claire's yearbook photo feels less and less concrete. Was she really wearing a blue dress in that picture, or is he mixing it up with the dream version of her sitting before him now? The details run together, impossible to pin down.

The skyline behind Claire melts and reforms. Sometimes Seattle. Sometimes New York. Sometimes something he can't name. Zane grips his chair, trying to stay grounded.

"I was so sure about everything," he admits, watching as his coffee mug phases through the desk like a ghost. "But now..." He gestures at the ever-changing room, where even the laws of physics seem optional. "I don't know what's real anymore."

Claire remains the only constant in the swirling chaos. Her presence is solid and unchanging while everything else refuses to hold its shape. Yet even this certainty feels dangerous to trust in a world made of dreams.

The dream apartment's edges begin to blur. The books on Claire's shelf melt into indistinct shapes, their titles becoming hard to read. The clock on the wall dissolves into a puddle of numbers that drip toward the ceiling.

Claire's eyes widen as she notices the dissolution. She reaches for Zane, but her hand passes through the space between them.

"Wait!"

Her voice cracks as the dream tears apart.

Zane jolts awake, heart racing. The dream sticks like static. He grabs for his journal, spilling water as he scrambles.

His hand trembles as he scrawls. The shifting scarf. The three journals. The blue stone with the white streak. He draws the room along with all the details, the furniture, rain pattern, coaster rings, frayed blanket, faded postcards. These aren't symbols. They're clues. Pieces of her actual life. His pen races to capture them before they vanish.

***

Claire's eyes flutter open to Sarah's bedroom. Her body feels lighter somehow, free from the usual weight of anxiety that typically greets her upon waking.

She sits up slowly, perching on the side of the bed. She runs her hand along the pattern of the quilted bedspread as she replays the conversation with Zane. The way he listened without judgment. The memory of his presence brings an unexpected smile to her face. It wasn't just the words they'd shared, but a recognition that defied explanation. For the first time, she doesn't push these thoughts away.

Her journal sits on the nightstand where she left it. Claire reaches for it, then pauses. Usually, she'd write the dream off as an escape from reality, a way to cope with leaving Liam. But this feels different. The specificity of details, the consistency of Zane's presence, the way he mentioned their shared past. It nags at her consciousness like a forgotten memory trying to surface.

She hugs her knees, thinking. What if it's not just dreaming? The peace lingers, wrapping around her like warmth.

Sarah moves in the kitchen nearby, the world calling. But Claire stays still, holding the dream close, allowing herself to believe, but only for a moment.

Chapter 19

ZANE'S FOOTSTEPS TRACE AN endless loop across his apartment floor, from window to desk to kitchen and back again. He walks with restless fingers drumming against his leg, mind replaying every moment of the dream. Claire's voice echoes in his thoughts, the way she'd opened up about leaving her relationship, how her words carried weight beyond mere dream-speak.

He pauses at his desk, scanning the scattered notes and diagrams. The purple scarf, the journals, the river stones, each detail feels like a breadcrumb leading somewhere real. His hand brushes over the sketch of her apartment layout, trying to piece together what these fragments might reveal about her actual location.

The morning sun catches on Emily's forgotten coffee mug, still sitting on the counter where she left it days ago. Zane barely registers it now, his thoughts too tangled in Claire's world. He resumes his pacing, running his hands through his disheveled hair.

"Think," he mutters, stopping at the window. The city sprawls below, countless buildings holding countless lives. She's out there somewhere, no longer trapped in her toxic relationship, finding her way forward. The thought that she's making actual changes while he's stuck here, unable to reach her beyond dreams, drives him mad.

His phone buzzes with another missed call from Emily. He silences it without looking, too focused on piecing together Claire's words about chronic pain and writing.

Each night brings new clues, but none have brought him closer to her.

A sharp knock breaks Zane's concentration. The door swings open before he can answer. Only Park has that particular knock-and-enter combo down to an art.

"Got your favorite leftover pad thai." Park waves a brown paper bag, his eyes sweeping across the chaos of papers and string covering the wall. "Though I gotta say, man, you're giving off major 'unhinged TV detective' vibes."

Zane doesn't turn from the window, still lost in thought. The smell of food fills the apartment, cutting through the staleness of his self-imposed isolation.

"Seriously, what's next? Growing a beard and writing 'WHO IS SHE' in red marker across your windows?" Park sets the food down, clearing a space among the scattered papers. His joke falls flat as Zane continues staring out at the city.

Park's reflection appears beside Zane's in the window glass. Though his friend maintains his usual smirk, concern edges into his voice. "You know, most people just use dating apps to meet women. This whole beautiful mind routine seems like overkill."

Zane settles into the worn leather couch as he recounts every detail of the dream. Park perches on the armrest, actually listening for once instead of cracking jokes.

"She talked about leaving someone toxic," Zane says, picking at his food without eating. "The way she described it, the control, the isolation, it wasn't just dream logic. You could hear the relief in her voice, like she'd finally broken free."

Park nods, his usual skepticism softening. "These aren't just, I don't know, metaphors your brain's cooking up?"

"She mentioned chronic pain too. Specific details about how it affects her writing career." Zane sets his container down, leaning forward. "And get this. She's staying with a friend now. Someone named Sarah. The entire dream took place in her apartment, but it was different this time. More solid. I could see books on shelves, smell coffee brewing."

"That's... weirdly specific," Park admits, running a hand through his hair.

"Exactly. And when she laughed, Park, it wasn't like a dream laugh. You know how dreams usually feel foggy? This was crystal clear. She has a quiet laugh, like she's not used to enjoying things."

Park studies his friend's face, noting the mix of excitement and frustration.

"So she's opening up more?"

"Yeah, but carefully. Like she's testing whether it's safe." Zane picks up his fork again, pushing the noodles around. "She asked why she felt like she knew me. I can tell she wants to believe this connection is real, but something's holding her back."

Park shifts on the armrest, his weight making the leather creak.

"So, what's the endgame here? Are you waiting for her to just knock on your door?" His voice carries its usual teasing lilt, but something deeper lurks beneath the surface, a trace of genuine curiosity.

Zane drops his fork into the container, the metal clanking against plastic. His hands spread across the papers scattered on his coffee table, fingertips brushing against sketches of Claire's dream apartment.

"I need to find her in the real world. These dreams are showing me pieces of her life. Her chronic pain, her writing career, this friend Sarah she's staying with. Every night brings new information. It's like putting together a puzzle, but..."

"But you're missing the box with the picture on it," Park finishes, leaning forward to examine the notes.

"Exactly. I know she's out there, living this life I keep glimpsing. The details are too specific, too consistent to be random." Zane plays with his hair. "When she talks about her writing or her pain, those aren't dream fragments. They're real things she's lived through."

Park studies the layout Zane has drawn. A coffee maker by the window, journals on a shelf, even the blanket's pattern. His skepticism starts to slip.

"You've got to admit," Park says, "this is pretty elaborate for just a dream."

Park sets down the sketch, a knowing smirk spreading across his face.

"You know, for someone who had such a massive crush on Claire back in school, it's pretty wild you didn't recognize her right away."

Zane's head snaps up. "What are you talking about?"

"Claire? Come on, man. We talked about this. You used to stare at her like she held the secrets of the universe. You were always too scared to talk to her though." Park chuckles, shaking his head. "You'd turn bright red whenever she walked past."

Zane's mouth opens, then closes. It was strange, realizing he hadn't been as invisible in his feelings as he once believed.

"I... I guess I buried those memories." Zane rubs his temples. "But now that you mention it..."

"So what's the plan here? Track her down because of some dreams?" Park's tone shifts from teasing to concerned. "What happens if you can't find her? Or worse. What if you do find her and she has no clue what you're talking about?"

Zane shifts away from the table. "I just feel this connection."

"Connected enough to risk everything? Your job? Emily?" Park leans forward. "What if you're building this whole thing up in your head and she's just some girl we went to school with that randomly popped up in your dreams?"

Doubt flickers across Zane's face, but he squares his shoulders.

"I'm not completely sure about anything anymore. But I know what I feel in these dreams."

Zane slumps back into the couch, closing his eyes.

"I don't know what the endgame is, Park. That's the truth." His voice carries a rawness he hasn't shown since the accident. "But these dreams - they wake something up inside me. Every detail feels significant, every conversation matters in a way nothing has since..."

He trails off, fingers brushing his cheek as the memory of screeching metal and shattered glass flashes in his mind.

"Since the accident," Park finishes quietly.

"Yeah." Zane picks up his cold pad thai, more for something to do with his hands than hunger. "It's not just about finding her anymore. There's something more, why we keep connecting like this. Why her? Why now?"

Park watches his friend, noting the spark in his eyes, a light that's been gone for months.

"When I'm there, on that beach or in her apartment, everything feels clear. Like I'm finally awake after being numb for so long." Zane sets the food down, leaning forward. "The accident took something from me, Park. Not just physically. But these dreams... they make me feel alive again."

Park watches Zane closely. The manic edge is gone, replaced by a quiet intensity he hasn't seen in a while.

"You know what's weird?" Park picks up one of Zane's sketches, turning it in the fading light. "For all your obsessing, these dreams might actually be good for you."

Zane looks up from his notes, brow furrowed. "What do you mean?"

"Well, for starters, you're actually talking about something besides quarterly reports and client pitches." Park sets the sketch down, gesturing at Zane's animated expression. "And I haven't seen you smile this much in months. Even if nothing comes from this, at least you're... I don't know, engaged with life again?"

The observation catches Zane off guard. He leans back, considering Park's words.

"Speaking of engagement," Park continues, his tone casual but deliberate, "Why sit around waiting for another dream when you have real leads? You know her job, her history, and even the Sarah person she's staying with."

Zane's eyebrow rises. "You mean actually looking for her?"

"Hey, you're the one with the wall of evidence over there." Park shrugs, nodding toward the piles of notes. "Might as well put those detective skills to use in the real world."

The idea hangs in the air. Zane taps his thigh, weighing it, doubt slowly shifting into consideration.

Zane stares at Park, processing his friend's unexpected offer. His heart races at the possibility of actual progress, of turning these ethereal connections into something tangible.

"You'd really help me find her?" Zane shifts forward on the couch, studying Park's face for any hint of mockery. But his friend's expression holds nothing but sincerity.

"Look, I still think this whole dream connection thing is weird as hell." Park slides off the armrest onto the couch proper. "But weird or not, it's the first thing that's lit a fire under your ass since the accident. And honestly?" He gestures at the wall of evidence. "You've got more details here than most stalkers."

"Thanks for that comparison." Zane rolls his eyes, but a smile tugs at his lips.

"I'm just saying - we've got a handful of details now." Park counts off on his fingers. "That's more than enough to start with. Plus, I've got some contacts who owe me favors."

"Contacts?" Zane raises an eyebrow. "Should I worry about how you know these people?"

"Please. I work in marketing, same as you. We all know people who know people." Park leans forward, his tone more serious. "If you really want to find her, you're gonna need help. And lucky for you, I happen to know a guy who's annoyingly persistent," he says, grinning at Zane. "It's either shit or get off the pot, man."

The thought of involving Park in something this intimate makes his stomach twist. These dreams have become his sanctuary, a private connection he's guarded fiercely.

"I don't know, Park." He stares at his notes, doubt creeping into his voice. "What if I'm wrong? What if this is just... nothing?" His hand drops to his lap, shoulders slumping. "I've already searched online accounts and social media. I can't find her." The admission feels heavy, like confessing a failure. "Maybe this is just one of those Mandela effects."

The leather creaks as Park leans back, studying his friend's face. His usual smirk softens into something more genuine. "It's a little late to worry about that. We will figure it out together." He nudges Zane's shoulder. "You're my best friend, man. I'm not gonna let you go full dream hermit on me."

The simple declaration sits between them. Zane looks at Park and sees the concern beneath the jokes, the loyalty behind the teasing. His chest tightens with unexpected emotion.

The wall of evidence looms over them. Zane's fingers tap against his thigh as he weighs the risk of sharing this piece of himself against the possibility of making actual progress.

Zane grabs a fresh notepad, his hand moving quickly as he jots down everything they know about Claire. The scratch of pen on paper fills the apartment while Park leans over his shoulder, pointing at what to add.

"Okay, so we've got: writer, staying with Sarah, originally from Canada, and whatever else you can remember from back in the day. Oh, and a photo!" Park taps the growing list. "What kind of writing does she do?"

"Travel pieces, I think." Zane circles the word 'writer' twice. "In one dream, she mentioned working on an article about hidden spots in Seattle."

Park straightens up, pacing the room. "That's actually useful. We can check travel magazines, blogs, freelance sites. How many Claires could be writing about Seattle?"

"Could work." Zane adds 'Seattle' to the list, underlining it. "But what if she uses a pen name?"

"One step at a time, man." Park drops back onto the couch. "For now, let's focus on what we know for sure. Maybe try to get more specific details in your next dream? Like which magazines she writes for?"

The suggestion makes sense. Even a simple plan feels better than spinning in circles.

"You're right." He sets the notepad down, looking at his friend. "Thanks, Park. I don't know how I'd do this without you."

Park's signature smirk appears. "You wouldn't. That's why I'm here." He stretches, kicking his feet up on the coffee table. "Someone's got to make sure you don't start assigning red string to your dreams."

Park glances at his watch, the leather band catching the dim light. "Look, man, I know this feels urgent. Like you've got to solve it all tonight." He shifts on the couch, turning to face Zane directly. "But you've still got a life to live. A job. Friends."

Zane taps his notepad, feeling the old rhythm of obsession take over. The scattered papers seem to pulse with possibility, each detail a breadcrumb leading to Claire.

"I know, I know." Zane rubs his eyes, the weight of sleepless nights showing in the dark circles beneath them. "It's just... when I'm working on this, everything feels like I'm doing something that matters."

"Hey." Park's voice cuts through the fog of Zane's thoughts. "Your actual life matters too. The people in it matter." He looks around. "This isn't going anywhere. We'll figure it out together, but you need to stay grounded."

The words hit home. Zane looks around his apartment, really sees it for the first time in days - takeout containers piling up, unwashed coffee mugs, the general decay of someone lost in obsession.

Park stands and stretches. "Come on, I'll help you clean up a bit before I head out." He starts gathering containers, a gentle reminder of reality. As they finish, he pauses by the door, keys in hand. He clasps Zane's shoulder, his grip firm and reassuring.

Zane moves to his apartment window after Park leaves, his friend's support still resonating in his chest. The city sprawls before him under the night sky. Each window represents another life, another story unfolding in parallel to his own.

His reflection overlays the city. He traces the window, dark circles echoing Park's warning. The garbage bags by the door mark how far he'd slipped. But Park's presence has turned this private mission into a shared one.

City lights shimmer like the spark inside him. One foot in the mystery, one still in reality. Park keeps him tethered.

Zane watches a plane cross the night sky. The weight of searching for Claire feels lighter somehow, shared between friends rather than crushing down on his shoulders alone.

Chapter 20

CLAIRE FINDS HERSELF IN a garden unlike any she's seen before. Moonflowers blooming, their petals catching starlight that seems too close, too bright. The path beneath her feet shifts between smooth stones and soft grass with each step.

Zane's hand fits perfectly in hers, his thumb tracing small circles against her skin. The simple touch sends warmth through her entire body. She sneaks a glance at him—the way his dark hair falls across his forehead, how his eyes reflect the strange, beautiful light around them.

"This feels different," Claire whispers, afraid to break the spell of the moment.

"Good different?" Zane's voice carries none of her hesitation. His grip tightens slightly, steadying her as they step over a small stream that wasn't there a moment ago.

Claire nods, letting herself lean closer to him. The garden responds to their movements, flowers turning to follow their path, vines curling away to clear their way. She can smell jasmine and something sweeter, more exotic.

His shoulder brushes hers, sparks flickering at every touch. It should feel strange, but it feels like coming home.

They pause beneath a willow tree dripping with lights like fallen stars. Zane turns to face her, his free hand coming up to brush a strand of hair from her cheek. The touch lingers, gentle and reverent.

Claire's pulse pounds, but she doesn't retreat. Here, she feels bold enough to close the distance, to let his embrace pull her in. His arms wrap around her, and she presses her head to his chest, letting the rhythm of his heartbeat settle inside her.

The garden hums with unreal beauty, but Claire feels only the warmth of his arms, their bodies fitting as if made for this.

A crystalline fountain appears, starlight dancing in its waters. Zane leads her to the edge. The sound is neither music nor whisper, but something between.

Zane turns to face her, his eyes soft with an emotion that makes her breath catch. His hand comes up slowly, giving her time to pull away if she wants. But she doesn't. His fingers tucking a wayward strand of hair behind her ear.

Claire leans into it, savoring the warmth of his skin against hers. In this moment, her chronic pain feels distant, overshadowed by the gentle press of his hand and the safety of his presence.

Zane draws her closer, his other hand settling at her waist. Claire's heart thunders in her chest as he leans in, his breath warm against her lips. When he kisses her, it's soft and careful, like he's afraid she might break. But Claire isn't fragile anymore. She presses closer, deepening the kiss.

The fountain sparkles behind them, but she barely notices. She feels only his arms, the perfect fit of their bodies, the safety in being seen.

No words pass between them as the kiss ends, none are needed. Claire rests her forehead against his chest, listening to his heartbeat while his fingers trace patterns along her spine. The connection between them pulses like a living thing, deeper than dreams, stronger than distance.

Claire melts into Zane's embrace, his hands tracing slow patterns across her back. The garden around them fades into soft focus, leaving only the warmth between them, the steady rhythm of their shared breath. His touch is gentle yet certain, each caress carrying the weight of unspoken understanding.

She meets his gaze. The tenderness in his eyes aches in her chest. His touch trails up her spine, melting every barrier.

Zane's hand cups the back of her neck, thumb brushing against her jawline. Claire leans into the touch, allowing herself to be held, to be cherished. Their foreheads press together, sharing the same air. The connection is raw and pure.

His lips find hers again, soft at first, then deeper. Claire's fingers curl into the fabric of his shirt, anchoring herself to this moment. The kiss feels both familiar and thrillingly new, as if they've done this a thousand times before and never at all.

The garden responds to their intimacy, starlight flickers like fireflies. Flowers perfume the air. But she's lost in his arms, in how his hands pull her close, like she's precious.

Their kiss breaks naturally, but they remain wrapped in each other's arms. Claire rests her head against his chest, while his fingers continue their gentle exploration of her back. The tenderness of the moment brings tears to her eyes from the pure rightness of being held this way.

Claire's eyes flutter open. She steps out of the bedroom the next morning, her cheeks flushed. Sarah sits at the kitchen counter, a knowing smirk playing across her face as she pushes a steaming mug of coffee toward her friend.

"Well, look who actually got some sleep." Sarah leans against the doorframe with each hand holding a steaming mug. Her red hair catches the morning light, creating a soft halo effect. "You're practically glowing."

Claire accepts the coffee, wrapping her fingers around the warm ceramic. "I forgot what it feels like to wake up without dreading the day."

"And no nightmares?" Sarah settles on the edge of the bed, tucking one leg beneath her. "You were sleeping like a baby."

"Just..." Claire pauses, remembering fragments of peace, of understanding eyes and a gentle voice. "Just wonderful dreams."

Sarah's teasing smile softens. "You look different. More like the Claire I remember from before."

Taking a sip of coffee, Claire realizes Sarah's right. The constant weight of anxiety has lifted, replaced by something lighter. Something like hope.

"Your coffee's still better than mine," Claire says, deflecting the emotion building in her throat.

"Everything's better than that swill Liam made you drink."
Sarah wrinkles her nose. "Speaking of which, we're burning that
awful mug he gave you. Consider it therapy."

A laugh bubbles up from Claire, unexpected and genuine. It
feels foreign but welcome, like stepping into sunlight after too long
in the shadows.

Claire scribbles a list of tasks for the day on a piece of paper at
the counter: find work, look for an apartment, schedule a doctor's
appointment. She adds smaller goals like buying groceries, organizing meds, and calling her insurance. Each one helps her reclaim a
piece of herself.

Reviewing her list, she feels calm. Every task is a choice for
herself like a roadmap to freedom.

As Claire powers up her laptop, the screen lights up with unread
emails from magazines and tourism boards. Each one reminds her of
the chances Liam's criticism cost her.

"You used to love this," Sarah calls from the kitchen. "Remember that piece you wrote about Vancouver's hidden cafes?"

Claire skims through her inbox. A travel magazine seeks stories
from solo female travelers. Her hands move before doubt creeps in,
pitching strength through solo adventures. The words come easier
than expected, like muscle memory returning.

She cringes at her outdated portfolio site, but her best pieces still
shine, like hiking in Montana and Toronto's art scene.

Opening her contact list, she spots names of editors who once
praised her work. She drafts a quick email to her most supportive
former client, explaining her absence and availability for new assignments. Before second thoughts can take hold, she hits send.

"I forgot how much I missed this," she mutters, sitting
straighter. Suppressed stories and quiet perspectives rise. Her fingers
dance across the keys, sketching pieces on resilience and rediscovery.

The blinking cursor stares back. Doubt slams into her. Work,
housing, chronic back pain, all without backsliding. She shuts the
laptop.

"I can't do this." The words slip out before she can catch them. She places her hands over her eyes, fighting back tears. "What if I'm not strong enough? What if Liam was right?"

Sarah looks up from sorting through Claire's clothes, catching the tremor in her voice. She crosses the room and perches on the arm of Claire's chair. "Hey, look at me."

Claire drops her hands but keeps her eyes fixed on the floor.

"Remember when you convinced me to try rock climbing?" Sarah nudges her shoulder. "I was terrified, but you told me to focus on one hold at a time. Not the whole wall."

"This is different." Claire's voice cracks.

"Is it?" Sarah reaches over and reopens the laptop. "You've sent a pitch. That's a hold. You sorted your stuff. Another hold," Sarah says, pointing to the to-do list. "You're not starting over. You're remembering yourself without him."

Claire glances at her list, then at the half-finished pitch on her screen. Each item represents a small step forward, away from Liam's influence.

"You're doing great," Sarah says, squeezing her shoulder. "One step at a time."

Claire curls into the window seat with her journal. She starts writing, describing the view. But it's Zane who fills most of the pages. His presence feels steady, calm, free of judgment. His hand brushing hers in the last dream felt grounding. His eyes hold understanding, not pity.

Her pen moves faster as she remembers their conversations, the easy flow between serious moments and shared laughter. The safety she feels in these dreams stands in stark contrast to her waking hours with Liam. With Zane, she doesn't need to measure her words or brace for criticism.

Sarah's voice breaks through her concentration. "You're smiling." She joins Claire by the window. "I haven't seen that expression in ages."

Claire closes her journal, but keeps her finger marking the page. "Just writing."

"About those dreams you mentioned?" Sarah's tone stays casual, but her eyes show genuine interest. "The ones with the mystery man?"

Claire fidgets with the journal's corner, weighing how much to share. "His name is Zane," she finally says. "And these dreams... they feel... good."

"Tell me about him." Sarah pulls her legs up, settling in to listen.

"He listens. Really listens." Claire opens her journal again, running her fingers over the words she's written. "When I'm with him, even in dreams, I feel like myself again. Like I can breathe."

Heat rushes to Claire's cheeks as Sarah's grin widens. She clutches her journal tighter, suddenly very interested in the Seattle skyline outside.

"You were quite... vocal last night." Sarah sips her tea with exaggerated innocence. "Something about muscular hands and gentle eyes?"

Claire buries her face in her hands, the journal sliding onto her lap. "Oh god."

"Don't worry, it wasn't anything scandalous." Sarah nudges Claire's foot with her own. "Just lots of happy sighs and mumbling his name. Zane, was it?"

"I don't remember-" Claire says. The way his fingers had traced patterns in the silver sand, how his shoulder brushed against hers as they sat watching the glowing waves.

"Your face is redder than my hair." Sarah sets down her tea, leaning forward. "Come on, spill. What exactly happens in these dreams?"

Claire tugs at a loose thread on her sleeve. "Nothing like that. We just talk. Walk along this strange beach. It feels... peaceful."

"Peaceful enough to make you purr in your sleep?" Sarah wiggles her eyebrows.

"Sarah!" Claire throws a small cushion at her friend, but can't help laughing. It feels good to joke about something so personal, to share these moments without fear of judgment or control.

"Hey, no shame." Sarah catches the cushion. "After everything with Liam, you deserve some sweet dreams. Even if dream-boy has you making sounds I haven't heard since college."

Sarah's eyes sparkle with mischief. "I don't know who this Zane guy is, but he sounds like the kind of distraction you deserve."

Sarah reaches across, squeezing Claire's hand. Embrace it. Maybe it's your subconscious telling you it's okay to feel good again.

Claire lets out a small laugh, nervous but genuine. "It did feel good. Really good. Like I could just be myself without worrying about saying or doing the wrong thing."

"See?" Sarah grins. "Your brain is literally creating the perfect man while you sleep. That's self-care right there."

Claire's confidence is finally taking hold. Maybe it was the pep talk she needed as she opens her laptop again. Three freelance writing proposals sit in her drafts folder, polished and ready. Her finger hovers over the send button as doubt creeps in, but she pushes through. Click. Click. Click. Each submission feels like a small victory.

She even feels like getting back into the kitchen after grocery shopping. It's always been a place she felt she had control over.

The apartment is filled with the rich aroma of herbs and vegetables. Claire tastes the soup she has been perfecting all evening and adjusts the seasoning without second-guessing herself. When Sarah returns from work, she stops in the doorway, inhaling deeply.

"Something smells amazing." Sarah drops her bag, peering into the pot.

Claire ladles two bowls, her chest warming with pride. "I sent out those pitches too."

"Look at you go." Sarah takes a spoonful, her eyes widening. "This is incredible."

The simple praise, given without conditions, makes Claire stand a little taller. She settles at the table with her own bowl, savoring both the taste and her growing sense of capability.

Curled in the window seat, Claire watches the purple sky and thinks of last night's encounter with Zane, his touch, his embrace, the garden.

She traces her fingers over the fresh journal entry, following the loops and curves of Zane's name. She can still feel the imprint of his hand at her waist.

"What if..." she whispers, then stops. Sarah's words echo. These dreams feel too vivid, like another world and not just a mental escape.

She hesitates, then types "shared dreams" into her laptop. Articles flood in, science, stories, strange theories.

She thinks of how Zane seems to have his own history, his own thoughts and reactions she couldn't predict. How their conversations flow naturally, building on previous dreams. The way he sometimes mentions things about New York that she's never known.

Claire shuts the laptop. For the first time, She lets herself wonder if the dreams are more than illusion, if somewhere Zane is dreaming of her too.

The thought should send a chill through her, but instead, it glows quietly inside. She lifts her pen, writing "What if?"

Claire slips under the covers, her body relaxed against the softness of the bed. The sheets smell of lavender fabric softener, so different from the harsh detergent Liam always insisted on using. She adjusts her pillow, finding that perfect spot where her neck doesn't ache.

Her phone glows briefly as she sets her alarm, but instead of her usual anxiety about the next day, a flutter of excitement stirs in her chest. She thinks of Sarah's teasing from this morning, how her friend's laughter made the dreams feel more tangible.

Rolling onto her side, Claire hugs her pillow close. A smile plays across her lips as she remembers the kiss. Now, she looks forward to dreaming.

The distant sound of Seattle traffic mingles with the soft patter of rain against the window. Claire's eyes grow heavy, but her smile remains as sleep begins to claim her. Her final thought is simple: the hope of seeing him again, of returning to the world where she feels fully herself.

Chapter 21

PARK TAPS A JITTERY rhythm on the table, grinning wide as Zane slides into the seat across from him. Two coffees steam between them, but Park doesn't touch his.

"You look like you're about to explode," Zane says, reaching for his cup. "What's going on?"

Park leans forward, his blue eyes bright. "Remember how I said I'd help you track down your dream girl?" He pulls out his phone, swiping through screens. "Well, I might have done some digging. And by digging, I mean I called in a favor from my cousin who works at our old high school."

"Park—"

"Before you go all ethical on me, hear me out." Park's fingers drum faster. "She had access to old records, and guess what? Claire is Claire Winters, and she didn't just disappear after graduation. She moved to Seattle."

Seattle. A real place. A real lead.

"I know that look," Park says, pointing at Zane's face. "That's your 'everything just clicked' expression. You mentioned the dreams showing Seattle, right?"

"Some details..." Zane sets his cup down carefully. "The rain, the architecture. I thought I was just filling in gaps, but—"

"But nothing. This is real, man." Park's excitement softens to genuine support. "This whole dream thing is crazy, but Claire? She's definitely out there. And now we know where to start looking."

Park slides his phone across the table. A Seattle address and a brief blog profile appear. Claire Winters, freelance travel writer.

Zane stares at the blurred profile photo. The smile, the head tilt—it matches the woman in his dreams.

"Breathe, man." Park leans back, studying Zane's reaction. "I know that look—you're already buying a plane ticket in your head."

Zane picks up the phone, zooming in on the details. His mouth goes dry as he reads her occupation.

"She writes about places she's never been," he says, remembering fragments from their dream conversations. "She told me once... she creates stories about destinations from research because her situation makes travel difficult."

Park's eyebrows shoot up. "That wasn't in any of the information I found."

Zane sets the phone down gently. What if he's wrong? What if this is just wishful thinking?

"I don't know, Park." He rubs his temples. "This could be nothing. Or worse—I could come across as some crazy stalker if I'm wrong."

"Or," Park counters, "you could finally get some answers."

Zane's gaze follows Park's finger as it outlines the etched letters. The morning bustle of the shop fades away, leaving only the crude knife marks in the wooden table—CBCK. His mind drifts back to that day months ago, before the accident, before Claire began haunting his dreams.

"You remember when you carved this?" Zane asks, running his own finger along the rough grooves.

Park's usual playful demeanor shifts to something more thoughtful. "Yeah, right before everything changed." He taps each letter deliberately. "Crossroads Between Chaos and Kismet. Seemed like just a random phrase then."

"And now?"

"Now?" Park crosses his arms. "Now I'm watching my best friend obsess over dream connections and mysterious women in Seattle. Pretty sure that qualifies as both chaos and kismet." His voice carries no judgment, only understanding.

Zane stares at the letters, their meaning pulsing like a sign he hadn't seen clearly until now.

"You're at the crossroads between chaos and kismet, man," Park says, his voice lighter but laced with meaning. "You've been chasing this for months. What's stopping you now?"

Zane traces the letters, then sits up. His eyes lock on the Seattle address like a compass pointing north.

"You're right," he says, steady now. "I've had pieces for months. Now I have coordinates."

Park pulls up a flight search on his own phone. "I can get time off work next week. We could—"

"No." Zane meets his friend's surprised look. "I need to do this alone. If I'm wrong, I don't want to drag you into my mess. And if I'm right..." He pauses, choosing his words carefully. "This connection, whatever it is, it's between me and Claire."

"At least let me help you plan." Park starts typing. "You'll need a hotel, rental car—"

"I can get a room at the Waterfront." Zane pulls out his laptop, already checking flights. "It's near the address you found."

"Look at you, all decisive suddenly." Park grins, but his eyes show concern. "What about work?"

"I've got vacation saved. I'll say it's a personal emergency."

"In a way, it is." Park leans forward. "When are you thinking?"

"Next weekend." Zane clicks through options. "Gives me time to prepare, but not enough to talk myself out of it."

"That's... surprisingly rational for someone chasing dream connections across the country."

Zane looks up from his screen with a slight smile. "Maybe because it finally feels like everything's been leading to this moment."

Zane's cursor hovers over the "Book Flight" button, his earlier confidence wavering. The coffee shop's rush has thinned, leaving behind the quiet hum of espresso machines and distant conversations.

"I keep thinking about Emily," he says, pulling his hand away. "I let that fall apart for dreams. What if I'm just..." He motions helplessly.

"Going crazy?" Park says, earning a sharp look from Zane.

"What if it's not her?" Zane's voice drops lower, the fear he's been holding back finally surfacing. "What if I fly across the country and find out I've been chasing shadows? What if I'm just setting myself up for disappointment?"

Park taps each one deliberately: C, B, C, K. The sound seems to cut through Zane's spiral of doubt.

"Look at these marks," Park says. "When I carved them, they were just random letters. Now?" He meets Zane's gaze. "Maybe they're a sign. Maybe they're nothing. But you don't get answers by standing still."

Zane traces the carving, thinking of every vivid dream. Too close to walk away.

"You've spent months collecting clues," Park continues. "Now you have a genuine lead. Are you really going to let fear stop you when you're this close?"

Zane's finger lingers on the laptop trackpad, his coffee growing cold.

Park stretches back in his chair, a familiar glint of mischief in his eyes. "You know if you find Claire, you're buying my coffee for life." He takes a slow sip from his cup, eyebrows raised. "And if not... well, Seattle's supposed to have incredible coffee. So either way, someone's winning here."

Zane laughs softly. Park's gift for cutting tension with humor lands again. Zane looks at him with deep gratitude for every late-night talk, every moment of support.

"I couldn't have done any of this without you," Zane says, his voice carrying the weight of months of friendship and understanding.

Park waves him off with an affable grin. "That's what wingmen are for." He picks up his coffee cup in a mock toast. "Even if the wingmanning involves chasing dream girls across state lines."

***

Three days later, Zane sits at his desk, finalizing reports before his upcoming absence. Mark from marketing stops by, leaning against the doorframe with a steaming cup of coffee.

"Finally putting in for some PTO?" Mark takes a sip from his mug. "About time. You've been wound tighter than usual lately."

Zane minimizes his flight confirmation email. "Yeah, taking next week off."

"Going anywhere good?" Mark's eyes crinkle with genuine interest. "You look like you could use a beach somewhere. Get some relaxation."

"Something like that." Zane shuffles papers on his desk, avoiding eye contact.

"Well, wherever you're headed, hope it helps you decompress. You've seemed... distracted lately."

Back at his apartment, Zane pulls his carryon from the closet. He lays out clothes methodically—practical items for Seattle's notorious rain. His hands shake as he folds each piece, the reality of his mission sinking in.

He pauses at his dresser, catching his reflection. The man staring back looks both terrified and determined. Taking a deep breath, he continues packing, trying to channel the calm he feels in the dreams with Claire.

His phone buzzes—a text from Park: "Don't overthink it. Just pack and go."

Zane smiles at the message. Park always knows. He keeps packing, steadier now, ready to face what waits.

On his bed, Zane runs a finger over CBCK carved into the journal's cover. The lamplight spills across pages of beaches and dream fragments. The crude etching feels different under his fingers than Park's version on the coffee shop table.

Crossroads Between Chaos and Kismet. The phrase rolls through his mind as he flips through the journal's pages. Chaos—the accident that should have ended everything but instead opened a door. Kismet—the inexplicable pull toward a woman he hasn't seen in what feels like forever.

The journal is littered with Claire's name, written in uneven strokes, some rushed, others deliberate. Scattered between the entries, CBCK lingers like a whisper he can't ignore, its presence as certain as the pull dragging him toward Seattle.

"Chaos and kismet," he whispers. The words settle deep, calming something inside. This isn't fantasy. It's destiny. It's as real as his scars.

***

Since booking his flight, nerves have settled into quiet certainty. Whatever's in Seattle, he's meant to find it.

Park's car comes to a stop at the airport terminal. Zane grabs his bag, the journal already tucked inside. The crisp air mirrors the charge running through him. "You sure you don't want me to park and walk you in?" Park drums his fingers on the steering wheel. "I make an excellent emotional support buddy."

"I think I can handle walking through an airport." Zane shoulders his bag, trying to hide his anxiety behind sarcasm.

Park kills the engine and steps out anyway, rounding the car with his signature grin. "Come here, you idiot," he says, pulling Zane into a tight hug, complete with the customary back-slapping that makes it appropriately masculine. "Remember, crossroads or not, you'll find your way."

"Getting philosophical on me now?" Zane adjusts his bag strap, deflecting the emotion building in his chest.

"Someone has to be the voice of reason while you chase dream girls across the country." Park's eyes crinkle with genuine affection beneath the teasing.

Zane turns toward the terminal entrance and weaves between travelers and their rolling luggage. The automatic doors whoosh open, airport noise washing over him.

"CBCK!" Park's voice carries across the busy lobby, drawing curious glances from nearby passengers.

Without turning around, Zane throws his fist in the air twice, acknowledging his friend's parting reminder. The gesture feels silly and significant, like everything else about this journey.

Zane settles into his window seat, watching ground crews scurry across the tarmac like busy ants. His carryon fits snugly under the seat. The familiar weight of Park's carved letters presses against his ankle through the bag. A kid squeals nearby as the plane taxis. Zane barely hears it. His mind drifts to nights in Park's car, Claire theories, quiet support. Those talks kept him sane.

The plane lifts off. Manhattan fades beneath clouds. Zane's stomach drops, not from the ascent but from the reality of what he's doing. Six months ago, he would have dismissed anyone claiming dream connections could be real. Now, he's living it.

Park's words echo: "You don't get answers by standing still." The warmth behind them quiets Zane's doubt.

The flight attendant offers drinks, but Zane declines. He's too wired on anticipation to need caffeine. Through the small window, sunlight catches on the wing, creating patterns that remind him of the glowing waves from his dreams. Everything feels charged with meaning now, like the universe is confirming his course.

Zane collects his things from the overhead compartment. His legs feel stiff after the cross-country flight, but anticipation pulses through him, making the discomfort barely noticeable.

He walks through crowds of reuniting families and hurried business travelers, following signs toward the exit. The automatic doors part with a whoosh. Seattle's famous gray sky stretches above him, a stark contrast to New York. The air here feels different—cleaner, with hints of pine and salt water that remind him of the beach from his dreams.

Zane pulls his phone from his pocket, opening the message where Park sent Claire's address. It's burned into memory, but he needs to see it. At the curb, he breathes in Seattle.

"Let's do this," he says, gripping the phone like a lifeline.

Chapter 22

CLAIRE SITS AT SARAH's kitchen table, stirring her coffee while memories from the last few weeks wash over her. The mug's warmth seeps into her palms, grounding her in the present while her mind drifts back.

Those first weeks after leaving Liam blur together with nights spent crying on Sarah's shoulder and days hiding under blankets. But Sarah never wavered, bringing tea and gentle encouragement. "Baby steps," she'd say, coaxing Claire to send out one more job application, make one more phone call.

The publishing company's response came faster than she expected, just days after her last application. Claire remembers staring at her laptop screen, hands shaking as she read the offer. Editorial Assistant position. New York City. A fresh start across the country.

"I can't move that far," Claire had protested, but Sarah's eyes lit up with possibility.

"Why not? What's holding you here besides fear?" Sarah pulled Claire into a fierce hug. "You're ready for this. I've watched you get stronger every day."

The memories shift to endless apartment searches, Sarah sprawled beside her on the couch with takeout containers, both of them scrutinizing New York rental listings. "Look at this one in Brooklyn," Sarah would point, dreaming alongside Claire until possibility felt real.

Now, just weeks after fleeing with only a suitcase, Claire holds the job offer letter. A new job. A new city. A new chapter.

Sarah appears in the kitchen doorway, sleep-rumpled but grinning. "Still can't believe it's happening?"

Claire traces the letter's edge with her finger. "Sometimes I forget I'm not that scared person anymore."

"Good." Sarah squeezes Claire's shoulder. "Because she's gone. You're something else entirely now."

"They want me to start right away," Claire had told Sarah earlier, her voice still shaky. "I can't believe it's all happening so fast."

"That's why you need to go," Sarah had said. "No more waiting. This is your life now."

The goodbye was rushed but full of meaning, Sarah's hug tight enough to carry across the miles. Now, as the cab pulls away, New York waits.

Claire steps out of the cab onto a busy Manhattan street, her small suitcase bumping against her legs. The towering buildings stretch endlessly upward, glass and steel disappearing into the morning haze. Her neck cranes back, taking in the dizzying height until she stumbles slightly. A man brushes past, jostling her bag. She snaps back to street level. The crowd weaves around her, energy vibrating underfoot.

She pulls her phone out, double-checking the address of her temporary sublet. The screen reflects neon and billboards in a dizzying kaleidoscope.

Steam rises from a hot dog cart. Coffee shop doors swing open and closed, releasing waves of rich aroma. Horns honk in an urban symphony she's never experienced in Seattle. Each sensation hits harder than the last, overwhelming her senses.

"You gonna move or what?" A delivery guy with boxes balanced on his shoulder breaks through her daze.

"Sorry." Claire steps aside, pressing closer to the building. Her fingers grip the handle of her suitcase more tightly. The city's raw energy threatens to sweep her away, but underneath the anxiety bubbles something else, excitement. Pure, unfiltered possibility.

Claire takes a deep breath and straightens her shoulders before joining the foot traffic. Her suitcase clicks along, her steps growing steadier. No Liam controlling her movements. No past holding her back. Just Claire taking on New York City, one uncertain step at a time.

She stands in her studio apartment, taking in the place that will become her home. It's small, but it's hers. A place to start over. She sets down the suitcase and begins unpacking, her clothes finding a home in the narrow closet. Hangers click softly as she arranges them by color, the familiar rhythm helping to settle her nerves.

At the bottom of the suitcase, wrapped in a sweater, she finds the photo of her and Sarah. She places it on the desk.

Her journals come next, stacked neatly beside her laptop. She arranges her pens in a ceramic mug, positions her lamp just so, creating a workspace that feels distinctly hers. Each item has its place, chosen with intention.

The kitchenette gets similar attention. She lines up her favorite tea bags in the cabinet, places her well-worn coffee maker on the counter. The familiar scent of coffee beans helps make the strange space feel more like home.

In the bathroom, she lines up her toiletries, avoiding the mirror. Her meds sit on the shelf as a quiet reminder of strength.

Back in the main room, Claire steps back to survey her work. The space has transformed from an empty shell into something uniquely hers. Simple, organized, safe. Her style. Her rules. Her new life.

The next day, Claire steps into the modern office space at Horizon Publishing, her heels clicking against the polished concrete floors. The open layout buzzes with activity, editors hunched over manuscripts, designers comparing color swatches, the occasional burst of laughter from a corner desk.

"Claire! Welcome to the team." Ashley, her supervisor, waves her over. Her bright smile and casual demeanor ease some of Claire's tension. "Let me show you to your desk."

Claire runs her hand along the desk edge. It's clean, simple. Hers. Ashley walks her through the morning tasks. "Start with these manuscript submissions. Flag anything that catches your eye." The familiar territory of reading and evaluating helps Claire settle into a rhythm.

At eleven, Ashley calls the editorial team for their weekly pitch meeting. Claire's stomach tightens as she takes her seat around the conference table. Eight faces turn toward her, curious but friendly.

"Before we dive in, any fresh perspectives from our newest team member?" Ashley's invitation catches Claire off guard.

Her throat constricts. The old voice, Liam's voice whispers doubt, but she remembers Sarah's words: take up space.

"Actually," Claire says, her voice steadying, "I noticed a trend in our recent submissions. There's a surge in eco-fiction that blends climate anxiety with hope. Maybe we could develop a dedicated series?"

The room falls quiet. Claire's heart pounds until Ashley breaks into a wide grin.

"That's exactly the kind of thinking we need. Let's explore that." Other team members nod, adding their thoughts to Claire's suggestion.

As the meeting continues, Claire feels something shift inside her.

Claire steps into the evening breeze. Instead of heading home, she walks without direction. The city hums with vendors shouting, taxis honking, music spilling from open doors.

A small café catches her eye, its window display filled with pastries and a hand-painted "Local Roasted" sign. A soft chime rings out as she steps inside, where the warmth of coffee and baked goods greets her like an old friend.

"What can I get you?" The barista's genuine smile puts Claire at ease.

"A vanilla latte, please." Her voice is steady. No second-guessing.

Claire claims a corner table by the window, watching people rush past outside while cradling her drink. The foam creates delicate patterns on the surface, and she takes a photo to send to Sarah. The mismatched décor feels welcoming, like a place she could belong.

A couple laughs over cake. An artist sketches, quick and sure. A man types furiously, pausing only to sip espresso.

Claire pulls out her journal and opens to a fresh page. Her pen flows freely, capturing a life taking shape. No one watching. No one questioning. The latte warms her hands through the ceramic mug as she writes, and since arriving in New York, Claire feels truly present in the moment. This is her time in this quiet corner, this peaceful solitude, this freedom to simply be.

The café hums around her, but Claire stays still, savoring the last sip of her latte before stepping back into the night. The walk home is quiet, the city softened by evening light. By the time she reaches her apartment, her thoughts have settled, her heart steady.

Claire pushes aside her dream journal, burying it under a stack of manuscripts. "Just stress dreams," she mutters, focusing instead on her coffee and her new work schedule. The publishing house needs manuscript reviews by noon, and she has three meetings to prepare for.

When fragments of the beach dream surface, his warm brown eyes, that gentle smile, Claire cranks up her music, drowning out the memory with bass-heavy beats. She throws herself into work, attacking each task with intense focus.

During lunch, Sarah had texted asking about "the dream guy." Claire left it unread. About the same time in a meeting, someone mentioned dreams, and Claire's pen pressed so hard against her notepad it tore the paper.

Claire's nervous habits kick in. She reorganizes her bookshelf by color, then alphabetically, then by genre, anything to keep her hands busy and mind occupied. The dream journal stays buried under work documents, its presence like a persistent itch she refuses to scratch.

In bed, Claire sets two alarms and plays a meditation app, determined to have dreamless sleep. "They're not real," she whispers to her ceiling. "Just my brain processing change. Nothing more."

Her thumb still hovers over the search bar where she'd typed "recurring dreams about the same person" before she caught herself and shut the app.

Claire shuffles papers on her desk, trying to focus on manuscript deadlines when Ashley pokes her head around the corner, grinning.

"Hey, a few of us are grabbing drinks at Murphy's after work. You should join us."

Claire's hand stops mid-shuffle. Social invitations still trigger that old panic response of Liam's voice warning about staying out too late, asking too many questions about who she'd be with.

"I don't want to intrude..."

"No intrusion! Just casual drinks, good conversation. No pressure." Ashley's smile remains warm, expectant.

Claire takes a deep breath, remembering Sarah's advice about baby steps. "Actually, that sounds nice. Count me in."

Later, Claire follows Ashley through Murphy's wooden doors into a cozy pub atmosphere. String lights cast a warm glow over exposed brick walls. Two other editors from work, Milton and Jen, wave from a corner booth.

"Claire! You made it." Jen slides over, making space. "What's your poison?"

"Wine?" Claire suggests tentatively.

"A woman after my own heart." Jen flags down a server. "Two house pinots, please."

The conversation flows. Milton reenacts awful submissions, making her laugh until it hurts. Jen shares dating disasters. Ashley offers juicy publishing gossip.

Warmed by wine, Claire joins in with perfect timing. Her comment about a purple-prose romance sends the table into laughter.

For so long she's felt like an outsider. But here, she's simply Claire. Here she's valued, heard, and unexpectedly funny.

***

Claire sits on her windowsill, legs tucked beneath her, as the city sparkles below. Steam rises from her chamomile tea, fogging the glass where her forehead rests. Three months ago, she'd barely managed to pack a suitcase. Now here she is, in New York City, with a job she loves and the beginnings of new friendships. Sarah would be proud of her. Hell, she's proud of herself.

Her phone buzzes with a playlist notification. As she reaches for it, Milton's words from earlier echo in her mind: "Sometimes the best stories find us in our dreams." He'd been talking about writing inspiration, but the phrase stirred memories of a beach and brown eyes that felt like home.

Claire shakes her head, setting her empty mug in the sink. As she slides into bed, the phrase lingers, gentle as waves. Just before sleep takes her, she wonders if maybe he's dreaming too.

Claire drifts to sleep, her body relaxing into the unfamiliar comfort of her new bed. The usual sharp edges of her dreams blur and soften. No vivid beach materializes, no direct encounter occurs.

Though she can't see him, Zane's presence wraps around her consciousness like a familiar blanket. His energy lingers at the edges of her awareness, neither intruding nor demanding attention. It feels like sitting in a room where someone kind has just been, their essence still hanging in the air.

The sensation follows her through various dream fragments: a walk through Central Park, a quiet moment in her office, a glimpse of waves breaking against rocks. In each scene, she feels watched over but not watched, protected but not controlled. It's different from the intensity of their previous encounters, more like background music that soothes without requiring focus.

When Claire wakes, the feeling clings to her like dewdrops on morning grass. She stretches, noting how her pain seems duller, manageable. The memory of the dream doesn't demand to be written down or analyzed. Instead, it settles into her bones, a quiet reminder that somewhere, somehow, she's not alone.

She makes coffee. The routine movements of measuring beans and heating water carry none of yesterday's anxiety about the dreams. The connection exists without consuming her, like a letter kept safe in a drawer.

Claire sits cross-legged at her desk, sorting through manuscript submissions while Milton leans against her cubicle wall, sharing his thoughts on the latest fantasy novel trend. His animated gestures draw laughs from nearby coworkers.

"I swear, if I see one more chosen one prophecy, I'm switching to romance."

"At least romance has kissing," Jen chimes in, rolling her chair over. "Speaking of which, lunch? That new Thai place opened around the corner."

Claire's old instinct to decline surfaces, but she pushes past it. "Count me in. Just let me finish these notes."

Ashley joins their growing lunch group, and soon Claire finds herself squeezed into a booth between Milton and Jen, sharing pad thai and trading stories about their worst first dates. The conversation flows naturally, no pressure to perform or measure her words.

Back at the office, her phone vibrates. Sarah's name lights up the screen, and Claire steps into the break room for privacy.

"There's my brave girl!" Sarah's voice carries the warmth of home. "How's the Big Apple treating you?"

"I just had lunch with coworkers," Claire says, unable to keep the pride from her voice. "Actual friends, Sarah. I'm making actual friends."

"Of course you are. You're amazing when you're allowed to shine." Sarah's words hold no trace of surprise, just pure joy. "Tell me everything."

Claire leans against the counter, describing her new routines, her growing comfort with the city. Sarah listens, throwing in the occasional "I told you so" that makes Claire laugh.

"I miss you," Claire admits.

"I miss you too. But look at you. Thriving, independent, living your life. Exactly what you needed."

Later, Claire curls into her reading nook. City lights blink outside. She skips the dream journal, opening her planner instead. Her pen hovers for a moment before touching the paper. The words flow differently tonight. There's no analysis of mysterious beaches or brown eyes, no questioning what each symbol might mean. Instead, she lists concrete goals: "Pitch travel series to Ashley. Join that writing workshop Milton mentioned. Find a yoga studio nearby."

The simple act of planning feels revolutionary. No one stands over her shoulder questioning her choices. No voice whispers that she's reaching too high or dreaming too big. Every goal she writes is hers alone.

Claire pauses, watching a plane's lights blink across the night sky. She adds another line: "Host a dinner party for the team." The thought of filling her space with laughter and friendship makes her smile. On a fresh page, she writes in bold:

"This is my chance to create something new."

Chapter 23

ZANE STEPS FROM THE cab into Seattle's mist. The red brick building rises, weathered but cared for. He grips the creased paper with Claire's address, Park's handwriting worn from use.

A couple exits the building, and Zane catches the heavy door before it closes. The lobby smells of lemon cleaner and old wood. His footsteps echo as he approaches the row of mailboxes, scanning the names. There it is. "C. Winters" in neat black letters.

In the mirror, he smooths his travel-worn hair. His eyes are tired, but focused. The brass elevator doors wait ahead, shining like a gatekeeper.

His phone buzzes with a message from Park. Zane sends a thumbs up, The knot in his throat makes words impossible. The weight of the moment crashes over him. After months of dreams, research, and obsession, he's standing mere floors away from answers.

The elevator doors slide open with a soft ding. Zane steps inside, his legs unsteady. As he presses the button for the fourth floor, doubt creeps in. What if she slams the door in his face? What if this Claire Winters isn't his Claire at all?

But he remembers the beach, the connection that pulled him across dreams and now across the country. The elevator rises, each floor bringing him closer to truth or disappointment. His reflection in the elevator's mirrored wall shows a man transformed by purpose, by the chance that something impossible might be true.

The doors open to a quiet hallway. Apartment 4C waits at the hall's end, its brass numbers reflecting the afternoon light filtering through a window. Zane walks toward it, each step deliberate, until he stands before her door. The hallway smells of old cigarettes and pine cleaner, a combination that burns his nostrils.

He raises his hand, knocks. The sound echoes. Silence follows. He waits, counts, knocks again. Still nothing.

Shoulders slumping, he turns to leave when a door creaks open behind him. A man emerges from 4A, keys jangling at his belt. His clothes hang loose on his frame, and deep lines crease his face.

"Looking for someone?" The man's voice carries the weight of too many tenant complaints.

"Yes, I'm looking for Claire Winters." Zane shifts his weight, conscious of how strange his request might sound. "She's about five-six, dirty blonde hair, green eyes. Probably keeps to herself, might do some writing work?"

The landlord's expression remains neutral, almost bored. He crosses his arms, keys clinking against his belt buckle. "And you are?"

"I'm Zane. I'm an... old friend." The lie tastes bitter on his tongue.

The landlord studies him, eyes narrowing slightly. His silence stretches uncomfortably long before he speaks again. "Can't help you with tenant information."

The landlord gestures for Zane to follow. His brow is furrowed. The elevator closes with a soft thud. Silence builds. Each floor drops him farther from his goal.

"Look, I know this seems strange." Zane's voice cracks slightly. "But anything you could tell me about her would help."

The landlord pauses by the mailboxes, running a hand over his weathered face. "She moved out. She was a quiet tenant, kept to herself mostly. Her boyfriend, not so much, but he paid the rent on time."

"Did she leave any forwarding address?" Zane's fingers grip the strap of his travel bag tighter.

"Can't share that kind of information." The landlord shakes his head.

Zane's heart sinks under a fresh wave of defeat. The weight of the cross-country trip settles heavy on his shoulders as he stares at Claire's empty mailbox, mocking him.

"That's all I can tell you." He turns away. Keys scrape in the lock, echoing through the still lobby.

Zane stumbles into the gray afternoon, legs unsteady. The lamppost's cold metal bites through his jacket as he slumps against it, watching traffic blur past. A bus splashes past, soaking his shoes. He barely notices.

His hand finds Claire's photo in his pocket, now creased and soft from constant handling. The girl in the photo stares back, her smile suddenly mocking his entire journey.

The old dreams flash through his mind in fragments. The beach. Her emerald eyes. The way she'd touched his hand, solid. But doubt seeps in with the drizzle, chilling him through.

"What am I doing?" The words vanish in traffic. Park's warnings echo. CBCK suddenly feels less like fate and more like desperation.

A couple hurries past, sharing an umbrella, their laughter carrying on the wind. Zane watches them disappear around the corner, their happiness a stark contrast to his hollow chest. He pulls out his phone, thumb pausing over Park's number. What would he even say?

The photo slips from his fingers, catching in a gust of wind. Zane lunges for it, but it dances just out of reach before settling in a puddle. He retrieves it carefully, but the water has already begun to blur the ink, distorting Claire's features into something unrecognizable.

Rain slicks his phone as he dials Park. Each ring widens the ache in his chest.

"Hey, dream detective! Tell me you found her." Park's cheerful voice cuts through the gray Seattle afternoon.

Zane leans against the brick wall, his forehead pressing into the cold surface. "The place is empty," he says, his voice cracking. "She's gone."

"Shit." Park's tone shifts instantly. "What happened?"

"Landlord wouldn't tell me much. Just that she moved out. And he mentioned a boyfriend." Zane kicks a chunk of concrete, watching it skitter through the wet. "I flew out here for nothing."

"Not nothing. Now we know," Park says, pausing. "Look, come home. We'll figure this out together."

"I feel like an idiot." Zane slides down the wall until he's crouching, not caring about the dampness seeping through his clothes. "You tried to warn me about getting too obsessed."

"Hey, I also told you to chase it. That's what you did." Keys jingle in the background of Park's call. "Want me to pick you up from the airport when you get back?"

"Yeah." Zane watches a taxi splash through a puddle. "Thanks, man."

"That's what friends are for. Even the crazy ones who fly across the country chasing dream girls."

Zane stares at the puddle-strewn sidewalk, his phone pressed against his ear. The Seattle drizzle soaks through his jacket.

"Look, sometimes the trail goes cold." Park's voice carries its familiar warmth, even through the tinny phone speaker.

Zane's fingers brush against the damp photo in his pocket. "I can't let this go yet." His voice catches. "You weren't there in those dreams, Park. The connection was…"

A long sigh crackles through the line. "I know that look in your voice."

"That's not even a thing."

"It is with you," Park says. "That stubborn sound in your voice means you're about to do something brilliant… or stupid."

Zane pushes himself up from the wall, his clothes leaving a damp outline on the brick. "The landlord mentioned a job opportunity. That's something, right?"

"You're not letting this go, are you?"

"Not yet." Zane watches a business woman hurry past, her umbrella fighting against the wind. "I came too far to turn back now."

Park stays quiet for a moment, then lets out another resigned sigh. "Just… don't go full stalker mode, okay? I'd hate having to visit my best friend in jail."

"I'll be careful." Zane's grip tightens on his phone. "Thanks for not telling me I'm crazy."

"Oh, you're definitely crazy. But you're my crazy friend, so what can I do?"

Zane slumps onto a soaked bench, phone in hand. Seattle's skyline floats in mist, the Space Needle pale against gray clouds. Water drips from his hair. He barely feels it.

He touches the ruined photo in his pocket. The pull defies logic and distance, heavy as gravity. Even now, with only an empty mailbox and vague mention of a boyfriend, the force of it threatens to break him open.

A seagull lands nearby, pecking at a discarded wrapper. Zane watches it hop closer, remembering Claire's dream confession about feeling trapped. The bird takes flight, disappearing into the gray sky, free in a way that makes his heart ache.

The city bustles while Zane sits still, caught between reality and something else. But the pull remains.

Park's words echo in his mind. "Sometimes the trail goes cold." But this isn't just a trail, it's a thread woven through dreams into reality, binding him to someone. The thought of letting go twists his stomach.

A glint of iridescence catches his eye, something small between wet leaves near the bench. He leans down, brushes aside debris, revealing a delicate spiral shell. Its mother-of-pearl surface catches the dim light. In one of their dreams, he'd given Claire a shell just like it.

He picks it up. The shell is smooth, cool in his palm. Finding this so far from any beach feels too precise to be coincidence. His thumb traces the spiral, remembering Claire doing the same.

Rising, Zane tucks the shell beside her photo in his pocket and walks. The neighborhood unfolds in coffee shops, boutiques, and apartments that might've been part of Claire's routine. A bookstore display draws his eye, but the curated bestsellers say nothing of her. He passes a café where two friends laugh over steaming mugs. It's a sharp contrast to his solitary search.

Each block pulls him farther from the Claire who whispered secrets beneath impossible stars. This busy, indifferent world feels miles from the one they made together.

Pigeons scatter as he rounds the corner, wings flapping against drizzle. He stops at the crosswalk, watching the light change. None of this fits the life he imagined for her.

Zane ducks into a small café as dusk settles over Seattle. Warm air fogs his glasses, and the sweet smell of coffee wraps around him. He orders something simple and finds a corner booth. The vinyl seat squeaks as he sinks into it.

The sandwich arrives, but it tastes like nothing. His thoughts circle the empty apartment, the landlord's vague mention of a job, and the hollow ache that settled in when he realized she was gone.

Steam curls from his coffee cup. He watches it fade and remembers what Claire once said about dreaming of him. Like trying to hold morning fog. The memory stings but also steadies him. The dreams were real. The shell in his pocket presses against his leg, small but certain.

He flips through his notes. Pages built from trust exchanged in sleep. The lead might be weak, but it still matters. The dreams brought him here. They showed her to him.

Zane pays and then steps into the misty night. Each step back toward the hotel drags. The city moves on while he carries the weight of what he didn't find.

The hotel lobby gleams with polished marble and warm lighting, different from the gray world outside. He nods to the front desk clerk with a faint smile and heads for the elevator. The mechanical hum fills the silence as he ascends to his floor.

In his room, Zane drops his jacket and slides the balcony door open. Cool air rushes in, rain and city mingling. He grips the railing, staring out over Seattle. Lights and shadows stretch across the skyline. Somewhere in them lingers Claire's ghost.

His fingers trace the shell's spiral pattern one more time before tucking it safely away. Below, the city doesn't stop, unaware of his search, the dreams that haunt him, and The weight of Claire's absence presses heavier than her presence ever did.

"I'll find you, Claire," he whispers, his words carried away by the evening breeze.

Chapter 24

CLAIRE WAKES TO THE throb of sore muscles and the scent of city air pushing in through the cracked window. Not pain exactly. Just the residue of rebuilding. For the first time, she doesn't feel fragile. She feels present.

New York stirs outside, but she doesn't rush to the window. Let it buzz. Let the horns blare and the vendors shout. This morning isn't about watching the world move past. It's about claiming her place in it.

The boxes still line the wall, half-unpacked. Her desk waits in the corner, a photo of Sarah propped beside the laptop. That small piece of home reminds her She didn't just escape. She stepped toward something new.

Pain flashes as she stands, sharp but fleeting. Manageable. In this city of endless motion, her struggles feel smaller. She can breathe here. She can build here.

Today, she belongs to the pace, the rhythm, the forward pull of a life becoming hers.

Claire moves through the crowded streets, laptop bag bumping her hip. The publishing office looms ahead, its glass doors reflecting morning sunlight. Inside, she settles at her desk, organizing manuscripts into neat piles.

"Coffee run?" Marcus from marketing waves a five-dollar bill.

"Next time. Deadlines." Claire opens her inbox and dives into work before her mind can wander.

Hours blur as she edits, red pen cutting clean lines through pages. The familiar rhythm grounds her, keeping her thoughts tethered to deadlines and words.

At lunch, she grabs a sandwich from the deli downstairs. The owner, Tony, greets her by name now. "The usual?"

At home, Claire chops vegetables. The steady thunk of the knife fills her kitchen. Steam rises from the pot. Garlic and herbs fill the air. No takeout tonight. Cooking gives her something she can hold onto. It's something she can control, once again.

Soon after dinner, she walks her block, learning its patterns. The bodega cat watches from its perch as she passes. Children play basketball in the fading light, their shouts bouncing off brick. An elderly couple sits on their stoop, nodding as she walks by.

She clings to the tangible—the weight of manuscripts, the smell of dinner, the rhythm of city life. There's no space left for dreams.

Claire catches a glimpse of dark hair and broad shoulders on the subway. He's a stranger who bears a passing resemblance to Zane. Her heart skips a beat before logic catches up. She forces her attention back to her phone, scrolling through work emails.

In the break room, a song drifts from someone's desk radio. The melody brings a flash of the beach and Zane's smile. Claire shakes her head and dumps the coffee.

These moments ambush her throughout the day, a laugh that sounds like his, a cologne that reminds her of the dream's salt air. Each time, she pushes the thoughts away, focusing on manuscript pages and meeting schedules.

Back home, she dims the lights and turns on soft jazz. City glow creeps through the fabric. Her routine, usually soothing, feels hollow now.

She opens the medicine cabinet, eyes fixed on the bottle of sleeping pills. Her fingers skim the label, recalling how the dreams deepened when she took them. Logic warns her that she's building something new. But the pull of those dreams, of him, lingers.

Claire twists open the cap, tipping a pill into her palm. Just this once, she tells herself. Just to know if he's still there.

Her consciousness drifts, the pill softening her grip on reality. City sounds fade, replaced by rustling leaves. She opens her eyes in a hidden garden with glass walls curved like waves, glowing with golden light.

Wooden bookshelves line the walls, their warm mahogany stretching up toward a glass ceiling that shows glimpses of a violet sky. Plush armchairs nestle between potted plants, their leaves casting intricate shadows across leather-bound volumes.

Her bare feet sink into thick moss as she moves through the space. The air carries the mingled scents of old books and fresh earth. A fountain bubbles somewhere nearby, its sound mixing with the whisper of turning pages.

"I was hoping you'd come back."

Zane sits in a worn leather chair, book in his lap. Golden light shapes his face, rendering him both solid and surreal. He looks up, and warmth floods her body.

"This is different," Claire says, running her fingers along the spines of nearby books. The titles shift under her touch, becoming whatever she imagines them to be.

"We create it together," Zane says, setting the book aside. "Somewhere quiet. Safe."

Claire settles into the chair opposite him, drawing her knees up. The fabric is soft against her skin. A cup of tea appears on the small table between them, steam curling in patterns too perfect to be natural.

The garden-library pulses with their shared consciousness, responding to their emotions. Vines curl and uncurl along the shelves, flowers bloom and fade in gentle waves, and the light shifts like liquid gold through the glass walls.

Claire watches as Zane reaches for his teacup, his fingers brushing against hers in a seemingly accidental touch. The connection surges through her. Her skin tingles where his fingers touch.

The garden-library shifts in response, the golden light intensifying, casting warm shadows across their faces. The moss beneath her feet seems to pulse with energy, and nearby flowers turn their faces toward them as if drawn by the surge of connection.

She doesn't pull away. His touch anchors her to this moment, making the dream feel more substantial than the waking world she left behind. The warmth of his skin lingers, spreading up her arm and settling in her chest.

Zane's eyes find hers, recognition flickering. Even here, the walls she's built and the distance she clings to start to crack. Her fingers tremble as she sets the cup down, aware of every place their hands touched.

The air thickens with everything left unsaid. Claire fights the urge to reach for him again, to confirm the touch was real.

Claire shifts in her chair, the leather creaking beneath her. The dream-library's golden light catches the steam rising from her tea, creating ethereal patterns that dance between them.

"I needed a fresh start," she says, her voice just above a whisper. "Everything before felt... suffocating. So I left. Packed up my life and moved across the country."

Zane leans forward, his presence steady and warm. "That takes courage."

"Does it? Sometimes it feels more like running." Claire traces the rim of her teacup. "But the city... it's different here. Like I can breathe again. When I walk past the Met steps—"

"The city has that effect," Zane says.

Claire's head snaps up. Their eyes meet, a current of recognition passing between them. Claire's heart races as she realizes the slip, but she continues, carefully now. "My office overlooks this little coffee cart. The owner draws hearts in every latte."

"Mario's cart?" Zane asks, then catches himself.

Claire files the detail away, heart racing. She shifts topics, describing her work with books without naming the publishing house. Zane shares a story about his career, just as cautious with details.

The dream responds to their dance of half-truths, the bookshelves shifting, titles blurring and reforming. Their shared knowledge of New York hangs between them, unspoken but undeniable.

"Sometimes," Claire admits, "I write about these dreams. About this place. About—" She stops herself, but her meaning is clear.

Zane's expression softens. "I've been trying to find you," he says quietly. "In the real world."

The garden pulses, golden light swelling. Claire opens her mouth, then hesitates. How much can she reveal? How much does she dare admit?

The light softens as Zane leans forward. Claire holds her breath. She can see the amber in his eyes, the slight curve of his mouth as he studies her.

Her defenses waiver. The carefully constructed walls she's built since leaving Seattle seem paper-thin under his gaze. The dream responds to her surrender, the air growing thick with possibility. Flowers unfurl along nearby shelves, their perfume sweet and heady.

"I've been fighting this," Claire whispers, her fingers gripping the arms of her chair. "Telling myself it wasn't real."

Zane reaches out, his hand hovering near her cheek. "And now?"

The space between them crackles with electricity. Claire leans in, his fingers brushing her skin. The contact sends warmth spreading through her body.

The bookshelves around them blur at the edges, reality bending to accommodate the intensity of their connection. Claire's pulse pounds as Zane's face draws closer. His breath mingles with hers.

Her doubts vanish like mist. Zane's hand cradling her face, everything else falls away, her careful plans, her rational arguments, her fear of letting someone in.

The dream shivers. His warmth begins to slip from her skin.

"No, wait—" She reaches, but her fingers pass through him. The garden melts away, colors running like paint. Zane watches her, as if memorizing every detail. It presses deep into her chest.

The dream slips through her grasp like water, leaving her grasping at empty air.

Claire bolts upright, breath ragged. Sweat clings to her skin. Her eyes adjust to the dark as the city's glow filters through the curtains.

She presses her fingers to her cheek, where Zane's touch still lingers. The details remain sharp in her mind. The way he mentioned Mario's coffee cart. That's too specific to be coincidence.

She reaches for her journal, then pauses. Writing makes it real. And real means accepting that Zane might be out there, remembering the same golden light, the same almost-kiss.

She hugs her knees and lets the city noise wash over her. Her mind insists dreams aren't real. But she can't shake the feeling of him or the charge between them. Maybe leaving Seattle brought her closer to something. Maybe it even brought her closer to him.

Claire stares at her reflection, exhaustion etched deep. Steam fogs the mirror, softening her features. Her fingers rise to her cheek, tracing the memory of his touch.

"Get it together," she mutters, turning away from her blurred image.

She goes through her morning routine with mechanical precision. She brushes her teeth, combs her hair, and chooses clothes. Each movement is precise and mechanical. Each task is a deliberate step away from the golden light of the dream library, from the electricity of almost kissing Zane.

But the smallest things pull her back. The spine of a book on her nightstand triggers the memory of endless shelves. The steam from her coffee reminds her of the tea they shared. Even the morning light filtering through her window feels pale compared to the dream.

She pours her coffee down the sink, unfinished. Twice, she drops her laptop bag before managing to sling it over her shoulder. Her clumsiness matches the disorder in her mind.

"It was just a dream," she says into the silence. But the words feel hollow. Zane feels more real than the mug in her hand or the floor under her feet.

She presses her forehead to the surface of her front door, taking deep breaths. The solid wood grounds her in reality, but even this simple touch reminds her of the dream's vivid sensations. Her body remembers what her mind tries to deny, the undeniable connection, how true it felt, how the dream pulsed with shared presence, how close they had come.

Chapter 25

ZANE STEPS OFF THE plane at JFK, his carry-on bag heavy against his shoulder. His shirt clings with damp, creased from too many restless hours. The familiar buzz of New York's airport feels hollow after chasing a ghost. He checks his phone. Three missed calls and a text from Park asking if he's landed. Zane's thumb hovers, then he pockets it. The failure feels heavier than his bag.

At baggage claim, voices and announcements blur. A couple reunites nearby, their joy sharp against his exhaustion. Zane grabs the same suitcase he packed with hope just days ago.

The taxi line winds on, but Zane barely notices. His mind replays every dead end: the empty apartment, vague neighbors, coffee shops full of blank stares.

A familiar horn blast cuts through Zane's brooding. Park's sedan idles at the curb, and his best friend steps out, arms spread wide.

"Man, you look like you lost a boxing match with fate." Park pulls him into a bear hug. "And fate won by knockout."

Zane manages a half-smile, dropping his bags into the trunk. "Thanks for the ride."

"What else are friends for? Besides, someone had to make sure you didn't wander off chasing another dream lead."

They slide into the car, and Park merges into traffic. The silence stretches until Zane breaks it. "I saw her again last night." His voice drops. "We were..." He trails off, remembering the brush of Claire's lips against his, the way her fingers tangled in his hair.

Park glances over. "That good, huh?"

"It was different this time. More..." Zane searches for the right words. "Intimate. Like we'd known each other forever."

"Hey." Park cuts him off. "One step at a time, remember? Let's get you home first."

The evening air hits his face as Park nudges him down the street. Zane's feet drag.

"You're thinking too loud," Park says, nudging him. "I can hear the gears grinding from here."

Zane shrugs, hands deep in his pockets. A couple passes by, their laughter carrying on the breeze. Every happy face feels like a reminder of what he couldn't find in Seattle.

Their usual coffee shop glows warm against the darkening sky. The bell chimes, and the barista waves, already reaching for their regular orders.

Park guides them to their regular table, his hand firm on Zane's shoulder. The carved CBCK catches the overhead light, and Park taps it twice. "Remember what this means?"

"Crossroads Between Chaos and Kismet." Zane traces the letters with his finger. "Lot of good that did me in Seattle."

"Maybe you're still at the crossroads." Park slides into his seat, leaning forward. "Look, you went to Seattle. You confirmed she exists. That's not nothing."

Their drinks arrive. Americano and dark roast. Steam rises between them. Neither speaks.

"You need a reset. Caffeinate and recalibrate." Park pushes Zane's coffee closer. "Sometimes you need to step back to see the complete picture."

Zane wraps his hands around the warm coffee mug, his stomach churning with a familiar anxiety. The shop bustles with traffic. The barista's laugh reminds him of Claire's from his dreams. A woman's blonde hair glows in the light. His heart lifts, then drops.

"You're doing it again," Park says.

Zane forces his attention back to the table, but his eyes keep wandering. A businessman in a crisp suit. Two college students sharing earbuds. A mother bouncing a baby on her knee.

The door chimes, but Zane doesn't turn. His fingers drum against the mug, his mind stuck between the past and what he can't let go of. Park keeps talking, but Zane barely hears him, the noise of the shop swelling around him like static.

"Stop torturing yourself," Park says, pulling Zane's focus back. "Every blonde isn't going to be her."

Zane drains the cup. The dregs are bitter on his tongue. His legs feel stiff from sitting too long.

"Gonna toss this," he mutters to Park, lifting his empty cup.

He weaves through tables, dodging a backpack sprawled across the aisle. As he approaches the trash bin, the bell chimes. A woman in a loose sweater walks by. But before his mind can catch up, she's already vanished into the crowd outside.

Zane dumps his cup and returns to Park, his eyes scanning faces with renewed intensity. "I swear, every person who walks in—" Zane leans in, lowering his voice. "I keep thinking—maybe..."

"You're turning into Sherlock. Just missing the accent." Park smirks, pushing his empty cup aside. "Next thing you know, you'll be wearing a deerstalker hat and carrying a magnifying glass."

"I'm serious, Park. What if she's right here in New York? What if I've walked past her a dozen times already?"

"Then fate needs better timing." Park checks his watch. "Speaking of timing, we should head out. Some of us have actual work to do."

Zane outlines the carved CBCK with his fingertip.

"I can't shake it, Park." His voice stays low, barely carrying across their small table. "Every time I'm here, it feels like I'm getting closer to something. I just don't know what."

Park sets down his cup and studies Zane's face. The circles under Zane's eyes have deepened since Seattle, but there's an intensity in his gaze that wasn't there before.

"You're sounding like one of those late-night psychics." Park sits back. "Next, you'll be reading tea leaves and carrying crystals."

Zane snorts, going along with the joke. "Yeah, about that..." He shifts in his seat, hand slipping into his jacket pocket.

Park's eyes widen as Zane pulls out a small, translucent crystal, its surface catching the coffee shop's warm light. "No way. You didn't."

"Look, I had two days to kill in Seattle after the landlord thing." Zane turns the crystal between his fingers. "Found this little shop tucked between a bookstore and some vegan café."

"Please tell me you didn't consult a fortune teller too." Park reaches for the crystal, but Zane pulls it back.

"The owner said it helps with dream clarity." Zane's cheeks flush darker.

Park lets out a laugh that draws glances from nearby tables. "Dude, you're literally carrying a magic rock in your pocket. This is beyond how it sounds."

Avoiding Park's amused stare. "Whatever. It was fifteen bucks."

"Fifteen-" Park chokes on his coffee. "Dude, someone saw you coming a mile away."

"It's different." Zane lingers. The crystal weighs in his pocket. The letters feel rough beneath his touch. "These dreams, this place... it feels connected somehow. Like I'm supposed to be here. Waiting."

"Waiting for what?"

"That's just it." Zane straightens, scanning the room again. "I don't know. But something about this spot... it reminds me of the dreams."

Park opens his mouth, probably to crack another joke, but stops when he sees Zane's expression. Instead, he just nods, letting the moment stretch between them.

"Sometimes," Zane continues, his voice barely above a whisper, "I swear I can feel her presence here. Like she's just around the corner, or sitting at another table. It's driving me crazy, but I can't shake it."

Park stands, tossing his empty cup into the trash. "Come on. You need sleep, man."

Zane lingers a moment longer, tracing the carved CBCK with his fingertip, the letters rough beneath his skin.

Zane rises slowly, the crystal pressing against his leg. He casts one last look around the shop, then follows Park toward the door.

The bell above the door chimes softly as Claire steps inside, pulling her sweater close. The warmth of the shop settles over her, but something sharp cuts through the coffee scent. It's a faint cologne that's oddly familiar in a way she can't place. It stops her cold.

She breathes in again, trying to hold on to it, but it slips away.

At the counter, the barista greets her with a smile. "The usual?"

Claire nods. "And a chocolate croissant."

As she waits, she glances toward the door. Two men are leaving, their backs already to her, stepping into the cool night. One of them hesitates, just for a moment, then follows the other outside.

She watches them go, something flickering at the edge of her awareness. But she shakes it off, turns to take her drink, and moves toward the tables.

Her eyes fall on an empty spot near the wall, still warm, crumbs scattered on the surface.

"Messy eaters," she mutters, brushing the table clean.

As she sets her bag down, her fingers graze something carved into the wood. CBCK.

She traces them slowly. A pull hums through her. A whisper from a place she's only known in dreams.

All the worn etchings, the scratched graffiti, the stories left behind. It feels like somewhere she's been before. It feels lived-in, as if it's been waiting for her.

"Nice. Might be my new favorite table," she says, and settles into the seat, the corner view and faded marks already making it her favorite.

She shakes it off, but her gaze keeps drifting back to the carving. The shop feels different. The exposed brick walls, the soft hum of voices, the light through the windows, it all feels like something remembered, not new.

Claire pulls her journal from her bag and flips to a fresh page. Her pen hovers. She scribbles fast, afraid the words might slip away.

Claire finishes her croissant and glances again at the CBCK. Her fingers trace the letters one last time.

As she gathers her things, the faint scent returns. She pauses, turning slightly, but there's no one there.

Chapter 26

A DREAM FORMS AROUND Zane with startling clarity. Leaves carpet Central Park's winding paths in rich golds and deep reds. His footsteps echo against weathered planks as he crosses Bow Bridge. The air carries a crisp sweetness, mixing with the earthy scent of fallen leaves. A flock of birds takes flight from a nearby oak, their wings casting fleeting shadows across the water below.

Zane stops at the center, gripping the railing. The lake ripples with colors deeper than reality. Claire appears at the far end, her hair glowing in the light.

She walks with effortless grace, her emerald eyes finding his. The usual warmth spreads across her features as she draws closer.

"I was hoping I'd find you here," she says, her voice carrying that familiar Canadian sound that makes each word feel like home. She stops beside him, close enough that he can see the subtle flecks of gold in her eyes.

The dream version of Central Park wraps around them like a cocoon. Claire shifts against the railing. Her shoulder brushes his, sparking a ripple through the dreamscape.

"Everything feels different lately," Claire says, her gaze fixed on the water below. "Like I'm finally moving forward, but..." She trails off, unable to shape the feeling into words.

Zane nods. "Sometimes starting over means letting go of who we thought we had to be."

A leaf spirals down between them, its edges glowing with shades of gold. Claire catches it, turning it over in her palm. "You ever feel like you're right where you're supposed to be, but also completely lost?"

"Every day." Zane studies her profile—stronger than before, but still guarded. "But lost doesn't always mean wrong."

The bridge sways beneath them, each plank groaning. "I keep thinking I'll wake up knowing exactly what it all means."

"Maybe we're not supposed to know yet." Zane's voice is gentle, but his words carry weight. "Maybe just feeling it is enough."

Claire turns to him, her expression open yet unreadable. "How do you stay so sure about things that don't make sense?"

"I don't." He smiles. "I just know some things feel true, even when I can't explain why."

They fall into comfortable silence, understanding that some connections need no words.

Zane watches her hand trace the railing, leaving fading trails of light. Her presence feels more solid than ever, grounded by the distant sounds of taxis and street music.

"Tell me something real," Claire says, her sweater shifting in the breeze.

Zane steps closer, drawn to the glow in her hair. "Sometimes I come here just to watch the leaves change. The bridge has a spot where the paint's chipped, right there." He points at a section that appears pristine in the dream. "I've probably crossed it hundreds of times."

Claire nods, understanding flowing between them. The lake below reflects scattered clouds and fragments of buildings, creating a kaleidoscope of city and sky. A horse-drawn carriage clip-clops along a nearby path, its sound muffled as if heard through water.

"It feels different here," Claire says, her voice blending with the rustle of leaves. "Like everything's both sharper and softer at once."

Zane notices how the dream bends reality as street lamps pulsing with their heartbeats, the wind carrying broken snippets of conversation. Yet Claire stays in perfect focus, more vivid than anything else in this altered version of his world.

Zane's heart pounds as Claire draws ribbons of light that vanish. His hand moves before his thoughts catch up. Fingers brush against hers, hesitant at first, then intertwining with quiet certainty. A wave of energy spreads from the contact.

Her hand is warm in his. She turns to him, emerald eyes bright with recognition and something deeper.

A smile touches her lips, gentle yet tinged with longing. "It feels like we're close..." Her voice carries that familiar Canadian lilt as she squeezes his hand. "But not yet."

Around them, the city plays its muted symphony of horns, murmurs, wind, but all Zane notices is how her fingers fit between his.

The crisp scent of fallen leaves drifts through the air as Zane leans in, pulled by something he can't explain. Claire's emerald eyes lock onto his. His heart hammers as the distance between them fades.

"Zane?" Her accent is familiar, but her voice warps, distorts.

The dream fractures around them. The bridge's iron railings blur and fade. Claire's warmth beside him begins to dissolve like morning mist.

"Zane! Wake up!"

Hands shake Zane's shoulders. His eyes snap open to find Emily's worried face hovering over him, her features sharp in the harsh bedroom light. Confusion floods his system. The solid weight of reality crashes back. Scratchy cotton sheets beneath him. The whir of the ceiling fan. Emily's perfume mixing with the staleness of sleep.

"You were talking in your sleep again," Emily says, her tone carrying an edge he can't quite place.

Emily shifts closer, her fingertips trailing along his arm. The familiar scent of her jasmine perfume fills his senses, pushing away the lingering images of leaves and bridge railings.

"I miss you," she whispers, her lips brushing against his neck. Her practiced touch echoes countless mornings.

Emily's hand slides beneath his shirt, warm against his skin. Her confidence radiates through every movement as she straddles him, her weight settling across his hips.

"Let me help you forget about dreams for a while." Her voice carries a playful edge as she leans down, pressing her lips to his collarbone. Her hair falls forward, creating a curtain around their faces.

Zane's pulse quickens as Emily's fingers trace patterns on his chest. Her touch becomes more insistent, deliberate in its intent.

Emily captures his mouth with hers, the kiss deep and demanding. Her body moves against his with a familiar rhythm, igniting responses built from years of intimacy.

Light filters through half-drawn curtains, casting shadows across the rumpled sheets. Zane stretches, muscles stiff from sleep. The space beside him is empty, the sheets cool to the touch where Emily should be.

Clattering sounds drift from the kitchen. Zane swings his legs over the bed's edge, running his fingers through disheveled hair. His mind drifts to pieces of last night's dream of the bridge and Claire's emerald eyes before he forces the thoughts away.

The hardwood floor creaks under his feet as he pads toward the kitchen. Emily stands at the counter, already dressed for work in a crisp blouse and pencil skirt. Her hair falls in loose waves as she measures coffee with practiced precision.

The coffee maker hisses and burbles, filling the silence between them. Zane watches Emily's shoulders tense slightly, the only indication she's aware of his presence. The air feels thick with the weight of what happened during the night.

"Morning," he offers, his voice still rough from sleep. Emily continues measuring coffee grounds, her movements mechanical and precise.

"There's fresh coffee if you want some." Her voice is flat, controlled. Water splashes loudly against the sink as she rinses the spoon.

Zane hesitates in the doorway, his thoughts slow to catch up. Emily moves with ease, her auburn hair warm in the morning light as she whisks eggs. The scent of coffee blends with butter heating in the pan, familiar yet unsettling.

She wears one of his old Columbia t-shirts, soft and faded. She moves barefoot, plucking herbs from the windowsill garden that somehow survived her absence.

Emily plucks basil. The leaves shimmer as she tears them. The scent reminds him of quiet Sundays and shared meals.

He keeps hearing Claire's accent, the way she stretched the "her" in herbs, turning a simple word into something unexpectedly charming. It caught his ear right away—"her-bs," she'd said, playful and proud. The memory tugs a smile from him as he recalls her playful indignation when she corrected his American pronunciation.

Emily's movements with the herbs are efficient. Methodical. Clinical, almost. Nothing like Claire's animated gestures when she explained the proper way to say her-bal tea, her emerald eyes sparkling with mock offense at his "barbaric American butchering" of the word by using a silent H.

The contrast is stark—Emily's practiced grace, Claire's expressive charm. He shifts uncomfortably, guilt settling in his stomach as he catches himself making the comparison.

The normalcy of the moment feels surreal. Dishes that had piled up in the sink are now clean and stacked neatly in the dish rack. The counter gleams, free from the coffee rings and takeout receipts that had become his new normal.

Emily glances up, catching his stare. Her smile carries that same warmth it always had, as though she never left. "I figured this place could use a little life again."

Emily slides a plate of scrambled eggs in front of Zane, the ceramic clinking against the table. Steam rises from their coffee mugs as she settles in across from him, her fingers wrapping around the warm ceramic.

"I've been doing a lot of thinking," Emily says, pushing her eggs around with her fork. "About us, about everything that happened."

Zane watches her hands. The engagement ring is still seated on her finger, how her fingers tap against the mug with nervous energy. The kitchen feels smaller somehow.

"I walked away when you needed me most." Emily's voice cracks slightly. She sets her fork down, meeting his gaze. "I told myself it was because you were different after the accident, obsessed with these dreams. But really, I was scared."

The admission hangs between them. Outside, a car horn blares, the sound muffled through the kitchen window. Emily reaches across the table, her fingers brushing against his hand.

"We had something good, Zane." Her touch is warm, familiar. "I don't want to lose that. Not when we could try again. Really try."

Zane stares at their hands. Hers small and delicate against his. The engagement ring is a quiet weight he can't ignore. His breakfast sits untouched, the steam long gone as the soft glow from outside drapes over the kitchen table.

He stares at her hand, memories flooding in. Their first date in the Village. Lazy Sundays. The way she danced while cooking. The familiar weight of her touch carries years of shared moments.

But Claire's voice echoes in his head.

"I appreciate you telling me this," he said, pulling his hand back. He wraps it around the mug instead. The ceramic burns, grounding him.

Emily's engagement ring catches the morning light, sending tiny prisms across the table. Once, that sparkle had represented their future. Now it feels like an anchor to a past he's not sure he can return to.

"You're right, we had something good." He sips slowly, the bitterness mirroring the mess inside him. "But I'm not the same person I was before the accident."

Emily leans in. "Neither am I. Maybe that's okay. Maybe we can build something new."

The hope in her voice makes his throat tight. Memories of their shared life war with images of Claire, real and dream blending together until he can barely distinguish between them.

"I need time," he manages, his voice rough. "I can't make any promises right now."

The words hang between them as morning light streams through the kitchen window, casting long shadows across their cooling breakfast.

The front door swings open without warning, and Park strides in with his signature grin, holding a paper bag and coffee carrier. He freezes mid-step at the sight of Emily at the kitchen table, his eyebrows shooting up.

"Well, well. Look who's back." Park's voice carries a mix of surprise and something sharper beneath his casual tone.

Zane's stomach drops as Park takes in the scene—breakfast remnants, Emily in his t-shirt, the lingering intimacy. The kitchen suddenly feels too small for three.

Emily straightens in her chair, smoothing her hair with one hand. Her smile doesn't quite reach her eyes as she greets Park. "Morning, James."

Park sets the coffee and bagels on the counter. He only uses the paper cups as props when he's buying time to think. His gaze flicks between Zane and Emily, assessing.

"Didn't realize we were having a reunion." Park leans against the counter, arms crossed. His casual pose contrasts with the tension in his shoulders. "Should've brought more coffee."

The silence stretches, broken only by the hum of the refrigerator and distant traffic. Zane feels caught between his best friend's protective concern and Emily's hopeful presence, the weight of unspoken words pressing down on all of them.

Emily rises from her chair with grace, her smile shifting to match Park's challenging tone. "I see your coffee choices haven't improved, James. Still getting those burnt beans from the corner shop?"

"At least I don't drink that fancy vanilla nonsense you used to bring over." Park's eyes crinkle with familiar mischief.

"Some of us have taste." Emily glances at her empty mug. "Speaking of which, I should get dressed. Unlike some people, I have actual meetings to attend."

She squeezes Zane's shoulder as she passes, the gesture automatic, born from years of morning routines. Her footsteps fade down the hallway, leaving Zane and Park in weighted silence.

Zane eyes the paper bag on the counter. "Since when do you bring artisan bagels?"

Park glances toward the hallway, making sure Emily is out of earshot. He leans in, voice dropping. "Remember when you mentioned Claire going on about Montreal bagels at breakfast? In the dream?" His expression softens. "Thought it might make you smile, man. Didn't expect..." He gestures vaguely toward where Emily disappeared.

Zane's chest tightens at the mention of Claire's name, remembering how she'd passionately defended Canadian bagels, her accent growing stronger with each point she made.

Zane stares at the bagel in his hand, its Montreal-style preparation suddenly feeling like a cosmic joke.

"Beyond crossroads now, Park." He lets out a hollow laugh. "Think I've graduated straight to chaos."

Park slides into Emily's vacated chair, his usual playful demeanor softening. "Don't exactly have a manual for this situation, huh?"

Zane's mind drifts to the dream bridge, to Claire's emerald eyes and that distinctive accent as she'd teased him about proper bagel preparation.

"You know what's crazy?" Zane keeps his voice low. "Emily's here, making breakfast like old times, wearing my clothes. It's everything I thought I wanted. But all I can think about is how Claire pronounces 'herbs' differently."

Park leans back, exhaling. "That's some grade-A chaos right there."

"Tell me about it." Zane tugs at his hair. "Emily wants to try again. Meanwhile, I'm comparing her herbs to dream talk about pronunciation."

The sound of running water echoes from the bathroom, making them glance toward the hallway. Zane's chest tightens with a mixture of guilt and longing. Not for Emily's return, but for a connection that exists only in dreams.

Park grabs his jacket from the back of the chair, stretching as he stands. He moves slowly, buying time as Emily's humming drifts from the hallway.

"Walk me out?" Park tilts his head toward the door, his expression leaving no room for debate.

At the door, Park turns. The lines around his eyes make him look older than usual.

"Look, man." Park's voice drops. "I get it. Emily's familiar. Safe. She represents everything you thought you wanted." He glances toward the kitchen. "But I've seen how you light up talking about those dreams. About Claire."

Zane's hands fidget with his shirt hem, a nervous habit from childhood. The sound of Emily's soft singing creates an oddly domestic backdrop to this moment of truth.

"You've got some decisions to make, buddy." Park's words carry the weight of years of friendship and understanding.

Chapter 27

CLAIRE PACES HER SMALL New York studio, phone pressed to her ear.

"You should see my place now, Sarah. Finally got those hanging flower pots set up in the windows." Claire's voice brightens with excitement.

Sarah's warm laugh crackles through the speaker. "Look at you, becoming a New Yorker. You'll be yelling at tourists to walk faster next."

"Already did that yesterday." Claire settles onto her window seat, tucking her legs beneath her. "Some guy stopped right in the middle of Fifth Avenue to take a selfie."

"That's my girl." Sarah's pride carries through the line. "How's the new job?"

Claire traces patterns on the window glass. "They actually listened to my pitch about the travel series. My editor wants three sample chapters by next month."

"Claire, that's amazing!"

"I know. It feels…" Claire searches for the right words. "It feels like I'm finally doing something. Something that's just mine."

"You earned this." Sarah's voice softens. "How are you really doing though? Beyond work?"

A pigeon lands on Claire's windowsill. "Better. The pain's more manageable since I started the new physical therapy. And I…" She takes a deep breath. "I haven't touched a pain pill in a while."

The line goes quiet for a moment. "I'm so proud of you," Sarah whispers.

"Thanks." Claire wipes at her eyes. "Sometimes I still can't believe I did it. Left Liam, moved across the country. Started over."

"You did more than start over. You started living."

Sarah hears the slight tremor in Claire's voice. "You're still having the dreams, aren't you?"

Claire tightens her grip on the phone. "I didn't say anything about—"

"You don't have to. I can hear it in your voice when you talk about starting over. That same distance creeps in."

"I'm fine." Claire stands, moving away from the window. "Really. The dreams are just... less frequent now."

"But more intense?" Sarah's question cuts through Claire's deflection.

Claire's silence answers for her. She moves to her desk, touching the spine of her journal.

"You know you can tell me anything." Sarah's voice carries the same gentle tone she used during those first nights after Claire left Liam. "Even if it sounds crazy."

"That's just it." Claire sinks into her desk chair. "Every time I try to explain it, The words feel wrong, like describing color to someone who's never seen it."

Sarah waits, letting the silence draw out Claire's thoughts.

"Sometimes..." Claire's voice drops. "Sometimes I wake up unsure of what's real anymore."

"Claire—"

"I know how it sounds." Claire cuts her off, straightening in her chair. "I'm doing everything right. The job. The apartment. Making new friends. I'm moving forward."

"But?" Sarah prompts, hearing the hesitation in Claire's breath.

Claire closes her eyes. "But every night there's this pull, like something's waiting just around the corner."

Claire traces the edge of her journal. "The dreams changed after I moved here. They're not just fragments anymore."

"What do you mean?" Sarah's voice carries through the speaker.

"We talk now. Like, really talk." Claire pulls the journal closer, opening to a drawing of Zane's face. "He tells me about his life in marketing, his best friend who sounds like this total goofball. Sometimes I swear I can smell his coffee breath when he leans in."

Her cheeks flush at the admission. "God, that sounds insane."

"It doesn't." Sarah's response is immediate, firm. "Tell me more about him."

Claire stares at her drawing. "His name is Zane. He has this tiny scar on his cheek that enhances his smile. And when we're together, it feels..." She swallows hard. "It feels safe. Like I can finally breathe."

"You've never mentioned his name before."

"I know." Claire's voice drops. "Because saying it out loud makes it too familiar. Makes me wonder if I'm losing my grip or if..." She trails off, running her fingers over the sketch.

"If what?"

"If, he really exists. If he's out there somewhere, having these same dreams." Claire presses her palm against her chest, feeling her heart race. "The way he sees me, Sarah. Like he sees past all my walls. Like he knows me."

Claire adds, "I think I'm falling for someone who doesn't exist."

"Sarah, am I crazy for feeling this way about someone from a dream?"

"No crazier than anything else in this world." Sarah's voice carries a thoughtful tone. "People fall in love with characters in books, with celebrities they've never met. At least your dream guy talks back."

"But what if..." Claire hesitates, her heart racing. "What if these aren't just dreams? He mentioned knowing me from school. He Said he remembered seeing me there."

"Wait, hold up." Sarah's voice sharpens with interest. "You never told me that part."

Claire curls into her chair. "Because I don't remember anything good from back then. But sometimes, when he talks about those days, there's this... echo. Like déjà vu, but deeper."

"Like a repressed memory?"

"Maybe." Claire closes her eyes, trying to grasp at fragments that feel just out of reach. "What if I knew him back then? What if I felt something for him but buried it so deep I forgot?"

"You were different back then," Sarah says softly. "We all were. Younger, more guarded. Maybe your mind is finally ready to remember."

Claire opens her eyes, staring at Zane's sketch. "But how can I trust these feelings? They're so intense. But they're based on dreams."

"Listen to me." Sarah's voice grows firm. "Love isn't always logical. Sometimes it sneaks up on you in the strangest ways. Maybe these dreams are your heart's way of remembering something your mind forgot."

Claire's fingers drift toward her bedside drawer, where the sleeping pills sit. Her hand trembles as she speaks into the phone.

"I've found a way to make the dreams more... consistent." She keeps her voice casual. "Just something to help me sleep."

"Claire." Sarah's tone shifts, a familiar edge of concern creeping in. "What do you mean by consistent?"

"It's nothing serious." Claire pulls the drawer open, the pills rattling softly. "Just over-the-counter stuff. Helps me fall asleep faster, that's all."

"How often?"

Claire's throat tightens at Sarah's direct question. "Most nights now. It's the only way I can relax enough to sleep."

The silence on the other end of the line stretches until Sarah speaks again, her voice gentle but firm. "You're using pills to chase these dreams, aren't you?"

"I'm not—" Claire starts to protest, but Sarah cuts her off.

"Remember what you told me about your pain pills? How they started as just something to help you cope?"

Claire pulls her hand from the drawer like it's hot. "This is different."

"Is it?" Sarah's words carry no judgment, only concern. "You've come so far, Claire. Built this amazing new life. I'm so proud of you for that. But this..." She pauses. "This feels like you're looking for another escape."

"I'm not escaping," Claire whispers. "I just want to understand what these dreams mean."

"By medicating yourself to chase them?" Sarah's voice softens. "I don't want you to lose yourself in this. Not when you've worked so hard to find yourself again."

Claire's fingers curl around the edge of her desk, knuckles whitening. "You're making this into something it's not. The dream s..." She swallows hard, fighting back the tremor in her voice. "They help me feel connected to something."

"Connected to what, exactly?" Sarah's question hangs in the air.

"To him. To possibilities." Claire pushes away from her desk, pacing the small space of her studio. "You don't understand. When I'm with him, I don't feel broken. I don't feel like I'm just surviving."

"And the pills?"

"They're just sleeping aids." Claire runs her fingers through her hair, tugging at the ends. "It's not like before. I'm not dependent on them. I just... I need them to quiet my mind enough to dream."

"You're right." Sarah's voice carries a gentle weight. "I don't understand. But I see patterns, Claire. And this one feels dangerous."

"It's harmless." Claire's voice rises slightly. "I'm not hurting anyone. I go to work. I'm building a life here. The dreams are just..." She trails off, struggling to find the words.

Sarah's sigh carries through the phone. "Maybe you're not hurting anyone else." Her tone softens but holds firm. "But chasing dreams with pills? That's a slippery slope, and you know it."

She clenches the phone in her hand. "You don't need to keep checking on me."

"Who said anything about checking up?" Sarah's voice carries a forced lightness. "I miss my best friend. And I have some vacation days I need to use before they expire."

Claire moves to her window, watching the city lights flicker. The thought of Sarah seeing her apartment, seeing the journals filled with Zane's face, makes her stomach twist.

"I don't know, Sarah. Work's been pretty intense lately."

"Perfect. You need a break." Sarah's tone shifts, becoming gentler. "Look, I'll come for a weekend. We can catch up properly, maybe hit some of those fancy New York spots you keep telling me about."

Having Sarah there would mean hiding the pills, the circles under her eyes, pretending the dreams don't consume her.

"I..." Claire's voice catches. "I guess it would be nice to have some company."

"Great!" Sarah's enthusiasm barely masks her relief. "I'll look at flights tonight."

Claire stares at her reflection in the window, seeing the shadows under her eyes, the slight tremor in her hand. Sarah would notice these things too. She always does.

"So, I've made a list." Sarah's tone lifts, light and hopeful. "And before you roll your eyes, yes, I'm that tourist who wants to see everything."

Claire steps away from the window, a small smile tugging at her mouth. "Everything?"

"Statue of Liberty, Empire State Building, that giant piano store from that Tom Hanks movie—"

"FAO Schwarz?" Claire settles back into her chair. The heaviness begins to lift from her shoulders.

"That's the one! Think they'll let me recreate the dance scene?"

Claire laughs, the sound genuine and warm. "I'm pretty sure they removed the floor piano years ago."

"Dreams crushed." Sarah sighs dramatically. "Fine, then you have to take me to that coffee shop you won't shut up about. The one with the fancy latte art?"

"The Beanie?" Claire's fingers relax around her phone. "Their barista made me a cat face in my foam yesterday. Complete with whiskers."

"Pictures or it didn't happen."

"Check your phone." Claire smiles as Sarah squeals at the incoming photo.

"Okay, that's adorable. But seriously, we're doing all the touristy stuff. I want selfies with street performers, hot dogs from those sketchy carts—"

"You'll get food poisoning."

"Worth it!" Sarah's enthusiasm bubbles through the line. "Oh, and we have to do one of those horse carriage rides through Central Park. I don't care how cliché it is."

Claire shakes her head, but her smile remains. "You're ridiculous."

"That's why you love me." Sarah pauses. "And maybe we can check out that writing spot you mentioned? The one with the great people-watching?"

After the call ends, Claire sets her phone down, the echo of Sarah's laughter still lingering in her ears. City lights flicker through her window like distant stars, casting shadows across her studio apartment.

Sarah's words about the sleeping pills twist in her mind, mixing with memories of past dependencies.

She places her forehead against the window, letting the glass ground her. Sarah's right. She's built something here. Her new job, the apartment, even the simple victory of ordering coffee without anxiety. Yet each night, she finds herself reaching for those pills, chasing moments with someone who might not exist.

The city sprawls before her, millions of lives overlapping. Maybe Zane is real, staring at the same sky. Or maybe he's just a dream her lonely mind invented as a perfect answer to the need to feel understood.

Claire feels the weight of Sarah's concern. Her friend had pulled her out of darkness before, recognized the signs when Claire couldn't, or wouldn't, see them herself. The thought of Sarah visiting brings both comfort and anxiety. How can she explain these dreams without sounding like she's losing her grip on reality?

Claire watches red lights disappear, reminded how easily things slip away. Her reflection meets her gaze, tired but steady, suspended between the life she's building and the dreams she can't release.

Sarah's words from their earlier conversation twist in her mind: "Chasing dreams with pills? That's a slippery slope."

Claire reaches for the drawer anyway, the familiar rattle of the bottle both comforting and accusatory. She tips one pill into her palm, studying its smooth surface in the lamplight. The pill feels heavier tonight, loaded with Sarah's concern.

"Just to help me sleep," she whispers, but the words ring hollow.

The bathroom mirror shows tired eyes and forced determination. The pill sits on her tongue for a moment before she swallows it with a quick gulp of water.

That night, the dream comes differently. The usual vividness seems muted, its colors less intense. Zane appears through a haze, his features slightly blurred around the edges. When he speaks, his voice carries an echo she's never heard before.

"Something's different tonight," he says, reaching for her hand. His touch feels distant, like a memory of warmth rather than the real thing.

She tries to step closer, but the distance doesn't change. The comfort of his presence is there, but it feels wrapped in cotton, dulled somehow. She can still sense his kindness, his understanding, but it's as if she's watching through frosted glass.

When she wakes, the lingering sensation isn't the usual warmth, but rather a hollow ache in her chest.

Claire blinks awake, her head fogged from the pill. The dream scatters like dry leaves, Zane's distant touch, his voice still echoing. She sits up, wincing at stiff muscles.

In the bathroom, the harsh light exposes every shadow under her eyes. Her reflection stares back, pale and drawn. The woman in the mirror looks like she's pretending to have it together.

She splashes cold water on her face, trying to rinse off the heaviness of medicated sleep. The dream's artificial quality clings to her thoughts. Even Zane had seemed hazy, more like a fading photograph than the warm presence she'd grown accustomed to.

Her thoughts tangle with Sarah's words, blending into the weight of old struggles. The parallel is there, undeniable now in the morning light.

Claire grips the sink. "Maybe Sarah's right," she whispers, barely louder than the tap. The admission sits heavy in her chest for a moment before she straightens her shoulders, turns off the water, and reaches for her toothbrush.

She has meetings to prepare for, a lunch date with coworkers, and Sarah's visit to plan. Real things, tangible things. The day stretches ahead of her, full of possibilities that don't require chemical assistance to reach.

Chapter 28

ZANE TRACES THE CARVED letters on the table. The wood feels rough, grounding. Across from him, Emily watches, familiar and beautiful, but just out of reach.

"I miss us," Emily says, her green eyes searching his face. "The way we were before... before everything changed." Her hand inches across the table. She stops just short of touching his.

The coffee shop bustles around them, but Zane barely registers the ambient chatter. His attention splits between the etched "CBCK" under his fingertip and Emily's presence across from him. She looks beautiful. Her auburn hair falls perfectly, and her expression is open and hopeful.

"Remember when we used to spend weekends here?" Emily's voice carries a gentle nostalgia. "You'd work on your campaigns, and I'd grade papers. We didn't need to talk. Just being together was enough."

Zane's nail snags on the 'K' as memories rise. But overlaying these memories are dreams of another woman.

Emily leans forward, her voice dropping. "I know things got complicated after the accident. But we can work through this, Zane. We always have before."

The letters beneath his finger seem to pulse with meaning, Crossroads Between Chaos and Kismet. Park's words echo in his mind as Emily waits for his response.

Emily's shoulders tense despite her attempt at appearing casual. "Remember when we first moved in together? That tiny apartment with the leaky faucet?" Her laugh comes out shaky. "You promised to fix it, but we ended up just timing our showers to the drips."

"I keep thinking about all those little moments," Emily says. "The Sunday crosswords. The way you'd bring me coffee in bed. How you knew exactly when I needed space after a rough day at school." She pulls her hands back, wrapping them around herself. "I miss that certainty. That feeling of knowing exactly where we fit in each other's lives."

"I know I walked out. But I was scared, Zane. Scared of losing you to something I couldn't understand or compete with." She reaches across the table again, her fingers stopping just short of his. "Being apart made me realize I'd rather face it together than not have you at all."

The tremor in her voice betrays the cost of this confession. "I'm not asking for everything to go back to how it was. I just... I just want us to try."

Zane's finger stills on the etching, the rough edges of each letter grounding him as Emily's words hang in the air. His chest tightens with a familiar ache. The weight of their shared history pressing against this new, inexplicable pull toward something else.

"Emily..." He lifts his eyes to meet hers, taking in the hope and vulnerability written across her features. "What we had... it wasn't just good, it was authentic. You were there through everything, even when I made it impossible."

His hand withdraws from the table, leaving the carved letters behind. "But right now, I'm not the same person who promised to fix that leaky faucet. I'm not even sure I know who that person is anymore."

Emily's shoulders tense, but she holds his gaze, waiting.

"I need space." His voice is quiet. "Not because I don't care, but because I need to understand what's happening to me. Pretending things can go back to normal wouldn't be fair to either of us."

Emily blinks rapidly, her composure wavering for just a moment before she straightens in her chair. "And these dreams? They're part of what you need to figure out?"

"Yes." The single word carries the weight of countless sleepless nights and vivid encounters he can't explain. "I know it sounds crazy—"

"It doesn't sound crazy," Emily interrupts, her voice steady despite the shine in her eyes. "It sounds like you're lost. I just thought..." She takes a breath. "I thought maybe we could find our way back together."

The coffee shop door chimes as Claire steps inside. The scent of roasted beans and warm pastries wraps around her as she takes her place in line, her shoulders relaxing after a tense morning at work.

Voices drift from a nearby table, cutting through the ambient noise. A man's voice strikes a chord deep within Claire. It's familiar, like a half-remembered song. Her fingers tighten around her phone.

Claire stares at the menu board, pretending to read it. The woman's voice carries notes of restraint and hurt, though Claire can't make out the exact words through the sound of the espresso machine and general bustle of the morning crowd.

The man speaks again, and Claire holds her breath. The voice tugs at something in her subconscious, but she resists the urge to turn around. Instead, she shifts her weight, moving forward as the line advances. Her heart beats a touch faster, though she tells herself it's just the anticipation of caffeine.

Claire focuses on the bagel selection on display, yet remains acutely aware of the continuing conversation behind her, like background music that refuses to fade.

"It's not fair to you if I can't give you all of me. I need to sort out my feelings before I can figure out what's next."

The raw honesty in his tone makes Claire's heart ache. She's heard similar words before. She's been on the receiving end of them, but something about this feels different. Less like an excuse and more like genuine struggle.

She glances over her shoulder. The man's back is partially turned, dark hair tousled, shoulders tense. Across from him, a woman. Her face is etched with unmistakable pain.

Poor girl, she deserves better than this, Claire thinks, recognizing the familiar mix of hope and hurt in the woman's expression. She's worn that same look herself, clinging to something that was already slipping away.

The barista calls "Next!" making Claire jump. She turns back quickly, hoping neither of them noticed her watching. But the man's voice lingers in her mind as she steps forward to order, carrying an echo of something she can't quite place.

Embarrassment flares in Claire's cheeks as she pulls away from the line. She slips between customers, making her way to the exit.

The bell chimes as she pushes through the door, the outside air cooling her flushed face. Her footsteps quicken down the sidewalk, putting distance between herself and the heavy conversation she'd intruded upon.

Claire shakes her head, trying to dislodge the lingering echo of the man's voice. She has no right to carry their private moment with her, yet something about his tone keeps tugging at her memory.

Stop it, she scolds herself. You're just projecting because you're lonely. Her boots click against the concrete as she rounds the corner, leaving the coffee shop and its occupants behind.

She's still caught in thought when a tall man brushes past with a mumbled "Sorry," the bell chiming behind him as he enters the café.

Inside, Zane looks up at the familiar sound of Park's entrance, grateful for the interruption. Park strides toward their table, his serene smile masking the assessment in his blue eyes as he takes in the scene.

"Did I miss the reunion special?" Park drops into an empty chair. His voice carries just the right mix of humor and warmth to break the tension. He sets his breakfast down and leans back. His gaze moves between Emily's tight grip on her cup and Zane's rigid posture.

Emily's shoulders relax slightly at Park's presence, though her eyes remain fixed on her cooling coffee. Zane watches his friend settle in, recognizing the calculated casualness in his movements. Park has always known exactly when to show up.

"You know me," Park continues, unwrapping his bagel with exaggerated care. "I hate missing the good parts of any show."

Emily's lips curve into a small smile as she gathers her purse. "I should go. Need some time to process." She pauses, eyeing Park's breakfast. "Another bagel? That's your third this week."

"These Montreal-style ones are incredible." Park bites in, then freezes mid-chew. Something crosses his mind. He swallows fast. "Have a good day, Emily."

She nods, adjusting the strap of her purse. The morning light catches her auburn hair as she turns, highlighting the tension in her shoulders despite her attempted lightness.

Park slides into her vacant seat. His half-eaten bagel sits forgotten as he fixes Zane with a pointed look. "So." He leans back, crossing his arms. "How much trouble did you just get yourself into?"

"I care about Emily. After everything we've been through, how could I not?" He looks up at Park, searching for understanding. "But these dreams. This connection with Claire. It's like nothing I've ever felt before."

Park sets down his bagel, wiping his hands on a napkin. His usual smirk fades into something more serious. "You know I'm the first to call you out when you're being dramatic, but I've never seen you like this."

"That's just it." Zane leans in, dropping his voice. "Every time I close my eyes, every dream... it feels more natural than sitting here right now. And Emily..." He exhales, fingers raking through his hair. "Emily deserves someone who's fully present, not someone chasing shadows."

"Or someone who has defined the meaning behind those impromptu letters on our table," Park adds, gesturing to the CBCK etching. His attempt at humor falls flat as he notices the genuine distress in Zane's expression.

"I can't shake this feeling that there's something bigger happening." Zane's voice carries a quiet desperation. "Like everything from the accident, these dreams, even Emily coming back. It's all connected somehow. And I need to understand this chaos."

Park's playful demeanor dissolves completely. He studies his friend's face, recognizing the weight of this confession. "So what are you saying?"

"I'm saying I have to follow this through wherever it leads." Zane meets Park's gaze. "Even if it means letting go of what Emily and I had."

Park's finger traces the etched letters, worn smooth by countless coffee-stained mornings. His usual playful demeanor gives way to something more grounded as he studies Zane's face.

"You're back at the crossroads, buddy." Park's voice carries the weight of their years of friendship. "Chaos on one side, kismet on the other. You've got to figure out which path feels right. It looks like you just came back from chaos, that leaves..."

"How do I know which is which?" Zane's coffee has gone cold, forgotten between his palms. "Emily represents everything stable, everything I thought I wanted. But Claire—"

"You're labeling everything," Park says. "Emily equals stability. Dreams equal chaos. But what if it's the opposite? What if clinging to the familiar is the chaos?"

The morning light shifts through the cafe windows, casting shadows across their usual table. Zane's finger finds the etching, following Park's path across the letters. The rough edges ground him in this moment, even as his mind tries to drift toward dreams of glowing beaches and Claire's presence.

"Sometimes," Park continues, "the craziest-looking path is actually the one that makes the most sense. You just can't see it until you're already walking it."

A crowd trickles into the café as Park stands, gathering his things. "Don't overthink it," he says, squeezing Zane's shoulder. "Sometimes you have to trust the universe's weird sense of humor."

Zane barely registers Park leaving. His focus stays on the carved letters. CBCK. Sunlight slides across the table, catching the ring of condensation beneath his cup.

Emily's words stick in his mind—Sunday crosswords, coffee in bed, the leaky faucet they never fixed. Each memory carries the weight of shared history, of comfortable routines and understood silences. He can still see the hope in her eyes, the careful way she'd reached for him across this very table.

But beneath those memories, something else pulls at him. The dreams of Claire feel just as vital. The way she looks at him, her presence both foreign and familiar. The connection defies explanation, yet it anchors him in ways he can't dismiss.

Emily is everything he thought he wanted. She offers stability. She represents history and understanding. Yet he sits here, unable to answer her, because the dreams won't release him.

Zane leans back, the café bustling around him. He stays motionless, suspended between what was and what might be.

Chapter 29

CLAIRE SHIFTS HER WEIGHT. Her eyes dart through the crowd at JFK's arrival gate. Her fingers tap against her thigh, matching the rhythm of her nerves.

A flash of red hair catches her attention. Claire's heart leaps as Sarah's familiar figure appears, dragging a purple suitcase behind her. Their eyes meet across the terminal.

"Sarah!" Claire breaks into a run, weaving through the crowd. She crashes into her best friend, nearly knocking them both over. Sarah's laughter rings out as she wraps her arms around Claire, squeezing tight.

"Easy there, you'll wrinkle my carefully planned outfit." Sarah pulls back, grinning. "Though I guess that's better than those awkward side hugs you used to give."

Claire wipes at her eyes, surprised to find them damp. "I didn't realize how much I missed you until right now."

"Of course you missed me. Who else is going to keep you from becoming a complete hermit?" Sarah hooks Claire's arm. "Now, please tell me you've found a decent coffee shop in this concrete jungle. The airplane stuff was basically brown water."

"Actually, I found this amazing little place near my apartment—"

"Lead the way then." Sarah grabs her suitcase handle. "And don't think you're getting out of telling me everything. I want all the juicy details about New York life."

Sarah watches Claire's profile as they navigate the bustling subway platform. The sharp angles of Claire's face have softened, no longer carrying that haunted look from her days with Liam.

"You look good," Sarah says, steadying herself against a pole as the train lurches forward. "Like, actually good. Not that fake 'I'm fine' face you used to pull."

Claire's lips curve into a genuine smile. "Amazing what happens when you're not walking on eggshells all the time."

But Sarah notices the shadows under Claire's eyes. She sees the way Claire fidgets with her sleeve. Those telltale signs of restless nights she recognizes from their years of friendship.

"Though I'm betting your sleep schedule is still garbage." Sarah keeps her tone light, but her eyes narrow as Claire's smile falters for a fraction of a second.

"Work keeps me busy." Claire shrugs, turning to watch the tunnel walls flash by. "You know how it is with deadlines."

"Mhmm." Sarah watches Claire's hand tremble as she brushes her hair aside. She has seen that habit before, always when Claire is holding something back.

Inside the small studio apartment, Sarah takes in the exposed brick, gigantic windows, and personal touches. Travel photos and arranged books line the walls and shelves. Her gaze lingers on the cluster of wine bottles by the recycling bin. She counts three, then looks away.

Claire moves through the kitchen, grabbing two glasses. "It's small, but it works." She grabs a bottle of red from the counter, already opened. "Plus, I can actually afford it on my own."

"It suits you." Sarah settles onto the worn leather couch, accepting the generously filled glass Claire hands her. "Very writer-chic."

Claire sinks into the armchair across from her, tucking her feet underneath her. She raises her glass. "To new beginnings?"

"To new beginnings." Their glasses clink. Sarah watches Claire take a long sip before asking, "So tell me everything. How's the publishing gig?"

Claire's face lights up as she describes her work. She talks about the manuscripts she's reviewing, her growing confidence in team meetings, and how her boss actually listens to her ideas. Her hands move with energy, wine nearly spilling.

"And my coworkers are great. No office drama, if you can believe it." Claire pauses to refill both their glasses. "It feels... normal. Good normal, you know?"

Sarah swirls the wine in her glass. "So, how are you really doing? Beyond the job and the apartment?"

Claire's fingers tighten around her glass. "I'm good. Great, actually. Got three new freelance pieces accepted last week." She takes another sip, avoiding Sarah's gaze. "And I joined this writing group that meets on Thursdays."

"Claire." Sarah's tone carries years of friendship and concern.

"What? I'm putting myself out there. Isn't that what you wanted?" Claire stands, grabbing the wine bottle. "Need a refill?"

Sarah holds out her glass, watching Claire's slightly unsteady pour. "You know that's not what I meant."

Claire sinks back into her chair, the wine making her movements loose. "I keep having these dreams."

"About him?" Sarah asks softly.

"Zane." Claire's voice carries a hint of longing. "They feel honest. Genuine, Sarah. We talk for hours sometimes. He listens, really listens." She traces the rim of her glass. "Last night, we were in this garden. The flowers glowed like starlight, and when he touched my hand..." She trails off, lost in the memory.

"You're sure these aren't just fantasies?"

"They're different." Claire leans forward, her voice picking up speed with the wine. "Sometimes he tells me things about New York, places I've never been. And when I check later, they're real." Her eyes shine with conviction. "The way he looks at me... no one's ever looked at me like that. Like I matter."

Sarah glances at the wine bottles near the recycling bin, then looks back at Claire. "How many of those are from this week?"

Claire shifts in her chair, pulling her knees closer. Her wine glass trembles slightly in her grip. "Don't start."

"I'm not starting anything." Sarah points at an orange prescription bottle she spotted on Claire's end table.

The color drains from Claire's face. "Those are just to help me sleep."

"Along with the wine?" Sarah's voice remains gentle, but her eyes hold steady. "The Claire I know fought like hell to get away from Liam, to build something fresh. Now you're trading one escape for another?"

Claire sets her glass down. Wine sloshes over the rim. "It's not the same thing."

"Maybe not. But you've come so far, Claire." Sarah leans forward, covering Claire's hand with her own. "I watched you rebuild yourself piece by piece. Find your voice again. Don't let anything hold you back now. Not pills, not wine, not even beautiful dreams."

Claire pulls her hand away. "The dreams... they feel like the only place where someone truly sees me."

"I see you." Sarah's voice cracks. "I see how strong you are, how far you've come. And I'm terrified of watching you slip away into something that isn't real."

Sarah springs up from the couch, grabbing Claire's hand. "Enough heavy talk. Get your coat. We're going exploring."

Claire groans, sinking deeper into her chair. "It's getting late."

"Perfect timing. The city's just waking up." Sarah rummages through Claire's closet, tossing a blue peacoat at her. "Come on, show me your New York."

"You're still your bossy self." Claire catches the coat. A smile tugs at her lips. "Some things never change."

"Somebody has to stop you from shutting yourself off completely."

They step into the crisp night air as they head toward Washington Square Park.

Musicians fill the park with jazz. Their notes float on the breeze. Sarah pulls Claire toward a chess table where two old men battle with intense focus. "Look at them, so invested in the moment."

Claire watches the players, noticing how one taps his fingers against the table while thinking, how the other's eyes crinkle when he captures a piece. Small details that ground her in the present.

"There's this great café around the corner," Claire says, pointing east. "They make these ridiculous chocolate croissants."

"Lead the way, tour guide."

The café smells of cinnamon and coffee. Claire chats with the barista while ordering, her voice relaxed as she points out her favorite table. Sarah watches the tension ease from her shoulders.

"See?" Sarah nudges Claire as they settle into a corner table. "The real world has its perks too."

A short time later, the scent of garlic and herbs fills the small kitchen as Sarah chops vegetables while Claire stirs a pot of pasta. Their shoulders bump in the tight space. The rhythm between them feels familiar and easy.

"Remember that time you tried to make risotto for that guy you were dating?" Sarah grins, sliding diced tomatoes into a bowl. "What was his name—Brad?"

"Brian." Claire rolls her eyes. "And thanks for bringing up that disaster. The rice was basically concrete."

"But your face when he actually ate it!" Sarah laughs, nudging Claire's arm. "Like he thought he earned a trophy."

Claire flicks water at her friend. "At least I didn't set off the fire alarm making toast."

Their easy banter continues through dinner, sharing stories between bites of pasta. After the dishes are cleared, Claire gestures to the couch. "You're welcome to crash here. The couch pulls out."

"Already booked a hotel." Sarah checks her phone. "My ride should be here in five. I want the full tourist experience—room service, tiny soaps, the works."

They hug goodbye, Sarah squeezing extra tight. "Remember what I said, okay?"

Alone, Claire pours a large glass of wine and starts her routine—washing her face, moisturizing, brushing her teeth. She pauses, staring at her reflection as she reaches for the prescription bottle.

Her hand hovers over the orange bottle. The wine glass rests on the sink. The pull to escape into dreams wrestles with Sarah's concern.

Claire sits on the edge of her bed, rubbing the glass rim.

Sarah's words echo: "Don't let anything hold you back." They sting, mingling with the warmth of their evening. Claire takes a smaller sip, letting it settle.

Her phone chimes with a message from Sarah: "Made it to the hotel. Get some sleep, okay?"

Claire sets her glass down. The mattress creaks as she lies back and pulls the blanket up. Her thoughts paint the ceiling—Liam's control, Zane's peaceful presence, Sarah's concerned eyes.

Claire shifts onto her side, eyes on the wine bottle beside the bed. The glass gleams dully. Sarah's voice lingers in her mind, steady and warm.

"I'll figure it out," she whispers to the empty room, her eyes drifting closed.

Chapter 30

SARAH WANDERS THROUGH CENTRAL Park, coffee in hand, the crisp air waking her up more than the caffeine. She snaps a quick photo of swirling leaves, already thinking of the caption. At the water's edge, ducks glide past mirrored towers. Nearby, a toddler squeals, tossing crumbs with wild joy. Sarah smiles and takes another photo. She knows the moment will look flatter than it felt.

Farther in, she follows a quiet path lined with cherry trees. She pauses only when a squirrel stares her down before darting up an oak. At Bethesda Fountain, she stops to catch her breath and leans on the railing. Artists sketch the angel statue. She lifts her phone for a selfie, then checks the time.

Sarah settles onto a stone bench near the Fountain, grateful for the rest after walking the park's winding paths. Steam rises from her coffee cup, warming her hands in the cool morning air.

She scrolls through messages. One shows Claire standing in her new office, a nervous pride in her smile. Sarah smiles, thinking of their weekend and Claire's growing independence.

She sips her coffee, watching tourists pose as violin notes float in, blending with the fountain's rhythm.

Sarah startles at a sudden burst of laughter that pierces the fountain's peaceful rhythm. She looks up from her phone to see two men standing near the angel statue, their animated conversation carrying across the plaza.

The taller one gestures wildly, his sandy blond hair waving in the morning breeze as he playfully shoves his friend. "Come on, man. You can't keep living like this. Emily deserves better than—"

"I know, Park." The other man cuts him off, running a hand through his dark hair. His shoulders slump as he leans against the fountain's edge.

Sarah shifts on the bench, trying not to eavesdrop but finding their energy magnetic against the quiet backdrop of the park. Park, the blond one, continues teasing his friend. Their natural rapport shows in their body language and casual banter.

The fountain spray forms a brief rainbow between them. Park's laugh fills the space. His friend's is smaller, uncertain.

Sarah takes another sip of coffee, her peaceful morning meditation now thoroughly disrupted by their presence. She considers moving to a quieter spot, but something about their interaction holds her in place.

Sarah can't help but watch as Park throws his head back, his laughter bouncing off the stone walls of the fountain. His entire body moves with each joke, hands painting stories in the air as he teases his friend.

"I swear, you're worse than my grandmother with her soap operas." Park clutches his chest dramatically, stumbling backward. "Oh, the dreams! The mystery! When will they meet?" His voice rises in a comical falsetto that draws amused glances from passing tourists.

His friend tries to maintain a serious expression but fails, cracking a reluctant smile. Park seizes on this, pointing accusingly. "Ha! See? Even you know how ridiculous this sounds."

Sarah finds herself mirroring Park's infectious grin, hiding her smile behind her coffee cup. His energy radiates across the plaza, warming the cool morning air like a spotlight. Even the pigeons seem to pause their strutting to watch his performance.

"The great romance of our time," Park declares, spreading his arms wide. "Star-crossed lovers meeting in their dreams! Shakespeare would be jealous." He pretends to wipe away a tear, his blue eyes sparkling with mischief.

A group of children running past slow their pace, giggling at Park's theatrical gestures. He gives them a conspiratorial wink, incorporating their presence into his routine with a graceful bow that makes them laugh harder.

Sarah's gaze drifts to the coffee cups in their hands. The familiar logo catches her attention. The same café Claire raves about, with its distinctive black and gold design wrapping around white paper cups. Her eyes narrow, focusing on the way Park gestures with his cup, coffee sloshing dangerously close to the rim.

The fountain's mist forms a gentle barrier of white noise, but Park's booming voice carries clearly across the plaza. "Look, all I'm saying is you can't keep chasing her forever. Even if this Claire person—"

Sarah freezes. She shifts slightly, angling to hear without drawing attention. The dark-haired man sips slowly before speaking.

"It's not just dreams anymore, Park. The details are too specific." His voice carries a weight that contrasts sharply with Park's theatrical tone.

Park rolls his eyes, pointing his coffee cup at his friend. "Right, because dream connections are totally normal. Next you'll tell me you're secretly a superhero."

"Like destiny?" Park interrupts with an exaggerated swoon. "Like the stars aligned just for you and this mystery dream girl?"

The cup wobbles in Sarah's grip as Park's words hang in the air. "And what if Claire isn't—? What if she's just some—?"

The name hits like a punch. Sarah's spine straightens. Her muscles tense as she fights the urge to turn and stare directly at them.

Park's theatrical gestures fade into background noise as Sarah's thoughts spiral. The sound of Claire's voice plays over in her head: "The dreams feel so natural, Sarah. He's always there, waiting..." She'd dismissed it as stress, as Claire's tendency to escape into fantasy. But now...

The coffee cups. The names. The dreams. Sarah's breath stalls as pieces align. She recalls Claire's sketch—dark hair, tired eyes, a man holding something heavy inside.

Her fingers dig into the cold stone bench as she forces herself to stay still and avoid giving away her presence.

Doubt settles in as the conversation by the fountain continues, the words blending into background noise while her mind races. Could she be reading too much into this? New York is massive—what are the odds of stumbling across the exact person from Claire's dreams?

She shifts on the bench, studying the dark-haired man's profile. His tired eyes and slight hunch match Claire's descriptions, but how many men in New York fit that same description? The coffee shop connection seems significant, yet it's one of the most popular chains in the city.

Walking up to strangers and asking about dream connections sounds absurd—like something from a bad romantic comedy. What would she even say? "Excuse me, but do you happen to be the man haunting my best friend's dreams?"

Park's theatrical voice carries across the plaza again, mentioning Claire's name, and Sarah's doubt cracks. The specific details are too precise to ignore, yet the rational part of her brain screams that this is crazy. She could make things worse by interfering, potentially embarrassing Claire or herself.

Her hand tightens around her phone. Should she call or send a photo? If she's wrong, how would Claire react?

Sarah stands halfway, then sits back down, earning a curious glance from a passing jogger. The urge to approach them battles with her natural caution. She's always been the practical one, the voice of reason in Claire's life. Now she's considering chasing a wild coincidence based on overheard conversations and coffee cups.

Sarah's heart races while Park and his friend gather their belongings. The dark-haired man, possibly Zane, crumples his empty coffee cup, tossing it into a nearby bin with practiced ease. Park sips the last of his drink, his theatrical gestures now subdued as they prepare to leave.

"Come on, dream chaser. We've got that meeting in twenty." Park claps his friend's shoulder, steering him away from the fountain.

Sarah's paralyzed by indecision as they turn toward the path leading out of the plaza. Their footsteps echo against the stone, mixing with the fountain's steady rhythm. Park's voice carries fragments of conversation—something about work deadlines and lunch.

They weave through the crowd, Park's blond head bobbing above it all. Sarah watches them disappear into the flow of foot traffic.

Sarah's legs tense as she rises from the bench. Her gaze locks on Park's retreating blond head bobbing through the crowd. She takes three steps forward, coffee cup still in her hand, before a tour group cuts across her path.

By the time the crowd thins, Park and his friend have vanished into the winding paths of Central Park. She rises on her toes, scanning the plaza. Nothing but strangers. Her shoulders slump as she drops back onto the cold stone bench.

The fountain continues its steady rhythm. Sarah stares at the spot where they stood moments ago. She replays Park's jokes, the man's tired eyes, and the café cups Claire always mentions. Their conversation about dreams and destiny, too specific to be mere coincidence.

She moves through the crowd, cup in hand, the fountain scene looping in her mind. Dreams. Claire's name. Every detail feels absurd and inevitable.

Park's voice echoes: "Star-crossed lovers meeting in their dreams!" The phrase that had seemed ridiculous moments ago now carries a different weight. Sarah thinks of Claire's journal entries, her detailed descriptions of dream encounters, the man with dark hair and tired eyes who matches the stranger from the fountain.

Could it really be him? The thought loops louder than the music. Claire's trembling certainty echoes in her mind—mirrored in the voice of the man by the fountain.

Chapter 31

THE DAY'S WEIGHT DRAGS Zane into his pillow, his body sinking into the mattress. His fingertips skim the leather-bound journal on his nightstand, its pages folded and filled with hurried thoughts of Claire.

He shifts onto his side, drawing his knees up slightly. The conversation with Emily at the coffee shop replays in his mind, but her face blurs, replaced by Claire's gentle smile from his dreams.

His breath steadies as exhaustion takes hold. His final thought lingers on Claire. Her face, her voice, more vivid than anything in the waking world. The journal slips from his hand, landing soft on the carpet. His thoughts drift into the space where reality bends. Claire's voice calls him forward.

His body relaxes as sleep takes over. The world shifts and blurs, colors bleeding together until they reform into the familiar dreamscape. He finds himself on their weathered wooden bench, its surface smooth from countless dream-visits. The park stretches before him, but not quite as he remembers it from reality—the trees shimmer with an otherworldly iridescence, their leaves casting prismatic shadows that dance across the ground.

Distant laughter echoes with memory, wind chimes ring from nowhere. The path ahead disappears into mist—a world with its own rules.

His heart skips as a familiar figure emerges from the mist-shrouded path. Claire moves toward him, each step light and deliberate. She wears the same sweater she always does in these dreams. It fits like a memory.

"I was hoping you'd be here," she says, settling beside him on the bench. Her smile reaches her eyes, crinkling the corners in that way that makes his chest tighten.

Claire pulls out her worn notebook. Her fingers rub together as she speaks. "Sometimes I wonder if I knew you before. In another life maybe." She laughs softly at her own words, but there's truth in her eyes.

The notebook falls open in her lap, and she begins to draw. Zane leans closer, drawn to the motion of her pen across paper. Her handwriting flows across the page in elegant loops, interspersed with small sketches taking shape in the margins.

"It feels different tonight," she says without looking up.

Zane watches the sky fade from violet to gray. "It always changes when we do."

"What are you drawing?" he asks, watching as lines become patterns, patterns become shapes.

Zane's eyes drift over Claire's shoulder as she sketches, following the graceful movements of her pen. The familiar shapes and swirls fill the margins until his gaze catches on four letters nestled between abstract patterns: CBCK.

He gasps. The same letters Park carved into their coffee shop table. They are the same letters that have haunted his waking hours.

"What's that?" He points to the scribble, his finger hovering just above the page. "Those letters there—CBCK?"

Claire pauses her sketching, tilting her head as she studies the letters. "That's strange. I didn't even realize I wrote that." She bites her lower lip, lost in thought. "I've seen it somewhere before, but I can't remember where."

Zane's pulse spikes. The coincidence feels too meaningful to dismiss. He watches Claire's face as she continues to stare at the letters, searching her memory.

"It just appeared while I was drawing," she says, her voice soft with confusion. "Like muscle memory, you know? When your hand remembers something your mind forgot."

Claire continues drawing, unaware of his stare. CBCK stands out, identical to the carving on their table. His fingers twitch, fighting the urge to grab her notebook and demand answers.

Instead, he leans back against the bench, forcing his breathing to steady. She hums softly, adding more swirls around the letters, each stroke fluid and natural.

Park's words loop in his head. "Crossroads Between Chaos and Kismet." It doesn't feel random anymore. But pressing Claire might shatter whatever delicate connection they've built in this space. The same four letters appearing in both worlds have to mean something.

Claire shifts beside him, her shoulder brushing his. The contact sends a jolt through him, grounding him in the present moment despite his buzzing thoughts. He watches her add another flourish to her drawing, her movements graceful and unconscious.

Some revelations, he realizes, need time to unfold on their own.

Claire closes her notebook, tucking the pen behind her ear. "These dreams feel different from normal ones." She trails her fingers over the worn leather, keeping her gaze away from Zane's. Claire pulls back, arms folding around herself. Doubt crawls in as her fingers grip the soft sweater.

"What if it's just my mind playing tricks?" She stares at the CBCK letters in her notebook, their meaning blurring before her eyes. "Maybe I'm just holding onto an idea."

The mist at the edge of the path seems to thicken, matching her clouding thoughts. She's been down this road before—finding meaning in coincidences, believing in connections that turned out to be nothing. Her time with Liam taught her how dangerous hope could be.

"Sarah keeps telling me I need to stay grounded in reality." Claire's voice catches as she closes the notebook. "And she's right. Dreams are just dreams, aren't they? Our minds creating patterns where none exist."

The weight of her sleeping pills and wine bottles flash through her mind. How many nights has she chased these dreams, desperate to return to this bench, to feel this connection? Her hands tremble slightly as she tucks a strand of hair behind her ear.

"I've spent so much time trying to escape reality." She forces herself to meet Zane's gaze. "What if this is just another way of running?"

Zane leans forward, his eyes finding Claire's with an intensity that cuts through her doubt. The light reveals every sincere line of his face.

"What if it's not?" His voice carries a quiet certainty that makes Claire's breath catch. "What if these dreams are trying to tell us something? Like breadcrumbs leading us somewhere."

His hand moves toward hers but stops short, hovering over her notebook where the CBCK still stands out stark against the white page.

Claire feels his words press into her, steadying her fears. His warmth unsettles her instinct to pull away, to guard herself from hope. But something in his voice, in his gaze, makes her want to believe.

Zane's presence beside her on the bench radiates a steadiness that anchors her swirling thoughts. Despite her doubts, despite Sarah's warnings, despite everything she knows about disappointment and false hopes, his words ring with a truth she can't dismiss.

The notebook lies open between them, the mysterious letters both a question and an answer. Claire stares at them, feeling the pull of their meaning just beyond her grasp, strengthened by Zane's unwavering belief.

"These dreams," he says, his voice steady despite the urgency building in his chest, "they're leading us somewhere. I can feel it." His fingers hover over the notebook, tracing the air above the letters without touching them.

He wants to tell her about Park's carving, about the coffee shop, about every connection he's discovered. But something says: not yet.

His mind races with possibilities. If the letters appear in both worlds, what else might connect? What other breadcrumbs have they missed while questioning the reality of their connection?

He needs to return to that coffee shop table, needs to examine every detail of Park's carving, needs to understand why these four letters keep appearing.

The edges of their shared dreamscape blur first—trees melting into abstract shapes, the path ahead dissolving into mist. Claire's notebook remains clear between them. The letters CBCK stand defiant against the fading world.

"If we're meant to understand, maybe it'll find us." Her voice carries a gentle certainty that contradicts the dissolving reality around them.

The dream folds inward. Claire's face vanishes, then the letters, then everything. Zane reaches for what's already gone.

His eyes snap open. The darkness of his bedroom feels solid. His fingers grip the sheets, seeking anchor in physical sensation.

Claire's notebook floats in his mind. The letters CBCK are clear, like they've been burned into his memory. Every detail of how her hand moved across the page, the exact placement of each letter, remains sharp despite the dream's end. His breath comes in short bursts as he processes the connection—those same letters carved into the coffee shop table, now appearing in their shared dream.

Zane snaps on the lamp. The light is too bright, but he needs it. His hands shake as he flips to a blank page. Claire's notebook glows in his memory. He writes fast, trying to catch every detail before it slips. His pen flies across the page as he tries to capture her hand's rhythm, the layout, and the swirls around CBCK. His sketch is clumsy. It looks nothing like her graceful lines.

Below the drawing, he jots down her words: "I've seen it somewhere before." The admission sends electricity through his veins. He pauses, tapping his pen against the page. He underlines CBCK three times. The pen digs in so hard it imprints the next page.

His mind locks onto the letters. Over and over. Park carved them into their coffee shop table. Now, without explanation, they have surfaced in Claire's notebook.

He leans toward the window, tracing CBCK into the fog with one finger. C-B-C-K. Each stroke leaves a ghostly mark that catches the city lights, glowing like Claire's pen strokes in the dream.

Zane remains still, his eyes fixed on the letters slowly fading from the window. He's certain they hold the answer now. Those letters bridge the gap between his world and Claire's, between reality and dreams.

"I'll figure it out," he says to himself as he focuses on the vanishing letters. "Whatever it takes, I'll decode what CBCK means."

Chapter 32

ZANE PUSHES THROUGH THE coffee shop door. Park trails behind, his grin visible in the reflection of the front window.

"You're starting to look like a private investigator." Park nudges Zane's shoulder. "Should I call you Detective Hart?"

Zane rolls his eyes. He can't hide a smile as they weave between tables toward their usual spot.

"I mean it," Park continues, sliding into his seat. "You've got that whole brooding detective thing going. All you need is a fedora and a tragic backstory." He taps the carved CBCK on their table. "And mysterious clues."

Zane stares at the etched letters.

"You're hilarious." Zane leans back, his chair creaking. "But something about these letters—they showed up in my dream last night. Claire was drawing them."

Park's teasing expression shifts. Curiosity replaces it as he leans in. "The same letters I carved? That's... weird."

"Exactly." Zane scans his notes, tapping a line with his finger. "She knew them but couldn't recall where from."

The morning crowd ebbs and flows around them, baristas calling out orders over the hiss of steam wands. His eyes drift across faces, searching for Claire's features in every blonde woman who walks through the door.

Park settles into his usual chair, coffee cup warming his palms. "You know, that etching's going to wear away if you keep fondling it like that."

Zane pulls his hand back, caught in the unconscious gesture. He wraps his fingers around his own cup instead, but his gaze continues to sweep the room. A woman in an oversized sweater catches his attention before turning, revealing features nothing like Claire's.

"I can't help it," Zane admits, his finger finding its way back to the C. "Every time I touch these letters, it feels like..." He trails off.

Park leans forward, studying his friend's face. "Like what?"

"Like I'm one step closer to understanding something." Zane's finger moves to the B, then K. "Ever since that dream, seeing Claire draw these exact letters—it can't be coincidence."

Zane's head lifts at the sound of the bell. Hope rises, then falls.

Zane shifts to face the entrance, scanning each table in practiced order. Walls. Corners. Center. His gaze drifts over faces, every movement filtered through one question—could it be her?

Park watches, unimpressed. "Your coffee's getting cold," he says. Zane doesn't answer.

A group of students crowds around the pickup counter, their backpacks creating a visual barrier to the window seats beyond. Zane cranes his neck but can't see past them. He thinks about moving but stays still.

"Your coffee's getting cold," Park says. Zane continues his methodical sweep, his own cup untouched.

The students shift, revealing a new section of the café, but the window corner remains hidden behind their clustered forms. Zane's fingers drum against the table, his usual patience wearing thin as this blind spot in his surveillance persists.

***

Claire hunches over her notebook in a corner seat, her oversized sweater pooling around her arms. Steam rises from her untouched coffee as her pen moves across the page. The carved wooden table bears scratches and stains from years of customer use, providing a stable surface for her hurried writing.

She pauses, chewing on her pen, trying to capture the exact shade of brown in Zane's eyes. The buzz of conversation and clinking cups creates a comfortable barrier between her and the rest of the café.

A group of students clusters near the counter, their coats and backpacks forming a wall that shields her from view. Claire appreciates the inadvertent privacy, sinking deeper into her corner as she writes.

She shifts in her seat, notebook balanced on her knees. She's too focused on the page to notice anything else. Her pen moves faster now, racing to capture the feeling of connection before it dissolves into the morning air.

Claire's fingers brush across the lined pages of her notebook. Her pen hovers over today's blank page, but something catches her eye. It's a familiar pattern of letters scrawled in the margin of yesterday's entry: CBCK.

She squints at the writing, trying to place it. Her head throbs with the effort of remembering, but the origin slips away each time she gets close.

Turning the page back, she finds the same letters again, this time underlined twice. When did she write this? The coffee shop chatter fades. She traces each letter with her finger. The letter C feels significant. She can't explain why.

Claire flips through old entries and finds CBCK scattered in the margins. Every instance tugs at a memory just beyond reach.

She taps her pen against the page and stares at the most recent CBCK. She wills her mind to bridge the gap between recognition and understanding. But the memory stays locked away, leaving her with nothing but the nagging sensation that these four letters mean something important.

***

"It's like she's always a step ahead," he mutters to Park, frustration creeping into his voice.

Park takes a long sip. "Or maybe you're chasing ghosts," he jokes, though something in his tone suggests genuine concern.

The door chimes, and Zane's attention snaps to a woman entering, her blonde hair catching the morning light. His heart rate picks up until she turns, revealing features nothing like Claire's.

Behind the wall of students, Claire glances up from her notebook as her name is called. Zane, focused on a blonde near the door, never sees her move.

Zane slumps back in his chair. "I don't know why, but it feels like I'm so close." His voice carries the weight of weeks spent searching, hoping, waiting. The café's ambient noise—steam hissing, cups clinking, muted conversations—seems to mock his frustration.

Park reaches across the table, his finger finding the familiar groove of the CBCK etching. "Maybe you're looking too hard. Sometimes things find you when you stop searching."

Behind the cluster of students, Claire tucks her notebook into her bag, careful not to bend the pages. Her coffee leaves a ring on the wooden table as she lifts it. The side door catches her eye—a quieter exit than pushing through the morning crowd.

She stands, adjusting her oversized sweater back onto her shoulder. The letters swim in her mind, persistent yet unclear. Her boots stay quiet on the café's floor as she weaves between empty tables toward the side exit.

The door closes with a click, swallowing her into the morning bustle of the city. Neither Zane nor Park notice her departure, the wall of students having hidden her presence entirely.

Zane sees a flash of movement near the side door. A sweater vanishes into the crowd. He blinks, then looks back at the etched letters.

"What if we're overthinking this?" Park asks. "CBCK could mean anything."

But Zane barely registers his friend's words, his mind stuck on the strange pull he felt watching that stranger leave.

"You still with me?" Park waves a hand in front of Zane's face.

"Yeah, sorry." Zane tears his eyes from the side door. "Just thought I saw..." He says, unable to articulate what drew his attention.

Park's voice breaks through Zane's thoughts. It pulls him back to their corner of the café. "I think you're going to drill a hole into that table with all the tracing. Jesus, watch for splinters." His eyes crinkle with familiar concern masked by humor. "Maybe the universe is telling you to let it go."

"Maybe I want something I can never have." The words slip out, heavy with resignation.

Park smirks. "Quoting old-school Nine Inch Nails now? What's next, a full-on existential crisis?"

Zane withdraws his hand, a faint smile breaking through. Park's banter grounds him, even as his eyes drift back to the side door.

Thunder rumbles outside, drawing Zane's attention to the darkening sky. The morning's golden light has given way to heavy clouds, casting shadows across their usual spot.

"And it looks like the universe is about to let loose with this storm coming in." Park taps his empty cup, the hollow sound echoing Zane's growing frustration.

Rain streaks down the windows. It blurs the world outside. Zane's reflection wavers, lost in the glass like the answers he still hasn't found.

"I know what you're thinking," Park says, leaning back in his chair. "But sometimes a coffee shop is just a coffee shop. And sometimes letters carved in a table are just... letters carved in a table."

***

Rain darkens the concrete as Claire stands beneath the café's awning. Her fingers tremble slightly as she opens her notebook again. The letters mock her, familiar yet foreign, like a word that refuses to form on her tongue.

"Why does this feel so important?" The question comes out as barely a whisper, lost in the growing patter of rain. Her thumb traces the letters, the indentation of her pen visible on the paper. Each curve and line feels significant, though she can't explain why.

Claire fumbles with her umbrella, then steps into the rain. The light rain creates a gentle rhythm against the fabric as she steps away from the shelter of the awning.

Inside the café, Zane's finger hasn't left the carved letters. The wood feels smoother now, worn down by his constant touching. Park's words hang with concern and skepticism.

"Maybe you're right about everything," Zane says, his eyes fixed on the etching. "But something tells me she's out there."

Park shakes his head, but a smile softens his expression. The gesture carries years of friendship, of standing by Zane through every obsession and challenge. "Then you better be ready when she shows up."

The rain picks up outside, drumming against the windows. Through the glass, Zane watches umbrellas bloom on the sidewalk like sudden flowers, but his attention keeps returning to the letters beneath his fingertips.

Claire steps into the drizzle, her umbrella offering minimal protection as the wind shifts direction. Her boots click against the wet pavement, each step taking her further from the café. The city moves around her in its usual rush—people ducking into doorways, taxis splashing through puddles, the constant symphony of urban life.

She slows near the corner, a ripple of unease crawling up her spine. The sensation reminds her of forgetting to lock a door. She looks back at the café, rain streaking the windows.

The letters from her notebook flash in her mind: CBCK. Her hand grips her umbrella handle as a shiver runs through her. The café's warm interior glows invitingly through the rain, and for a moment, she considers turning back.

"Stop it," she whispers to herself, adjusting her bag strap. "It's just a feeling."

She forces herself forward, the pull of the café still pressing at her back. The rain drums against her umbrella in an erratic pattern that matches her unsettled thoughts.

***

Zane gathers his things, his movements slow and distracted.

"We should head out before this rain gets worse," Park says, but his attention fixes on something through the streaked window.

Zane shrugs into his coat, the heavy fabric catching on his sleeve. His wallet slips into the chair cushions without notice. It's lost in his distracted movements.

Park's gaze follows a woman outside, her movements hesitant beneath the umbrella. She stands still amid the rushing crowd, turning in place as if searching for something lost. Her oversized sweater makes her look small against the backdrop of hurrying pedestrians.

"When it rains, it pours," Park mutters. His eyes follow her uncertain movements.

Claire pulls her umbrella closer, the wind threatening to turn it inside out. The letters loop in her mind, insistent and unresolved. CBCK. Again. Again. She steps off the curb and disappears around the corner.

Chapter 33

PARK ADJUSTS HIS JACKET collar, squinting up at the darkening sky. "Well, since we're already out and getting soaked, might as well catch that new sci-fi flick at the Regent. It's only three blocks away."

"I should probably head home," Zane says.

"Come on, man. When's the last time you did anything besides obsess over dreams and coffee shop etchings?" Park steps off the curb, dodging a splash from a passing taxi. "Plus, I heard the special effects are insane."

"The movie starts in twenty minutes," Park says, checking his phone. "If we don't leave now, we'll miss the trailers. And you know how I feel about missing trailers."

Park leads the way, sneakers splashing through puddles. Zane trails behind, the neon reflections blurring in the rain.

They weave through the evening crowd. Their shoulders hunch against the strengthening rain.

They join the line snaking beneath the marquee's golden glow. Zane reaches for his wallet. His hand finds empty space. He pats his coat pockets, then his jeans. Nothing.

"Don't tell me," Park says, looking up from his phone. "The infamous coffee shop cushions struck again?"

"Must've slipped out while I was sitting." Zane runs a hand through damp hair.

"Those cushions are like the Bermuda Triangle of personal belongings." Park shakes his head, chuckling. "First my keys last month, now your wallet. That couch is building quite the collection."

Park tugs his jacket collar higher against the rain. "Look, head back to the coffee shop. I'll grab our tickets and save the seats."

"You don't have to wait—"

"Just go get your wallet, man. You're buying the popcorn when you get back." Park waves him off with a grin.

Zane jogs and dodges pedestrians as the rain intensifies. His shoes splash through puddles and soak his cuffs.

Water drips from his hair as he weaves between umbrella-wielding crowds. A taxi horn blares as he cuts across the street, earning a shout from the driver. But Zane barely notices.

His soaked jacket clings to his shoulders. Rain drums on his head, running into his eyes. He blinks it away and speeds up as the sign comes into view.

The weather has cleared most of the usual evening crowd from the sidewalks, leaving Zane almost alone as he sprints the last block. His footsteps echo off the building facades. They mix with the steady patter of rain.

The bell chimes as Zane bursts through the door, water dripping from his hair and jacket onto the worn wooden floor. Only a few customers remain, scattered among the tables like quiet afterthoughts.

Behind the counter, Katie looks up from wiping down the espresso machine. Her eyebrows raise at his disheveled appearance.

"Let me guess," Zane says, flashing a sheepish grin as he pushes his wet hair back from his forehead. "You thought you were done with me for the day."

Katie sets down her cleaning cloth. "You do seem to practically live here."

"I should invest in some stocks." He gestures toward their usual table by the window. "My wallet decided to play hide and seek with the cushions."

Zane weaves between the empty tables, leaving wet footprints on the wooden floor. The cushions on his usual seat still hold the indent from earlier. He kneels beside it, ignoring how his wet jeans cling uncomfortably to his skin.

His fingers probe the gap between the cushion and backrest, finding only crumbs and forgotten receipts at first. He shifts the cushion, tilting it forward, and spots the familiar leather edge of his wallet wedged deep in the crevice.

"There you are," he mutters, easing it free. It resists, then pops loose. He brushes off lint and coffee grounds, checking inside.

Katie walks past with her cleaning supplies, smirking. "Found another victim of the couch?"

"This thing's like a magnet for lost items." Zane tucks the wallet into his back pocket, making sure it's secure this time.

Zane slides into the damp seat, wincing as his wet clothes make contact. The leather wallet feels familiar in his hands as he flips it open, methodically checking each compartment. His driver's license stares back at him, the forced DMV smile a reminder of better days. Credit cards line up neatly in their slots.

In the billfold section, several twenties remain crisp and untouched. He smooths them flat, arranging them all facing the same direction. A movie ticket stub from years back catches his eye. It's from some action flick he saw with Park. He tucks it back behind the bills.

His fingers find a photo of him and Emily in Central Park, laughing at something long forgotten. The edges are worn, but the smiles still shine. He pauses, studying them.

A business card from his first job interview slips out. He'd kept it as a good luck charm, though the company logo has nearly worn away. Sliding it back into place, he feels the familiar rhythm of organizing, of putting things in order. Each item has its spot, its purpose.

The bell chimes again, pulling Zane's attention from his wallet. A woman steps inside, shaking raindrops from her umbrella. Her blonde hair falls loose around her shoulders, slightly damp from the weather.

"Back again?" Katie calls from behind the counter, already reaching for a cup.

"Actually, I think I left my calendar here earlier." The woman's voice carries a slight Canadian sound. She folds her umbrella, creating a small puddle on the floor. "Black, about this big?" Her hands frame an invisible rectangle.

Zane glances up briefly before returning to his wallet organization, only half-listening to their exchange. He slides his credit cards back into their slots, making sure each one clicks into place.

"Oh yeah, I remember seeing it." Katie wipes her hands on her apron. "Want me to check the lost and found?"

"If you wouldn't mind." The woman approaches the counter, her footsteps soft against the wooden floor. "I've been writing in that thing for months. Kind of attached to it."

Zane's fingers pause on his wallet as the woman's voice carries across the quiet shop. Something about her accent tugs at him. He glances up, watching as she shrugs off her rain-dampened coat.

His wallet creaks softly in his grip as it tightens. Her movements are graceful. She shakes the coat, droplets scattering across the wooden floor in tiny constellations.

His heartbeat quickens. She reaches up, fingers running through her blonde hair. The motion seems to slow, becoming dreamlike as she tosses her head back.

The shape of her jaw, the gentle lift of her nose, he knows them. He has memorized them in dreams and scribbled them onto journal pages. His wallet slips from his hands, landing on the cushion with barely a sound.

The impact is instant. Claire stands just feet away. No doubt.

She turns, she pushes a loose strand behind her ear, her emerald eyes finding Zane's. The café noise slips away. Only the charged silence remains between them.

Zane goes breathless. Those eyes. He knows those eyes. He's seen them countless times across dream-filled nights, watching him with that same mix of curiosity and hesitation.

Claire freezes. Her fingers remain tangled in her hair. Understanding hits first, then doubt. Her lips part in a quiet "oh" as the blood drains from her cheeks.

The space between them thickens, like a storm on the verge. Zane clutches the table's edge, holding steady as the ground beneath him feels less certain.

Claire shifts back, her shoulder meeting the counter. Her gaze stays locked on his, searching and uncertain. She traces the same face that has filled her dreams for months.

Neither moves. They're locked in recognition and disbelief.

Katie's voice snaps the silence. "Found it!" She emerges from the back room, waving Claire's calendar. But Claire doesn't turn, can't turn, locked in this moment of profound realization.

Her face. God. Her face. Every detail matches his dreams with precision. The slight arch of her eyebrows as they draw together in recognition. The way her bottom lip trembles slightly. Her beautiful pale skin framing her green eyes.

Sweat slicks his palms. They slip slightly against the table. The space between them feels infinite and close, electric against his skin.

Claire's hand drops from her hair in slow motion, coming to rest against her throat. Her eyes are wide with the same shock he feels, reflecting back the reality of this moment.

Zane wants to stand, to reach her, but can't move. He just stares, drinking in the truth. She's real. The thought repeats like prayer. His chest aches with recognition so sharp it hurts. Every dream and search led here. Now he can barely breathe.

Jazz murmurs in the background as Zane stares, frozen, hand still pressed to the table. Katie's cheerful voice cuts through the thick silence between them.

"Here's your calendar! Found it behind the register." She waves the leather-bound book, but Claire remains frozen, her eyes locked on Zane's face.

Words stick in his throat. A small beauty mark rests at the center of her chest, visible above the neckline of her sweater. The slight tremble of her lower lip, the way her fingers touch her neck. Every detail matches with devastating accuracy.

"Claire?" His voice comes out rough, barely above a whisper. The name feels both foreign and familiar on his tongue.

A single tear breaks free, rolling down Claire's cheek as she stares at him. The droplet trailing silver down her pale skin before disappearing beneath her jaw.

Chapter 34

CLAIRE'S LEGS MOVE WITHOUT thought, carrying her to Zane's table in slow, measured steps. Her pulse thunders. The soft jazz fades.

The space between them shrinks with each of Claire's steps. Three feet. Two feet. Her hands tremble at her sides, and she curls them into fists to steady herself.

Shadows cross Zane's face, pulling the scar on his cheek into focus, the one she remembers from the dreams. His throat works as he swallows hard, his chest rising and falling with quick, shallow breaths that match her own.

Claire stops just out of reach, close enough to see gold flecks in his brown eyes. The same eyes from her dreams stare back with wonder and disbelief. Her lips part, but no words come. What could she say in this crazy moment?

Claire's heart hammers against her ribs as she takes in every detail of his face. The scar. The warm brown eyes. The slight tremor in his hands that mirrors her own. Her throat feels tight, each breath a conscious effort.

"It's you, isn't it?" The words barely escape, her voice trembling with emotion.

Zane nods, his eyes never leaving hers. "It's me. And you're here." His voice breaks on the last word, thick with disbelief and something deeper.

Katie calls out another order. Claire jumps. The sudden intrusion of reality sends a tremor through her body. She grips the strap of her bag as Zane takes a small step closer. His movement is cautious, as if approaching a wild animal that might bolt at any second.

Her eyes land on the CBCK etching in the table. Her breath catches. Recognition hits her.

Claire's legs weaken. She sinks into the chair across from Zane. She traces the table's edge, feeling every groove. The café hums around them, but the sounds feel far away, muffled by the weight of this moment.

Zane's eyes dart around the space, taking in the ordinary scene of customers typing on laptops and baristas calling out orders. His hand trembles as he slides his wallet aside. Everything familiar now feels changed by Claire's presence.

Only a few feet separate them. It feels both too near and too far. His cologne hits her again, and her heart races. She watches his fingers drum the table.

Claire blinks against the sudden brightness, using the moment to gather her thoughts. Her mouth opens and closes before she finally manages to speak.

"I don't know what to say." Her voice comes out soft, almost lost in the ambient noise of the café.

Zane exhales, fingers raking through his damp hair. "I've imagined this a thousand times." He meets her eyes. "Now that you're here, I don't even know how to begin."

Zane leans forward, his elbows resting on the worn table surface. His heart races as he struggles to organize the cascade of memories and emotions threatening to spill out all at once.

"It started after my accident," he begins, his voice low and intimate. "I was engaged. My life was..." He pauses. "Normal. Predictable. Then one night, everything changed."

The coffee shop's ambient noise fades as Zane loses himself in the retelling. "The dreams got more vivid. I kept journals, researched lucid dreaming, tried everything to make sense of it." He exhales. "My friends thought I was losing it. Maybe I was. But I couldn't shake the feeling that it meant something."

His voice grows softer, more vulnerable. "I followed every lead. Searched through old yearbooks, social media, even flew to Seattle." A hint of frustration creeps into his tone. "Always one step behind, always just missing you. But these dreams kept pulling me forward. Like breadcrumbs leading me here, to this moment."

Zane inches his hand toward her on the table. "I know how crazy this sounds. Trust me, I've questioned my sanity more times than I can count. But sitting here now, seeing you..." His voice trails off as emotion overwhelms him.

Claire's hands twist in her lap as she absorbs Zane's story. The intensity of his search and the depth of his connection to their shared dreams crash over her like a wave. It threatens to pull her under. Her throat tightens as guilt mingles with an overwhelming sense of inadequacy.

"I don't remember much from high school." The words come out barely above a whisper. She forces herself to meet his gaze, watching as something flickers across his expression. "I'm sorry."

The apology hangs between them, heavy with the weight of her perceived failure. Claire's fingers grip the edge of her chair, anchoring herself against the urge to flee. The familiar self-doubt creeps in. The same doubt that plagued her through years of toxic relationships and emotional wounds.

The memories he described feel like they belong to someone else. Her own high school years are a blur, filled with anxiety and isolation. The thought that she might have crossed paths with him back then, might have shared some quiet connection she can't even remember, settles over her like another layer of shame."

I should remember. Shouldn't I?" Her voice wavers slightly as she looks back at him. The question carries all her uncertainty, all her fear that she's somehow failing him in this moment they've both dreamed about.

Zane's expression softens as he watches Claire wrestle with her memories. He can't help but smile.

"You sat in front of me in one of our classes. Every day, you'd flick your hair around as if you were trying to get my attention." His eyes take on a distant look, lost in the memory. "Sometimes, when you weren't paying attention, I'd catch the end of your hair between my fingers in an attempt to let you know I noticed you."

Claire's brow furrows, trying to piece together these fragments of their shared past.

"Park. James Parker. My best friend. He used to tease me mercilessly about my crush on you." Zane's cheeks flush slightly at the admission. "Called you my unicorn because you were this... magical, unreachable thing in my life."

His voice grows quieter, more intimate. "I never told anyone this, but..." He pauses, running a hand through his hair. "I spent weeks working up the courage to ask you to prom. I had an entire speech planned. Then I found out someone beat me to it." The old hurt flickers across his face. "I still remember watching you with him, wearing a blue dress that caught all the lights."

Zane's eyes meet hers, warm and earnest. "You were always there, Claire. In the background of my life, in the margins of my memories. Even before the dreams, you were this constant presence I could never quite reach."

Claire's vision blurs as tears well up in her eyes. She realizes Zane had noticed her during those dark years. He had seen beyond her carefully constructed walls.

"I felt invisible back then," she whispers. "Like a ghost drifting through the halls." A tear rolls down her cheek. She wipes it quickly, but more follow. "I never thought anyone was really seeing me."

Zane's words shake something loose. After years of feeling worthless, believing she didn't matter, he's describing moments she lived but never noticed, where she was someone's center without even knowing.

Zane leans in, voice dropping to a murmur. "I think we were meant to find each other again, Claire." His eyes fill with quiet conviction. "Something's been pulling us together. Always."

His voice is warm, steady. Claire lets the words settle, each one pressing against something long-guarded. The coffee shop seems to fade around them, leaving only this moment, this connection that defies explanation.

She lifts her gaze to meet his, struck by the raw hope in his expression. The eyes from her dreams look back at her, but now they hold something deeper. Maybe it's a history she can't remember, a connection she can't explain.

Her throat tightens. Memories of past disappointments surface. Every time she'd believed in something bigger than herself, life had knocked her down. Yet here sits Zane, solid, defying her careful walls of disbelief.

Claire exhales, breath shaky. "I don't know if I believe in fate, but..." She meets his eyes. "This doesn't feel like an accident."

The confession strips away a layer of protection she isn't ready to lose. Claire watches as Zane's eyes crinkle at the corners when he smiles, a detail she'd noticed in dreams.

"You know what's strange?" Zane leans forward. His voice carries a hint of amusement. "In our dreams, you always smelled like jasmine." He gestures to her coat. "And here you are, wearing the same scent."

Claire touches the sleeve of her jacket, surprised. "My mother used to grow it in our garden. I never told you that in the dreams, did I?"

"No, but I remember the way you'd always run your fingers through the plants when we walked through that surreal garden." His expression softens. "It's weird how many little details were real. I gathered you love to be in a garden."

Claire lets out a laugh, sudden but sincere. "Like your habit of playing with your watch when you're nervous?" She nods toward his hand, where he's doing exactly that.

Zane glances down, startled, then joins her laughter. The tension fades, replaced by a comfort that feels too natural for strangers.

"This is a lot to take in, but..." She meets his gaze. "I think I'd like to keep talking."

"I'd like that, too." Zane's smile reaches his eyes, relief evident in the way his shoulders relax.

The café slows as night settles. Katie wipes the counter. The cloth squeaks under the soft pulse of jazz.

Zane barely notices the surrounding shift, too absorbed in watching Claire's expressions as she speaks. Her hands move gracefully as she describes her work, and he finds himself mesmerized by the way she tucks her hair behind her ear. It's a gesture so familiar from their dreams, yet brand new in this reality.

Claire pauses mid-sentence, noticing the empty tables around them. "I didn't realize how late it's gotten." Her voice carries a hint of wonder, as if the hours had melted away without permission.

Katie stacks chairs nearby, the scrape of metal against wood a gentle reminder of the closing time. But neither Zane nor Claire moves to leave. A comfortable silence settles between them as they watch the last customer gather their belongings.

He leans forward slightly, his voice quiet but certain. "I've waited so long for this."

Chapter 35

Zane opens the coffee shop door, holding it for Claire as they step into the night. Steam curls from manholes, adding to the surreal feel of their meeting.

Claire pulls her coat tight, though she isn't cold. Water beads on the fabric like tiny stars. She glances at Zane, still processing how his presence feels both foreign and familiar.

Their footsteps splash quietly through puddles as they drift down the sidewalk. Neither speaks, but the silence carries none of the awkwardness typical between strangers. Instead, it feels like a continuation of their countless dream conversations. Comfortable. Natural. Meant to be.

Zane matches her pace perfectly, just as he had in their shared dreams. His shoulder occasionally brushes against hers, each touch sending sparks of recognition through him.

A taxi splashes past, sending water across the road. Claire's hair darkens with moisture, and Zane fights the urge to brush away a drop that trails down her cheek. The gesture feels too intimate for this delicate moment between dreams and reality.

They pause at a corner. Rain beads on Claire's lashes as she gazes up at the mist-shrouded buildings. Zane watches, struck by how she fits this rain-washed city like a dream slipping into his world.

Mist curls around their feet. Zane stares at the ground, his heart pounding loudly in the quiet. He gathers himself, and the words he's been holding finally break free.

"You've always been my unicorn," he says softly, watching water droplets splash against the concrete. The phrase hangs in the damp air between them.

Claire turns toward him, brow creased in confusion and curiosity. A car passes, headlights cutting across their faces.

Zane feels her gaze on him but keeps his eyes fixed on the wet pavement. His hands fidget in his pockets, thumb running over the rough edge of his house key. The weight of the moment presses against his chest, making each breath deliberate.

A drop of water falls from Claire's hair onto her collar. She reaches up to brush it away, the movement drawing Zane's attention. Their eyes meet briefly before both look away, the intensity of the connection almost too much to bear.

"In high school," he continues, "I remember wanting to talk to you, but..." He shakes his head, water droplets falling from his hair.

Claire's eyes widen slightly, recognition flickering across her features. Her hand moves to brush back a wet strand of hair.

"Then the dreams started, and there you were again. Just as unreachable." Zane's voice catches. "Every time I thought I was getting closer, you'd slip away like smoke. Even when I flew to Seattle..." He trails off, watching a raindrop trace its way down her cheek.

"And now you're here, and I still can't believe you're here." His words rush out, like she might vanish before he finishes.

Claire stops abruptly, raindrops sliding down her face as she processes Zane's words. Her brow furrows. She stares at a puddle reflecting fractured neon from the storefront behind them. The perfect image he's created of her feels like a crushing responsibility, another expectation she can't possibly meet.

"Zane, my life has never been magical," she says, her voice barely rising above the patter of rain. Each word carries the heaviness of her past, of countless nights spent seeking escape in dreams and medication. She shakes her head, damp hair clinging to her face, trying to shake the fantasy he holds.

"You've built this perfect image of me," she says, her voice catching. "But back in school, I was already broken." She takes a shaky breath, the cold air burning her lungs.

Zane stands still, watching as Claire's carefully constructed walls begin to crack. Her shoulders curve inward. She makes herself smaller, trying to disappear.

"Why didn't you tell anyone?" The question comes out soft, barely audible above the patter of rain on concrete. His throat constricts as he watches her shoulders curl inward, making herself smaller.

Claire laughs without humor, the sound full of resignation. She stares into a puddle, her reflection shattered by ripples. "Because I didn't think anyone would care. Or notice."

The simplicity of her answer hits him. All those times he had seen her in school, quiet and withdrawn, always alone, take on a new meaning. He had romanticized her solitude, never once considering the pain behind it.

Water rolls from his hair onto his collar as he processes this revelation. The girl from his dreams and the woman before him merge into someone far more complex than his imagination had allowed. His unicorn wasn't magical or untouchable. She was wounded, surviving, human.

"I learned early that being quiet meant being safe," she says, voice just above the passing cars. "In school, I sat in the back corner, made myself so small even teachers forgot me." A bitter smile flickers. "It worked too well."

Zane watches her fingers twist around the strap of her bag, a nervous habit he recognizes from their shared dreams. The gesture carries new meaning now, speaking of years spent holding herself together.

"When the first guy started isolating me, it didn't feel strange." Her eyes fix on a crack in the sidewalk. "I was already used to being alone. He'd say, 'You don't need other friends,' or 'Nobody gets you like I do.' And I believed him because... being invisible was all I knew."

A taxi splashes through a puddle nearby, but Claire barely notices. The words she's held back for so long spill out like the surrounding rain. "With Liam, it was the same pattern. He'd tell me I was special, different from other girls. But that was just another way of cutting me off from everyone else."

She brushes wet hair from her face. "After a while, you start to think maybe they're right. Maybe you don't deserve better. Maybe this is all there is." Her voice catches. "And trusting anyone else feels impossible because you've forgotten how."

Zane watches Claire struggle with her confession. His hands ache to reach for her, to offer comfort, but he holds back, sensing her fragility in this moment.

"I'm sorry," he says. "I didn't know." The words feel inadequate against the weight of her pain, but he continues. "But I see you now. And I care. More than you realize."

Claire's shoulders tense at his words, her eyes locked on the ground between them. The rain creates expanding circles in the puddles at their feet, matching the ripples of emotion crossing her face.

"I've carried all this for so long," she says. Her grip loosens as she looks at him. "Hearing you say I'm magical." She shakes her head, drops flying. "It's hard to believe when I don't see it."

He watches as she blinks against the rain, or perhaps tears, her guard lowering for the first time since they met in the coffee shop. Without thinking, he reaches out and takes her hand. Her skin is cool and damp from the rain, but her fingers instinctively curl around his.

Claire's eyes widen slightly, but she doesn't pull away. Instead, she stares at their joined hands as if trying to convince herself this is actually happening.

"You're still magical, Claire," Zane says softly, his thumb brushing across her knuckles. "Not because your life was perfect, but because you survived." He feels her hand tremble slightly in his, but her grip tightens. "You're here now, standing in the rain with me. That's what makes you extraordinary."

Her lips part slightly as if to speak, but no words come. Instead, she stands there, holding his hand in the rain, letting his words sink in.

Zane sees her, really sees her, not as the untouchable dream or the broken survivor but as someone beautifully, perfectly human. He studies her face. The pain is still there, but so is strength.

Claire's eyes meet his, clear and direct despite the rain. Her fingers tighten around his hand, and her voice comes soft but steady over the sound of falling water. "Thank you. For seeing me. For... believing in me."

"Maybe there's a reason we're both here," he says.

They begin walking, their footsteps falling into an easy synchronization. Water splashes beneath their feet, creating small ripples in the puddles they pass. Claire sneaks glances at Zane's profile, noting how his expression has softened from earlier intensity to something more peaceful.

Each step forward seems to shed another layer of doubt, another shadow of her past. Their joined hands swing gently between them as they walk, and Claire realizes she can't remember the last time she felt this safe with someone.

The city moves around them. Cars splash past. People hurry under umbrellas. Neon signs reflect off wet surfaces. But they remain in their own bubble, moving at their own pace.

By the time they reach her building, rain clings to their clothes and hair, but neither seems to care. Claire's hand tightens around Zane's as Sarah appears in the doorway. The familiar teasing tone makes Claire's cheeks flush.

"I got a bit..." Claire glances at their joined hands, droplets falling from her wet hair. "Distracted."

Sarah's eyes dance between them, recognition dawning on her face. Her earlier encounter in Central Park suddenly clicks into place. This must be Park's friend. The one obsessed with finding Claire.

"So you're the dream guy," Sarah says, arms crossed as she leans into the frame. Amused, but protective. "I was starting to think Claire made you up."

Zane shifts his weight, caught off guard by Sarah's directness. He remembers Claire mentioning her best friend's fierce loyalty. "I'm Zane," he offers, his voice steady despite his nerves. "And I promise I'm very real."

Claire watches the exchange, her heart racing as her two worlds collide.

"You're both soaked," Sarah observes, her expression softening as she takes in Claire's unusually bright eyes and relaxed posture. She hasn't seen her friend look this at peace in years.

Zane reluctantly releases Claire's hand to fish his phone from his pocket. Park's name flashes on the screen, and he answers with a grin he can't suppress.

"Yeah, I found it." His eyes lock with Claire's, warmth spreading through his chest. "And something else too."

"What's that supposed to mean?" Park's voice crackles through the speaker. "You're doing that cryptic thing again, aren't you?"

Sarah steps closer to Claire, wrapping an arm around her shoulders. Claire leans into the embrace, grateful for her friend's steady presence as she watches Zane talk.

"Remember how you said things find you when you stop searching?" Zane's voice softens. "You were right." He pauses, his free hand running through his wet hair. "She's here, Park. Claire's here."

The line goes silent for a moment. Then Park's laughter bursts through. "No way. You're kidding me!" Another pause. "Wait, you're not kidding, are you?"

"I'm not." Zane's eyes never leave Claire's face. "She's standing right here."

"Holy shit," Park breathes. "The universe has a weird sense of humor, doesn't it? All this time searching, and she shows up when you're just looking for your wallet."

Zane laughs into the phone, running his free hand through his wet hair. "Found my wallet wedged in those money-eating cushions you mentioned. But get this, Claire walked in right after." His eyes meet Claire's, and warmth spreads through his chest. "Talk about timing."

Park's enthusiasm crackles through the speaker. "This calls for celebration. Meet me at Jerry's in twenty? Best greasy spoons in the city."

Zane shifts his weight, glancing between Claire and Sarah. Rain drips from his collar as he lowers the phone slightly. "There's this diner nearby, Jerry's. Park wants to meet up, if you're interested? Nothing fancy, just good late-night food."

Claire pushes wet strands of hair from her face. "Greasy diner food sounds perfect after getting soaked." She turns to Sarah, who stands with arms crossed, studying Zane with careful consideration.

Sarah's protective instincts show in the slight furrow of her brow. "I'll grab my coat," she says after a moment, her tone carrying a mix of caution and acceptance.

From the doorway, she glances back at Claire. "It's probably still buried in my suitcase. You head out and I'll meet you at Jerry's."

She disappears inside, leaving Claire and Zane in the doorway.

"Park's going to flip when he sees you," Zane says into the phone, grinning. "See you in twenty." He hangs up, pocketing his phone as rain continues to drum against the sidewalk.

Zane steps to the curb, raising his arm to flag down a passing taxi. The yellow blur speeds past, splashing water onto the sidewalk. Two more cabs follow suit, their "off duty" lights glowing in the misty night.

Claire pulls her wet coat tighter, watching his failed attempts with growing amusement. "We could just walk," she suggests, gesturing down the street. "Jerry's isn't far."

Zane drops his arm, turning to face her. The rain has plastered his dark hair to his forehead, but his eyes shine with warmth. "You sure? You're already soaked. I don't want you getting sick."

"Can't get much wetter," Claire says, a playful edge creeping into her voice. She takes a tentative step forward. Zane falls into stride beside her.

Zane's lips curl into a mischievous grin as he leans closer to Claire, his breath warm against her ear. "That sounds like a challenge." His voice carries a playful edge that makes Claire's pulse quicken.

Heat rushes to her cheeks despite the chilly rain. She pushes his shoulder, but can't hide her smile. "I walked right into that one, didn't I?"

"More like splashed right into it." His eyes dance with amusement as they continue walking, their shoulders occasionally brushing.

The rain falls as they make their way through the glistening streets, the tension between Claire and Zane crackling like electricity in the damp air.

Zane points out details as they walk - a hidden courtyard, an ancient deli sign, stories of late-night adventures with Park. His voice carries easily over the gentle patter of rain, and Claire finds herself leaning closer to catch every word.

With each step, the tension eases. What's left feels familiar and new. Claire's hand brushes against Zane's as they dodge a particularly large puddle, sending electricity through her rain-chilled fingers.

Water drips from Claire's hair onto her shoulders, but she barely notices. She should be cold, but she's not. Each glance and touch warms her more than the rain can chill.

Chapter 36

THE RAIN EASES AS Zane and Claire move through the city. Claire lifts her face to the sky, letting the mist cool her skin.

Zane watches her, surprised by the calm between them. The ease in their steps. The quiet they share.

Steam drifts from a nearby grate, softening the outlines of passing cars.

"Still can't get over that glowing beach," Claire says as she steps around a puddle. "The sand looked like stardust."

"And the waves were that vibrant shade of blue," Zane adds, his hand brushing against hers as they navigate around a newspaper stand.

Claire slows her pace, watching the light dance across puddles. She lowers her voice. "For the first time in a long time, I feel like things could get better."

Zane stops beside her, turning to meet her gaze. His eyes hold steady confidence, warm and certain in the golden light. "They will. We'll figure it out together."

Claire's heels click softly against the wet pavement as they turn down a narrow street, leaving the bustling main road behind. The sound of car horns and chatter fades into a distant hum, replaced by the gentle patter of rain. Warmth spreads through her chest as Zane's arm brushes against hers.

A sharp echo cuts through the quiet, footsteps that don't match their rhythm. Claire's muscles tense as she picks up the sound of shoes scraping concrete behind them. Before she can turn, movement catches her eye ahead.

Two figures step out of an alley, their dark silhouettes blocking the path. One is tall and broad, the other wiry but just as menacing. They move with practiced precision, spreading out to cut off any escape route.

The taller one steps forward, streetlight catching the glint of metal in his hand. His voice cuts through the rain like ice.

"Bag. Now!"

Claire's heart pounds against her ribs as her fingers instinctively tighten around her purse strap. She feels Zane go rigid beside her, his breathing shallow but controlled.

Zane steps in front of Claire, his body tense, every nerve alert. His heart pounds, but he doesn't hesitate. He used to imagine moments like this back in the day, times he wished he could stand up for her and protect her. Now he does.

"Take it," he says, voice steady despite the adrenaline coursing through him. He reaches for his wallet. His movements are deliberate and slow.

The taller mugger sneers, knife glinting as he moves closer. "Wallet's not enough." His eyes slide past Zane to Claire. "Pretty thing like that's worth more."

Rage burns in Zane's chest. He shifts to keep Claire behind him as the second mugger circles left and footsteps approach from behind.

"You don't want to do this," Zane warns, tracking their movements. The rain drums against his shoulders, each drop heightening his senses.

Claire's breath comes quick and shallow behind him. Her fingers grip the back of his jacket. He can feel her tension, matching his own.

The mugger lunges forward, blade slashing through the rain. Zane pushes Claire clear, catching the man's wrist mid-strike. The knife clatters to the pavement.

"Run!" he shouts to Claire, but the words barely leave his mouth before the second attacker moves in.

The second mugger reaches into his jacket, movement fluid and practiced. Time seems to slow as Claire watches his hand emerge, gripping a black handgun.

Her grip tightens on Zane's arm. She freezes as the gun turns toward her. The details sear into her memory.

Zane's muscles coil beneath her grip. She feels the shift in his stance, the gathering tension. His breath comes short, but he doesn't move, doesn't give the gunman any reason to pull the trigger.

Rain drums against the pavement, each drop echoing like thunder in Claire's ears. The mugger Zane disarmed scrambles for his knife, cursing. Footsteps splash behind them as the third attacker closes in.

The gunman's finger tightens on the trigger. Claire's heart pounds so hard she can taste it. The moment stretches, elastic and fragile, ready to snap.

The world explodes into chaos as Zane's muscles uncoil like a spring. His hands slam into Claire's shoulders, propelling her backward. The gunshot cracks through the night like thunder, echoing off wet brick walls.

White-hot pain tears through Zane's side. His body jerks violently, the impact spinning him halfway around. His hand flies to the wound, warm blood seeping between his fingers. The coppery scent fills his nostrils as rain mixes with the spreading crimson stain.

His knees buckle, but he forces himself to stay upright. Each breath sends daggers of pain through his ribs. Through the haze of agony, his only thought is of Claire. He needs to keep her safe.

"Zane!" Claire's scream pierces the night, raw and desperate. He wants to tell her to run, but the words don't form.

The world tilts and blurs around him. Rain pelts his face as he sways, his blood-slicked hand pressed against his side. The gunman's face swims in his vision, features twisted in shock at what he's done.

Pain pulses through Zane's body with each heartbeat, but he plants his feet wider. He is determined to stay between Claire and danger. Blood soaks through his shirt, hot against his skin despite the cold rain.

His breath comes in ragged gasps. The edges of his vision darken, but he blinks hard, fighting to stay conscious. He can hear Claire behind him, her voice breaking as she calls his name again.

Claire jerks backward as the attacker lunges, his arm swinging toward her shoulder. She stumbles, thrown off balance. Her arms windmill as she tries to stay upright, but her heel catches on the uneven pavement. The world tilts, sharp and sudden, before she crashes to the ground.

The impact comes with brutal force. Her head cracks against the curb. Pain erupts, followed by darkness creeping in.

Rain pelts her face as she lies there. Each drop feels like needles against her skin. Sounds become distorted. She can hear Zane's voice, the shuffle of feet, the distant wail of sirens, all warping together into a nauseating symphony.

She tries to push herself up, but her arms feel like lead. Her stomach lurches. The pavement seems to roll beneath her.

Through hazy vision, she makes out Zane's figure, a shadow against the streetlights. She tries to call his name, but her tongue feels heavy, uncooperative. A sharp taste of blood coats her throat.

The world continues to tilt and spin, reality becoming as fluid as the rain running down her face. Each heartbeat sends new pulses of pain through her skull, matching the rhythm of the spreading warmth she feels beneath her head.

The two muggers stare at Zane's bleeding form, their faces draining of color. The gunman's hand shakes, weapon clattering to the ground. Without a word, they bolt down the alley, their footsteps splashing through puddles as they vanish into darkness. A car rushes past the street entrance, its headlights cutting through the rain for a brief moment, illuminating the blood mixing with water on the pavement. The vehicle continues on, leaving them alone in the dark once more.

Claire's head throbs with each heartbeat, but she grits her teeth, forcing her limbs to move. The world tilts and spins as she pushes herself onto her hands and knees. Sharp pain lances through her skull, making her vision swim. Her arms tremble, threatening to give out, but she keeps moving.

"Zane," she gasps, barely audible through the ringing in her ears. Pain flares with every crawl forward, but she keeps going.

Water seeps through her clothes, cold against her skin, but she doesn't feel it. Her fingers find Zane's blood, thin and bright in the rain. The metallic scent clings to the air as she pulls herself closer.

Claire crawls to Zane's side. Her vision blurs as she fights through waves of dizziness. He lies curled on the wet pavement, one hand pressed against his side where blood seeps between his fingers. The red spreads across his shirt, mixing with the rain in growing circles.

Her hands shake as she presses them over his, trying to stem the flow. The warmth of his blood against her palms makes her stomach lurch, but she holds steady. Rain pelts her face, washing away the tears she didn't realize were falling.

"Stay with me," she pleads, her voice cracking. Her head throbs with each word, but she focuses only on Zane's face. His skin has gone pale, lips taking on a bluish tinge that terrifies her.

Zane's eyes flutter, struggling to stay open. His chest rises and falls in short, shallow gasps. His lips part, voice barely carrying above the sound of rain hitting pavement.

"Told you..." he whispers, his fingers twitching toward hers where they press against his wound. "I'd keep you safe."

Headlights sweep past, illuminating Zane's pale face for a moment before plunging them back into shadow. The car continues without slowing, its tires hissing against wet pavement. Music thumps from a nearby bar.

Something hot trails down Claire's cheek, dripping onto Zane's shirt. She can't tell if it's blood from her head wound or tears. Her chest clenches as she watches his unsteady breathing, each rise and fall too shallow.

"Hold on," she whispers. She presses harder against his wound. The pressure makes him wince, but she doesn't let up. "Just hold on."

A siren cuts through the night, its wail bouncing off brick walls. The sound grows louder, closer, but Claire's vision swims. She blinks hard, trying to stay focused on Zane's face, but the edges of her sight keep darkening.

The siren's pitch changes as it draws nearer, the sound drilling into her aching head. She can feel her arms weakening, her body wanting to collapse beside Zane on the wet pavement. But she keeps her hands pressed firmly against his side, anchoring herself to this moment, to him.

Red and blue lights strobe across the wet pavement. Uniformed figures rush toward them as Claire keeps pressure on Zane's wound, her fingers numb.

"Ma'am, we need you to step back." A firm hand touches her shoulder, but Claire doesn't move.

"Please," she whispers, watching Zane's chest rise and fall in shallow bursts. His eyes have closed, his skin ashen under the harsh emergency lights.

More hands grasp her shoulders, gently but insistently pulling her away. The loss of contact with Zane feels like physical pain. Her blood-covered hands hover uselessly in front of her as paramedics swarm around him.

"You're hurt too," someone says, turning her face to examine the wound at the back of her head. The touch sends fresh pain through her skull.

"Just help him," Claire chokes out, trying to push away the hands that hold her steady. Her eyes blur as she watches the paramedics surround Zane, their sharp, urgent voices rattling off numbers and medical terms that mean nothing to her.

The rain continues to fall. It mixes with blood on the pavement. Emergency lights paint everything in alternating washes of red and blue. The pain in her head and the sticky warmth of Zane's blood on her hands tell her this is real. Horrifyingly real.

Hands press something soft but firm against the back of Claire's head. The pressure sends fresh waves of pain through her skull. She tries to focus on Zane, but the strobing lights blur and stretch, making her stomach lurch.

"Stay with me," a voice says, calm but urgent. Claire blinks, fighting to stay awake. The paramedics' voices distort, like they're underwater.

Her body feels heavy, disconnected. The rain bites at her skin, but the sensation is dull. A voice reaches her, asking questions she can't process. The words tangle before they reach her lips.

The world tilts sharply. Strong hands catch her as her knees buckle. She tries to stand, to reach for Zane, but her limbs won't obey.

Through narrowing vision, she watches as the paramedics lift Zane onto a stretcher. His arm hangs limp over the side, fingers curled slightly, still stained with his own blood. She wants to call out to him, to touch his hand one last time.

Claire reaches toward him, her arm moving as if through deep water. The darkness closes in faster now, turning the flashing lights into dim, distant stars. Her fingers stretch toward Zane's still form. The void claims her before she can reach him.

Chapter 37

FLUORESCENT LIGHTS PULSE BEHIND Claire's eyelids as awareness comes and goes. The steady beeping drifts in and out, distant and strange.

Her body feels weighted, pressed into crisp hospital sheets by invisible hands. Even breathing takes effort, each inhale catching slightly in her chest. The sharp scent of antiseptic mixes with something metallic. Maybe blood.

Voices drift around her, clinical and detached. Words float past like debris in a stream. "Concussion." "Observation." "Responding well." Only one thought breaks through the fog: Zane.

She tries to form his name, but her tongue lies useless in her mouth. The drugs pull at her, dragging her down into velvet darkness. She tries to resist, but the sedation wins.

The hospital sounds grow distant, underwater. The lights blur. The beeping dissolves into a distant murmur of waves. Sand stretches before her, familiar and strange. Claire lets go and steps into the dream.

Claire opens her eyes to the familiar beach, but something is off. The sand shimmers as if alive, reflecting light from nowhere. The waves roll in smooth patterns, more precise than nature allows.

Her body feels weightless here, free from the ache and heaviness of her hospital-bound form. The air smells clean and unreal, as if nothing human has ever touched it. Above her, the sky shifts in colors. Ribbons of light dance across an eternal twilight.

She steps forward, bare feet sinking into sand both solid and fluid. Ripples of light shimmer with each motion, as if the beach responds to her presence.

The horizon bends slightly at its edges, reminding her this isn't quite reality. Water meets sky in a seamless blend of colors that shouldn't exist together but somehow do. The waves curl in slow motion, their foam glowing with light that pulses like heartbeats.

Claire wraps her arms around herself, scanning the endless shoreline. The beach stretches endlessly, yet somehow feels like it belongs to her alone. She's been here countless times in dreams, but never has it felt so immediate.

A flicker of movement catches Claire's attention. There, where the ethereal waves meet the shore, a familiar silhouette stands against the shifting sky. Her heart skips as recognition floods through her, Zane.

He faces the water, his stance both strong and vulnerable. Light moves over him in colors she can't name but instinctively understands. As if sensing her presence, he turns.

The expression on his face steals her breath. Love radiates from him, pure and unguarded, but beneath it lies a profound sadness that makes her chest ache. His eyes hold hers across the distance, conveying everything words cannot.

Light pulses between them as the waves lap gently, steady and synchronized.

Claire's feet remain rooted to the spot, her body unwilling or unable to close the distance. The glow wraps around him, blurring the lines between solid and unreal, close enough to see yet always just beyond her grasp.

Claire steps forward, pulse hammering. The sand stirs with each movement, glowing softly. His name slips from her lips, stretching across the dreamscape as if the world itself is listening.

"Zane."

His smile deepens. She hurries forward, drawn by the pull between them. Space collapses until they stand face-to-face.

Zane's presence feels solid and ethereal, as if he exists between two worlds. His eyes hold hers with tenderness, speaking volumes.

They fall into step beside each other, their footprints leaving trails in the sand. Waves curl around their ankles, warm and cool at once, defying the laws of nature. The water glows where it touches them, as if responding to their connection.

Claire's shoulder brushes against his as they walk, the contact sending ripples of awareness through her. The horizon bends at strange angles, but the moment feels close and private.

Their pace matches naturally, each step in perfect sync. The rhythm of their movement blends with the gentle percussion of waves, creating a melody that exists only for them. Time drifts unnoticed.

The rhythm of their steps falters as Zane slows to a stop. Claire turns to face him, catching the shift in his expression, a mix of peace and urgency that makes her chest tighten.

"I don't have much time," Zane says with clarity. The sand, shimmering silver and gold, coils around their feet, stirred by the weight of his words.

His eyes lock with hers, deep and earnest. "Before I met you, I was just... existing. Going through the motions, building a life that looked right on paper." He reaches for her hand, his touch sending ripples of warmth through the surrounding air. "But you gave everything meaning."

The surreal sky brightens. "Even when I didn't know what I was searching for, you were there—the light pulling me in." His thumb traces glowing circles against her hand. "You made me believe again."

Each word sinks into her like heat. It spreads through the dream's rhythm.

"Thank you," he whispers, his voice thick with emotion, "for being the mystery that gave my life purpose, for being worth every step of the search."

Claire stops abruptly, her feet sinking into the luminescent sand. The dreamscape pulses with her rising emotions. The grains swirl in agitated patterns. Her chest tightens as reality crashes over her. He's saying goodbye.

"You can't leave me," she chokes out, tears spilling down her cheeks. The drops fall like crystals, each one catching the light before disappearing into the sand. "Not now. Not after everything."

She tightens her grip, trying to hold him in place. The waves crash harder, matching the rhythm of her racing heart. The ethereal colors above them darken, responding to her distress.

Her tears fall unchecked, blurring her vision as she sobs. Her body trembles with the effort to hold it in, each breath a battle against the tide of grief threatening to overwhelm her.

"Please," she whispers, the word carrying across the dreamscape with devastating clarity. The air feels heavy with everything she hasn't said.

She refuses to let go, her hand clinging to his. The beach stretches endlessly around them, but their world has narrowed to this single point of contact between them, this last desperate attempt to hold on to what they've found.

The dreamscape pulses with Claire's anguish, but Zane's presence remains steady, anchoring her against the storm of emotions. His eyes hold a depth of love that makes her heart ache as he slowly shakes his head.

The sand shifts beneath them, unsteady under the weight of her trembling. Zane's smile, heavy with tenderness and sorrow, pulls the air from her lungs.

"You were always my unicorn, Claire," he says softly. Each syllable leaves ripples in the air between them, like stones dropped in still water. "And you always will be. But now it's your turn to shine."

His steady voice makes her legs give way. Above them, the sky's shifting colors move like a living canvas, reflecting the moment's bittersweet beauty. Claire feels each word settle into her bones, even as her heart rebels against their meaning.

Claire's legs give out beneath her, sending her crashing to her knees in the sand. Her tears soak the sand as light flickers beneath her. Her fingers clutch at Zane's clothes, desperate for any hold on him she can maintain.

"I can't do this without you," she whispers, her voice shaking. The dreamscape responds as waves crash and the sky darkens.

Her body trembles with each sob, shoulders rising and falling as she buries her face against him. His scent, solid and familiar, cuts through her, making the pain sharper.

The ground beneath her pulses with each sob.

Claire feels the solid warmth of him against her cheek, making the knowledge of his impending absence cut even deeper. Her fingers twist in the fabric of his clothes as another sob tears through her. The sound echoes across the dreamscape like a wounded animal's cry.

Zane kneels beside Claire in the sand, moving with quiet ease. The soft glow outlines his form as he cups her face, warmth seeping into her tear-streaked skin. The dreamscape shifts, light blooming where their hands touch.

"You can, Claire," he says. His words leave glowing trails in the air. "You've always been stronger than you think."

His thumbs trace along her cheeks, slow and steady. The otherworldly sky sways with color, pulsing in time with their shared breath.

"Live for both of us," he whispers, the words settling into the space between heartbeats. The sand swirls around them, responding to the weight of his declaration. His eyes hold hers with unwavering certainty, reflecting all the love and faith he carries for her.

Claire feels his words settle deep, their truth undeniable, even as her heart refuses to accept the end. His hands press gently against hers, tethering her to this place where reality and dreams still blur.

The waves inch closer to where Claire kneels, their usual gentle rhythm taking on an urgent quality. Each surge reaches further up the beach, the water glowing with an inner light. The horizon narrows as if the world is shrinking around them.

Zane rises slowly beside her, his movement causing ripples in the ethereal air. He extends his hand down to her, palm up, an offering and a farewell wrapped in one simple gesture. The light brightens his fingers, making them appear both solid and translucent.

She slips her hand into his, fingers interlacing with desperate strength. His skin feels warm against hers. As he helps her to her feet, she grips tighter, trying to memorize the exact pressure of his touch, the exact way their hands fit together.

The waves lap at their feet. Each touch of water sends shivers of energy through the dreamscape. Claire's grip on Zane's hand becomes almost painful, her fingers white-knuckled with the effort of holding on.

Claire hesitates. Tears slip into the tide as her body refuses to move.

The waves pulse brighter as Zane turns to face Claire, his eyes holding a depth of emotion that steals her breath. His hand tightens around hers as the water swirls at their feet.

"I've loved you since high school," he says, his voice carrying across the dreamscape with perfect clarity. "I just didn't know how to tell you." His voice steadies. "Your smile made everything brighter."

Claire's heart clenches as he continues, each word resonating through their shared space. "I'd hear you in the hallways, see you in the cafeteria, and something inside me would scream. But I was too caught up in who I thought I should be to understand what that meant."

"Tonight, when I saw you in that coffee shop, everything clicked into place. My whole life, I've been standing at the crossroads between chaos and kismet, and every path led back to you."

The water rises around their ankles, its pull growing stronger. Zane takes a step backward toward the deeper waves, his movements slow and purposeful. His eyes never leave Claire's face as he whispers, "I'll always be with you, Claire. I love you."

The tide pulls harder now, waves climbing higher with each pass. Claire feels his grip slipping, though his touch still holds the same deep warmth. His figure softens at the edges, fading into the shifting light around them.

Claire's scream tears through the dreamscape, raw and primal. "Zane!" The sound echoes across the beach, each repetition carrying the weight of her desperation.

She lunges forward, trying to follow him into the deeper water. But the waves rise up before her like a wall of liquid light. The tide presses against her legs. It holds her in place despite her struggles. Each attempt to move forward meets with stronger resistance, as if the dream itself conspires to keep them apart.

She reaches for him, fighting the rising wall of water. It swirls around her feet, its usual warmth now feeling like ice against her skin. The force of her movement sends ripples through the dreamscape, distorting the colors above them into frenzied patterns.

"Please," she begs, her voice breaking. "Just let me reach him." But the waves remain firm, creating a shifting barrier that gleams with inner light. Each surge of water pushes her back another inch, even as she fights to maintain her position.

Her tears strike the tide. Circles of light merge into the waves. The sky darkens, pulsing with her anguish. Still, she strains forward, trembling. Her body shakes with the effort of resistance, but the barrier holds firm, keeping her anchored to this spot while Zane drifts further from reach.

What sounds like his fading voice carries across the water, clear despite the distance growing between them. "This isn't the end, Claire." The words ripple through the air, leaving trails of light in their wake. "You'll see. Just keep shining."

Each syllable resonates through Claire's body, settling deep in her bones even as she fights against their finality.

His last words echo through the dream, carried on waves of light. "I love you." The sound lingers in her chest, aching and final.

Claire's eyes snap open. Her chest heaves as reality crashes back. The sterile hospital room comes into focus with harsh lights, beeping monitors, the sharp scent of antiseptic. Her cheeks are wet, tears mixing with dream ones.

Her hand clutches at her hospital gown, fingers twisting in the thin fabric above her heart. The pain there isn't physical. It's deeper, rawer, as if something vital has been torn away. Zane's last words echo in her mind, each syllable burning like a brand: "Just keep shining."

The monitor quickens beside her, a sharp contrast to the dream's silence. She presses her other hand to her mouth, trying to contain the sob building in her throat, but it escapes anyway. Her body shakes with grief.

The warmth of his touch lingers on her skin like a phantom. It makes the reality of his absence cut deeper.

She still sees it—the sand, the color, the light. But none of it belongs here.

Fresh tears spill down her cheeks. The full weight of loss settles over her.

"Come back," she whispers into the empty room, her voice raw and broken. "I love you too." But only the rhythmic beeping answers, each sound marking another moment in a world without Zane.

Chapter 38

THE LIGHTS BLUR INTO a hazy glow as Claire's eyes flutter open. Her limbs resist movement, each breath dragging pain through her chest. The antiseptic smell burns her nostrils, mixing with the metallic taste in her mouth. A steady beeping pierces the fog in her head.

She tries to lift her hand but finds it weighted down. Blinking slowly, her vision sharpens enough to make out Sarah's familiar red hair. Her friend's head rests on the edge of the hospital bed, fingers intertwined with Claire's.

Through the window in the door, blurred figures shift in the hallway. Claire squints, making out Park's broad shoulders as he paces. Emily stands against the wall, arms wrapped around herself, her usually perfect posture crumpled with exhaustion. Their hushed voices filter through the glass, though the words are indistinct.

Sarah stirs, lifting her head. Dark circles ring her eyes, and her makeup is smeared. "Hey," she whispers, squeezing Claire's hand. The pressure sparks sensation in her fingers.

Park notices the movement through the window. His face tightens with an emotion Claire can't quite read. He touches Emily's arm, gesturing toward the room. Emily's shoulders tense, and she shakes her head, stepping back from the door.

Claire's throat constricts as memories flash through her mind. The rain on pavement, a gunshot, Zane's blood on her hands. The heart monitor stutters and beeps faster.Claire's fingers tighten around Sarah's hand. "Where is he?" The words scratch her dry throat.

Sarah shifts in the plastic chair, her eyes fixed on their joined hands. "Claire, you need to rest."

"No." Claire pushes against the mattress, ignoring the stab of pain in her skull. The heart monitor spikes its protest as she struggles to sit up. "Take me to him."

"Please, lie back down." Sarah's palm presses against Claire's shoulder.

"Stop treating me like I'll break." Claire yanks the pulse monitor from her finger. The machine erupts into a shrill tone. "Just tell me where he is."

Sarah's lips tremble. She reaches up and brushes a tear from her cheek. "He—he didn't make it, Claire."

The words hit like a physical blow. Claire's chest caves in, her lungs refusing to work. She shakes her head, the motion sending sparks of pain through her temples. "No. No, you're wrong."

"The bullet..." Sarah's voice cracks. "It hit an artery. There was nothing they could do."

Claire stares at her hands, remembering the warmth of his blood seeping through her fingers. The world lurches, her stomach turning."

He held on long enough to make sure you were safe." Sarah cups Claire's face between her palms. "He saved your life."

A raw sound tears from Claire's throat. She folds into Sarah's arms, shaking with sobs she can't contain. Sarah cradles her close, rocking her like a child.

"It's not fair," Claire whispers into Sarah's shoulder. "We just found each other."

Sarah strokes Claire's hair, her own tears falling. "I know, sweetie. I know."

Claire's fingers twist in the hospital sheets. "No, you don't understand. I just saw him."

Sarah's brow furrows. "Claire, you've been unconscious for—"

"On the beach." Claire's voice cracks. "He was there, Sarah. The same beach from our dreams. He walked into the waves, but..." The words stick in her throat as reality crashes against memory.

She touches her lips, chasing the last trace of his voice. "It felt so real. He was right there."

Sarah reaches for her, but Claire pulls away. "He can't be gone. I can still feel him." She says. "He was just telling me to keep shining, to live for both of us. He told me he loved me, Sarah."

"That was a dream, sweetie." Sarah's voice is gentle, careful.

"No." Claire grabs Sarah's wrist. "You weren't there. You didn't feel it. He was warm, and solid, and..." Her words dissolve into a ragged breath as the memory of his touch starts to fade.

Claire stares at her hands, now empty, now still. The same hands that had tried to hold his life in him on the wet pavement. The same hands that had reached for him on that dream-swept shore.

"But he promised," she whispers, her voice small and lost. "He said this wasn't the end."

Through the window's rectangular frame, Claire watches Park and Emily like actors in a silent film. Park's broad shoulders hunch forward as he gestures, his hands cutting through the air with sharp, desperate movements. His usual easy smile is gone, replaced by tight lines around his mouth.

Emily stands rigid against the wall, arms crossed over her chest. Her posture is calm, but her hands betray her tension. She shakes her head at whatever Park is saying, her auburn hair falling forward to shield her expression.

Park steps closer, lowering his voice, though his agitation shows in the way he rocks on his heels. Emily's shoulders rise, her chin lifting. Whatever battle of wills plays out between them, Emily holds her ground.

A nurse passes between them, breaking their tableau. Emily uses the interruption to step back, creating distance and masking her face with her hands. Park's hand drops to his side, defeat evident in the slope of his shoulders. He runs his fingers through his hair, a gesture so like Zane that Claire's chest constricts.

Emily's lips move, forming words Claire can't hear. Park's reaction is immediate. His whole body stiffens, and he turns away, pressing his fist against the wall. Emily reaches for him, then stops, her hand hovering in the space between them before falling back to her side.

Claire turns away, unable to watch any longer. Their grief feels too private, too raw, like a mirror of her own pain that she's not ready to face.

Through the window, Claire happens to catch Emily's gaze. The other woman's eyes lock onto hers, sharp and unflinching. Emily's face remains carefully composed, a mask of practiced control, but something deeper flickers beneath the surface.

Claire expects to find anger or blame in that stare. After all, she's the reason Emily's fiancé ran into danger. Instead, she finds a well of understanding so profound it steals her breath. Emily's eyes hold the same raw ache that Claire feels burning in her chest, the same hollow space where Zane used to exist.

Their shared loss stretches across the sterile hospital corridor like an invisible thread. Emily's fingers press against the glass and leave a faint impression that fogs with her breath. For a moment, she looks like she might enter the room, might bridge the gap between them.

Park touches Emily's elbow, breaking the connection. Emily's expression wavers for just a second, then she turns away. But that brief exchange has already carved itself into Claire's memory. The silent acknowledgment that they both loved the same man, albeit in different ways, and now they both must learn to live in a world without him.

Claire turns away from the window, her body curling inward as the tears break free. Each sob pulls her tighter into herself, her chest seizing with the effort. The hospital sheets twist in her grip as she presses her face against the thin pillow, trying to muffle the sound of her breaking.

Zane's words from the dream echo through her mind, crystal clear despite the fog of medication. "Live for both of us," he'd said, as if it were that simple. As if she could just pick up the pieces and move forward when half of her heart lies shattered on the rain-soaked pavement.

"Keep shining," his voice whispers in her memory. Claire's fingers dig deeper into the sheets, her knuckles white with strain. How can she shine when the light inside her feels extinguished? When every breath hurts more than the last?

The memory of his smile on that surreal beach cuts through her like a knife. The warmth in his eyes as he cupped her face, the gentle press of his fingers against her skin. It had felt so real. Now the warmth is gone, leaving a silence she can't explain.

"This isn't the end," he'd promised. But it is. It is the end, and she's drowning in the reality of it. No more shared dreams. No more chances to build the future they'd barely begun to imagine. Just this crushing weight of grief and the bitter taste of words left unsaid.

Sarah's hand brushes Claire's back, but she barely feels it through the numbness spreading through her limbs. His final moments repeat in her mind. The way his body shielded hers, his voice fading.

Sarah's fingers thread through Claire's hair, a gentle rhythm that anchors her to the present. The touch is familiar and reminiscent of countless nights when Sarah helped her through panic attacks and moments of despair.

"He cared about you more than anything." Sarah's voice cuts through Claire's sobs. "He would want you to be okay."

Claire's breath hitches. She turns her face toward Sarah, tears tracking down her cheeks. "How can I be okay? Everything hurts."

Sarah shifts closer, her hip pressing against the hospital bed rail. Her eyes are red-rimmed but steady. "Because that's who you are, Claire. You've always been a survivor."

"I don't want to keep going." Claire's voice cracks. "I just want him."

Sarah wraps her arms around Claire, careful of the I.V. lines. "I know, sweetie. I know."

They stay like that, Sarah's presence a steady warmth against the cold hospital air. Her fingers continue moving slowly through Claire's hair. Each touch is a silent reminder that she's not alone.

"He would want you to be okay," Sarah whispers again, her words soft but certain. "He protected you because he believed in your light. Because he loved you for who you are."

Claire closes her eyes, letting Sarah's comfort wash over her. The pain doesn't lessen, but somehow it becomes more bearable with her friend's arms around her.

**

Days blend into a hazy stream of faces and voices. Claire signs papers without reading them, her signature a weak scrawl across hospital forms. The doctors' instructions fade into white noise. They tell her to rest, stay hydrated, and return for follow-up appointments.

Sarah's presence remains constant. She is a quiet anchor in the fog. She handles the details Claire can't process. The apartment looks the same, but nothing feels right anymore.

Park stops by with groceries, for Sarah and Claire, his usual energy dulled. Sometimes he just sits, sharing stories about Zane Claire can barely absorb.

Nights stretch endless. Claire stares at the ceiling, afraid to close her eyes. Sleep brings nothing. Not even dreams.

Time loses all meaning for Claire. Breakfast bleeds into dinner, sunset into dawn.

The pain medication bottles line up like soldiers on her dresser. Claire takes them mechanically when Sarah reminds her, though they do little to dull the deeper ache.

Her phone buzzes with messages she can't bring herself to read. Work emails pile up and go unnoticed. The world continues spinning while Claire remains frozen in that moment on rain-slick pavement, Zane's blood warm on her hands.

Sarah sorts through Claire's clothes, picking out funeral attire with gentle efficiency. The black dress feels like a costume when Claire tries it on, the mirror reflecting someone she doesn't recognize. She barely recognizes the pale, lost woman in the glass.

Claire stands at the back of the hall, her dress stiff against her skin. Photos of Zane's smile mock her from every corner. They show his graduation, family gatherings, and moments with Emily and Park. Their shared dreams feel distant now.

Mourners cluster in small groups, their hushed voices echoing off marble floors. Some share stories of Zane's kindness, his work ethic, his infectious laugh. Others simply stand in silence, dabbing at tears.

Emily sits in the front row, her auburn hair swept into an elegant knot, her spine straight despite the weight on her shoulders. Park stands beside her, one hand resting protectively on her chair. His usual energy is subdued, his movements careful as if the air might shatter.

A woman who shares Zane's warm brown eyes, his mother, Claire realizes—approaches the podium. Her voice trembles as she speaks of her son's passion for life, his dreams, his recent engagement. The word engagement hits Claire like a physical blow. She presses her fingers to her ribs and tries to hold herself together.

Sarah squeezes Claire's hand, grounding her in the moment. These people knew a different Zane. They knew the marketing executive, the devoted friend, and the fiancé. They didn't know the man who walked with her on dream-swept shores, who understood her broken pieces because he carried his own.

A slideshow begins playing on the wall. Images of Zane's life flash by. They're mostly childhood birthdays, college graduation, and office parties. Claire searches each photo for some hint of the connection they shared, but finds only glimpses of a life she never truly knew.

She stands apart from the crowd, an outsider looking in on grief she's not sure she has the right to claim. Their few precious moments together feel like a secret she must keep.

Claire's legs feel like lead as she approaches the memorial display. Her fingers grip a folded note, its edges worn from being carried in her pocket since she wrote it that morning. The note trembles in her hand as she stares at Zane's photo. His smile is bright and unguarded, his eyes holding that warmth she remembers from their shared dreams.

She unfolds the note carefully, smoothing the creases. Her handwriting looks small and fragile on the white paper. "You were my reason, my dream, my protector. I'll carry you with me forever."

The words blur as tears well in her eyes. She slides the note beneath the frame, pressing it into place. Her fingers rest on the photo's edge, tracing his face through the glass.

"Thank you for finding me," she whispers, her voice barely audible above the quiet murmur of conversations behind her. The words fall short of everything she wants to say, but they are all she can offer without unraveling.

Claire wipes her eyes, stepping back from the memorial display. Before she can fully turn, Park approaches with quiet hesitation, something tucked in his hand. He holds out a thin envelope, his voice softer than usual.

"I found these a few nights ago," he says. "Didn't know if I should bring them, but I think they're yours now."

She takes the envelope carefully. A strange stillness settles over her as she pulls out the contents. Inside are several photos. One draws her in instantly, triggering a memory so vivid it steals her breath.

It had been impossible to forget—the far corner of the downtown Houston high-rise where prom was held, transformed that night into a beach escape lit by strings of golden light. Sand-colored flooring softened each step, and a painted backdrop of ocean waves and fading sky made the city outside feel like a distant illusion.

In the photograph, a tall guy is kissing her. His face is partially hidden behind dark sunglasses, the kind Zane wore as a joke that night, but the intent in his posture is unmistakable. Her hand rests gently against his chest, caught mid-moment between instinct and surprise. In her other hand, clearly visible between them, is a small boutonniere of orchid and lily—tucked into her palm with quiet purpose, as if the kiss alone hadn't spoken enough.

"I remember this," she says quietly. "I'd just slipped away from my boyfriend. I was trying to breathe, just standing near the photo setup, thinking no one would notice. Someone bumped into me from behind. He didn't say anything. Just leaned in... and kissed me. I never saw who it was. Then he slipped a flower into my hand and walked off before I could even react."

Park watches her with a quiet sort of weight. "I saw you standing there alone," he says. "You looked like you were trying to disappear into the wall. I had my camera from the yearbook staff and thought, give it a minute—Zane will find her. I didn't expect that to happen, though."

Claire runs her thumb along the edge of the photograph. Her voice is barely above a whisper. "Oh my god. That was Zane."

The dream version of the beach had always felt unreal, too perfectly lit, too peaceful to be tied to anything concrete. But now, looking at this image, with its soft light and dreamlike haze, she sees the truth. It was never imagined. It had always been there, waiting to be remembered.

"He tucked that moment away," Park says. "He never told me. He never told anyone. I think when you disappeared from school after that, he just buried it. But he never really let it go."

Claire nods slowly, the memory blooming now in full color. "This was the start of it. I never connected it before, but this was it. That one kiss stayed with me for years. And the flowers..."

Park places a hand on her shoulder with quiet finality. "You were always part of his story, Claire. Even before the dreams. Even before he understood why."

She holds the photo close, heart pounding, the weight of it both grounding and impossible. In that quiet corner of another city, years and miles away from where she now stood, they had unknowingly written the first line of something far bigger than either of them understood.

Claire feels a presence behind her and turns from the memorial display. Emily stands across the room, her eyes fixed on Claire with an intensity that makes her pause. The connection crackles between them. Two women who loved the same man, both left with empty spaces where he used to be.

Emily's composure remains intact. Her shoulders are straight. Her hands are clasped in front of her black dress. But her eyes hold a depth of understanding that cuts through Claire's defenses. In that look, Claire sees everything they share—the pain, the loss, the bittersweet memories of a man who touched both their lives.

Without words, Emily gives a slight nod. The gesture carries the weight of acknowledgment, acceptance, perhaps even forgiveness. It's brief, barely noticeable to anyone else in the crowded room, but to Claire it feels monumental. In that small movement, Emily validates Claire's right to grieve, to have loved him, to be here.

Claire's fingers tremble against the photo frame as she returns the nod, her throat too tight for words. The moment passes quickly, but its impact lingers like an echo.

Claire steps out of the memorial hall. The heavy doors close behind her with a soft thud. The air hits her face, crisp and clean compared to the stuffy atmosphere inside.

She looks up. Blue sky breaks through gray, like Zane's eyes when he laughed. Leaves swirl at her feet, dreamlike. She moves forward into the unknown and carries Zane's memory like a quiet flame in her heart.

Chapter 39

CLAIRE FUMBLES WITH HER keys, the metal scraping the lock before it clicks open. Inside, the apartment is dark. Wine bottles crowd the coffee table. Torn labels and half-filled glasses clutter every surface.

Her purse slips from her shoulder, landing among scattered papers and clothes. Tissues near the couch, shoes abandoned mid-stride, a sweater over a chair. Everything is left where it fell.

She sinks onto the couch, her dress snagging slightly on the cushions. On the table, reminders of Zane sit where she left them.

She spots the edge of her journal under the papers. The leather is worn, her fingers knowing its texture without thought. It feels heavier now.

She flips through the pages. Dreams, hopes, scattered notes from nights she barely remembers. Her fingertips trace over the letters "CBCK" sketched in the margin, the lines now permanently etched into her memory like scars.

Each entry captures their story. The beach, the conversations, the feeling that they were meant to find each other are now confirmed with the photos Park gave her. Her vision blurs as she reaches their last dream, where golden sand stretched forever and Zane stood at the shore, framed by an endless horizon.

Her fingers freeze. Under "CBCK," new ink. Sharp, slanted letters: "Crossroads Between Chaos and Kismet."

She knows that handwriting. Zane's curves. Zane's slant. Her fingers follow the grooves his pen left behind. The journal rests open in her lap.

"He knew I'd find this," she thinks.

The questions come fast, but no answers follow.

She lifts the journal closer, studying every detail of his writing. The ink looks fresh, darker than her own faded entries. A tear falls, soaking the page. His words blur beneath it.

Claire clutches the journal to her chest, feeling the weight of these final words from him. His last message, hidden in plain sight, waiting for her to discover it. The ache in her chest deepens, a physical pain that threatens to consume her.

Claire stares at Zane's handwriting until the letters blur into shapeless smudges. "Is this what you meant?" Her whisper breaks in the empty room as she presses the journal against her chest.

Each curve and line feels like a piece of him she can still touch, still hold on to. The message waits, clear and cruel. Like he knew where it would all end.

Bottles line the counter, some spilled, some empty. Stains on the floor. Crusted glasses untouched.

Next to the sink, a small orange bottle catches the dim light. The sleeping pills rattle softly when a truck rumbles past outside, the sound drawing her attention to how many remain. The label bears yesterday's date, but the bottle is already half empty.

An overturned wine glass reflects the chaos—clothes strewn across chairs, takeout containers stacked in precarious towers, tissues scattered like fallen leaves. The mess grows outward, reaching everything within arm's length.

Claire lifts the wine glass to her lips, the burgundy liquid sloshing against the rim. Her other hand grips the journal, its pages soft and worn from countless readings. The light fades. She doesn't move.

She takes a sip of wine, longer this time. It does nothing for the hollow ache inside, but it softens the edges. The journal lies open to a familiar page, the one where she recorded their first conversation in the dream. Her handwriting moves across the paper, capturing the way he had approached her on that strange shore, the way his eyes had known her before a single word was spoken.

The wine glass trembles in her hand as fresh tears fall, dotting the pages like rain. The tears soak into the page, and she lets them. They belong there.

A soft knock echoes through Claire's apartment, followed by another, more insistent one. Claire doesn't move from her position on the couch, her eyes fixed on Zane's handwriting in the journal.

The door opens, letting in a shaft of hallway light that cuts across the dim room. Sarah's sharp intake of breath breaks the silence as she takes in the scene—wine bottles scattered across every surface, clothes strewn about, and takeout containers creating a maze on the floor.

"Oh, Claire," Sarah whispers, her footsteps careful as she navigates through the chaos.

She doesn't lift her gaze, her fingertips trailing the inked letters. The cushion sinks under Sarah's weight, bringing her near enough to notice the smudges left by dried tears on the pages.

Sarah's gaze sweeps over the mess, lingering on the half-empty pill bottle by the sink. Her hand finds Claire's shoulder, squeezing gently. "How long have you been sitting here?"

Claire shrugs, barely moving.

Sarah reaches for the nearly empty wine glass balanced on the coffee table's edge. Her fingers close around it just as Claire's hand shoots out to stop her.

"Don't," Claire's voice cracks. "Please."

Sarah's expression softens as she takes in Claire's disheveled appearance.

Sarah sets her purse down and pulls out a small paper bag from the pharmacy, placing it on the table with deliberate care. The white bag crinkles as she smooths it out, the prescription label visible through the thin paper.

"I brought your meds," Sarah says, her voice gentle but firm.

Claire's eyes drift to the bag but don't quite focus on it.

Sarah glances across the kitchen counter, taking in the collection of empty wine bottles. She picks up one bottle, examining its label before setting it back down with a soft clink.

"You know," Sarah says, keeping her tone casual as concern tightens her chest, "you should really be careful mixing those pills with all this wine." She moves closer to Claire, her hand hovering near her friend's shoulder. "I don't want you waking up feeling worse."

Sarah rises, adjusting her bag. "I hate to rush, but I have to meet someone." Sarah checks her watch.

Claire doesn't respond.

Sarah hesitates by the couch, her shadow falling across Claire's lap. A faint smile crosses her face as she adds, "I'll be back soon, though. I'll bring dinner, so don't even think about living off wine and crackers tonight."

The promise of food draws no reaction from Claire. She remains frozen in her position, shoulders hunched over. The soft sound of Sarah's heels against the hardwood floor marks her retreat, but Claire doesn't look up to watch her go.

Sarah pauses, adjusting her purse strap. "And don't worry... I'll tell him you're okay." Her voice carries a knowing undertone, a slight emphasis on 'him' that makes Claire's fingers still on the journal page.

Claire's head lifts slightly, the first movement she's shown since Sarah arrived. The words pierce through her wine-induced haze, stirring something in her chest. Park. The thought of him waiting for news about her condition sends a fresh wave of guilt through her body.

"Try to rest, okay?" Sarah's voice softens as she steps into the hallway. The door closes behind her with a gentle click, leaving Claire alone with her thoughts.

Now Park's face mingles with her memories of Zane. She remembers his steady presence during the memorial, the way he'd stood guard between her and well-meaning mourners, and how he'd slipped her the photos along with his number with a gruff "Just in case."

The pharmacy bag sits quietly, a reminder the world is still turning. Her name on the label stares back in bold black ink.

She reaches for the wine glass again, muscle memory taking over. The glass is cold against her hand, a sharp difference from the warmth of the journal resting in her lap. She lifts it, and the wine swirls, dark and still.

"I don't know how to do this without you," she murmurs, eyes locked on the photo in her hands. "Not now... not when I'm just starting to remember."

Chapter 40

CLAIRE SITS CURLED ON her window seat, watching raindrops chase each other down the glass. The rain sounds like it did that night at the coffee shop, the night everything changed. Her breath fogs the cold surface as she leans closer, creating a small circle of opacity that she traces with her finger.

Her gaze drifts to the coffee table, where her journal lies open. Its pages are illuminated by a single lamp. The familiar "CBCK" stares back. It is Zane's handwriting, unchanged while everything else is gone. She pulls her knees closer to her chest, holding herself together.

Claire presses her forehead against the cool glass, closing her eyes. That night feels both distant and immediate. She remembers the way Zane had looked at her across the coffee shop, how his voice trembled when he said her name. The memory cuts deep, fresh as a recent wound.

She moves from the window, her legs stiff. Empty wine bottles clutter the table and counter, casting dull reflections. A half-finished glass of wine sits precariously close to her open journal.

Her doctor's prescriptions mock her from beside the leather-bound book. The zolpidem for sleep, alprazolam for anxiety. These little white pills that promise relief but remind her of everything she's trying to forget. She picks up the bottle of zolpidem, rolling it between her palms.

Sarah organized the medications earlier, setting them in neat rows with typed instructions taped to each bottle. The kitchen shows signs of abandoned meals, a plate with toast crumbs, an apple with one bite taken out. Dishes pile in the sink, coffee mugs leaving rings on every surface.

A tangled blanket on the couch marks another restless night. Clothes spill from the basket. Mail piles unread by the door.

The alprazolam bottle stands upright next to her journal. Its white cap is a stark contrast to the dark leather cover. Claire reaches for it, then pulls back, her hand trembling. The doctor's words echo in her mind—"Take as needed for panic attacks." But what about the constant, gnawing anxiety that never quite leaves?

Claire's fingers trail across the leather-bound journals spread on the coffee table. Zane's is darker, more worn, filled with hurried notes and fragments of his search. Her own are stacked beside it, the oldest one fraying at the edges, its spine soft from years of being opened and reopened.

She lifts the cover gently and turns to the first pages. Tucked between two early entries is a delicate orchid and lily boutonniere, its colors faded, the stem carefully pressed flat. She never fully understood why she kept it. She only knew that it mattered. She used to tell herself it was just a memento from prom, a fleeting kiss that belonged to someone she would never see again. But deep down, she had always hoped it had been Zane. Even before the dreams, even before the memories began to surface, a quiet part of her had wished it was him.

Back then, she did not trust what she remembered. Too much had been buried beneath pain, guilt, shame, and the need to survive. Trauma had carved away parts of her past, leaving her with scattered pieces she could not bring herself to look at. She spent years holding everyone at a distance. She believed keeping someone who truly loved her at arm's length was safer than allowing herself to be vulnerable.

Now, holding the photograph in her hands, she feels the full weight of what she kept from him. Zane had lived quietly in the edges of her memory, waiting. She wishes she had reached for him. She wishes she had asked the questions. She wishes she had been brave.

She would give anything to go back and fix it all. But the past only comes in fragments now, and too much of it can no longer be changed.

She shifts her gaze to the photograph, propped against an empty wine glass. The painted waves and golden lights from that night surround their kiss, casting the moment in a glow that feels both surreal and heartbreakingly real. That version of herself, a girl just trying to breathe, never imagined a single touch would carry forward into another life.

She reaches for the photo, careful not to smudge the glossy surface. That kiss had never let go of her. And now, neither could she.

Beside the photo, their journals tell the rest. Hers is filled with dreams of him before she ever knew his name. His is a record of longing, each page reaching for a face he could never fully recall. Together, they tell a story threaded through time, memory, and all the moments they never dared to claim.

Her eyes settle on the open page of her journal, where his handwriting remains, steady, certain, and completely unlike the chaos that once ruled her life. He had written it the night they reunited at the coffee shop, his fingertip tracing the letters into the table. Four letters. CBCK.

Crossroads between chaos and kismet.

She finally understands it now. This was never about fate handing her something perfect. It was about choosing to step forward when everything else tried to hold her back. Zane had always seen something in her worth chasing. And for a little while, she let herself believe it too.

Claire lifts the glass of white wine to her lips. She watches the pale liquid catch the lamplight. The grigio burns slightly as it goes down. She takes another sip anyway. Her fingers trace the stem again and again, chasing nothing.

The rain continues its beat against the windows, but something else catches her attention. At first, it's barely perceptible, a gentle rushing sound underneath the rainfall. Claire stills, tilting her head slightly. The sound grows clearer, waves lapping at a shore, their rhythm distinct from the rain's staccato beat.

She swirls the wine again, watching it create a miniature whirlpool in the glass. The sounds grow louder, mixing with the rain in a perfect harmony. Claire closes her eyes. The two sounds merge into something deeper. The familiar crash and retreat of water against sand feels so close she can almost smell the salt air.

Her hand trembles slightly, wine threatening to spill over the rim of the glass. The waves continue their gentle symphony, weaving through the rainfall like threads of memory, too precise to be imagination.

Claire sets the wine glass on the coffee table, her fingers lingering on its stem before reaching for her journal. The leather feels cool against her skin as she traces the words "Crossroads Between Chaos and Kismet." Zane's handwriting flows across the page, each letter a testament to his existence, his search for her, his belief in their connection.

The phrase echoes in her mind now—not just a message, but a map.

The waves continue beneath the rain, but she barely notices now. She is lost in the curves and lines of his writing. Her thumb brushes over the 'K', where his pen pressed harder, leaving an indent in the paper she can feel.

Memories flood back—his voice in the coffee shop, soft and trembling as he said her name. The way his eyes lit up when she walked through the door. How his hand felt in hers as they walked through the rain-slicked streets.

Her throat tightens. "Why couldn't you stay?" she whispers. "You were the only thing that made sense." Her voice catches on the last word.

She clutches the journal closer, as if holding it tight enough might somehow bring him back. The leather cover creaks under her grip, but she can't let go. Not yet. Not when it's one of the few tangible pieces of him she has left.

Claire shakes the bottle of pills. The tablets rattle inside the bottle. The prescription label lit by the lamplight—her name printed in stark black letters, the dosage, the warnings. Take as directed. Do not exceed recommended dose. May cause drowsiness.

The sound of waves grows stronger, pulling at the edges of her consciousness. She closes her eyes, and suddenly she's back on that surreal beach, golden sand stretching endlessly beneath a kaleidoscope sky. Zane stands at the water's edge, his silhouette sharp against the horizon.

"Live for both of us," his voice echoes in her memory, clear as crystal. The waves had lapped at his feet, drawing him away while she remained frozen on the shore. His smile—so full of love and acceptance—burns behind her eyelids.

The pill bottle feels heavier now. Claire sets it down, her fingers lingering on the white cap. The waves crash louder in her ears, drowning out the steady patter of rain against her windows. That final dream moment replays with perfect clarity. His last words carried across the beach: "This isn't the end. Just keep shining."

She opens her eyes, but the sound of waves doesn't fade. If anything, it grows stronger, as if the dream beach exists just beyond her apartment walls. The pills promise sleep, promises dreams, but she knows they won't be the same. They'll never be the same without him there.

Claire lifts the dried flowers from between the pages of the journal, the once-vibrant petals now pale and fragile. The flowers tremble in her unsteady hands, each brittle petal a delicate reminder of their shared moments. The stem crackles softly as she cradles it, afraid it might crumble at the slightest pressure.

Tears well up, blurring her vision as she holds the flowers against her heart. The petals scratch against her sweater, their texture both foreign and familiar—like memories that fade but never quite disappear.

"I don't know if I can do this without you," she says. A tear falls, landing on one of the petals. The moisture darkens the dried flower, threatening to dissolve what little remains of its former beauty.

The wine glass drops. It rolls once, spilling across the floor. The pale liquid spreads across the floor in irregular moon shape patterns.

Tears fall from her eyes, mixing with the spilled wine. The sight blurs as more tears come, dropping steadily like the rain outside her window.

Claire sinks back onto the couch, her body heavy with exhaustion. In her left hand, she grips the dried flowers. The brittle petals crackle softly with each breath. Her right hand closes around the pill bottle, the plastic warm from being held so long.

Her chest rises and falls in uneven rhythms as she clutches both items tighter. The journal represents everything she had found—connection, understanding, love. The pills promise escape, relief, maybe even dreams of him again.

The sound of waves continues beneath the rainfall, a ghostly reminder of their shared experience. Claire's face remains neutral, masking the war raging inside her. Her fingers trace the ridges of the pill bottle cap.

She lies there, perfectly still except for her breathing, suspended between two choices. The wine spreads further across the floor, reaching for the couch like fingers stretching toward her.

The waves grow louder, crashing against Claire's consciousness with increasing force. Each surge drowns another layer of reality. The sound fills her apartment like water rushing into a sealed room.

Vertigo hits. The room tilts. Furniture blurs. Her eyelids grow heavy, fighting to stay open as the waves thunder in her ears.

The dried flowers slip and fall in slow motion. She tries to catch it, but her movements feel sluggish. It's as if she's already underwater. The couch beneath her seems to undulate with each crash of invisible waves.

Her eyes fight to stay open. Through half-closed lids, she watches the spilled wine ripple across her floor, moving against gravity. The liquid shifts and flows like tiny tide pools, reflecting various colors in the lamplight.

The waves roar now, drowning everything else. Her head falls back against the couch. Her eyes close. She can't resist anymore.

The journal slips from her lap and lands beside the pill bottle. The cap rolls across the floor, circling once before tipping onto its side.

Water surrounds her. It pulls her under.

The roar fades to rhythm. Claire stands barefoot on the beach. The tide touches her ankles. The sand glows like crushed glass. The horizon blends into the sky, soft and strange.

She steps forward. The water curls around her feet, gentle and sure. Each breath feels further away. The air tastes like memory.

Her form begins to blur. The dream starts to take her.

Something moves in the distance.

She doesn't call out. She doesn't need to.

The waves hush to a whisper.

Then silence.

Author's Note

THIS STORY CAME FROM a place I never expected to return to.

Years ago, I had a near-death experience. Most of it is a blur now, but one part never left me. I found myself standing on a shoreline surrounded by colors I cannot describe. The sky, the light, the air, none of it felt like the world I knew. And then I saw her.

She was someone I recognized. We had known each other not long before, but life had taken us in different directions. What surprised me most was that it was her. Of all people, it was her. That is the part I still cannot explain.

We spoke, and the conversation felt real in a way I still struggle to understand. Every detail of that place, and that moment, stayed with me long after I woke. In many ways, this story would not exist without what happened there.

In Dreams, We Love Again is fiction, but it carries the shape of something that truly happened. The world inside this story was born from that vision. The emotions behind it came from a place I never expected to touch again.

Thank you for reading.

About the Author

Casey L. Bennett is a storyteller with a background in film, television, and digital media. He began writing in high school and later expanded into screenwriting, video production, and children's publishing. His work as an award-winning video producer spans educational content, television, and digital storytelling.

His adult fiction is shaped by real-life experiences and a natural focus on emotional honesty and personal connection. Influenced by authors like Edgar Allan Poe, Robert Louis Stevenson, and James Patterson, he brings a cinematic eye to the page and a deep interest in the emotional moments that define us.

In Dreams, We Love Again is his debut novel. He writes across genres and continues to develop new projects in both written and visual formats.

To learn more about Casey's books, upcoming releases, and personal updates, visit:

www.CaseyLBennett.com

A Note to the Reader

Thank you for spending time with this story.

If you made it to the end, then you already know this wasn't just a love story. It was about the quiet moments that shape us, the timing we can't control, and the choices that find us at the crossroads between chaos and kismet.

Personal stories like this aren't easy to write. And they only matter if they're read. So if something here stayed with you, I'd be grateful if you left a review or shared it with someone who might need it.

Thank you for being part of it.

Want to know when the next book is ready?
Join the official CBCK Creative newsletter for updates on upcoming releases from all our authors and imprints.
Visit:

www.cbckcreative.com
Facebook.com/cbckcreative